I0637919

# Everything
## by the
# BOOK

# Everything
## by the
# BOOK
## Things aren't always black and white

Nicola Dunn

First published in the United Kingdom in 2015
by Dunnsix Publishing

ISBN 978-0-9571362-1-2

Produced by
The Choir Press, Gloucester

# 1

## 1979

A s he stood on the warm echoing stage he wished he'd managed even a small slice of the toast he'd left on his plate at home that very morning. If his belly rumbled he knew everyone in the softly-lit theatre would hear. He stood calmly and breathed heavily, hoping the eager onlookers wouldn't notice.

He felt the vibrations of music under his feet. He tapped his foot on the stage, closed his eyes and inhaled the deepest of breaths; he absorbed the moment of pure freedom. The smell from the previous performers' sweat and perfume whirled around him. He moved his body slowly from one side to the other, which brought a smile to his face. The lights left a tingling sensation on his warm glowing skin. He danced across the stage, tapped his feet hard, and moved with all his force. The audience would stand and cheer at such a spectacle of elegance and skill.

His blood pumped hard and vibrantly around his quickly moving body. It flowed and swayed with elegant movements. Every space of the stage used, he smiled and absorbed the wonderful attention; flowers were thrown in gratitude onto the stage and landed at his feet, as the over-contented audience applauded him with wide eyes. The sound of clapping from the happy onlookers who stood with their hands above their heads; each time the heavy red velvet curtain was pulled back they would still be cheering, another standing ovation, each night the same.

'Encore, encore!' the audience cheered. Their roared demands to see him again filled the theatre; the noise echoed through his tired and exhilarated body, which overflowed with adrenaline and excitement.

'Lucas. Hey Lucas!'

He opened his eyes, hearing his name being yelled by the man in charge, who stood watching him from the side of the stage. Feeling embarrassed, he looked down quickly at his black leather shoes. The spilt on the side had been there for some time. At the front his black sock was protruding slightly. He laughed to himself and shook his head, reaching for the broom. The orders came for him to hurry, every night the same, as the doors would be opening soon. The awaiting audience would be soaring down the aisle to find their expensive numbered seats from which to admire the dancers who waited backstage in their dressing rooms. The dancers were always laughing and sharing food together; they'd be the ones with flowers at their feet, not him.

Gripping the broom tightly with his sweating hands he began to push it forcefully, only hearing the bristles against the stage floor. Sadness rushed through him as he knew the stage he was cleaning was the only pathway to his dreams.

Lucas stopped sweeping and put his hands through his brown curly hair. Knowing he'd never be taken seriously, he'd keep sweeping and emptying the overused bins in the dressing rooms. At the end of each performance he'd enter the rooms again and imagine feeling part of the dancers. They'd sit enthusiastically at the powdered tables, the bright bulbs around the mirror lighting up the multitude of colours smudged on the glass. Powder dust lay on stale sandwiches, empty bottles of expensive champagne placed next to dirty glasses wherever there was a space.

Each evening as he finished his duties the dancers seem to glare at him in a kind of pitying way; to him they were always smirking. He was simply the cleaning boy, the one with holes in his shoes.

Lucas pulled on his large grey coat, pushing his hood down to feel comfortable, wrapping his long red scarf around his neck. As he squeezed the soft wool between his fingers he inhaled a deep breath, feeling the cool air at the back of his throat from the opening of the heavy back door. Sadness began to consume him at what he'd chosen to do; it was silly to think he could get away with it.

Tucking the end of his scarf into his coat, Lucas's thoughts went to his bicycle, left outside next to the rubbish sacks, the green and black sacks he'd pile high. Fearful one day he would go to make his way home and his rusty old bike would have been stolen, he always attempted to hide it behind the rubbish, hoping it would still be there when he left.

Whatever he felt cleaning or simply standing enthralled at the side of the stage, he loved to be there; it was the most amazing feeling of complete freedom he'd ever experienced. There was only one other time when he felt such a way: when he was with her, whenever he thought of her.

'Bye, Lucas; cheerio, dear!' The tall dancer, wearing a costume covered in feathers, passed him as she chuckled to her companion who mirrored her attire. Lucas watched her as she seemed to disappear into the mass of sequins and high heels. She was extremely pretty; Lucas frowned and shook his head in disbelief as it seemed her long legs in her skimpy feathered costume went on forever. To admire her black fishnet tights he looked around once more.

Walking outside to the back of the theatre, he grabbed his bike from the protection made by rubbish bags and tied the small blue plastic bag onto the back with an old piece of cord he'd found in the full dressing-room bin. Pulling his scarf up over his mouth as the cold air was beginning to bite, he pedaled slowly home, swaying in the quiet road from side to side, as he had in his imagination on the stage earlier, humming to himself all the way.

As he went tiredly into his small flat he switched on a light, huffing as the bulb barely lit the room. He would get round to buying a shade for it one day. The cold air hit him; he pulled his coat around his tired body and fell slowly onto his bed, bringing his knees up to his chest to protect himself from the cold a little more. The dark blankets and greying sheet slid to the floor as he lay still, looking at the damp ceiling; the brown marks seemed to get darker the more he stared above his head. It had become a routine for him, lying quietly every night, breathing into the air, seeing his breath in the cold room. The wallpaper around the uncurtained window was peeling, showing more brown patterns of soggy plaster.

Lucas let out a long sigh, and thought about making some food. Taking the blue plastic bag from his pocket he held it to his chest, hearing the plastic crumpling. He knew he wasn't ready to look inside, the guilt overwhelming him, knowing and feeling in his heart it was all going to turn out wrong for him.

Sitting up, he could see his cold toast and unopened post on the side, and he suddenly felt it had all become too much for him. The sense of nervousness inside gave him a sickening feeling in the pit of his stomach. He knew he was going to have to face her sooner or later and smile like he normally did.

Placing the bag under his bed he pushed aside old application forms for dancing schools. Some hadn't even been written on; he screwed up all up the ones he'd tried to fill in. He was desperate to dance at the theatre where he swept and cleaned. He couldn't believe they hadn't replied, even if it was a flat-out no; he was sure he'd sent his application. Some forms he had only put his name on, while he waited for them to get back to him, and they were piling up in the corner of his cold room. He would sit on his dampening mattress at night making paper planes with them. They had been unsuccessful in gliding across the room, as he knew they'd be if he'd made the decision to place them in an envelope.

Lucas began pouring beans into a dirty saucepan, warming them through on his small oven; there was no need for a plate, and once they were to his satisfaction he grabbed a fork from the cluttered drawer and began eating straight from the pan. Sitting alone at the small table, all he could hear was the pan being scratched with his fork, the noise making him shudder. He used the cold dry toast from breakfast to wipe around the saucepan, fully cleaning the sides of any sauce and colourful orange remains. Cooking himself dinner and making paper planes had become the highlight of his lonely evenings; he always felt alone and empty when he wasn't with her. Maybe he could open the window, as the condensation from the small radiator where he placed his underwear to dry had made the window seal and the net go mouldy; he had a new stain to look at now, which brought a small smile to his face.

Change fell from his pocket as he moved to place his empty pan in the sink, the small coins landing on the dusty floorboards, his last few pounds rolling under the turned-up edges of the green rug. Huffing, Lucas bent down to retrieve them, thinking about buying some stamps once he had gathered them safely in his pocket again.

Catching a glimpse of the blue plastic bag under his bed as he was on his hands and knees, he leant forward, pushing the bag under the bed further out of his view; he didn't want to feel guilty any more.

If he could take one more look he'd hide it for good.

Scurrying on his knees again on the hard floor, he took the bag from its place, his fingers absorbing the feel of the soft plastic. He could tell the sandwiches he had quickly thrown in the bag before he had left the theatre had been squashed on the journey home. Sitting on the floor at the bottom of his bed, he placed it on his knees and took the sandwiches out, smelling them; he hated salmon. Inhaling a deep breath, he took one more dreaded look inside the fish-scented bag.

# 2

---

Natty had been tossing and turning in her bed for nearly two hours. Each time she looked over to the small sideboard next to her bed she could see the flashing numbers on the white digital clock, bringing her a sense of dread; she really didn't feel like getting up that morning, wishing to stay within her flowery covers forever. Leaning over abruptly, she turned the clock around, desperately not wanting to be reminded how long she didn't have.

She had spent most of the morning awake, thinking over and over and over. Thoughts and songs going through her mind constantly. Seizing her large soft pillow, she placed it over her face and bashed it with her hands, praying she could stop her mind running away with her, her empty thoughts rushing in and out of her head.

Giving in to her overworking thoughts she sat up, promptly leaning against her headboard, her pillow between her fingers, gripping onto the cotton.

'Oh my God, why can't you sleep?' Natty spoke out loud, puffing her cheeks and blowing out a long breath, tugging her hair in frustration. Wondering what else she could do, she placed her fingers on the pink bow that held together all of the cream lace concealing her elegant shapely body. She had finally grown into the beautiful swan of the ugly duckling story.

Seeing her breast slightly brought another thought to her already-full mind. There was no getting away from it; she longed for him to touch her, needed him to stop inventing and hold her in his arms and simply kiss her like she had never been kissed before. Knowing she'd feel the magical tingly sensation when he placed his lips onto hers for the very first time, just as in the awaited end moments in the movies. She was certain he wanted her, thinking how each time they spoke he'd lean across her a little more than

6

was really necessary; she always yearned to push herself closer to him, to his lips, but he never seemed to get the message. If she were to completely throw herself at him, he'd fall to the floor and then she'd have the chance to feel her small breasts pressing against his strong chest. She happily relived the moment of having her eyes intently on him as he came out of the bathroom with a towel wrapped tightly around his waist. His skin always slightly wet, showing the outline of his muscles rippling, when he walked, strong, appealing and innocent, to Glenn's old bedroom.

Natty thought eagerly about him touching her. It was insane even contemplating him throwing his inventions into the air and holding her close, touching her as she desired him to. Natty touched her breast in excitement and gently squeezed it, moving the soft lace and ribbon away so she could feel herself properly; closing her eyes and moving her hand slowly down her soft slim stomach. Her exhilarating thoughts were with him the whole time. She moved her body under the bedclothes, wriggling down, hiding in case he could somehow sense what she was about to do. From under her floral covers her own satisfaction echoed around her quiet surroundings, the sound of pleasure.

The feeling became awkward for her, having difficulty breathing stuck under the hot heavy blankets, beginning to have an overwhelming attack of claustrophobia but determined not to stop her own pleasure to the very end, until she heard a gentle knock at the door.

'No, no! Oh, for goodness' sake, not right now!' Natty pulled the heavy blankets from herself and sat up, her sweaty hair sticking to her face, flustered and hot, pulling strands of her hair out of her mouth. Her cheeks were flushed as she kicked her covers back into place, huffing as she hadn't succeeded in giving herself the complete sexual moment she longed for, her breast still out of her nightdress. Pulling up her shoulder straps, she leant over in haste to turn the clock around again.

'Oh, God.' Natty could see how late for work she was going to be.

'Natty, you are going to be late!' Her father's soft voice came from behind her closed door.

'Thank you Dad!' Natty spoke through her teeth with a sense of embarrassment, her voice almost squeaky as she screwed up her face, as if she somehow wanted to pretend she wasn't in the room. She was twenty-four, for heaven's sake, and her dear father still worried about her punctuality.

Her bed was beginning to feel hot and uncomfortable; she pushed her blankets onto the red carpet with her feet and rushed to the bedroom sink to wash her hands extra hard. Wiping the steam from the small mirror with her wet hand, she washed her face, her skin feeling soft and warm. Spitting quickly into the sink after brushing her teeth, the thought of him went through her mind again, causing a feeling of excitement to stir in her; a throbbing emerged between her legs again. She would definitely be late if she didn't push the thought away and concentrate on getting ready.

Rushing to her wardrobe, she could see it needed to be tidied after work. There was never enough hanging space, so she'd end up having to squeeze her grey uniform into the smallest gap; it always needed a good shake before she put it on. And today was no different. Checking her black tights for holes and taking a pair of knickers from her messy drawer, she felt irritated seeing her underwear in such a state. It was a must for her to choose knickers to match her bra; fully aware that she had no time to make a fuss, she grabbed the first set she could. The glowing red numbers on the clock reminded her every time she glanced over that she'd have to rush breakfast.

Going back to the sink where she had left the hot tap running, seeing the steam mist on the mirror, she wiped the wet residue away. Natty tied her hair into a neat ponytail with a small bobble. Straightening up her small watch pinned to the front of her uniform, she smiled. She gave her cheeks a pinch to add a little colour; her makeup was going to have to wait.

Finally, she left her warm steamy bedroom to quickly retrieve the breakfast she'd smelt her father making.

'Morning, Dad, thanks for waking me.' Natty went to sit at the table, having to remove a couple of handfuls of papers and notes before she did so. Sitting on the edge of the chair, she flicked through the newspaper. Glancing at the corner of the page, she could see it was the 11th of January 1979.

Shouldn't be too long before he hears, she thought, as the

anticipation and excitement of hopefully seeing his surprise built up in her empty stomach. She clapped her hands together quietly in jubilation at his forthcoming news.

'Here we are. I wasn't sure if you were asleep with all the noise going on up there.' Her father spoke softly, placing her tea and toast on the newspaper, and went back to take more bread from the bag. As he slid the soft bread into the toaster he sipped his hot drink, leaving the other milky tea on the side to cool a little more.

Natty coughed and looked at the floor as she could feel her face flushing. She didn't need to pinch her cheeks after all. As she bit into her warm toast, a drip of butter fell onto her lap.

'Bugger!' Licking her finger, she tried to wipe it clean while admiring her dear father standing with his back to her, thinking how his hair had become greyer at the sides over the last few years. He still was handsome, almost charismatic. Whenever Natty saw him immersed in his thoughts she could relax a little. It seemed to her it was the only time he'd find peace, gaining a relationship with himself and no other but the characters deep within his mind. She prayed he could find the same happiness away from his words.

'Dad, thank you, I must be going now; thank you so much for breakfast and waking me! Strawberry jam next time would be nice.' Natty smiled in a joking manner, kissing her father's soft face.

Grabbing her coat from the coat rack, she quickly checked her pockets for her keys, happy she needn't hunt for her coat under her sister's any more.

As she turned the key and started her car she looked over to see her father waving his arms around at the front door, his blue dressing gown keeping him warm. She sighed, knowing how late she was now going to be.

'What is it, Dad?' Natty shouted from the opened car door, keeping one leg in the car so she could make a quick exit.

'Natty, it's the phone for you. He says it's really urgent.'

Natty huffed to herself again; she wished she had stayed hot and flustered under her bed covers and finished her own little pleasure. Putting her own needs to the back of her mind, she slammed her car door shut and made her way back indoors.

'Hello, Mr Lucas. Look, can't be long; I have to make it to work

9

within fifteen minutes. Have you found the answer?' Natty spoke with eagerness as the feeling of excitement rose in her again; she had been waiting for a call from him, but his choice of time wasn't very well thought out.

'Hello, Miss Natty. How are you on this chilly morning?'

'Yes, Mr Lucas, I will be fine on this chilly morning if you hurry and I'm not late. And if I don't have to deal with the really difficult people like yesterday. Maybe a few bed baths for some handsome gent may make this day a little warmer.' Natty chuckled slightly before she closed her eyes and shook her head at the thought of how bad the previous day had been in the hospital, and of how, if she continued making remarks about wetting the bodies and chests of handsome men, she would never get the chance to feel her own chest against his.

'I wanted to show you something, Miss Natty, if I could be lucky enough to have your company this evening.' Lucas's voice was shaky and gentle.

'OK, Lucas, I could meet you at eight. That is, of course, if I get in on time! Which means, by the looks of it, I will be meeting you sometime next week. Lucas, I really have to go; I will see you later!' Natty left hastily again. Realising how cold the hall felt made her shiver.

'Bye, Dad!' she shouted as she closed the door.

Natty sat in her car and inhaled a deep breath. She couldn't believe she had to face him later after her thoughts; come to think of it, her actions.

Sitting with her hands on her steering wheel, she watched her air freshener swaying slightly, the shadow seeming to enlarge on the dashboard. The strawberry fragrance blended with her sweet perfume as she looked at the shadow for a little longer; she found it very calming. The small piece of black card with three coloured circles filled with scented oil, resembling a small traffic light, made her realise how many sets of lights she would have to endure before she even reached the busy hospital car park. Once she got there it could take her over ten minutes to find a parking space.

'Why does everything always have to be so complicated?' Speaking out loud and still leaning forward on her steering wheel, gripping the black leather, Natty glanced at the home she shared with her father. It was such a large house; it always had been. Everything and everyone had always been so lost inside its stylish walls, and they still were. The front garden looked so pretty, as it always had. Her father worked so hard keeping the flowers free from weeds; they were going to blossom vibrantly in the spring. The grass was green and cut, the morning frost like an ice carpet making it almost seem magical. She could sit and admire it all day, but it was no good; she was definitely the latest she had ever been in her three years as a qualified nurse. All she needed now was to pull a thread in her black tights and she was going to give in and head straight for her bedroom, where she was going to think of Lucas, the crazy man; he was the excitement that filled her day. The unpredictable moments with him where she'd be excitedly left waiting for the next.

Flicking the air freshener with her finger, she started her engine and left for more complaints. The people and incidents she witnessed every day at work would have her dear father's toes curling in his red slippers. With a laugh she pushed the tape into the cassette player, praying it wasn't going to be chewed up and leave her with a lap full of brown stringy plastic. Sighing at such a thought, she made her way to the first red light.

The silence echoed in his ears as he wiped the sides down. Looking over at the table, Natty's father smiled, contented, as Natty had finished her tea and eaten her toast, only leaving the crust on the plate. He absorbed himself in watching his children move through their lives from afar. Having all of them home together always gave him a small degree of completeness.

Sitting at the table, pushing her plate to the edge, he began folding the newspaper. He would have to get round to cancelling the delivery each morning, he was tired of being reminded of how long he had been without his Eve. The date printed in black bold letters informed him every day.

Taking his notes from the chair where Natty had placed them, he began to fill his day with his escape to another place only he knew about. His pale hands felt cold; he rubbed them together and pulled his dressing gown across his chest a little more.

His permission to allow his imagination to flow would be coming to an end soon, which made him feel lonely. He paused. He knew once it was over he'd be sitting at the table again, remembering and punishing himself for everything he had and hadn't done when he'd had the chance to get it right. Feeling the only choice he had now was to live without one.

The clang from the letterbox took him from his thoughts. Taking a long breath, he continued and suddenly felt excited when he finally came within sight of the moment he'd share his achievement. He'd make sure they were all together again. Perching himself a little more upright, he ruffled the small green cushion behind his back, the very same cushion his Eve had held when she'd sat in her chair. Where she had survived in her own existence. He remembered how she had liked the sensation of the soft velvet on her fingertips. She had thrown it at him in their one and only pillow fight; he'd held on to the vision of her smile ever since.

Fulfilled in the thought of her happy image, he questioned why. Every morning he'd walk into the cool silent kitchen and wait for the kettle to boil; he'd stand with his back leaning against the worktop, his ageing hands in his dressing-gown pockets, not allowing himself to believe how everything around him had miraculously changed in a moment. The moment of her damaged mind. She had now given them her choice, for them to live with each day and to carry within themselves for the rest of their lives. He had to accept she was gone, his wondrous beauty.

He thought it wouldn't hurt to make her one more. As always he took an extra cup from the cupboard and pretended only for a short while she was with him. One more drink with extra milk, of course.

# 3

Lucas nervously placed the heavy black phone receiver down after calling her. The phone box smelt of stale urine and under his feet he could see he was standing in the remaining stains it had left. Some disturbed person had tried to set fire to the phone book, the yellow-and-brown burnt edges still leaving most phone numbers and addresses intact. The culprit had been as successful in their quest as Lucas was in making paper planes, which brought a sense of satisfaction to him. Such people were scoundrels with nothing better to do than to damage property which didn't belong to them, simply scoundrels.

His change fell into the small compartment; pushing his large fingers inside with difficulty, he retrieved what was left of his stamp money. It was lucky his call had ended promptly. Since his feast of beans and stale toast he hadn't slept; he was having an evening with Natty and hopefully he'd rest a little more before she graced him with her loveliness. If he was to stay in the repulsive phone booth with its odours, burnt paper and old chewing gum stuck to the small panes of glass, he wouldn't have to tell her the truth. Looking at the concrete floor, stained and damp, he could see the chewing gum he'd picked from the earpiece; it would have no doubt been entangled in his mass of curls.

'Whoever did this was troubled, surely.' Lucas became annoyed, feeling the filthy remains of the dirty sticky saliva ball on his fingers.

As he pushed open the door to his temporary safe haven the fresh air fulfilled him; he breathed strongly through his nose, desperately needing to clear his lungs of the stench. Buttoning up his grey duffel coat he saw the lining was ripped even further; it had another small hole under the arm. Each time he put his coat on he heard it rip stitch by stitch.

Walking home he kept his head down, making his way back to his small dingy flat only a road away from the germ-infested and graffitied playground. He wanted to get home; he wanted to rest his tired but strong body on his damp bed and simply sleep his worry away. He knew it had to be OK. There had to be a happy ending for him finally; if not he'd simply have to invent one.

Finally he was back in his four walls which kept him safe from the outside world; it was only a little warmer than the cold air outside. Throwing his coat and scarf on his bed, he sat at the table. He had emptied the blue plastic bag's contents onto the stained, crumb-covered wood, touching the only thing which was to determine if he were always to be alone, always to be without her. Wondering with a pain beginning to burn in his stomach why he had left it so long.

As he began to feel an overwhelming tiredness, a tear left his eye. Lucas cupped his hands to his chest and put his head on the table in disbelief, desperate to sleep; wanting it to stay the way it always had been, even if it was only for one more hour.

'Come on, Lucas, open the door; it's freezing out here!' Natty stood outside, knocking frantically as she held on to her sleeves in the hope of keeping her hands warm.

She had been more than aware she was going to be at his later than planned after placing the phone down on him earlier that day. Forty minutes behind time exactly. She had known before even hanging her coat up at the hospital. She had attempted to sneak to her locker and begin her duties before anyone noticed. It was guaranteed that the new arse-lick student nurse who did everything to get her gold star of the day would grass up anyone who walked in a minute late or left a minute early, and she did her very best to stick to her newfound reputation.

'Lucas, it's me, come on!' Natty shouted through the small letterbox, slamming it again and again, hoping he'd wake.

'Do you mind not banging away on that door, young lady? It's nearly nine.'

Natty turned around quickly in shock to see Lucas's neighbour bellowing at her; he was fat and balding, and miserably failed to cover his large belly with his dirty vest. Focusing on his dark hairy belly button made her cringe; thank goodness she wasn't giving him a bed bath, she thought. The staining on the front of his beige trousers matched the smell coming from his open door. His television must have been at full volume in his flea pit, which surely was more disturbing to the other tenants in the block than her simply knocking.

'Sorry! I didn't mean to upset you!' Natty smiled politely but wanted to shout at him, to tell him to use the toilet and not the front of his trousers, to mind his goddamn business and go and eat another piece of fried chicken. And how he was a rude fat man who she wouldn't treat, if ever he happened to give her the misfortune of meeting with him again, even if his legs were falling off. Not that he could ever get himself to hospital, of course, without stopping at the nearest doughnut shop. Taking a deep breath and trying to remain ladylike, Natty continued to smile, waiting for him to retreat into the hole he'd come from.

'I should think so. Youngsters of today; what's it all coming to?' The unwelcome neighbour turned his back to Natty and went inside his flat. Before closing the door he gave her a snarling look; as the door was closed the smell from him again emerged into the already mouldy corridor.

'Did you just fart?' Natty snarled back at his door, holding her hand over her mouth and nose. She didn't care much for remaining outside Lucas's front door much longer.

Holding her breath and striving to get his attention one more time, she began to bang on the door with her fist. This had better be worth it, Mr Lucas, she thought.

Suddenly Lucas opened his door. Pushing past and shutting the door promptly, Natty exhaled as she reached safe oxygen levels.

'Hello, Miss Natty. You look calm.' Lucas rubbed his eyes from his broken sleep. Placed his hands in the pockets at the back of his jeans. A nervous, sickening feeling filled his hungry stomach.

'Oh my God, and he had the impertinence to say "what are the youngsters coming to?" Oh, that smell! Couldn't you invent something to make your fat neighbour disappear? Oh, what a day.' Sighing, Natty threw her brown leather bag onto Lucas's bed and went straight to the kettle. She turned and turned the tap, but still no water came. The handle kept going round and round; the squeaking of the stainless steel started to irritate her as much as the neighbour had.

'Come here, Miss Natty, you are doing it all wrong.' Lucas went forward, taking the kettle from her, feeling very aware that, although he'd thrown the blue plastic bag back under the bed, it could be seen from where he was standing. He pushed down hard on the tap and turned it slowly, filling the kettle with ease. 'See? Easy peasy lemon squeezy.' He smiled.

Pretending to be interested in the recovery of the broken tap, Natty gave him a returning smile. Her only interest was throwing herself at him. Tit squeezy would be nice, she thought. She'd give him lemon straight in his gorgeous brown eyes if he didn't make the first move soon. She pressed her lips together, attempting to hold back her amusement, but her efforts were wasted as she burst into laughter. Her own thoughts of titty squeezing only stopped now and then when she paused for a breath, hoping she'd contain herself before the rusty old kettle had boiled.

'What are you laughing at?' Standing next to the overflowing steam with two teabags, he began to feel unsettled.

'Sorry, Lucas, I will stop now ... sorry ... don't look at me, then ...' Thoughts of *easy peasy titty squeezy* went through Natty's mind. Looking over at the front door, she was tempted to go outside to calm herself, but then the idea of having to be subjected to the fat man again suddenly stopped her laughing.

'Right, who's making the tea?' Her voice was uplifted, a slight chuckling still under her breath. Lucas always made the tea when she went to see him. She'd always offer, knowing full well he'd refuse.

She pushed her coat down her arms and placed it upon her bag, and made her way to the table. Noticing what he'd had for dinner, she began scraping the dried orange sauce from the table with her fingernail. She crossed her legs on the high stool. The tiny butter stain had almost doubled in size over the course of the day.

'Lucas, this table needs a good scrub!' Natty raised her voice over the whistling of the boiling kettle.

'Miss Natty. You must not concern yourself with such worries as a little dried sauce here and there.' Lucas spoke with humour in his voice. He grinned as he spoke to the young beauty sitting at his dirty table. Her uniform looked grubby; she was tired, he could see. But she still found the energy to come and see him. No one had ever been as kind as she was to him, apart from her father. 'See, Miss Natty, life is like this little teabag; it looks like a very simple thing. Come over here and I will show you.'

Natty pushed herself from the table and went to stand next to him. She began wondering if her breath perhaps smelt from her dinner, something which was meant to resemble spicy meatballs from the hospital canteen. She feigned a cough so she could bring her hand up to her mouth to check while approaching him slowly.

'Now watch, Miss Natty. You see how very simple this little bag is; it's the tiniest thing, but look what's inside. Your life, that's what.' Lucas pushed the teabag nearer to her face so she could see.

Lucas continued with his wisdom. 'This extremely purposeful bag has been beautifully and skilfully made. The holes placed apart with precision so the contents flow in just the right amount. It's like our lives, you see. We all acquire sad emotions and happy ones at different times, but only in the right amounts. Just watch closely, Miss Natty.' Lucas poured the hot water into a cup and gently and respectfully lay the teabag on top. 'Watch, Miss Natty, watch how the tea flows slowly through the water. The tea leaves inside are like your life, Miss Natty. They are not sure where they are going, but they are filling every wonderful space; every part of the water will be imbued with the bag's presence.' The water changed to a dark brown and Lucas took the bag out of the cup. 'Would you like me to add something else to your tea, Miss Natty? Like milk, which is me, or sugar, which is you?' His eyes sparkled as he spoke to her softly.

Natty stood next to Lucas, mesmerised as always by his craziness. Was this his way of saying he wanted to share his life with her?

'I would like, Lucas, to have milk in my tea: extra milk if you wouldn't mind!' Natty felt the tingling in her stomach she had earlier in her bedroom; she leant forward to kiss him. She closed her eyes and waited for his lips to touch hers, her heart thumping.

'Here you go, extra milk,' he said in innocence.

As Natty opened her eyes to see him holding a cup of tea in one hand and a bottle of milk in the other, he was smiling in delight.

'Thank you, Lucas!' How confusing did this man have to be? Everything about him enthralled her; he was unpredictable, but predictable at the same time. It had always excited her.

Natty knew Lucas never really had anything to eat in his cupboard; maybe a few tins of beans here and there, and always a half-eaten crusty loaf. She always left hungry, not fancying toast or a stale cucumber sandwich. She remembered how he'd save her a slice of chocolate Swiss roll whenever he had been given a plate of food at the theatre; he'd always be thrilled. She really fancied tucking into the soft chocolate sponge right at that moment. It was always the most endearing thing. He'd happily eat everything apart from the chocolate sticky treats, knowing how much she loved anything sweet. Natty desired him even more for such kindness. Her thoughts were on him as she took from her bag a packet of chocolate digestives. 'I have brought some biscuits for you; do you mind if I share them with you?'

'Miss Natty, thank you for coming to scc mc; thank you for thosc wonderful treats. Shall we sit? I want to talk to you. I have to let you know something so very important.' Lucas picked up his tea and sat on his bed, moving her bag onto the floor; straightened up the blankets and sheets with one hand so as not to spill his cup of life with extra sugar. He began to feel cold, and his beautiful guest must have been feeling it too as she was also shivering slightly. He gazed at her as she tore open the delightful biscuits; he loved them too. He'd hold the chocolate-coated crumbly disc in his tea, so he could suck all the brown sweet covering off with ease.

She was so pretty, so elegant; even in her grubby uniform her beauty was always there. His thoughts were to be the same whatever she wore. He admired, not for the first time, how long her legs were; she could have been a dancer with feathers in her hair and fishnet tights. Her own black tights had a small hole at the ankle. He wondered if she knew.

'Miss Natty, come and get warm; I will put a blanket around you while we talk.' Lucas put his drink on the floor and pulled up a dark grey blanket, looking at her and smiling.

'Yes, please. You need to get something done about the heating in here; one radiator simply isn't enough, Lucas.' Natty took her drink and a handful of biscuits to share and rushed over to sit on

18

his bed. Instantly Lucas placed the itchy grey blanket around her cold shoulders.

'Thank you, Lucas. What was it you wanted to tell me? With me moaning about your neighbour I completely forgot to ask; I do apologise.' Natty took a sip of her tea, trying to work out if the sudden stale odour was coming from the neighbour again or the blanket.

Lucas drew a breath.

'Oh, my goodness, look at that; now can you believe it? It doesn't matter how long I go; I end up with a stupid hole. Aaaah!' Natty got up swiftly and unlaced her black shoes, kicked them off, lifted the bottom of her uniform and grabbed the edge of her tights, pulling them down her legs in frustration. She quickly rolled them into a ball and placed them into the bottom of her bag. 'Damn things, they drive me mad! Lucas, can you make tights which never get ladders in them, please, please, please ...'

Natty stopped in her panic, realising Lucas had just witnessed her as she pushed her uniform up over her knickers. She tried desperately to remember the ones she had put on, even if the sheer embarrassment of what she had just done was bad enough, praying they were her blue lace pair with red around the edges.

'Sorry, Lucas! Please pretend you never saw anything!' Natty spoke softly with flushed cheeks, but the chill from his flat on her bare legs made her feel aroused as she saw him transfixed on her.

The urge to be really daring went through her already-busy mind. She had to, she *had* to do what was on her mind before she went stir crazy. But what if she made a fool of herself, and her slim body and small breasts didn't appeal to him? What if he was to laugh at her, to think her silly enough to believe he would want her? She stared at him longingly as she thought.

*What am I to do? Please, God, let this work, don't let him reject me, don't let him laugh. Let me be the woman I long to be. I want to be touched by him. I'm a young woman and women have needs. I'm a woman who has right in front of her what she needs right now, this moment in my life. You can do this, live for this moment; you can. Just go for it, Natty, you silly woman, now go on.*

She would have to get under the smelly blankets to keep warm sooner or later. Natty wanted the handsome man sitting simply gorgeous in his damp flat to keep her warm.

This was it, and she wasn't going to change her mind. Her thoughts appeared again: *Go on, Natty, you can do it, girl, put your shoulders back – no, leave it, you're looking nuts just standing here, he's waiting for you to do something; oh, for goodness' sake.* Over and over she thought until she finally began to open one button at a time. It was so cold she couldn't quite believe it, unsure if the shivering all over her body was from the lack of heating, nerves or both. Not sure if she should be giving him a kind of seductive pouty look, or move her hips from one side to the other. She didn't have a clue; she just had to go with what she had, and that wasn't much. Her bra was showing; she knew it was too late to stop even if she wanted to. She was cold with nerves and excitement. The throbbing in between her legs was becoming more intense. *God, it's cold,* she thought.

Any thought of rejection now had to be pushed to the back of her mind, as she was eagerly watching Lucas. Her dress now lay around her feet, her body shaking. Praying the handsome man who sat and stared at her with wide eyes would make some kind of move, even if it was to take his shirt off; why should she be the only one getting cold?

'Miss Natty, you are shivering and you are the most beautiful woman I have ever seen.' Lucas finally moved from his frozen staring position. Taking a step toward her, he finally unbuttoned his chequered shirt. His chest tanned and near her at long last. He put his hands onto her cold shoulders, rubbing his hands up and down her arms slowly. Pulling her closer and wrapping his arms firmly around her cold and aroused body.

A sense of safety rushed through her at the warmth and strength of his grasp; an overwhelming affection and love consumed her; she could stay like this forever. He'd always been so gentle and kind with her, and she was sure whatever was going to happen next wouldn't be any different.

Seeing a glimpse of her greying white bra and her old knickers brought a pang to her stomach. Of all the days in the entire world to have taken the worst underwear she had in her pretty lace-filled drawer. She believed she was unattractive to him in her attire, and realised as he held her there was nothing in the world she could do about it. It was all up to him now; she was going to feel wanted by this man. Allow him to take the lead and just feel it, feel his touch and his warmth. Allow him to take control of her.

The sensation of holding her was exquisite to him; she was precious, every little thing about her. He thought her little yellow knickers were like she had sat on the sunshine, finding them sweet and very sexy. Finally he was experiencing her soft untouched skin.

'I want to make love to you, Miss Natty. I would like to very much. May I?'

'Mr Lucas, you may.' It was too good to be true; she wish he'd just take her and talk later.

He unclasped her bra and pulled it from her breasts, touching them with the edges of his fingers, taking the fabric from her soft skin, her breasts firm and wonderfully round. Moving his hands over them, softly and intently absorbing every single inch of her figure.

He pushed her knickers down her legs as she remained standing; he could smell her soft skin, her gentle fragrance awakening more of his senses, as she gently lifted her heel to aid him. Starting from her ankles he moved his fingers up toward the insides of her legs, stopping only for a brief moment as he felt her wetness. Teasing her, he carried on touching her stomach, then softly taking his fingers over her nipples stimulated his own body and emotion, feeling himself becoming firm. Grabbing her arm softly, he pushed her hand onto him, so she'd know how he was, what she did to him and how happy he was going to make her, how he was going to make her burn with passion inside her body, make every part of her surrender to him. Her mouth widened for him to firmly kiss her, feeling her tongue pushing hard on his; she was wet like the saliva building between their forceful kiss.

He took her to the bed, pushing his fingers into her while he concentrated on her seductive eyes.

He lay his strong body gently on her, her breasts pert and her nipples rubbing on his chest, kissing her neck and moving down to her breast, pushing her nipples into his mouth, her nipples' softness and firmness in his mouth, her breast wetter with his movements, his mouth feeling the warmth from her skin making him want to dominate her, to let her know he wanted to feel every part of her. Moving her legs apart and pulling them firmly but gently around

21

his waist he thrust himself into her, her body naturally responding to him, their fingers locking. The desire and sensual arousal as her unblemished skin bled into his pores. The tightness inside her and wetness helped him move and feel each push with intense emotion, her moans becoming louder, telling him it was time for her; suddenly his stomach felt tight as he released himself inside her satisfied body. They breathed heavily together; he leant on his arms to watch her breathing hard. Moving her damp hair from the side of her face softly, touching her lips with his fingers. This beautiful woman who wanted to lie with him, a woman who held him close and a woman he knew he would never see again.

'Miss Natty!' Lucas spoke heavily, his breathing out of rhythm.

'Yes, Lucas.' Natty felt as though she had fallen in love with him. She could stay in the stale itchy covers forever, his kindness and loving heart protecting her, and his strong body was her amour against the world.

'Are you all right?' Lucas looked into her glistening eyes. 'I love you, Miss Natty.' He felt a sense of overwhelming exhilaration.

'And I very much love you.' She was complete finally.

Moving from her body, Lucas leant with his elbow propped on the greying pillow beside her and his hand on his head, looking at her beauty.

'Miss Natty, shall we completely devour all those chocolate biscuits?' Smiling and jumping from the bed to retrieve them and to pass her the cooled-down tea, he wondered what her cup of life was helping her with at that very moment, how much water she was to release once she knew. A heaviness overcame him suddenly; he was to speak to her now. If he waited he could keep her soft body next to him a little longer.

Sitting up side by side with their legs arched and the grey blankets covering most of their bodies, they placed the biscuits in between them. Chatting and laughing about how she had stripped in front of him. Imagining if it had all gone completely wrong and Lucas had said 'no, thank you' to her offer. Both wishing they never had to leave the cold, smelly bed.

Grabbing the last chocolate biscuit, Natty began laughing again. 'See, Mr Lucas, look closely. This chocolate biscuit is like your life. Its simple circular shape is crafted with dedication and love, each biscuit having the same amount of milk chocolate on top. But if you look close enough one may have a little extra splodge; that's you, by the way.' Chuckling, she waved the biscuit cheekily in front of him.

Lucas quickly grabbed it from her grasp and pushed the whole thing into his mouth, crunching frantically; crumbs were falling out of the side of his mouth onto the blankets.

'Hey, you!' Natty roared with laughter as she hit his shoulder. A sense of happiness overwhelmed her. She hadn't told him she had brought two packets.

Once Lucas had stopped chewing he slid his body from the bed and walked slowly to the small window. He stood naked at the radiator and mouldy net. He began to check if his socks were dry, wondering how he was to begin; how was he going to tell her now?

He could sense her eyes on him. He wanted to cry for what she would say; he wanted to say sorry, but he knew it was going to be too late.

'Lucas, you OK over there? Come and get warm.' Missing his touch already, Natty felt too far away from him.

He turned around to face her, his brown eyes full of tears.

'What's wrong, Lucas?' Her stomach began to churn with sadness for him as he looked so lost standing near the cold window. 'Lucas, come and sit next to me; you don't have to stand alone any more.' Natty touched the bedsheet with her hand.

Lucas slid under the blanket next to her, his body now cold.

'Lucas, you have made me feel so very happy. My life has been such a crazy rollercoaster since my mother left us. And to think after all that has happened we end up sitting here eating biscuits and being together, even though you ate my last one! I can feel something is very wrong, Lucas. You can tell me; you can say anything to me.' Natty felt she had done something wrong; why did he seem so sad after such a wonderful evening together?

'How did we both get here anyway? After everything, how did we? How can we make sense of it? Lucas touched her cheek softly. He knew how they had got there, all the moments which had brought them together. He wanted to hear all about it again. 'Can we do it all again?'

Immersed in fear, Lucas rushed to fill the kettle up to make another cup of tea; if he kept her talking he could prolong the moment.

'La-de-da, it doesn't matter; we are here now, and cold too.' She was shivering. 'Best get the other packet out my bag then. Do we really need to make sense of it all, Lucas?' Natty leant forward, stretching for her coat, which was crumpled up on the floor. Needing to cover her naked body more; spotting her underwear made her cringe. They were surely to be speaking to the early hours of the morning, and she was determined to be warm and, of course, eat the last biscuit.

# 4

---

**1975**

Matthew had sat at the top of the stairs for nearly an hour since he had placed Eve's once-discarded doll onto her pillow. Rubbing his hands together slowly, rocking gently to and fro. His head down while he tried to make sense of his feelings; how was he to untangle the web of pain forming inside him? Alone in self-torment, desperately yearning to enter the bedroom once more and take hold of the pretty porcelain figure, to wrap her gently in a soft blanket and protect her, let her know he'd never leave her again, he'd never stay away long enough for her to feel lost in the confusion of her day.

Pushing himself slowly up, he wiped his clammy hands down his black trousers. He was going to speak into the air, as though she was still with him. It wouldn't matter; he wasn't hurting anyone. Allowing her to finally understand how the love he held burnt inside him each and every day.

He stood close to the white door, his heart thumping, breathing heavily, smelling his own breath as his face was gently pressed to the wood. Sadness and a rush of excitement overwhelmed him. Hearing his girls' muffled voices echoing from the rooms downstairs, he slowly turned the brass handle.

His knees were firm against the covers as he stood next to the bed, consumed with nerves. She was simply exquisite. Adrenaline came flooding back to him as though it was the first second, the first moment when he fell in love and his life began and ended at the same time. As he touched the porcelain face with his unringed hand, he released a long sigh, knowing deep in his shattered heart she was real. She was going to hear his every word and every thought; she was going to understand. His speech was soft and a little unsettled.

'My darling Eve, I love you so. I always have. I will continue to love you until my heart comes apart, until my breath has gone from my body. I yearn to share this crazy unpredictable world with you, for you to be a witness to our beautiful daughters' lives, their joys and their heartaches. Share all the rainy mornings with you, watch you dance and splash in puddles until your pretty shoes get so wet I have to pick you up and carry you in my arms until we reach the shore. We could run on the soft cool sand holding our arms out on the highest point of the hill as the wind takes our breath away, giving in to it all, so we can simply be. We'd walk and be the only ones for miles; we'd make love until the glorious sun rose upon the horizon, burning with vibrancy and magic to begin another day, the sun burning into the calm sea. It's how our days could be, Eve: like the sun, simply magnificent. You'd smile at the spectacle of such beauty and I'd adore watching your happiness. The sun's reflection would embrace you within its glow, shine upon you, showing how beautiful you are, and how lucky the sky would be to have you welcome it with such radiance. I promise to give you all the understanding and truth you deserve, with all the strength I have left in my body. I'm ready, Eve, to walk barefooted with you on the warm sand.'

Lifting his head and gazing at the ceiling, Matthew knew it ought to have been the life for them, the way he'd always planned it to be, a magic to be created every day they were together. He pushed his chest out and inhaled a deep breath; his emotions whirled inside him. He still remained the luckiest man alive; he had had a chance to know her, and she had touched his skin and loved him.

The tears began to fill his eyes; he closed them firmly, desperately wanting to prevent them from falling. His despair was immense; his stomach began to ache; he longed desperately to be given another chance, even one more day to get it right, how it was meant to be.

'Hey, Dad, what are you doing up here?' Glenn called, rushing up the stairs. 'You have been—' She stopped in shock at the bedroom door. Almost holding her breath she stepped slowly, praying he wouldn't open his eyes until she reached him.

Feeling uncertain, Glenn glanced around the bare walls of the elegant bedroom where her father stood crying, holding on to a small china doll. Glenn firmly held on to her mother's makeup bag, cautiously perching herself on the edge of the bed so as not to mess up the covers.

'That's a pretty doll.' Glenn slightly raised her voice with a false excitement. She began feeling tense with worry. She didn't want to see him cry any more; hearing him every morning and night was hard enough to ignore already.

'It was your mother's.' Her father held it in his hands as he slowly opened his eyes, seeing Glenn's innocent expression; she had always looked so very lost, and still did. Silently reassuring her, he took her hand, accompanying her on the bed.

'I wouldn't have thought she was into dolls, Dad. Funny, isn't it?' Glenn frowned as she touched the pretty pink dress with the tips of her fingers. She thought the doll was beautiful, like her mother.

'Anyway, what have you got there?' Her father placed the doll back onto the pillow, pressing down on its body with his hand for his Eve to absorb his love and protection.

'It's Mother's makeup bag. I spoke to the others; they said it's OK. I probably won't use it; well, not the blue eye shadow, anyway.' Glenn chuckled nervously as she tapped the bag with her hand, pretending she felt comfortable with her father, who was still sniffing from his tears and wiping his face on the cuff of his brown sweater. She was trying to work out why he even wore it at all; the sleeves were too short and the threads were coming undone slightly around the edges. If he were to take one yank on it, the whole jumper could unravel itself to a mass of wool. She was going to hide it the next time she did the washing. She didn't like seeing him scruffy. Her mother wouldn't like it much either.

'What's wrong with blue eye shadow?' Her father's voice crackled as he tried to hold more tears from welling up in his throat in front of his daughter. They'd all been through enough. He couldn't have his daughters worrying about him any more; they'd spent all of their young lives doing it. It was their time now, to make their own choices in life to get them on the right paths, the walkways they deserved to be on, not the ones which no one else dared to tread. He had to help them to stop thinking about him; he prayed their lives could reflect the life he wished for his Eve.

'Nothing; it's just not my colour, that's all,' she said, realising their father had no idea their mother had covered her natural beauty. It was always such an upsetting thing to see.

'Come on, you. I think it's time we all went home; we have done enough here for one day.' If he'd had his way again he never would have left; he'd have locked the bedroom door and lain with her forever. He spoke gently but firmly as he had managed to push his tears back into his stomach; he'd hold the pain in for another time, when he was alone again. It felt like he was always alone.

Glenn slid herself from the bed and smiled back at him, wishing she had asked Natty to see if he was OK. 'Can we come again soon, Dad? I really like it here.'

Glenn suddenly realised how crazy her words were, how she felt so very at home in her mother's bedroom for the first time since she was small. Her mother was nowhere to be seen; she couldn't push her off the bed again, not this time. Glenn remembered only needing a small cuddle. One morning she had bravely clung onto her mother's bedclothes, her little legs kicking to give her extra strength as her small hands grasped the fabric. Believing for one short moment as she crawled slowly over to her mother's sleeping body that she could lie softly upon it, and her mother would wrap her soft arms tightly around her small frame. It had been a wasted attempt. As she gazed at the very same part of the carpet she had fallen to, the thought made her shudder. Her father's request to leave suddenly sounded like a good idea.

'What have your sisters been up to?' her father asked as he walked out of the bedroom and made his way down the stairs.

Glenn stood at the door and watched her father heading toward her sisters. Glancing over at the bed she saw their mother's doll. She took a deep breath, feeling uncertain of why she was going back in.

The porcelain figure was covered with a pink silk dress, with a pink sash around its tiny waist. Glenn grabbed it; its legs flopped, the beautiful little legs with delicate cream lace tights and shiny black shoes. A small pink ribbon tied the black ringlets back from the exquisite features, the purest bright red lips; its blue eyes twinkled like diamonds, protected by thick black eyelashes. Glenn looked hard at its face and felt angry suddenly. All she could see was her mother looking back at her. Glenn felt uneasy as she could sense her mother's smug expression, and her mother was reading her mind. She knew how Glenn wanted to throw her against the wall and smash her, shatter her beauty and her perfection. Every part of the doll reminded Glenn of how meticulous and unflawed she and her sisters had to be. They were their mother's china dolls; they were beautiful on the outside, but under the immaculate clothes and faces their bodies were stuffed with sawdust.

'Glenn! Glenn, come on; we're going!' Natty stood at the bottom of the stairs, tapping her fingers on the bannister. She had made a promise to herself she was never going to enter her mother's bedroom again, not after what had happened. Seeing her mother's lifeless body, still and harmless but just as beautiful; she was so peaceful finally, probably for the first time in her life. The picture Natty had painted when she was young next to her open hand. Natty wondered if she could ever understand how her sisters managed to go in and out of the room so freely, as if they didn't care.

She remembered how Ruth had stood in the bedroom doorway the evening it happened, her hands over her ears, pleading for her to wake, shaking uncontrollably, her tears soaking her face. Glenn's commands had only lasted briefly as their mother lay motionless; she had stood the closest, as though she really wanted to make sure she was gone. But she was gone; they all had to watch their father cry over her body, scream over her as he pulled her close. They all wanted him to stop shaking her, to leave her alone. But it felt worse when they watched him carefully taking her belongings from the bed and placing them one by one gently into the open box, like it hadn't really happened. The crazy thing was that they all took their bags back to their father's house the next day. Their mother wasn't in her home alone when she chose to sleep forever; she knew they were there.

'*Glenn!*'

Natty became fed up of waiting and made her way for the front door, holding a small bag; inside was her mother's apron. It was all she wanted to keep. Everything in her memories of their mother was tied up in the small perfect butterflies and the colourful loose silk threads. Their mother had wiped her hands and her tears on the front so many times, her soul and life were woven through the cloth for Natty.

'OK, I'm coming!' Glenn raised her voice, laying the doll on the bed. 'Lucky escape!' she said out loud, smirking, as she swiftly pulled at the bed covers to ruffle them. As she left the bedroom she felt as though she wanted to cry.

'Sorry, Nat. Where's Ruth? I thought we were in a hurry.'

'I can have a guess: she's in the garden again. Arranging Mother's flowers we bought.' Natty knew she had stirred an emotion in Glenn, as she was the one who liked to arrange them.

'I did them when we got here, for goodness' sake; is there nothing sacred around here?' Glenn rushed off to the garden, huffing under her breath. She threw the makeup bag on the kitchen table before she went outside.

'Ruth, what are you doing?' Glenn shouted out into the air before she could see Ruth. 'Ruth, where are you?' *How many more years does she want to climb these stupid trees?* she thought.

'Girls, will you hurry up, please?' their father shouted from the kitchen door. As he went back inside he shook his head. He knew Ruth was hiding in a tree; he had watched her from the window as he stood next to Eve's chair. He had watched her pull herself into the tallest one at the back of the garden.

Watching his daughter run away from them all, he finally understood how quiet Eve's life must have been. The window to the garden was her screen to only a very small part of her world. From where she sat she could never have seen anything else in the room, only the flowers and the trees blowing in the soft wind. The days when it snowed she'd lean forward a little to really admire its beauty. She had told him once how pure and untouched the snow was, and that it was nature's way of cleaning all of the old and beginning again with the new. If only they could have lived that way, if only he had tidied the garden more for her, but yet again he knew it was too late.

Ruth sat in between the strong branches, waiting for one of them to go out and find her, covering her mouth with her hands as she was giggling.

'Ruth, come on; Dad wants to go.' Glenn could hear her sister's giggles. It made her laugh as she was more than aware she was in full view of Ruth.

'I can see you, I can see you!' Ruth's giggles filled the air.

'Ruth, we are going; hope you fall and bash your head!'

'Hey, that's not very nice, is it?' Ruth dangled from the branch and landed on her feet. Placing her hands on her hips, she paced up to Glenn. 'I take it you banged your head at birth, Glenn, did you?' Ruth winked and walked past Glenn into the kitchen, picking up the makeup bag and hiding it under her jumper. She began to laugh again as she went out of the front door to meet Natty.

'What has got you laughing so much?' Natty asked.

'Just wait a couple of minutes, Natty.' Ruth sat in the back of their father's car, lowering her body so her sister couldn't see her.

'Ruth, where is it? Give it back!' Glenn ran down the path in haste. She was thinking that once she got hold of dear little Ruth she was going to wring her neck. 'Natty, have you seen. . . what's so funny?' Glenn felt like screaming.

'Nothing, Glenn; relax, will you?' Natty tried desperately to hold her laughter back as she could see Ruth bent down in the back of the car, holding the makeup bag above her head.

'Natty, you lot don't change. . . there she is.' Glenn pulled open the door and grabbed the silver bag from her hiding sister. 'Cow!'

Glenn sat in the passenger seat of the car; she pulled her seatbelt over and folded her arms in resentment.

Natty and Ruth's laughter echoed from the back seat.

'Not funny, you two, really not funny, you really are not funny, not even the slightest bit funny.' Glenn spoke through gritted teeth.

'I'm sure it was a little joke, Glenn. Ruth knows it obviously belongs to you now.' Their father started his car, looking up at the bedroom window before he went to drive away, knowing they would all be returning very soon. It was where his Eve slept. As he drove away he knew she'd been alone far too long.

'But it really isn't funny. You wait, Ruth. . .' Glenn turned and frowned at Ruth, who was still laughing in the back seat.

Ruth stuck out her tongue at her elder sister.

# 5

---

Hearing his name being called, he tried to ignore her shrieking demands; she hadn't stopped talking since he'd accompanied her back to his house. He'd only been at the party an hour and she had made her attack. She was a very pretty thing who he'd notice later on in the evening, only after guzzling down a whole bottle of champagne. If he ever was unlucky enough to be a man who had to scurry around the dance floor at the end of the night to see who was left for the taking, she'd probably be the chosen one, to his relief. She smelt as she looked, which was nice. He didn't like to feel suffocated all evening, though, with his movements constricted; she made it a tiring effort, standing by his side all evening, chatting and giggling over nothing in particular. Making eye contact with her seemed impossible; he just watched her mouth moving hastily, her lips only still long enough to swallow the contents of her champagne flute, and to devour canapés which were offered around all evening on silver trays. Maybe if he could take the tray from the smart waitress he'd place it on her lap in the corner for a while.

There was no chance of speaking to and congratulating the bride and groom. It was probably a mercy in disguise as he wasn't too keen on the groom anyway; he always cheated at cards on a Friday night. Harry could have done without going to the wedding reception in the first place; he'd had a really busy day at the garage, and simply felt like having a few beers and a bite to eat quietly on the sofa alone. He knew it was time to stay at home and cry for the loss of Eve, needing to do it for as long as the emotions were poisoning his stomach.

From the second he had arrived home on the day of the funeral and sat on the sofa with his black tie in one hand and a beer in the other, he had known it was asking too much for him to be part of the day, to have permission to comfort his family, after what he had done. He'd built up the courage to knock on the door, holding tightly onto a bouquet of white roses, praying they would be accepted by his brother; he wouldn't have been able to place them onto her grave himself, as he wasn't allowed to for his own mother. Matthew had been cruel that day. He needn't have been, knowing the last time Harry had seen Eve alive was at the net curtains, sweeping them across her body so he could see her; she was making him go away, telling him to leave with the movement of her hands and mouth. He had thought the dinner invitation all those years ago was something too good to be true.

Matthew had told him to go away too; strangers were not welcome, and he was to take his flowers with him. When Matthew went inside, Harry didn't turn around; it was when he placed the soft-scented flowers onto the doorstep. He felt like someone was watching him the whole time. He only wanted to say goodbye, only to have a minute with her, to tell her how sorry he was for falling in love with her.

He hadn't seen her name in the newspaper either, not straight away, confirming to the world she was really gone. The newspaper had remained on his couch the whole time, even next to him when he'd got drunk and had the worst sex ever with some lady who smelt too much of alcohol. Her makeup was smudged around her eyes; her breath was stale too; she was horrid, even more so after she had stolen money from his wallet. It was his punishment for not discovering her name in print straight away.

**MRS EVE HOPKINS**, 1922–1974. LEAVES A HUSBAND AND THREE DAUGHTERS. FOREVER IN THEIR HEARTS.

He didn't believe it at first; how could he have missed her name in bold black letters? He remembered throwing the newspaper across the living room; he felt like his body was going to erupt in pain.

'YOU LEFT ME TOO, EVE! YOU LEFT ME TOO, GOD DAMN IT!' Harry screamed into the air that day as he held the paper firmly to his chest. He screamed hard, causing pain to the back of his throat. 'I'M PART OF YOU ALL, ALL OF YOU, AND I'M SORRY, GOD DAMN IT! I DON'T WANT TO BE ALONE ANY MORE! IT'S BEEN TOO LONG!'

It was now March 1975. He should have let all his feelings out that day, knowing it was his time, but chose to go to the local bar and drown his sorrows with the hope of picking up another revolting example of a woman who was desperate for some drunken attention. Hidden away at the back of his mind, as he stood alone with a row of empty beer glasses in front of him, he felt that hidden in the background of it all someone did care. She didn't have to call him; she did. The sound of her voice was beautiful.

Since then he had buried his pain along with Eve; it was something he had become very good at, but the night of the wedding he could feel it becoming stronger than his own will, so to prevent his emotions beating him he had picked up the over-decorated invitation and begun to get himself pretending again. He hadn't planned to be holding on to a woman with one hand and the dearest champagne with the other before the night was up; drinks on the house, of course, and the only place for any woman would be his cold bed and out of the front door promptly the following morning, or even the same evening. It seemed to be the only way to put an end to the normal awful subjection to verbal emptiness.

'Harry? That is your name, isn't it? Could you do the back of my dress up, please? I can't see why it's taking so long; you were quick enough to undo it.' The young lady spoke gently, walking in front of him; she turned around with her hands on her bum and the back of her dress hanging down on each side, showing her soft skin. Harry began feeling quite contented with his consolation prize.

As he pulled the small zip up her shapely body his thoughts went back to the evening before. It had been bugging him all morning; he couldn't quite put his finger on it, knowing he had seen the bride somewhere before she resembled a glorified toilet-roll holder, knowing it was going to irritate him until he remembered who she was.

The newfound stranger stood prettily in front of him. He wondered if he should see her again, if she would be able to give him a moment's peace. At least she hadn't spoken while they'd had vigorous sex against the bedroom door. As his thoughts of her physique began to run away with him he became slightly excited at the thought of pushing his hands into the front of her dress. Something which had never happened before; any beautiful woman in his home would never have stayed for longer than necessary. Perhaps it was time to give it a go? What would it be like if he tried having a woman in his life for longer than eight hours? A sense of loneliness consumed him whenever they left, whoever they were, or however drunk they were. He was always left alone with the remnants of lipstick on his pillow; it was always a reminder someone had been there and someone had left, leaving him space to think of Eve. He had to keep himself busy or it would seem too hard to bear.

Harry stood in his black trousers, his white shirt undone at the front. His black bow tie and tuxedo jacket lay on the floor with a pile of oily overalls and jeans; from underneath the heap of used clothing a small gold sequinned handbag protruded slightly. Moving away from the temptation of his new acquaintance rapidly he bent down to reach for his jacket; as he picked up his hired attire he slowly pushed the small bag further into the disorder. He had a plan; he had to make it work. He didn't understand why; he just knew he had to try something.

'It has been a great evening, Sus ... Sal ... Susan.' Harry felt slightly embarrassed for the young lady who was sitting on his sofa with her legs crossed, leaning forward, elegantly poised and slowly buckling the straps on the front of her black stilettoes. Her blonde hair flowed around her knees. As she swept it up onto her shoulder, Harry felt a sudden exhilaration in his stomach again; she really was very sexy. Beginning to feel almost cocky he chuckled under his breath. He was nearly fifty-three and was more than capable of attracting women much younger than him.

It was no good; he had to see this one again. It was time. He finally had to come to terms with the fact he was never going to feel the same way about anyone else after Eve. Imagining he could still smell the scent from Eve's perfume on his skin after so many years.

Harry placed the tuxedo jacket on a wire hanger; the aroma of stale tobacco made him cringe. He was becoming gradually accustomed to the idea of seeing her again; her nails had been painted a glossy red, her toenails too, and her legs were smooth and soft. The plan he was conjuring up simply had to work, as he became more and more impressed with her.

'It has been fun,' the unknowingly accepted woman chanted under her breath as she frantically hurled old newspapers into the air, lifting each brown suede cushion and throwing it down again with a huff.

'What's the matter, Susan? Hold on; let me turn the radio down.' Harry knew what she was looking for. He had to find a reason to see her again. There was no way he'd just say; he certainly wasn't brave enough.

'Have you seen it? Bloody hell! What have I done with it? Where is my goddamn bag?' The young lady began to raise her voice in her panic, sweeping her blonde hair up behind her ears.

'I don't remember seeing it. Maybe you left it at the party.' Harry's voice was low as he cautiously covered the shiny gold bag with his clothing.

'I'm going to have to go! I can't believe I can't find it; I am sure ... oh, God, I pray someone has handed it in. I've only just got paid; my wage packet's in it. Oh, why do I have to do such ridiculous things?' The young lady promptly looked at Harry, bashing her forehead with the palm of her hand, seeming as though she was going to cry.

'Did you want me to lend you some? Some cash, I mean.' Harry was amazed by his words and the whole plan; who did he think he was? The realisation that he was actually going to see the whole plan through concerned him. To put such a pretty thing through such torment for his own gain: the thought brought a pang to his stomach, his very hungry stomach.

'I will see you out, then, Susan.' Harry was certain she had read his mind and deep down she knew. Nerves overwhelmed him as she took her sequinned jacket which matched her missing bag, checking her pockets frantically.

'Thank goodness for small mercies; at least I can get home.' Before she burst into tears she rushed up to Harry and quickly kissed him on the cheek. 'Bye; it's been nice.'

Feeling anxious and hoping he would say something, she went outside. It was a beautiful morning apart from the loss of her handbag; the dew was settled on the hedges, the sun behind the rooftops waiting to awaken the day. As she walked quickly to her car, a week's wages down, she turned one more time and smiled.

36

Standing at the car door she looked at him standing on the untidy porch.

'By the way, my name's Suzy!' *Arrogant arsehole,* she thought.

Harry rubbed the top of his head with his hands in sheer embarrassment for not remembering her name, but worst of all: under his dirty clothes were her handbag, her pay packet, her possessions.

'Matthew was right; you really do hurt people,' Harry said to himself, turning slowly as he went back to his messy surroundings and the predictable lonely feeling.

Walking despondently to the fridge, he opened it slowly; the smell of old chicken suddenly surrounded him. Grabbing the plate, he inspected the leftovers which he hoped to be eating with a bag of chips. Turning his nose up, he threw the chicken into the bin and the plate after it. As he huffed and sighed and made funny noises with his mouth, he ruffled his black hair, feeling desperate. All he wanted to do was have a cold beer for breakfast. As he pulled out the bottom compartment to retrieve one, an awful feeling of wasted hope engulfed him, as he remembered drinking them all with the lady with the golden handbag.

'Bollocks!'

# 6

---

Matthew felt his head beginning to hurt, finally parking outside his home. Wishing he could be left alone for only a while so he could collect his thoughts. He hadn't felt part of the world since Eve had gone to sleep. Everything seemed like make-believe; the trees, the grass, the flowers had been put there to make everything look normal. But it wasn't normal; nothing ever was. Going from one house to the other wasn't how he had ever planned anything to be; he had gone that day to stay forever with his girls and to be part of Eve's life once more, whatever she had in store for him, choosing to sit on the rollercoaster of emotions one more time.

The girls insisted they were to be with him at all times; they said they were going to help him. Especially Ruth; she'd already informed him it was always going to be the two of them. Matthew gave Ruth a half-hearted grateful smile in the car mirror. They needed to stop fussing; he was quite capable of messing everything up alone.

Ruth never saw their father's smiling reflection; sitting with her fingers stuck in her ears, she was hoping to ignore Glenn, who had been calling her childish names all the way home.

'Dad, you see your daughters? Do you fancy telling them to stop being such a pain?' Ruth quickly inhaled a deep breath, hoping her father hadn't heard; it wasn't meant, not in the way it sounded anyway. She felt relief he hadn't noticed, but it lasted for only a moment before she saw his fist clenched on his lap.

Natty leant across from the back seat so she could see him more, as his eyes were beginning to fill with tears. She wasn't sure why she didn't get out of the car; she was fixated on watching him. Her sisters were being unkind to him, being noisy all of the time. He was always so sad; his eyes couldn't lie any more. Natty believed he missed their mother like he had lost his own ability to breathe without her by his side; even though she hadn't been part of his life for such a long time, he had surely always been part of her soul.

Natty became aware suddenly of how hard it must have been all those years ago when he walked away from her, walked away from her life. She swallowed hard and recalled the day when he walked away from them all. Remembering like it was only yesterday. Seeing him go, she ran after him, dropping her picture on the floor in the hallway, praying he was going to turn around and come back to pick it up for her, but even at her tender age she knew he wasn't coming back; she knew he wasn't going to pick her picture up or read her a bedtime story again.

She quietly sat back in the car. She understood why he had left; she had understood even at such a small age, but she couldn't work out what made that day different to all the others. Why? She knew she was never going to know.

'Hello? We getting out of this car sometime in the next twenty weeks?' Glenn ruffled Natty's hair. Ruth roared with laughter at her sister's action, and was happy she was being left alone finally.

'Look, Glenn, no one is stopping you going indoors. Dad isn't ready yet!' Natty held on to her mother's apron, her fingers wrapped tightly around the soft fabric. She wanted to bring it to her nose to smell it but thought she'd wait until she was indoors. The aroma of sweet perfume and cooking lingered on it; she could smell it through the paper bag. If she closed her eyes their mother could have been sitting in the car with them. Pushing the brown paper bag under her jacket, she wondered if their father could smell it also; it was the perfume he gifted their mother with each and every Christmas. Natty had found a couple of bottles in their father's kitchen cupboard; the ungiven gifts still remained there in the polythene. He hadn't given them to her. Natty bet he wished he had.

In the midst of her thoughts her sisters were still giggling and calling each other names.

'Sorry, what's that, girls? Oh, yes, sorry.' Their father sighed and quickly opened his car door. He suddenly fell to his knees as he stepped from the car, his knees cracking onto the cold pavement.

'Oh God, Dad, no!' All three girls rushed from the car, dropping their new possessions, their stomachs full of anguish and fear. They all ran to help him up, each one grabbing at his arms and waist, attempting to pull him to stand high as the man he was, proud and strong, underneath all of his pain.

'Dad, please get up; it's going to be all right, we promise; it's going to be all right, we promise.' They all pleaded with their father; his anguish burnt through his chest. They could see his body becoming weaker with each plea.

'Dad, you can't do this any more; you just can't. It has to stop. You will make yourself sick, like Mother was, Dad; you will be so helpless.' Glenn's body was shaking with adrenaline and fear at not knowing what was happening to him. She wanted to scream at him like he was her child, to get him from the cold damp pavement.

'I'm so sorry, so sorry. I miss her!' His screeches echoed through them, shattering pieces of their hearts.

'Please, Dad, get up, please. Do it for Mother, please; you have to, Dad, you have to get up.' Ruth tugged at his jumper; she wanted him not to be stared at any more. The net curtains were moving in the street, the busybodies standing behind them. She didn't want them to laugh at him; they didn't know him. They couldn't feel what he was feeling. They didn't have the right to see such a man broken. Not their father.

# 7

---

'Natty, what are we going to do with Dad?' Glenn threw her brown wool coat onto the sofa, looking up to the ceiling, hearing his footsteps on the landing at the top of the stairs; he was pacing up and down again.

Glenn had left her makeup bag in the car. The thought made her huff and then chuckle as she wondered what all the fuss was about. It was only a silly bag full of old makeup; it wasn't important. It didn't matter if she had the bag or not, and in any case it would be rude to go outside and retrieve it after what had happened to their father. She would leave it a while.

Flattening her short black hair down, she gazed confused at Natty, who still hadn't answered her question. 'Hey, deaf ears, did you hear me? I said "what are we going to do with Dad?"' she said, shaking her head and pulling a funny face at her uninterested sister.

Natty sat in the armchair in her jacket, the apron still stuffed inside. She was gazing into the corners of the ceiling, looking for cobwebs; she was going to get her hand and take a swipe at them, take the little spiders' homes and lives away, give them a taste of her own life. She was fed up with being kind and understanding.

'Natty, you look like you've been stuffed. Will you talk to me?' Glenn picked up a small cushion and threw it firmly at her sister.

'Hey, what are you doing that for? Just don't, Glenn; I'm really not in the mood.' She felt numb; her arms were still shaking from the weight of their father. As her aching arm fell to the side of the chair she felt the box of colourful Christmas decorations which hadn't been put up. The gold tinsel fell to the carpet; Natty leant over the side of the chair to put it back in its rightful place. Smiling, she looked to the other side of the living room, almost

41

looking straight through her sister who was standing in full view of the undecorated Christmas tree, each branch bare and green, lonely without its normal coverings of candy sticks and little sparkly stars. Maybe any poor little spiders could find some comfort on one of the branches after she destroyed their homes.

Their father had taken the decorations from the attic and placed them in the middle of the room. The Christmas tree had remained on the floor in its green netting for at least two days, until one morning Natty and Glenn had gone down early and managed to put it up together without waking him and Ruth. That was three months ago. The decorations were still untouched. The box had become like forbidden treasure which had been cursed, each of them fearful of rummaging through what lay inside its protective cardboard. It wasn't going to happen. Natty wasn't going to do it, anyway; not a chance. It was something they'd always do together, but each of them waited for the others and none of them ever mentioned it.

Finally bringing her attention back to her overreacting sister, she looked at Glenn, who by this time was standing in the middle of the cold living room with her arms folded firmly, tapping her foot on the carpet.

Natty began to chuckle slightly. 'What's the matter with you, Glenn?'

'Oh, you want to talk to me now, do you? You know, when you have finished dreaming of Ben?' Glenn pushed her folded arms tighter into her chest, pursing her lips and raising her eyebrows, her eyes appearing to bulge.

'Oh, well, that's funny. Really sensitive, Glenn; didn't have you down for someone who had a care about your heartbroken sister.' Natty unzipped her jacket and took out the over-creased brown bag, placing it on the side of the armchair, rubbing her hands on it to flatten it as much as she could.

'I could have told you he was going to be a bum. But hey presto, good old clever-clogs Natty knows best.'

'I don't think so; your googly eyes were on him all the time. "How's Ben, Natty? Is he coming over?" Talk about obvious.'

'What's so obvious?' Glenn placed her hands on her hips as she looked over at Ruth, who was leaning up against the doorframe, watching her elder sisters at each other's throats again.

'Glenn, look, I really don't care if you fancied Ben, OK? Only care to forget about him.'

'Ruth, would you say I fancied that arsehole?' Glenn brought Ruth into their dispute.

'Glenn, I don't know; did you?' Ruth smiled slightly, glancing over at Natty, who was rummaging through the Christmas box with one hand, without looking.

'Oh, God, give me strength! You what? I can't believe you two. Talk about on the funny juice.' Glenn was now pacing up and down the living room with her hands on her head.

'Glenn, shall say this to you once only? If you continue to act like a mad ex-boyfriend lover any longer, I shall take this silver bauble and shove it gently up your huge knickered backside.' Natty held the retrieved Christmas decoration in her fingers, moving it from side to side with a smug look on her face, desperately trying to refrain from bursting into laughter, just as Ruth was at the door.

'Do what you like, because he liked me more anyway.' Glenn stopped pacing and gave Natty a snarling look, which could have provoked even the most patient person. Suddenly she felt the sting of the bauble smacking the front of her head.

Natty and Ruth roared with laughter at the fabulous shot.

'I suppose you think you're clever, do you? Well, you're not.' Glenn couldn't help laughing at the thought of how a silver bauble flying through the air and smacking her perfectly in the middle of the forehead must have looked. A sudden churning came to her stomach as she realised Natty must have known a little how she liked Ben; her stares must have made it obvious. Glenn remembered getting caught once, watching them both sitting in front of the TV together holding hands. Ben had looked up and asked if there was something wrong with her neck because her head had been in the same position for ages. The burning sensation on her cheeks resurfaced. Glenn suddenly felt bad for her sister, who sat laughing with another silver bauble in her hand. Glenn would make sure she ducked down next time.

Natty knew speaking to Ben again would be far too much for her to bear. She clenched her fist, wanting to burst into tears under her laughter. It was easy for her to remember the day. It wouldn't leave her; she'd wake up every morning and it'd be there in her already mixed mind. His smile, a gorgeous smile; he knew how to make her laugh. Her overwhelming sense of admiration for him each and every time they met. How happy it always made her when he'd buy her a thick chocolate shake with two straws, so they could sit and enjoy it together while watching a film in the cinema, holding hands all the way through. On more than one occasion they were ordered to keep their noise down through the showing as they'd insist on chatting; it made them both laugh more, and they'd shuffle down into their seats further so as not to disturb anyone while they chatted quietly and finished their shake. He'd kiss her softly, always holding her gently as he did. She thought he was the one for her; she believed he would be there when she needed him. Who cared about chocolate milkshakes, anyway?

Natty swallowed hard, wanting to burst into tears, feeling the lump building up in her throat beginning to hurt. Why couldn't she cry as she should?

Sitting with her fingers touching the tinsel she remembered again how she had run to him for comfort. Dashing up his path to his front door, she had felt it was her sanctuary; it was going to be all right once she was there. She needed him desperately to hold her tightly, to let her know she was safe in his arms, and how much he loved her. But most of all Natty needed to know it was OK to feel so lost and confused about everything. She prayed he could be honest with her and tell her with all the truth and belief inside him that it wasn't her fault her mother had taken her life. That even though her mother had been so ill she still loved them, and that Natty had done all she could for her mother in making her life just a little bit happier and a little more bearable. It was all she wanted to hear from him, only a few white lies.

She had waited for him to answer the door; in her desperation she cried, 'Come on, Ben, please answer, please!'

He didn't care; he opened the door in a smart shirt and jeans. His aftershave was freshly sprayed. She liked it. She'd smell it on her coat the morning after seeing him.

Why couldn't he tell her it was all going to be all right? He was unhappy in her presence, just like her mother. It was the moment Natty didn't feel safe. She left him at his door, as he had other plans, another heart to break.

44

Natty had paused before making her way up the street. *The audacity, the cheek,* she thought as she took her door key from her pocket. She gazed at his freshly waxed car, his green pride and joy. She grinned recklessly.

# 8

---

'Did you have a happy birthday, Ruth?' Her father sat on the kitchen chair, bending over, and began to undo his shoelaces. As he kicked off his shoes he glanced at the full plastic bags which he'd just placed on the floor.

Ruth began to take the groceries from them, looking at each item with care, feeling a little uncomfortable with his forgetfulness. Her fifteenth birthday had been nearly four months ago. It was now April 1975. Had he gone mad? And if he wanted her to really be honest, then her response was a big fat 'no'; she hadn't had a nice fifteenth birthday. He hadn't given her a card. She remembered how she had sat at the table holding the unwritten gesture still in its plastic; the neon orange sticker in the corner had '45p' written in black biro. Natty had been given a beautiful blue dress on her fifteenth birthday and he couldn't even be bothered to do that for her. She wondered if her Uncle Harry would have written one for her. On the day of her birthday she heard her father walking down the stairs and slid the card back under the fruit bowl. He kissed her gently and said he'd write it later. It didn't matter; she was just happy he'd washed that morning. She could smell his clean face as his stubble rubbed gently against her young skin.

Ruth continued looking through the freshly bought groceries.

'Dad, it was different, thank you. Glenn even managed to get me a card. I nearly fell off the chair. Then again, she did take it back again a little later cause I made her so angry. What a surprise, Dad, me making Glenn angry.' Ruth giggled at her father, who was rubbing his feet together, smiling as he leant back on the wooden seat. Ruth felt he was only humouring her; his mouth barely moved and he hadn't made eye contact with her once. All the bags were empty and Ruth grabbed up all the plastic, screwing it up, squeezing it extra hard, just like she wanted to do to Glenn's head for using her bubble bath.

'Ruth, my dear Ruth, please forgive me for making your birthday so awful. I promise I will make it up to you, you know, when things settle down. I didn't write it, did I?'

'No, Dad, it's OK.' Ruth wanted to run over to her father as he leant forward as if to get up from his chair. She wanted to hold him, help him somehow.

Looking into her eyes he could see them sparkling like the blue sea; she was immensely beautiful, stunning for someone so young. She was his daughter, his own very grown-up surreal image of beauty. He had to keep saying it over and over again in his head. He knew every time he looked into her eyes, her blue shining eyes. She wrote with her left hand; she liked to sit and read with a cushion on her lap. She had the ability to draw from memory after seeing something for only a few minutes. They were all traits he knew were not from him. He couldn't have drawn a matchstick man if he tried. And every time he looked into the mirror, he made a point of looking at his own eyes, his grey eyes. He cringed to himself in disbelief at having behaved so atrociously, especially after all the promises he made to her the day he bathed her sores.

His thoughts were disturbed by the chinking of cups.

'Cuppa, Dad?' Ruth stood holding two white china cups, waiting for the answer, smiling gently as she pinched a chocolate from the box Natty was devouring. She was nearly onto the second tray, only leaving coffee creams and Turkish delight, so Ruth knew she had better get in quick.

'I would love one, Ruth.' Swallowing hard as he felt he wanted to cry, her father picked up his black leather shoes and went to place them in the hall underneath the coat rack. Bending down underneath the coats he began to cry, pretending to sort out the shoes that had been thrown there. He wanted to curl up in a ball and pull the woollen coats and scarves upon his tired body and hide away, scream into them, not ever be seen again as a broken man. The sharp high heels that belonged to Glenn digging into his knee.

'Tea's ready, Dad!' Ruth's voice echoed from the kitchen.

Hardly able to put his words together through his sobbing, he blew his cheeks out, almost holding his breath. Breathing in and out slowly and using a scarf to rub his face dry, he answered at last, 'I'm coming, my little angel; I will be in soon,' his voice so soft it was almost a whisper.

His stomach twisted when he heard footsteps.

'Ruth, go back in the kitchen, please, Ruth.' A despair overwhelmed him as he had vowed to himself he couldn't allow his girls to see him like this any more, and hey presto, his youngest daughter was a witness to his failure, his body burning with embarrassment.

Ruth rushed forward, placing her hand on his shoulder, her own body shaking violently.

As she felt panic she looked at the kitchen door. Natty was only sitting at the table, getting through the bottom tray. The door blocked her from Ruth's view; it left Ruth alone with their father. Was she to call her sister?

'Dad! Oh, my dear dad! Please stop being so sad, stop hurting, please! I can't bear it.' Ruth knelt down to her father's level and found the ability to rub his back gently, noticing how cold he felt, her shaking hand on his body.

Looking at the kitchen door, she prayed Natty would appear to help her. It wasn't going to happen. She was alone with their father, a man who was always alone with himself, their father who struggled to survive a moment longer without their mother. If only it was Monday morning, when she'd be sitting in her class doodling on the edge of her Maths book. But it wasn't; she was sitting under the coat rack on the cold tiles in the hall with her father.

Taking her hand from his back as her father sat under the coats, still holding on to Glenn's damp scarf, Ruth slid her body next to him. They huddled close, shoes and coats soft and shielding them, a word not exchanged between them. Ruth pulled Glenn's grey coat onto her lap, and began gently tugging at the small thread hanging from the button; all of a sudden the brown leather button rolled onto the floor. Glenn was going to be moaning later. In Ruth's sadness the thought of pulling the remaining buttons from her sister's favourite coat felt quite cathartic. Placing her fingers onto another button, she twisted and pulled it until it was in her hand.

Her father looked at her with a gentle expression. 'Ruth, your

48

sister is going to be furious with you, you know.' His voice was husky from all of his crying.

Ruth looked up at him, smiling gently, looking mischievous. 'I know, Dad, but how funny?' Looking into their father's face she saw a small glint in his eye, which made her feel he was going to be part of her practical joke. She held the coat toward him. 'Want a go?' She began to giggle, and sensed an overwhelming relief when she heard her father giggling too.

'Give it over here, then.' Her father tugged at the helpless button, as his sadness turned into hysterical laughter.

Ruth's belly began to hurt; she was frozen with joy, almost unable to take a breath as she watched her father yanking at the button.

'Here you go, your turn.' The grey coat was passed back to Ruth for its final attack. Their laughter echoed through the hall.

'Shall we just leave her one? Seems it's unfair to take them all. Are we going to hide the evidence, Dad? I did lose one under the telephone table.' Ruth found it hard even to speak as she laughed through every word.

'You, young lady, are a bad influence.' Her father took a deep breath, hoping to contain himself, unable to remember the last time he'd allowed himself to feel such freeness. Keeping his focus on Ruth, he smiled, and without her knowing it dawned on him how much she resembled his brother.

'You OK now, Dad?' Ruth looked at his strong features and felt so proud to have such a handsome father.

'I am now, Ruth, thank you. I'm sorry for not being able to hold it together for you and your sisters; you have been so good to me.'

'And you have been good to us too, Dad; remember what you did for me? You know, keeping me. So you really haven't got to say sorry, not to me.' As Ruth spoke to her father she giggled now and then, the feeling of laughter still in her belly.

'Keeping you?' An unsettled feeling surged through him.

'You didn't have to, Dad. I mean, my dad – I mean Uncle Harry – has never wanted me, and you still kept me; you didn't have to. That's all.' Ruth wished she'd kept her mouth shut after their fun together.

'There is no other way it could have possibly been, Ruth. You

49

have always been mine. I certainly didn't keep you. You have always been part of our family and you always will be; you are mine, Ruth. My beautiful, grown-up, very fun-loving daughter, and if there's ever any thanking to do, it's from me. I thank you for coming into my life, our lives, and bringing such kindness and love to us all.' Feeling himself becoming tearful again he grabbed hold of her hand and tried to squeeze his tears into her grip. The real truth was, he never really knew deep in his heart if Harry had abandoned her; deep down, did he really yearn to be part of his daughter's life?

'Anyway,' he said, 'I thought we were having a drink. Shall we get these coats tidied up? I think we should put Glenn's on first.' He stroked her cheek and gave her a comforting smile.

'I think that sounds like a good idea.' Ruth looked at Glenn's coat on her lap and smirked.

They stood and began to pick up the coats, smiling at each other.

'Hey, what are you two looking so pleased about?' Natty walked from the kitchen. 'Left you some chocolates, Ruth: your favourite ones.' Making her way up the stairs, Natty giggled at Ruth, knowing how much she hated coffee creams.

They both watched her until she was completely up the stairs, then glanced at each other and smiled.

'I love you, my little Ruth.' The thought of Harry rushed through him again.

'I love you, my big dad.' The thought of getting a beating from Glenn rushed through her, as she gripped the buttons in her hand.

# 9

---

Crunching the empty beer can between his hands, Harry walked despondently to the fridge to retrieve another. The cold air escaped from the open fridge, making him shiver. Rubbing his hands up and down his bare chest, he rearranged the old takeaway cartons, the half-eaten noodles from the evening before and most likely the night before that, placing them to one side, discovering to his desperate need the relief to his thirst. Realising he had the remains of sticky Chinese sauce stuck to his hand, Harry huffed and wiped it onto the back of his jeans.

When he slammed the door shut, the clothes and the papers on the top of the fridge fell forward, revealing the edge of a beautiful gold sequinned handbag. Placing his beer on the side he was reminded of his dishonesty, and wished it could be discarded as quickly as the sticky sauce. Pulling the bag slowly from its protective place he held it in his hand, moving it to his nose so he could smell it. It smelt nice: the scent from the lady who had been in his home not too long ago. One month exactly. He hadn't heard from her, and wondered why he had forgotten about his plan. He had to get it together, make the first move, take the bag to her in the bookshop where she worked. The image of her crossed his mind quite a few times, but he still felt reluctant in his idea. Maybe she had no intention to ever set her eyes on him again; after all, he had stolen her handbag. It had been too long to attempt it now.

He bashed the handbag onto his head again and again. 'You stupid man, Harry. You've blown it again.'

Grabbing his last can of beer from the side he walked into the living room and threw the bag onto the sofa, sat and pulled the ring from the top of the can, guzzled down nearly all of its contents. He contemplated going to buy more; he had emptied the can enough to scrunch it in his strong hand. His home felt lonely as he gazed over at the armchair where Matthew always sat when he used to visit. Harry himself was sitting in the exact place he had met Eve for the very first time.

As he exhaled a deep breath a memory of the whole life he had thrown away engulfed his thirsty body. He had a daughter from the only woman he had ever loved, a part of them both entwined in one being. How he longed to say sorry to her for behaving in such a way, for leaving her. She wasn't Matthew's; she was his.

Harry knew he had destroyed everything between himself and Matthew: his brother who he'd always admired and looked up to, wishing he were him. After all they had gone through together when they'd sit on a wall with their grey school shorts on, chatting and making catapults with their father's pen knife, their father unaware. Matthew had always taken the blame for Harry when they were boys, and would always put a little of his dinner on Harry's plate if he thought he didn't have enough. *Here you go, little Harry; you need building up more than me.*

Harry chuckled to himself, feeling sad, remembering his brother's words. How could he have ever betrayed him in such a way? Why couldn't he have left what belonged to his brother alone? She wasn't his to have; she wasn't his to share, not like their dinner.

Sitting alone as usual in his messy home, memories filling his mind and body, Harry sat back a little further, taking the small handbag in his hands, moving it from one to the other.

'Come on, Harry, what are you going to do about it?' The small sequins rubbing against his dry skin, he knew he was holding on to something else which didn't belong to him.

'Come on, Harry, so what are you going to do?' Hearing the old newspapers crumpling behind his back, he wondered if the shops would still be open. It was 3.30pm; he'd have plenty of time.

'Just get off the sofa and go, God damn it.'

The thoughts went over and over in his head until finally, at 4 pm, he decided to get off the sofa and make his way out of the front door. Grabbing his shirt from the back of the chair, he began making his way promptly to the bookshop in town. The thought of buying beer went completely out of his mind.

\*

52

As he leant on the large decorated window cupping his hands around his eyes to see properly, his actions brought a pang to his stomach; he remembered peering through Matthew's window and seeing his daughter and Eve for the very last time. Fifteen long years ago. With every year he became older he knew she would surely more closely resemble the only woman he'd ever made love to.

Finding it hard to see through the darkened window, he could barely make out an outline of the young woman as she placed a book on a shelf. He knew it was her, not missing her beautiful blonde hair falling around her shoulders.

Holding tightly to her handbag, he stepped back from the window and took a deep breath. As he turned the brass handle he saw how his hands looked, old and oil-stained. He wasn't getting any younger, so if he was ever make to anything of his life he'd have to continue in his quest. An unrecognised nervous feeling began stirring in his stomach.

Entering the shop a stale aroma swept over him; it was unpleasant and musty, reminding him of his father's cellar, where he and his brother would play army battles. The place seemed stuffy; there wasn't very much space for customers to walk around, books piled in corners and shelves rammed with old pages bringing an added darkness to the shop. Harry wondered who'd buy such a thing. If he had his way, he'd be sticking them in the trash.

The only lightness in the shop was seeing her again, with a small pile of books in her arms; her black polo neck fitted her body to show its slender shape and her chequered cream slacks emphasised her long slim legs. Harry hadn't realised how adorable she was; she was very much to his approval.

Harry coughed to get her attention and found he had to cough even louder as she was immersed in her duty.

'Excuse me, can you help me, please?' Raising his voice slightly and smiling gently, he began to get his needs met.

She walked toward him, after placing the books onto the counter.

'Yes, sir – oh, it's you? The woman was taken aback for a moment and then collected her posture, pulling her hair gently around her neck so it lay exquisitely on one side of her shoulder, revealing its real beauty and length. She was very conspicuously glaring at him up and down, almost scowling.

'Yes, it's me.' Harry wanted to disappear into the maze of letters, jump into a book and become lost within the heavy bindings. He'd gallantly become a knight, returning from pursuit of the most terrifying dragon.

His wandering mind was disturbed by her voice echoing in his ears.

'How can I help you, Harry? That is your name, isn't it?' The young woman raised her eyebrows, her voice laced with sarcasm.

'Hello, Susan. I found this at mine. It still has your wages in; you can treat yourself now.' Harry needed to bellow and scream. He felt embarrassed holding out her handbag; surely she was aware of his antics, his ridiculous plan. He wasn't sure he had her name right either. Destroying the fire-blowing dragon or even getting eaten by one, chewed and spat out again would surely be easier than having to stand in a stinking bookshop feeling so humiliated.

'You've only just found it? Wow! Thank you; I love that bag too. I can't understand how it took you so long to bring it to me. I did tell you where I worked. I suppose you weren't thrilled to be seeing me again? And my name isn't Susan; it's Suzy. Honestly!' She shook her head; she had already felt annoyed with him for forgetting her name after their night together, and doing it again was plain stupid. Still, she felt she could put her stubbornness aside; after all, he had returned her favourite handbag. He was also far more handsome than she recalled.

'Yes. Not "yes" as in I'm not thrilled to see you again – I mean I'm thrilled, very much so – I mean yes, I have only just found it.' Harry knew he wasn't off to a very good start with her. If they could have sex behind the wooden counter, then his feeling so useless would come to an end.

'Thank you for bringing it to me, really. I can't imagine you read much? I'm sure there isn't much in this sort of shop which interests you.' She blushed slightly.

'Actually I love to read, if the football isn't on.' Harry laughed and began to feel relaxed instantly, to his relief.

'What kind of books?' Happily holding on to her returned handbag, Suzy spoke with interest.

'Normally the ones that have pages in and smell a little different.'

54

Harry folded his arms, forgetting about his dragon fight and the aroma of the shop; a sweet scent of perfume now pleased him.

'OK, you got me with that one. I know it does get a little stifling in here sometimes. They're old, you see; most of them are donated to us. It seems rude sometimes, turning such generosity away. Anyway, I'd best get on. It has been lovely seeing you again, and I hope you can stay and have a little browse; you may find something you like here, with plenty of pages. Thanks again for my bag.' She turned and went to place her bag behind the counter, then continued sorting through the small pile of books.

Harry was left standing in the middle of the shop with his arms still folded. The stale smell came back to him. As he went to leave, his back now to her, what he was thinking came out of his mouth without any planning.

'Only you; I'd enjoy spending a bit of time with you.' His voice was rattled. Should he turn around or simply grab hold of the brass handle again? Blowing a gasp of air out, his cheeks puffed, he decided he wasn't going to let his unpredicted words go to waste.

He continued to speak to her; this time he knew what he was going to say.

'Maybe we could make up our own story, you know: beautiful damsel in distress who lost her bag and the heroic prince gallantly returns unharmed from his courageous adventure, returning it to her, to await his prize of a night out for dinner in the great kingdom.' Speaking with eagerness and excitement, he knew she was not going to resist such a line.

She burst into laughter and rolled her eyes, shaking her head gently. 'That has to be the corniest invite out on a date I have ever heard. And anyhow, what makes you think I was a damsel in distress, Mr Prince Charming?' She continued to smile, noticeably blushing.

'Your prince will return on Tuesday to release you from your humble abode.' As Harry spoke he felt he was winning her over. The urge to stand behind her and have forceful sex entered his mind. She was leaning over the counter, tapping a pen on the surface; it was a perfect place for him to stand behind her and relive their first evening together. He pushed the thought reluctantly from his mind, as he knew it wasn't what he was looking for; he needed more than sex in his life, and he wanted a life, another chance to get it right finally. All of a sudden he felt like he was the dragon being slain as he'd never followed anything properly through in his life before.

'Oh, well, seeing as I am in such distress, I take it the honourable prince will be buying, as I lost my bag, remember?' The young lady continued tapping the pen on the side and moved her body gently in a flirty manner. As she licked her lips her eyes were wide and sparkling. 'I would be happy to be rescued from here at around six, as long as you're not saving any other damsels, and you remember my name.' She was full of childish giggles as she winked at him; pushing herself a little over the counter, she gave him a quick peck on his cheek.

'I think it'll be hard for me to forget. See you Tuesday, then. Bye – what's your name again? I'm only joking!' Harry touched his cheek where she had left the remains of her glossy red lipstick.

He stood outside the bookshop for a moment, happily absorbing the fresh air into his lungs, as the dusty shop had begun to burn the back of his throat. 'You Prince Charming, you.' Speaking aloud he smiled, turning to have one more look at the gloomy windows. Patting his back pocket to make sure he had his wallet, he made his way to the off-licence to buy some more beer.

# 10

The quietness surrounded him in their home, his girls out amongst the world, absorbing their young lives. They had so many wonderful moments to live. Matthew only prayed they'd believe they deserved them. A sense of pride overwhelmed him: Natty becoming a nurse, Glenn working for a newspaper company, and Ruth having her school journey still to follow.

As he sat on the edge of his bed he imagined his beautiful Eve sitting next to him holding his hand. He knew she wasn't real; he was fully aware he'd never entwine his fingers into hers again. He found comfort from his vision.

His bedroom was cold and dull; the brown duvet covers and carpet always seemed to close the room in. The dark mahogany wardrobes and dark cream walls were not a good choice. All those years ago he hadn't had time for pretty surroundings, putting a new home together for him and his girls. He hadn't cared about anything when he'd scoured the old flea markets for a batch of furniture that served a purpose. He'd toss and turn in his uncomfortable bedroom nearly every night, desperate to sleep, hoping to find some peace in his dreams.

Placed on the chest of drawers lay Eve's wooden box, full of her memories, the last meaning to her life she had embraced. He'd had to bring it back to his home; he'd not leave it at hers, not like her doll. Matthew hadn't touched the box since the day he had brought it home. He thought of how he'd stared at her belongings gathered around her breathless body. Respectfully taking each item quietly as if she wasn't in an everlasting sleep, he had prayed she'd wake. He had seen only Eve; he was unable to recollect seeing the girls, speaking to or comforting them in any way. How'd he forgive himself he never knew.

Despondently moving from the edge of his bed he stepped slowly to the box. It was all he had left of her: an old box with dried petals and pictures. Without any conscious warning an overwhelming surge of anger fuelled his body. Grabbing the box he held it high and hurled it through the air, smashing it against the wall of his dreary room.

'WHY, EVE? WHY?' Screaming like never before, his throat felt as though it was tearing. He could barely breathe, his repetition of breath becoming erratic and short. Panicking, he tried to inhale; his chest was burning as his breathing became more difficult. He had to sit again. He took slow steps to the edge of the bed as he held his chest and gripped his shirt.

The emotions surged through him, his tears falling from his eyes. He had to calm himself down; he had to. His body felt like lead.

Closing his eyes he took himself back to his thoughts only moments earlier. In the midst of his breathing and tears he took his mind away, holding Eve's hand again, imagining her sitting beside him: his vision of her smiling, her long black hair framing her beauty. As Matthew slowed his breathing down, enabling him to inhale a full breath, he opened his eyes.

Pushing his tired body from the bed, he walked slowly out of his room without looking at the remains of his torment. His tears had suddenly subsided as though they'd frozen inside. The cream walls on the landing were almost closing in on him, stifling any breath he'd managed to regain.

He knew exactly what had to be done. Walking down the stairs in haste, Matthew grabbed his coat; the other coats fell to the floor. He didn't notice or, if he did, he didn't care. Swiping his keys from his second-hand telephone table, he left the immense feeling of suffocation.

# 11

---

The large clock hung high above the platform; it was just past six o'clock. The number twelve was barely noticeable as the pigeons' mess had defaced most of the glass; the pigeons would find refuge on nearly all the high metal structures in the station, disrespectfully leaving traces of their visit.

Glenn stood amongst the noise of excited birds and commuters who all seemed to purchase their clothes from the same department store, resembling mannequins as they stood side by side modelling the latest fashion, the women nearly standing as tall as the men with platform heels and flared trousers. Glenn stared into the air, feeling apprehensive of being attacked with debris from the smelly grey birds. Her black suit jacket could never have hid such misfortune.

'Stupid birds, why don't you go and crap on yourself?' Glenn muttered under her breath. She hated waiting for anything, especially a delayed train; it had been due in at 5.45, but of course her rushing from her desk that day and squashing herself into the packed lift had been yet again completely unnecessary. She had been left standing at least twenty minutes over her time again, rubbing the blisters left on her feet by her high heels as she'd hastily walked to the station; her attempt to seem as dignified as possible in her dash had ended up turning into a very inconspicuous jog.

Standing near the edge of the platform Glenn began to tap her feet, humming, still avoiding any contact with the pigeons who skimmed past too frequently for her liking.

'Listen, you little flying smelly shit machines: if you come anywhere near me again, I'm going to get up there and pull your little beaks off. Now scram!' Glenn waved her hand in the air, speaking much louder than she had anticipated.

'Do we seem to have a problem with little flying shit machines?'

Glenn froze; her eyes widened, nearly popping out of her head in sheer disbelief at hearing such a deep husky voice coming from behind her. She felt her face becoming warmer and knew that if she turned her cheeks would match her shirt. It was one of her favourite work shirts with winged collars and large cuffs; the buttons were embroidered with flowers and chequers. He sounded gorgeous and strong.

All of a sudden the doors of the incoming train were flying open and other cloned workers dismounted; she hadn't even realised it had arrived. The station was buzzing with noise; the doors being slammed closed vibrated through the vast spaces above. Everyone knowing what they had to do to get home, like robots set on one motion, commuters wouldn't smile or acknowledge anyone else around them; they were in their own little corporate existence. The silent men and women pushed and shoved each other, desperately attempting to gain the seat by the dusty window for their journey home. The commuters who had left the train huddled together like the pigeons, all going in the same direction, all leaving the noisy infested station. Before pushing forward onto the train, Glenn swiftly glanced behind her to see the young man's face.

*Oh my God, he's old,* she thought. He was surely old enough to be her father. She felt disheartened, but only for a moment as the feeling was softened by her managing to find a seat: black-and-orange chequered, and surely not designed to be sat on for more than five minutes.

Nearly all the doors had been closed. It was going to be another journey home surrounded by silence; for some reason her fellow travellers seemed terrified of making eye contact with anyone at all. They would sit with their legs crossed, turning the pages of the oversized newspapers until they reached their destinations. Maybe one of them would cough from behind their printed sheets, giving confirmation to Glenn that she was sitting amongst humans.

Her moment of relief at finding a seat was short-lived as the stranger had found a seat directly opposite her.

Glenn wished she had a newspaper too so she could also pretend she didn't exist behind it. After working with them all day, the last thing she wanted to do was read them.

The stranger sat poised wearing a pinstriped suit and a beige raincoat; his crisp white collar and blue tie were slightly showing. His black shoes were highly polished. Glenn found it difficult to take her eyes from him, now and then glancing out of the window hoping to get a look at the trees and hills; the train always went too fast and she never could take it all in properly. There was handsomeness to him under his ageing skin; his grey eyes sparkled in the evening sunlight as the orange light was reflected through the window. His hair was completely grey, though cut into a very young and tidy style. He wasn't too bad for an old guy. She began to wriggle her toes in her shoes as they felt sore; then again, she always wriggled them when she felt nervous, not that anyone had ever known about her little habit.

The train pulled into the next station and some commuters departed, leaving her a little more leg room, and also leaving their newspapers on the seats for the next set of clones to hide behind. The stranger remained on the train, to her unexpected pleasure.

Glenn began to feel chilly as she shivered a little, glancing in the opposite direction again. The stranger gave her a soft smile; his eyes seemed to sparkle more as his lips moved. Her belly began to churn with anticipation. Glenn kept thinking she had to come to her senses; how she could possibly fancy such an oldie? Looking around the gradually emptying train, she could see there were plenty of younger men she could flutter her thick eyelashes at. Though the grey-haired stranger stirred an emotion inside her, something she had never felt before. Not even from Natty's melon-head of an ex-boyfriend.

Commuters had been departing the train for another three stations. Glenn had one more to go and in a funny way hoped the stranger would be flinging the doors open at the next stop also.

That was it; the train screeched to a halt. Glenn now had to stand in some kind of dignified way and reclaim any embarrassment she had given herself only forty minutes ago.

As she stood patting her black trousers down, the stranger moved his legs back a little so she could pass him without any problem, giving her a lingering smile as he did.

'Thank you, and by the way I don't like smelly flying shit machines.' Glenn smirked as her stomach tightened in complete bewilderment at what had left her mouth. Dashing past him and almost leaping out of the door, she hurried along the platform, praying the train would leave straight away. As the train left the station, which thankfully wasn't bird-infested, Glenn stood and looked up to the overcast sky. How could she have been so stupid? She could not believe she had said that. She pulled her shoes off at the station to take a slow and regretful walk home and maybe contemplate throwing herself off the nearest bridge, after sticking her fingers in her eyes.

It was nearly seven o'clock by the time she reached her front door. The soles of her feet were black with grit. She didn't care any more; there was no purpose in living for her. Even her short black hair felt knotty and tangled.

Throwing her shoes on the pile of coats on the floor in the hall, she walked straight up the stairs to go and bang her head on something hard. Slowly walking up the stairs with her dirty feet, the grit rubbing onto the carpet, she could hear someone crying in her father's bedroom. Leaning around the door she saw Ruth in the corner picking up broken wood, piece by piece, as something had shattered amongst colourful confetti and remains of dried yellow paint.

'Look what he's done, Glenn. Just look.'

# 12

---

The wind was picking up, the sky was overcast; it was going to be raining again soon. April showers never failed. The cool wind seemed to absorb the tears from Matthew's clammy face; he had cried all the way. He hadn't been alone in there since she had taken her life, taken his life along with hers. It had always been such a large house, too big for her all alone. All she had to do was simply ask and he'd have gone home. All those wasted years; why couldn't she have asked him?

For the first time in a very long time he felt emotionless. Matthew wasn't sure what he'd planned was a good idea; how were they going to feel? After all, their mother wasn't there any more; she was meant to be. He wondered as he unzipped his brown canvas jacket: if they hadn't gone for apple pie that day, would she still be sitting in her chair, wrapped warm and safe in her soft blanket, scenting the room with her perfume?

He stepped forward, slowly walking to the front door; the pots outside displayed beautiful flowers. He now was prepared to feel her loneliness, to imagine how it must have been for her with only her bottles of pills to keep her company, in the large spaces which had surely imprisoned her.

As he threw his keys onto the small telephone table, he gazed up the large stairs. The space was immense; the high ceilings seemed to go on forever. Why had he never noticed before?

A sense of numbness suddenly overtook his body as the image came of his three beautiful daughters running to him, calling his name over and over. His vision seemed so real he found himself almost stretching his arms out to take them in his strong grasp and twirl them around; their pretty dresses would flow around their small legs as he held them high, absorbing their giggles.

Shaking his head and tutting, he held on to the bannisters tightly, taking his first step up the stairs. How many years his girls and Eve had walked up and down them. He rubbed his hands softly against the wood to feel them. The crystals on the chandelier were dusty and overtaken by cobwebs; he wasn't there to clean them for her. His body remained numb; he was seeing and not feeling, something he never recognised.

Passing Eve's bedroom he made his way to his daughters' old rooms, rooms where they'd be sleeping if life for them all hadn't taken another unpredictable turn. A smile came to him as he looked at Glenn's pretty pink blankets with small flowers, her heavy floral curtains which matched beautifully. A pink carpet the platform for elegant white carved furniture, handmade glass handles on each drawer. A chuckle came to him as he thought of the girls with their brown covers at home. Touching her bed, he smiled. *She's such a funny thing,* he thought, walking over to straighten her perfumes and powders on her dressing table. Most of their belongings had stayed there; he had never had the heart to take everything of them away from Eve.

He made his way into Ruth's bedroom, remembering her pushing her body to and fro on the white wooden rocking chair with its small floral lemon pillow, how her legs dangled as she was too small to feel the soft cream carpet on her little toes. He took a moment to run his hands across all of her favourite fairy-tale books, then took one from the organised shelf, sat on the floral covers and opened it, feeling the pages with his cold hand. He had never read it to her. The little girl in red reminded him of Ruth as it was a colour she had always loved to wear. As he began to read the story out loud to himself, an undesirable emotion began to unfold in his stomach. He was determined to read the book, inquisitive, wanting to know how it ended for the pretty little girl in the red cloak. Slamming the book closed once his curiosity was fed, thoughts of his brother Harry engulfed him; he was the big bad wolf in the little girl's life. Matthew had to protect her, not let her go into the woods alone.

Leaving the book on the bed he turned to leave Ruth's room; at the corner of his eye he saw a picture of a castle surrounded by red roses stuck to the side of her dressing table. A smile came to him with the memory of how she had told him he was her prince. 'You're my princess too, Ruth.' Speaking into the air, he left his daughter's castle and walked only a few steps across the hall to Natty's room.

Matthew waited for a brief moment before making his way into his eldest daughter's room. He saw the white wardrobe's doors were open, only revealing the few empty metal hangers. Closing his eyes and shaking his head, breathing in hard through his nose, he tried to understand how he could have put some clothes in a bag when he and Dr Peters went to speak to his Eve, to tell her her daughters were not going to be sleeping in their glorious bedrooms again. It felt like yesterday as the doctor easily spoke to her, while Matthew went into each wardrobe quietly and gathered a few items, giving the metal hangers no purpose, just as he was doing to their mother.

'Huh.' He saw Natty's toothbrush still in the small glass on the little basin.

Matthew sat on the edge of the green covers; only the curtains and the pillows were floral. Her bedroom furniture matched her sisters', but one of Natty's handles had broken. Getting onto his knees Matthew tried to find it, to mend the antique furniture. Like all their hearts needed mending.

Kneeling on the soft green carpet, Matthew closed his eyes and from nowhere unexpectedly felt an overwhelming sense of peace. Embracing the intensity of such comfort he squeezed his eyelids tighter.

'We're coming home again, Eve; we are coming home.'

Matthew had finally experienced peace for the first time in his life, a moment he'd hold on to as long as he could. It was in him somewhere; surely his body stored such a thing, a part free from pain and guilt. It was hidden in everyone; he'd put his life on it.

Pushing his fingers into the soft carpet he pushed himself back up to his feet, opening his eyes and placing the delicate handle into his pocket. He closed the wardrobe doors, unaware of Natty having to scurry though the hangers in search of her blue silk dress to no avail all those years ago.

# 13

Clicking her heels on the pavement outside the bookshop Suzy waited for the arrival of the man with a useless memory for names. Her legs began to feel a little chilly. The brown tartan miniskirt and brown winged shirt weren't keeping her very warm. She was happy she had chosen to put on her cream tank top which matched her plastic knee-length boots wonderfully. She hated being cold. If she felt any chillier she would surely be making her way home.

As she swung her bag by its long strap back and forward by her bare legs she realised how heavy it was. Tuesday was always her day for closing the shop; the huge set of keys had to be pushed into her small brown bag, filling the entire space, the clasp barely clinging together, her crumpled cigarette packet sitting on the top.

'You have got to be joking. Come on, I've had enough now!' Suzy decided to take a cigarette from her bag and attempt to light it, flicking her hair to one side as she moved away from the direction of the wind, clicking her lighter again and again. She inhaled a deep breath to her satisfaction, blowing the smoke into the air, her bright red lipstick staining the butt. She was still only thirty-three, wondering why the hell she was standing on a chilly pavement waiting for a guy to come and take her out, and twenty minutes late too. She'd finally had enough; she wasn't waiting for anyone.

'Bloody hell. Sorry, old boy, missed your chance.' Suzy threw her cigarette into the drain, blowing out the last intake of smoke, and began to make her way home. Her heavy bag swung in front of her as she folded her arms to keep a little warmer.

The failure of his efforts began to irritate her as she walked toward her car.

'Hey. Hey, Suzy.' Harry sounded breathless as he walked quickly behind her.

Suzy continued to walk, feeling his presence, hearing he was out of breath.

'Really sorry I'm a little late; not very good for a knight in shining armour, am I?'

'You're crap!' Suzy turned around quickly, raising her eyebrows.

'At least I remembered your name!' Harry gave her a charming smile, his blue eyes glistening in the early-evening sun. She was a very sexy lady, he thought.

'Mmm, I don't do timewasters, Harry!' Suzy didn't want to smile at him straight away; he needed to suffer a little for his carelessness. She expected a little more grovelling than a glint of his gorgeous eyes. Folding her arms a little tighter, she waited for the begging.

'You don't look very happy. I'm truly sorry I'm late; I had to finish a job, and a customer was behind my back checking his watch too. Really, if I had my way I would have told him to shove his starting motor up his backside, but hey.' An unusual sense of desperation rushed through him; he hoped he'd said enough. To his sheer relief he saw her beginning to smile. 'Fancy a beer?' Harry moved his head from side to side, giving her a childlike look. It had never failed him in the past.

'Cheese and onion crisps too; that's the least you can do after that grovelling. Rubbish, absolutely rubbish!' Suzy laughed as she stared at the man wearing an old pair of jeans and a blue jumper, his blue flowery shirt collar over the neckline. Chuckling at the thought of how his mirror must only be from the waist, she looked him up and down. He was too old to wear such a shirt, she felt, but apart from the jeans and scruffy brown suede boots he was passable for the pub anyway, even though he'd already promised her dinner.

As they entered the aroma of tobacco and stale beer, the dark tables and burgundy curtains made the place feel dingy. The brown patterned carpet felt sticky under Suzy's boots as she made her way to a small table next to the window.

'What you having, Suzy, apart from crisps?' Harry watched her

67

as she began walking to the table as though he wasn't even there.

'Gin and tonic, please.' Without turning around Suzy made her request. Sitting at the oval wet table where stains from the bottom of old glasses were almost ingrained, she took the oversized set of keys from her bag and placed it on the sticky surface. Attempting to remould her cigarette box to its normal shape, she looked inside to see four cigarettes bent slightly, creasing the white paper which held her addiction together. One by one she straightened them up and placed them back in the fixed box, keeping one in her hand. *God, I need a fag,* she thought as she waited for the second time that evening for the man at the bar.

'Pint and a gin and tonic, please.' Leaning on the bar, Harry unintentionally absorbed the moisture from the beer towel, his jumper now wet, showing a darker blue circle on each elbow. 'Bollocks; well, that's just bloody swell.' Harry sighed as he squeezed his jumper with his hands, not even understanding why he was there, as this entire dating lark seemed to be a bloody waste of time. Why couldn't he just take her home and have rough sex with her? It was the only thing that never caused him such an ordeal.

He rolled his eyes before walking slowly across the sticky carpet with two drinks in his hands and a packet of crisps in his teeth. He hadn't even got a kiss from the dashing blonde and he was already worn out.

# 14

'Oh, God bless him; give him some money, Glenn.' Ruth fixated on the heap of dark stagnant blankets outside the entrance of the train station; it had momentarily seemed like nothing more than a pile of filthy blankets until she had seen his legs protruding from the bottom of the self-made shelter. The dark blankets, their colour unrecognisable through grime and stains, were not big enough to cover him properly. There were no socks protecting his feet from the cold concrete; his bare foot was showing through the bottom of the worn-out leather that fell from his filthy black shoes; no laces held the soft grungy pieces around his feet. A body was huddled under the dark shelter, hidden away from commuters walking casually past in their expensive suits.

Ruth wondered to herself if she was the only one who could see him lying so alone and desolate. She felt strangely enthralled by the existence. The freedom and the movements he could make as an invisible man. No one saw him; he simply blended in with the concrete and the surroundings. If he were to wear the latest fashion and do his hair and be a part of the world, he'd be judged and criticised. She knew how much sacrifice it must take to live in a way, to finally be left alone, to be and feel every part of who he was, raw and wonderful.

'Ruth, Ruth! Are you coming, for goodness' sake? I was walking up the road talking to myself!' Glenn stomped back to her younger sister, her fingers burning with the weight of the shopping, the plastic handles pushing into her hands.

'Sorry. Look at him, Glenn; I'm going to give him some money.' Ruth placed her glossy bags on the pavement and began to search for her purse; she knew she had thrown it in one of them and was attempting to find it amongst new shirts and trousers when she felt Glenn grab her arm. A sense of guilt rushed through her for all the newly bought items she would never wear; they were going to be thrown into the wardrobe with the rest of her labelled items, as she normally chose to borrow Glenn's, without permission of course.

'Don't be stupid; what are you giving him money for? It'll go on drugs and drink, for Christ's sake. Oh, don't you know anything? I'm going to get him a cup of tea; are you coming or not? Here, take them.' Handing her bags over to Ruth, Glenn made her way to the café, taking some change from her pocket of her flared jeans.

'Hey, Glenn, I want to give him some money; why can't I?' Ruth shouted at her sister, who was not too far away.

Glenn huffed and slowly walked back to her confused sister surrounded by plastic bags. 'Look, you know what these kinds of people are like; they bum around all day waiting for money to pay for their fix. Why else would he need money? Not going off to buy a lampshade, now is he?' Huffing again at Ruth's stupidity, Glenn went to buy the newly labelled addict a cup of tea.

'Glenn, you do amaze me.' Ruth quickly scurried through the bags and found her purse. Grabbing all of the notes and change she could, she threw them swiftly into the small pot, which held no more than six pence. 'Go and buy your drugs if you want to.' Ruth began to shake a little, knowing that if Glenn had seen her, she'd empty the small pot again in disgust, including the measly amount of money which had already belonged to him.

Glenn returned feeling almost smug she had won the battle with her sister. She placed the freshly filled polystyrene cup near the foot of the hidden stranger. She didn't fancy getting too close; fleas were certainly not her thing. She noticed empty polystyrene cups next to the blankets with tooth indentations all around the edges; one had been torn into small square pieces. It brought confirmation to her that the option of tea was also on the minds of the other passers-by who had been forced to stop and do something honourable by their own annoying family member.

'Come on, you; I want to get home now.' Glenn beckoned for Ruth to follow her. Her belly was rumbling and they had been shopping most of the day.

'Hey, you, these aren't all mine.' Ruth felt annoyed as she tried to gather all of the bag handles into her hands while she mumbled under her breath, 'You're such a lazy cow, Glenn Hopkins.'

As Ruth stood, feeling her arms beginning to ache, she took one last look at the sight of freedom and slightly smiled.

# 15

Matthew embraced the freshness of the air. As he slowly walked around the garden the memory in his mind overtook him: how Eve would fill the front of her apron with a few apples, how she'd slowly walk through the maze of trees, breathing in the aroma of flowers and freshly cut grass and looking up into the sky, pausing in her movements before stretching and twisting the ripened apple from its long branch; the leaves would fall around her feet. As he looked over to her small gravestone he knew the leaves could always fall upon her, she was always to be near the apple trees and the beauty as nature intended it to be; she was part of nature itself.

Yanking at an apple, Matthew held it in his hands and smiled. He had finally made the move to come back with his daughters; they seemed happy too. They never told him otherwise.

'Now how do I turn this apple into a pie, Eve?' He felt comfort as it was something which had always made him smile. He'd watch her rolling pastry, humming to herself; she'd be lost in her own happiness.

Throwing the apple up into the air and catching it, his smile became wider as he made his way back into Eve's house, which now belonged to them all once more. He checked behind the kitchen door for her apron, hoping to place the apple in the front pocket; he knew she'd like it.

'Where's that gone now?' He sighed as he placed the apple into the empty fruit bowl, holding on to it longer than needed. He checked behind the kitchen door again briefly before making his way up the stairs to his daughters. Deep down in his heart he was uncertain of how they truly felt about the decision to move back.

As he took each step of the stairs his thoughts slowly filled him. How he'd arrived home only a month ago. Making his way in the front door of his old home, he'd hung the coats on the floor back on to the coat hooks. His Glenn and Ruth had been sitting on the top of the stairs. Ruth had had upon her lap small pieces of broken wood, her tears falling onto her young features. Glenn's arm had been wrapped around her shoulders as she attempted to give her comfort.

Ruth had stood up and turned her back on him as he made his way toward them. Glenn had raised her eyebrows in disgust as she went to join her. Over and over in his head were Glenn's words before she turned away from him too. 'Dad, you really hurt her.'

They had all sat around the dinner table that evening; it was then he had included them in his idea. He had informed them they'd be getting all of their things together as they would be moving in the following week. He hadn't meant to be so direct and thoughtless of their feelings; it had to be done and that was that.

Natty had placed her knife and fork down on the edge of her plate; she had smiled at him that day, a smile he hadn't seen for a long time from her. Ruth had dismissed herself from the table; she had placed her uneaten dinner on the kitchen side. And Glenn had just continued eating.

'Can we swap rooms, Glenn? Your room is so much bigger than mine. I have to find a place somewhere for my old books.' Natty leant on Glenn's white doorframe, her jeans over her arms. She was the eldest, after all, and had never managed to work out why Glenn of all people had a much larger room than her. She felt as though her efforts were going to be completely wasted; she knew she never managed to get anything from Glenn unless Glenn was to be given something in return. Touching the soft denim with her fingers, she began to wonder.

'Hey, deaf ears, did you hear me?' Natty watched as her sister sat on the floor with her legs crossed, sorting through a bag of makeup and perfumes, placing each one onto her carpet, smiling in gratification with her complete collection finally back together. Bouncing her knees up and down in her cross-legged position, absorbed in her sorting.

Glenn hadn't even acknowledged the fact her elder sister had been hovering in her doorway for at least five minutes.

Natty turned to see their father on the landing. 'Oh, hi, Dad,' she said, thinking how tired he'd looked since the move.

'Still sorting, are you?' Standing next to Natty their father could see what a mess Glenn's room was in, not understanding why she was lining up all her belongings in shades of colours all over the floor; he'd thought she was meant to be putting them away. Her bed was covered in bags of clothes and boots she still had to sort through. Matthew shook his head, aware she'd never be done by tea time, and it was her turn to help him cook.

'You OK in here, Glenn?' Matthew took a step into her cluttered bedroom, as the disorganisation around him took his thoughts back to Eve's small flat when they had first met. Seeing his daughter happy in her own space brought him a sense of comfort. He wasn't going to say a word to her about getting tidy, not like he had his Eve.

'I'm lovely in here, Dad, thank you. It's such a super room. I love my room so much; it's the largest in the house.' Glenn looked up at Natty and smirked, shrugging her shoulders, giggling.

'Oh, so you did hear me, then?' Natty felt like throwing the pile of jeans at her dear sister's head.

'It's a very nice room, Glenn. I will leave you to it.' Smiling at both of them, their father made his way in to see Ruth. He needed to make her understand it had been an accident; he hadn't meant to smash the box.

He became nervous as he tapped gently on Ruth's door with his knuckles.

'Come in.' Ruth's voice was soft. She had sat on her bed crying, wondering why she was back amongst her make-believe stories. Everything in her life seemed the same way; they were all pretending she was part of the family, as she was to them. Their father pretended he cared for their mother; if he did, he'd never have broken her memories like he had.

'Hello, Ruth. Have you been crying?' Her father sat next to her on the bed, gazing at her for only a few seconds before wiping her soft tears away with his finger. Praying she would speak to him. Give him a chance to explain.

Ruth swallowed hard as she felt his soft touch on her skin.

'You hate her, Dad, don't you, deep down?' Ruth's stomach felt immersed in pain. Her words were unfair; they'd hurt him. Ruth

74

began to sob as she gently moved his hand away so she could place her own hands over her swollen eyes.

Inhaling a deep breath and pulling her to his chest, her father kissed the top of her head, allowing her to empty the pain from her young body.

'Shh . . . shhh, little Ruth, it's OK.' Her father began to move to and fro gently. All he needed was her pink blanket which he wrapped tightly around her when she was a baby, the soft wool he once wrapped around her to protect her sores and aching heart, to protect her from the pain her mother put upon her, only for them to still miss her so.

'I don't want your tiny-arse jeans, get out of my room.'

'But they're my favourite. Go on, Glenn, how many years have you had this room?'

'Look, lanky legs, I don't care if I've had this room longer than you, and I don't care if you feel unloved because I was given the best one, and of course you can offer me your crappy jeans all you like, I'd never get in them, so no: no jeans, no room, so get out, will you?'

'No, I am not leaving.'

'Nat, get out of my room and go into your little space, jealous head.'

'Guess what, Glenn? I don't want your stupid room anyway! Stupid person in a stupid room, with your stupid frilly covers.'

'Jealous, jealous, Natty's jealous!'

'Glenn, you're such an idiot sometimes. Thought you might actually do something kind for someone for the first time in your life.'

'And what makes you think I ever need to do anything nice for you, Natty? Tell me what you have ever done for me, you know, apart from getting on my tits.'

Ruth began to chuckle on her father's chest as they both sat listening to their other family members. Moving from her comfort, Ruth wiped her face with her hands and began to smile.

Matthew wondered why they both had to be so cruel. They had all been through so much; when were they ever going to realise? Chuckling with Ruth, he slowly moved from the bed and gently pushed the bedroom door shut, seeing Natty standing over her sister.

75

'I think I will deal with those two a bit later.' He wanted to cry for Ruth sitting on her bed smiling through her tears; it was all so hard for her to understand.

Sitting back on the bed he took Ruth's hand, hearing mumbling in the background as his other daughters continued in their battle. As he felt Ruth's hand shaking he felt thankful as it covered his own shaking body and fear of speaking of her mother.

'Ruth, my darling Ruth, I don't hate your mother. I never have, not for a moment.' Instantly he remembered how his stomach had been overwhelmed with such a feeling on the catastrophic day he had discovered Ruth abandoned and hurt in her cot. He was already lying to her; he had promised himself he was going to be honest before he knocked on her door. She needed him to open up to her, give her a sense of belonging; he felt it.

'Dad, I found her box all smashed. How can you change so?' Ruth took the edge of her duvet cover to dry her eyes a little more. 'If you didn't hate her, then how could you have been so careless with all we have left of her?' Ruth spoke softly, her voice a little shaky, staring straight into his eyes.

Her father let out a long breath, his body pumping with nerves.

'Let me be honest with you, Ruth. I am not actually sure if I'm saying the right thing.' He gave Ruth a reassuring gaze, his voice soft and slow. 'Please try to understand, I'm not liking myself very much for allowing you all to simply exist, to work out all the things that happened, yearning for the answers to why your lives were so crazy.' His tears mirrored Ruth's. 'I stood outside the front door the day I left. I could have come back to you all, helped you to finish your pictures, been there more for your mother, helped her. I never can forgive myself for letting her go, not taking care of her. She was so sick, wasn't she?'

'Yes, Dad, she was.' Ruth's voice was full of tears waiting to erupt. She was going to be strong for her father; she could see he was hurting.

'I was thinking of myself, Ruth, myself and that was all.' He paused. 'I don't hate her; she was sick and so perfect all at the same time. I promise you, Ruth, she never meant to cause you any pain. And I am sure, deep down, not even me.' Seeing his beautiful daughter listening with intent, he felt at that moment he wanted to share more. He had to let her know who her mother was.

'Did you want some of my duvet, Dad?' Ruth offered him the edge of her flowery bedding for him to wipe his eyes.

'No, thank you; your mother would have had a fit if she saw you doing that.' He began to giggle and continued sharing the quiet and unique moment with her. 'Do you know she was the most fun-loving, free-spirited woman you've ever wanted to meet? Always cracking jokes; well, that's what she thought they were. She'd smile as she'd glide around; she was part of everything and everyone around her, until she became too weak to fight her illness. And messy, oh my goodness, so messy; she'd hang her stockings over the lampshades, cups and plates and magazines everywhere. Thinking about it now, it was kind of fun to be around.' He spoke enthusiastically, his voice gentle at the same time, feeling a comfort with an underlying sadness as he shared his memories of his Eve. He watched his daughter wiping her face dry and chuckling.

'I could never imagine Mother being like that. She became so ill, Dad, didn't she? It wasn't fair for her to change so. I have all her things from her box in my drawer, hid them under all my paintings. I was scared you were going to throw them away when you came home. I looked at your face as you hung the coats up and I knew you were sorry for what you had done.'

'Ruth, I am sorry for so many things: having to sacrifice you all for my own fears, having to disown my dear brother for betraying me. Bringing you back here and never giving any of you a choice in anything. Right up until this very moment, sitting here with you, I never realised how very much. I love your mother; I have always, and you are all part of her and I love you all more than life.' He felt a burning in his stomach as tears began to fill his eyes with intensity.

'Don't cry, Dad, please don't cry any more.' Ruth wrapped her arms around him and held him close, hearing his heart beating, the wetness from his tears on her face.

'Yeah, and I remember the time when you used all of mine, so I will have one of your nail varnishes, thanks; give it over, Glenn.'

'You bite your nails, Natty. What the hell would you need nail varnish for? State of them.'

77

'Nails can grow, Glenn; you can't change your face.'

'They're still going in there, Dad.' Ruth pulled away from her father and smiled as she patted his chest with her hand softly.

'Yes, they are, dear Ruth.' Breathing heavily through his nose, attempting to halt his tears, he turned his body, looking over at the small bookshelf. Leaving Ruth on the bed he moved his fingers across the colourful bindings; the image of the little girl in the red cloak brought a smile to his face.

'Ruth, would you like to listen to a story?' Wiping his face with the cuff of his brown shirt, he sat back on the bed, kicking his shoes off, and leant up against the wall.

Ruth smiled as they snuggled close, pushing her arm through his so she'd be as near as possible.

As they both looked up they saw Natty and Glenn standing at the door, finally peaceful.

'Are you coming to share the story, girls?' Their father prompted them over with a movement of his head as he and Ruth shuffled up the bed a little so they'd be comfortable.

Glenn and Natty gazed at each other before rushing forward. Glenn managed to sit on the other side of their father and automatically followed Ruth in gripping his arm. Natty knelt down on the soft carpet and put her chin on her hands.

They all felt comfortable and warm as they eagerly waited for their father.

Opening the book slowly, he began to read.

# 16

---

'How do you like your eggs?' Suzy kissed Harry's bare chest and moved her body from his to sit on the edge of the bed. She leant over and grabbed his shirt from the floor, pulled it around her, covering her slender naked body, her blonde hair flowing and messy. Turning to him, she smiled and leant over once more to kiss him hard on the lips. Sex with him was good, she thought as she merrily made her way to the kitchen.

Harry lay in his spacious empty warm bed with his arms behind his head, looking up at the ceiling. Wondering when she was going to leave. He wanted to be left alone for a while, and the thought of eggs in the morning was far from appealing, not that he hadn't found the night before wonderful. It was an experience he had never encountered before, hearing someone in the morning. Normally he'd pull on his jeans and a shirt, grab a quick coffee and walk out the door. He didn't have to make an effort; he needn't care for making conversation.

Rubbing his hand up and down his chest, feeling pressured into having to leave his warm bed, he quickly moved the blankets away, pushing them to the floor, where they lay amongst dirty clothes. Scurrying around the floor for his creased jeans, he pulled them on. He'd never taken much notice before of how he lived; it really was a mess, he thought. Scooping the nearest pile of clothes up, he threw it on the bare sheet and discreetly covered it with a blue blanket, bashing it down with his hand, pretending the clothes were not there and he wouldn't have to deal with them, like he was pretending he couldn't hear her in the kitchen. He held the waist of his jeans with his other hand, his belt buckle swinging in front of him.

'Harry, you have no eggs!' Suzy shouted from the kitchen as Harry heard the fridge door being slammed.

Relief filled him as all he wanted was a black coffee.

Making his way out of his slightly tidied bedroom Harry went into the kitchen, stepping up to her quietly as she stood looking through the cupboards. His shirt covered her body wonderfully; he admired her long slender legs, wrapping his bare arms around her waist and beginning to pull the shirt up over her bum a little.

'I know what I would rather have than eggs; fancy coming back to bed?' Harry felt aroused instantly, content in getting back to the same feeling he'd had the night before. Moving his body from side to side and moving her hair away from her neck so he could kiss her, he knew instinctively where they were to be going in the next few minutes as his persuasion had never failed him in the past; the bulge in his undone jeans confirmed his feelings.

'How come you don't have eggs? Everyone has eggs.' Pulling away from him, she filled the coffee jug with water.

'Hey, Suzy, come on, come on; let's not worry about breakfast, eh?' Harry felt dumbfounded as he watched her filling the glass jug and taking coffee from the jar with a spoon. How was it she wanted coffee and eggs and not passionate sex with him? Brushing the front of his jeans down with his hand he tightened his belt, feeling a little embarrassed. He'd never been turned down before; he'd never had coffee or goddamn eggs made for him before.

'How about bacon? You do have bacon, don't you?' Suzy stood at the arm of the sofa as Harry moved the newspapers to sit. She was beginning to feel a little frustrated with him; breakfast was a must for anyone.

'No, Suzy, I don't really want bacon either. Coffee will be just fine, just black.' Huffing, Harry looked at his watch and knew it was going to be a long morning.

Hearing her making unnecessary noise in the kitchen, he began to wish he'd covered himself over and not his dirty laundry. How long did it take to make coffee, anyway?

'Here you go.' Suzy passed him his awaited drink, slumping her body next to him, pulling her legs up on the brown sofa. Her breasts were showing slightly as she hadn't finished buttoning up his old work shirt to the top.

Harry wanted to put his coffee down and grab the temptation before him. Looking into the hot brown water he blew a little before sipping from his cup, having to drink his offering before making a move to her breast or he was surely to get a smacked wrist. He chuckled to himself a little in his thought. The urge of excitement worked its way through his body as she sat next to him, sexy and in easy reach, her smooth legs up and her long blonde hair ruffled on her shoulders. He didn't want her to cook him breakfast, not ever. It wasn't his plan to be fed to the brim after simply taking her to the pub.

'I had a little sort-out in the kitchen, Harry: all those newspapers you have, stuck them in the rubbish sack for you. ' Suzy sat calmly and wondered why he hadn't made a comment on her breasts; she had been pushing them up a little with her arms as she held on to her cup, knowing it worked every time to have them showing a little. Her idea to get him going hadn't worked at all.

'Not all the papers? You didn't throw all of them, did you?' Harry placed his cup down on the small table promptly as he began to fear the worst, his voice full of panic.

'My God, Harry, they're only newspapers.' Suzy spoke in a high-pitched voice, almost mimicking him. She watched him move hastily from the sofa, nearly making her spill her drink. What was the big deal?

Harry was back with a newspaper in his hand, feeling a complete sense of relief, sliding the happily found paper behind the cushion he had been leaning on.

'Thanks for your help and all, I really think it's great, but do you mind not throwing stuff away without asking me?' Harry smiled reluctantly as he began fixating on her breasts, his eyes moving down her appealing frame.

'Harry, what was all the fuss about? You can buy more; it's not as if they're going to disappear from the face of the earth.' Suzy couldn't be bothered with him, extremely aware he was looking at her breasts and knowing she was more than ready to be leaving his messy home within the next ten minutes. She had eggs at home and she was not going to miss breakfast for anyone, especially not some newspaper hoarder.

What was written in the hidden newspaper had already gone from the face of the earth. Something which held her name, her existence, he wouldn't discard as her life had been.

Sipping slowly from his drink, he thought he'd try to explain.

'It's this particular one I wanted to keep; has some important stuff in it I like to read now and then. You can read things more than once, you know.' Harry's voice was rough. He needn't have spoken; it was simply nothing to do with the pretty blonde with gorgeous firm breasts.

'Oh, I see, yeah, like the football scores.' Suzy attempted to smile at him as he protected the paper with his body. 'I'm getting dressed, Harry; I think it best I go home.' Suzy leapt from the sofa quickly and thought he could shove his scores where he felt necessary.

'You don't have to go, Suzy; I'll take you for breakfast if you like.' He wondered why she seemed so upset with him. It was his paper; she didn't have a right to touch it.

Harry remained on the sofa as he heard her getting dressed in the bedroom.

'Have you seen my brown shirt, Harry?' Suzy shouted from the bedroom, as she had from the kitchen only ten minutes earlier.

Harry thought quickly about his quick clean-up and knew its whereabouts exactly. He sighed, raising his voice. 'It's under the blanket.'

'You what?'

'It's under the blanket on the bed!' Sighing again, Harry didn't move from the sofa to help her. He felt a sudden pang in his stomach, aware he was pushing her away, allowing himself to be alone again.

'That's a mad place to put it; why on earth did you stick it under there?' She shook out her creased shirt and smelt the arm; it had a sudden stale aroma to it. Shaking her head gently and raising her eyebrows, she leant over quickly and kissed Harry on the lips. 'See you around; thanks for the cheese and onion crisps!'

Suzy left without looking back, annoyed as he hadn't seen her out, or even cared she was leaving; she had given him the best oral sex the night before and this was the way he was treating her. 'What an arse,' she said under her breath as she paced up his path.

The aroma of freshly made coffee still lingered in his house. Harry took the newspaper into his bedroom with a refill. Sitting on his mound of clothing and blankets he read the small print, touching the crumpled paper with his fingers, reading her name again and again. *EVE HOPKINS, EVE HOPKINS, EVE HOPKINS.*

# 17

Hearing the coins fall into the small plastic pot awoke him from his sleep. The ground was hard under his body; the papers didn't protect him much. Every day before he slept he'd push the dirty thin blankets under himself the best he could. They weren't big enough; he had to put up with the familiar sensation of pins and needles in his bottom and legs every day.

He yanked the blankets up to his chin, his legs now completely covered, his black corduroy trousers faded at the knees and dirty from where he'd wipe his hands, the dust and dampness from the ground staining the thin fabric. His flies were broken at the front; he'd always make sure to cover them with his big baggy knitted jumper. It was black, his favourite colour, even if it was filthy and too big for him.

Sitting cautiously, he waited for people to walk past, protecting them from his presence, not wanting to frighten them by quickly jumping up from a shop doorway. Watching their legs as they hurried past him: the fashionable platform shoes and shiny red and white boots. Everyone seemed to be going somewhere. He wondered what they were rushing for; what were they rushing to? Swallowing hard as the chilly air in the night had made his throat a little sore, he coughed, placing his dirty hand over his open mouth.

An old lady rushed past him hastily; she held a long black umbrella and wore a cream woollen coat which nearly reached her ankles. Her grey hair was covered with a small see-through plastic hat. He never saw her face but she looked like she was expecting rain.

Pushing his fingers into the blankets he tried to understand what made them walk away, the busy people in wonderful shoes. They needn't; he had so much to share with them, if only they would take the time to chat for a while.

Pushing his body up to sit on his numb bottom and leaning against the white-tiled wall, he finally discovered the small cup at the bottom of his feet. Taking a quick glance to his side, he knew it was new; he hadn't imprinted his teeth marks in it and it was still as gloriously moulded. Feeling happy he hadn't knocked it over, he smiled and wondered who was so kind as to leave such a thing for him. Slowly he leant forward to retrieve his awaiting gift. Cupping the warm polystyrene in his hands, he held it in front of his face, studying how it was made, pulling the lid off and putting it back on. It was such a simple, brilliant thing to him. How could the hot fluid not burn his fingers? What was this amazing invention which protected his hands from the boiling water inside? The thoughts filled him just as the drink was going to fill him with warmth.

At last he pulled the lid off and took a sip; the sensation of the steam touching his face was immense for him. He chuckled to himself as they hadn't asked him if he took sugar.

He sat drinking, wondering, staying quietly out of the way of everyone as best he could. He never seemed to be out of view of the small children holding their parents' hands; they'd stare at him the whole time as they moved past him. He'd hear them innocently enquiring as they looked up to their protectors, 'Mummy, what is that?'

As he bit into the soft edges of the cup he knew he longed to share all his dreams and ideas, tell them all he'd done and how much more there was for them all to do, instead of rushing and walking up and down in front of him all day. They never realised how much time they were wasting. All the shopping they'd carry around, there was no need for any of it; instead they could be following their dreams, and not hiding themselves amongst other non-dreamers with over-filled glossy bags. How could he let them know if they simply didn't want to listen? He'd not take too much of their empty busy days.

Whirling around the remains of his tea, seeing the congealed sugar at the bottom of his damaged cup, he placed it with the other polystyrene carcasses. Standing slowly he felt his blankets fall to his feet, his toes finally protected with some warmth. Rubbing his legs up and down he bent over and began gathering his worldly possessions, which fitted into the crumpled box that he always used as a pillow. Taking each edge of the dirty coverings, he shook them gently; the foul aroma wafted under his nose. Folding them neatly and as small as possible he began pushing them safely into their home. The sides of the light brown box would give way soon; he knew he had to be extra careful.

Taking a deep breath he looked into his small plastic pot and began to shake it as he had the remains of his tea. He felt his heart almost miss a beat as the feeling of kindness overwhelmed him; someone, whoever they were, had been very generous. Pushing his fingers onto the crumpled pound notes, looking up to the clear sky, he thanked God for such a kind offering, feeling extremely lucky. Fixing his gaze into the sky a little longer he could see the old lady had bought her umbrella out for no reason at all; it was going to be a beautiful clear warm day, and he was going to make the absolute best of such a moment. Humming to himself and gathering up the rubbish he'd slept next to, he walked away from his temporary home.

The people on the streets passed him quickly, spurring their steps as he made his way closer to them; some crossed the road when they saw him leaning into the bin. He wasn't going to hurt them; he was only throwing away his bitten polystyrene, praying someone would speak to him, to share his wonderful ideas. They were all scared of him and they didn't even know him.

His pockets were finally empty when he stopped outside a small café. Opening his hand he looked at the scrunched green paper. His grubby hands had made them look dirty, his three pound notes; he'd been given the chance to live like a king for a day and he was going to do it brilliantly. He paused for a moment, hoping the extremely generous giver would be happy in wondering how they had changed this very day with their offering. An excitement rushed through him and his cheeks hurt through his smiling; he was happy he was going to have conversation over food and be amongst other dreamers, who only had to take a risk and their lives would change and they wouldn't have to shop any more. The anticipation absorbed him. As he entered the café the aroma of fried bacon and freshly cooked toast was amazing; the intense warmth filled his pores.

'Hey, you, get out of here. Go and find somewhere else to eat.'

Hearing a voice ordering him to leave, he was unsure of where it had come from. It was apparent everyone in the brightly lit café was staring at him. He wasn't doing anything wrong. He had money; he could sit at the empty table next to the window, out of the way.

As he walked back out of the door a man pushed past him, taking a seat at the table next to the window.

'Sir, could you get a sandwich for me, please? I have money.'

The man ignored him and continued reading the menu of hot greasy delights.

'Please, young lady, could you get a sandwich for me? I have money.' He held his notes out to the shoppers; they ignored his pleas, lowering their heads as they scampered past him.

'Please, please.' He tried again and again, praying someone would help. He'd buy them a sandwich also, or they could sit and chat and share one. He didn't understand them, as he hadn't understood his parents.

Stepping slowly past the glorious shops, he wasn't sure where he was going, unable to get anything to eat. He had money in his pocket; he wasn't going to hunt through the Chinese restaurant's bin for their leftovers.

'Please, sir, could you get me something to eat? I have the money.'

Opening his hand once more, he gazed at his money. The dirt from his hands was rubbing off on it. He could still see the queen's face, and thought how pretty she was. Maybe she'd buy him something if he asked her.

Sitting on a small wall next to the post office he gave his attention to the people going in and out. Gazing at the red post box, a thought filled him. He wasn't sure if his dark-haired friend would remember him.

He made his mind up; he was going to have a go. Despondently gazing down at his shoes and trousers, he spat on his fingers and wiped his face. Taking a piece of newspaper from his box he wiped over the front of his shoes, spitting again on the paper to give them an extra shine, pushing his fingers into his matted curly hair. He made his way up the busy street, walking straight through, as always, the avoidance of people creating his own path.

# 18

'Seriously, Glenn, tell me you're not going out dressed like that.' Natty stood at the bottom of the stairs in her pink dressing gown with her lips apart in amazement, secretly admiring her sister walking down the stairs barely clothed.

'And what's wrong with it?' Glenn pushed past her, smirking, touching the front of her hair and quickly taking a look down at her chosen outfit. She was happy with her short black miniskirt and white blouse with a black diamond pattern; her black patent shoes with a small heel and a leather buckle on the front pleased her. It was the first time she had worn them, as they had been thrown in the back of her wardrobe since the day she had purchased them. Feeling sexy with a sense of nervousness, as it was something she had never dared to go out in before, she knew how envious Natty was of her look.

Natty followed Glenn into the kitchen, tightening the cord to her dressing gown around her small waist. Leaning on the doorframe, she watched Glenn brushing down her skirt and opening an extra button at the top of her blouse to reveal her cleavage further.

'Glenn, Dad is going to kill you; you know how he said he doesn't want us wearing those skirts.'

'Relax, will you, Natty? I'm nineteen in six months. God, anyone would think I was still five.'

'You do act like you're five, Glenn, and you're wearing a skirt which would have probably fitted you then.' Natty felt envious of how pretty Glenn was, imagining their mother's approval of Glenn's beauty. Taking a look at down at her pink dressing gown with small flowers around the edge of the collar, she felt like a scruffy old woman; all she needed was a set of rollers through her loose wiry brown hair.

'Get lost, will you? You're getting on my nerves.' Glenn quickly poured herself a small fresh orange juice and drank it down, her pink lipstick staining the side of the glass.

'I hope you change before Dad sees you. Aren't you going to pour me one?' Natty asked in a sarcastic manner.

'What's your problem, Natty?' Glenn pushed past her to the door and grabbed her grey coat from the coat hook. 'See you later, miserable cow.' She slammed the door, chuckling to herself.

Standing outside the front door away from the misery of Natty, Glenn began feeling a little exposed as the change from her usual blouses and black trousers surely was going to make an impact with everyone she knew. She hoped the stranger at the station could find approval in her efforts. Of course, she had to travel to work on the crowded train and most probably be subjected to wolf-whistles on the way; she was definitely going to give them the two-finger salute if they dared.

The thoughts of seeing him again gave her butterflies in the pit of her stomach; she was flooded with anticipation for the smart stranger. She was going to have to do a whole day at the newspaper printing office before she made herself late for the train.

Her belly began to rumble; she had sacrificed breakfast to have extra time building her eyelashes with thick black mascara.

Natty stood in the hall and knew where her sister's beauty came from. There was no way she'd ever look so good in a miniskirt such as hers. Huffing to herself she walked slowly up the stairs, her hands gripping the bannisters; she didn't want to wear her nurse's uniform, not after seeing her sister so adorable.

Natty paused for a moment as she stood outside Glenn's bedroom; she had a chance to take a good look inside with her sisters absent, to feel what it was like to have the biggest bedroom in the house even if it was only make-believe. She still wished Glenn had agreed to her request.

Stepping softly onto the carpet, Natty could feel the fibres between her toes before jumping onto the flowery covers, bouncing up and down and laughing.

'How d'you feel now, Glenn dearest?' Natty continued to bounce up and down on the bed, looking over to the much-organised dressing table: bottles and powder boxes of all colours, the bedroom filled with fragrance. The mirror was grubby, and as Natty leant forward a little she saw the outline of her sister's lips on the glass.

'Lips! Oh my God, Glenn, you've been snogging your mirror!' The marks from pink lipstick remained on the glass; Natty could see where Glenn had been touching the mirror with her tongue. She wondered why Glenn needed to be perfecting her kissing skills all of a sudden. She was going to be asking her a few questions when she finally arrived home later in the evening, for sure.

Sitting curiously amongst blouses and dresses as Glenn had emptied most of her wardrobe onto her bed, Natty took one of her polo necks and held it in her hands. Smelling the soft wool, she wondered if she'd look as sexy in it. Pushing her dressing gown from her shoulders, her bare chest feeling the chill, she pulled the blue jumper over her head, pleased with how it felt on her bare skin. She tugged it back over her head and tossed it onto the bed, leaving it inside-out. Natty grabbed a pink bowed blouse, moving her arms into the soft silk, and stood in front of the full-length mirror to take a look. Moving her hands over the blouse she was satisfied in what she saw, laughing as she stared at the rest of her naked body. 'Not bad, young Natty; I think pink is your colour!'

Taking Glenn's cream corduroy trousers from the bed Natty pulled them up to her bare bottom. Pushing the fastenings together, she roared out loud with laughter as they were slightly baggy on the legs. As Natty went to the wonderful array of perfumes she could feel the trousers falling down; she held on to the waistband. With one hand she pushed the top from Glenn's favourite bottle of perfume, spraying it generously onto her unclean neck.

'See, Glenn, I can look and smell as good as you.' Natty danced in front of the mirror, jumping from one side to the other, her long hair hitting the side of her face.

'Ouch!' Natty bent over abruptly, holding her waist; a sharp stabbing sensation in her side had stopped her dancing. 'Stitch, stitch!' Natty bent over, attempting to slow her breathing down so the pain could ease. Her attention went onto Glenn's small clock on her wall.

Rushing through the pain, Natty pulled off the trousers and took the blouse over her head as quickly as she could, the buttons still fastened. Picking her dressing gown up from the messy floor, Natty knew she was going to be late and it was entirely Glenn's fault.

Leaving the refused bedroom Natty headed straight for her room naked and holding on to her dressing gown, unaware the cord was still amongst Glenn's clothes on her bedroom floor.

Glenn stood despondently tapping her hands on her side as she waited in the lift after work, sick and tired of all the attention she had unhappily received from the young suited men. The wolf-whistles and the honking of horns had happened as she had anticipated before she had even got to the station. One car that had passed her had the owner's name scratched on the side, *DICK*; whoever it was surely was a prize one as he hadn't stopped honking his horn until he was out of her sight. She was desperate to get home and throw the small piece of material to the back of her wardrobe with her shoes; the blister on her heel was burning and she knew she'd be walking home barefooted once she got off the train.

The lift was silent and tense as always. Glenn knew her ordeals of the day were not yet over. Smelling the consumption of cigarettes and food on the breath of the bearded man behind her, feeling the sensation of hot air up and down her neck, she prayed he'd be getting out on the next floor. Fifteen floors down seemed too much to bear. Sensing his body getting uncomfortably closer to her while he chatted to his friend, she knew she would never deliberately leave work late again and be subjected to such inconsideration.

The bell rang and the lift emptied on the tenth floor.

'Excuse me. Excuse me.'

The witnesses to her ordeal and repulsive company left her alone with him. Her body froze in dread as he remained standing behind her. There was plenty of space; why couldn't he simply remove his body from near hers and take his smelling breath and bushy beard into the corner?

Stepping forward as close to the large metal doors as possible, Glenn sensed his stare on her, imagining him looking up and down her legs. The bell would ring soon and then she could make her escape out of the building, away from him.

The ground-floor light shone above her head; the relief

90

overwhelmed her. Holding tightly on to her bag, she left the feeling of torture.

Checking her watch, Glenn hoped she wasn't going to miss her stranger. Walking hastily to the station, she could feel her heel becoming worse, her armpits still sweating from her earlier ordeal. She had been looking forward to going to work the evening before and the whole day seemed to be turning into a complete nightmare.

'For Christ's sake!' Glenn said out loud, feeling unsettled and uncomfortable in her attire.

Limping into the busy station, her hair ruffled, sweating and sore, Glenn felt unattractive and this was the moment she'd been waiting for all day, to see him again amongst the pigeons and fashionable strangers, the aroma of coffee and mingled perfumes and aftershaves. As she pulled her coat around her body a panic filled her.

'You have got to be kidding me!' she exclaimed, noticing her buttons from her grey coat were missing. There was one small button hanging from a thread at the bottom of her coat; she needed to get rid of it quickly, to make the whole thing match, and with a hard tug the button fell into her hand.

'No, no!' It was him, she knew it; he was walking toward her in his cream mackintosh. Squeezing the helpless button in her hand tighter, she stretched her neck to get a better view of him; a sudden sadness filled her as she realised she was mistaken.

Tutting, Glenn placed the last remaining button in her pocket, confused as to how they had all disappeared. The adrenaline and uncomfortable feeling made her angry; she felt out of control and wanted to go and hide in the station toilets and scream. Her stomach was churning and she wasn't sure if the whole idea of seeing the stranger again was a silly one.

Glenn walked slowly to the front of the platform; the train would be arriving at any moment.

'Damn.' Brushing down her coat and quickly ruffling her short hair, she knew she was right this time; she could see him standing at the other end of the platform. Certain he hadn't seen her, she wanted to see him; she pushed herself forward a little and stretched out her neck to make sure.

From that minute the lift situation was a piece of cake. The tall grey-haired stranger made his way forward amongst the other passengers, working his way up behind her. Swallowing hard and feeling her body almost freeze, she contemplated turning around; dare she?

The screeching from the train came to a halt; feeling the bodies of people pushing past her, Glenn managed to find a seat in the carriage. She tried to pull her skirt down a little, noticing how much of her thighs were revealed when she sat down, and the glances from the men in the carriage indiscreetly confirmed it; surely they wouldn't be hiding behind their newspapers on their way home.

He wasn't there; she couldn't see him. Downhearted, Glenn bent down, pushing her shoe off slightly, rubbing her heel, thinking she'd have to pop the blister when she finally got home. He was too old for her anyway. She was only eighteen and had never even been kissed before; he was old enough to be her father. The train began to move, and she sat back defeated, looking out of the window, lost in her thoughts, the outline of the trees and houses blurry as the train moved quickly past them.

'I take it you're not being a bird-hater today?' A soft husky voice came from the other side of the carriage; she saw the goose pimples on her legs as she felt a sudden surge of excitement and disbelief.

She looked up, unsure of where he'd come from; she was convinced he hadn't been there when she had sat down. It was him, the grey-haired stranger; he was sitting right opposite her.

'No, not today. I was lucky; they kind of missed me.' Glenn spoke softly, her voice shaky, thinking how yummy he was for an old boy. Inhaling a deep breath she stared out of the window again. The pain in her foot had suddenly disappeared as the nerves rushing through her overtook all of her senses.

She watched him out of the corner of her eye as he took his paper from his briefcase. That was it, Glenn thought; he'd be hiding behind the pages. His paper was folded and placed on his lap; taking a pen from his suit jacket, he began to write. Glenn was aware he was glancing at her as he did so.

'What's six letters and you do it over and over again?' The stranger looked at Glenn, smiling, tapping his pen on his paper.

'I was always told never to speak to strangers.' Glenn smiled softly at him, wishing she had the answer to his question.

92

'It begins with R. If you'd like me to be a stranger then I shall continue my crossword in peace. I'd be rather disappointed as I was hoping to complete it before I got home. May I say you're doing a very good job at speaking to strangers and, of course, pigeons?' The stranger laughed; as he smiled his eyes glistened in the evening sunlight coming through the grimy window.

'I have no idea. Sorry; crosswords aren't my thing.' Glenn felt as though she was going to be sick. She began to wiggle her toes in her shoes as she was fuelled with nerves.

'So what is your thing?' he asked inquisitively.

Glenn sat for only a moment and thought how she had no idea of what she loved to do; there was no pastime she'd find herself immersed in.

'Talking to strangers, I guess. REPEAT! Six letters, over and over again, begins with R.' Glenn raised her voice in excitement and self-approval as she was sure it was the answer he was looking for.

The stranger counted the letters and filled in the gaps with ease. 'Well, thank you; you don't know what you're good at until you try. What makes you travel on this dreary line each and every day anyway?' He placed his paper at his side, holding the pen between his fingers.

'Same as you, I guess: work and escaping.'

'Escaping from what?' The stranger frowned.

'From myself?' Glenn knew she had blown it; she hoped he'd give her another crossword clue to answer rather promptly.

'Oh, like that, is it? A young woman feeling in such a way; it's when you get to my age you find the need to escape from yourself.' The stranger leant forward slightly as the passengers who sat next to him began to cough, seeming unhappy with conversation around them. He gave Glenn the softest of smiles, ignoring the deliberate interruptions around him.

Glenn felt safe speaking to him, looking into his gentle blue eyes. He was older than her by a lot of years; the feeling she had rushing through her kept her from caring. There was something in his smile, something kind and warm and reassuring behind his sparkling eyes, his soft wrinkles marked as though he'd been smiling his whole life.

More tutting and shaking of newspapers built around them as

they continued to speak. Glenn felt relaxed and it didn't matter how all the other fuddy-duddies felt.

'So why do you need to escape now? You know, now you're old and all?' Glenn laughed as she rubbed her bare legs.

'Old! I like that. It's a myth, you know, age. I didn't need to escape from myself; I never realised, that was all. It's what you do in your life that matters; do you agree?' Tapping the pen on his hand he spoke with compassion and ease. 'I've chased happiness for so long and travelled up and down this line wanting someone or something to help me discover it. It's been in old me all along. I haven't achieved much in my life apart from searching for this mythical, imaginary outside happiness. I've never felt the urge to speak to anyone on this train, and I gave up on the idea of ever needing to, until I saw you.' Leaning back against the firm seat he smiled; the sun still shone upon his ageing face, allowing Glenn to see even more of the beauty coming from him.

Glenn felt a warmth rush through her exhilarated body. Her emotions confused her. She trusted him; he was sincere and honest and free with his expression. Comfort overtook her. From the moment he'd begun talking to her, she had known he was never going to hurt her. She'd absorbed every word; she didn't want him to be a stranger on the train any more, for both of their sakes.

'So what's your name, then, stranger on the train?' Glenn leant forward a little. Finally the view out of the window served her no purpose.

'The stranger's name is Stanley, Stanley Jefferson. Very nice to meet you. So I take it we are no longer strangers on this dreary line?'

'That's such an old man's name!' Glenn exclaimed, raising her voice. She covered her mouth as she realised how she sounded.

'Exactly.' He chuckled.

'Sorry, that was rather rude of me. My name's Glenn, Glenn Hopkins.' She raised her eyebrows, hoping she would be forgiven. He was going to be sitting in another carriage the following day to avoid her; she knew it.

'See the thing is, Glenn Hopkins, if I were a younger man in this ageing body I'd simply ask you to marry me. Just simply get married and share amazing years together. I'd ask you to marry me.

We could have children and do all sorts of wonderful things, witness each other's ideas and dreams and smile at each other every morning when we woke.' His eyes were soft, his voice calm and meaningful. 'You see I'm not that man any more, not outside anyway; inside it's all there, all burning to be released and explored with such a young woman as you. It's hard for people to see and feel what's really inside when they see an old man.' His eyes became glassy; his tears did not fall.

Glenn sat a little dumbfounded and saw his eyes filling with tears, reminding her of her father when she saw him cry for the first time. She wanted to put her arms around him, make sure he was OK. Was he for real? By the time he had finished speaking she had actually started to think about it.

'You haven't been married, then?' Glenn pulled her coat around her stomach, paranoid her belly was bulging too much, as her skirt had begun to feel a little tight around the waist. As old as he was, she still felt the need to impress him.

'No, I've only ever been with strangers in my life.' He smiled, taking his paper and placing it on his lap, looking down at his crossword.

There was a sudden silence between them.

Glenn began to blush; it was all madness, she thought.

'You don't know me at all; I could be anyone.' Glenn's voice was high-pitched.

Looking up from his newspaper and smiling, he spoke slowly and steadily as if he wanted her to hear every word. 'You could be anyone. That's what I mean; is there a reason why we couldn't be anyone together? Who says it's wrong? Is there a right and a wrong when living and loving is what's on offer?'

'Come to think of it, Stanley, I don't think there is.' Glenn didn't want the train to ever stop; she'd be getting off soon, but she prayed the train could travel to the ends of the earth just for that moment.

'Shall we?'

'Stanley, we don't know each other.' Tutting, Glenn looked out of the window, wishing she'd go with what she was feeling; go with her heart and not her head.

'Yes, we don't know each other, and what a brilliant way to start. Shall we go and have sex in the toilet, Glenn?' Placing his newspaper in his briefcase he stood slowly, reaching for her hand, pulling his tie down a little at the neck and unclasping his white collar. Complaining passengers began to move further up the carriage in disgust.

'Pull the emergency cord, will you? These people are crazy,' a passenger said angrily as he walked up the aisle.

'Leave them alone; they're not hurting you.' A heated discussion began at the other end of the carriage amongst disagreeing passengers.

Glenn stared at the handsome man, his hand reaching out to her. It was all she had to do; was there anything in this world really stopping her but herself? Nerves gripped her bulging stomach. *No way,* she thought.

The train stopped at the station; the passengers left the carriages, slamming the doors behind them, taking themselves through the congestion on the platform. The aromas and noises blended in with the whistle being blown, giving orders for the train to take another journey.

The guard waited at the end of the platform. As he stopped blowing the whistle he was tapped on the shoulder.

'Can I help you, madam?'

'Yes, you damn well can. I think you need to do something about your train service. They are having sex on there, you know; it's disgraceful!' The old lady walked away from the guard quickly, waving her umbrella in the air, chanting her displeasure under her breath.

The guard placed the small black whistle in his waistcoat and smiled.

*Lucky buggers,* he thought.

# 19

He walked slowly down the pretty road, vigilantly checking each house number. Eventually he paused as it had been a long walk; his feet were sore and his belly rumbled as always. He dropped the box onto the concrete, hearing the thud.

He recalled living in such a lovely place, with cut hedges and glossy front doors, pretty gardens and shiny cars parked outside. He took a look down at his grimy dark clothes. His house now sat on the concrete; the damp box filled with newspapers and blankets represented everything he'd become. His parents would punish him; they'd say they were right all along. A sadness filled his tired body as he bent over, picking up his only belongings. They couldn't take them from him like everything else; they were his and only his.

He glanced from one side of the clean road to the other. He knew it was number fifteen; he was sure of it. His friend had told him, 'Any time, Lucas, you can come and visit when you're better.' He'd never forgotten those kind words. It was the last time he had seen him. He prayed his temporary friend was true to his word.

For a moment he stood with his dirty hand on the gate, uncertain of which house to approach. At one side of number fifteen the front lawn displayed small trikes and a space hopper. That couldn't be it; his friend's girls were much older now than when he had seen them in the home. He remembered how sad their father had seemed when he had come in with them. His small girls would run to the pretty lady who sat in the corner humming lullabies, away from everyone.

There was a certain girl who seemed to stand out from the rest; she'd bring a sadness to him. She'd cling to her father's jumper; she didn't leave his side. Her hair was a beautiful blonde. She was the prettiest thing Lucas had ever seen; he had never forgotten her. His friend's pain had leaked from his body to the already sad isolated surroundings; he understood Lucas without even having to say a word.

The people in and out of the four walls were imprisoned by sorrow. Lowering his head, Lucas had known why he had to get out of there, knowing if he threw the metal chairs across the visiting room hard enough, jumped on the table and screamed they'd put his straitjacket on him and move him out, for him to again be on his own, the only thing he'd ever known. He'd be locked away again like when he was a small boy. His parents had always left a plate of food outside his bedroom door. He'd always be a prisoner. They never tried to understand him, never listened.

He wasn't put in the white buckled heavy cotton, thankfully, simply confined to a more secure home, for a few days behind closed doors. He learnt from his lesson; always on his best behaviour, smiling and being amongst the other patients, he bided his time before they allowed him to leave.

Finally he had walked away from the mental home, and he had walked the streets ever since. He couldn't go to his parents. They had brought him into the world, but when he was with them it was clear they simply didn't want him any more, not the way he was; it simply didn't suit. Their scolding confirmed it each and every day. He only wanted to invent something magical, something to change the world. They didn't like his silly story or his dreams. There wasn't anything about him that they admired, apart from his brown locks of hair. Neighbours would comment on him as they'd walk by. It was the only time his parents would pull him to their legs and be proud; they'd smile as the attention they would obtain thrilled them.

They had never understood him like his friend had. His parents only had to leave him alone in his ideas and dreams; he'd never hurt anyone. They were so tired of his mess and confusing conversation that he'd feel the belt on the side of his legs from them. They'd take it in turns. His parents always made sure they got everything right; they always did everything together.

The day after the most severe beating he shaved all his hair off, sitting in the bottom of his wardrobe; he wasn't going to let them smile again, not after what they had done. It was the last time he'd entered his bedroom or even felt the wrath of their hands and hurtful words. Saying they didn't know what to do with him any more, that he had been possessed by the devil and it was the last time he was going to hurt them, they got someone to take him away. They shook their heads in disgust as the stranger led him away down the garden path. No tears were shed. He was nothing to them; he was a nobody.

His only thought of them came to him when he'd take his blankets from the old cardboard and see the small Christmas picture at the bottom of the box. He had to keep it; he had to know why he had ended up in such a way. The thoughts of a Christmas beating came too often for him; it was one thing he couldn't get away from when he looked at his mother and father standing each side of him. One day when he discovered his dream he'd throw the picture away. He was going to do it, he was sure.

As he tapped his fingers on the wooden gate, his thoughts were interrupted by seeing the nets ruffling in the house next door.

'Doreen, will you come away from that window? He's a tramp.'

'He looks so lost; I think I will see.'

'Doreen, don't you dare go out there. I will have to call the police.'

'Oh, shut up, will you, for once in your life?' the old lady demanded as she made her way out of the front door, feeling the tugging on her arm from her unhappy husband.

Watching the old lady walking toward him wearing a pink flowery dress, Lucas felt emotionless, understanding finally it was his parents who were possessed; they wanted to make him suffer. Glancing behind her, he noticed her angry husband at the front door with the phone receiver in his hand.

'Young man, are you OK?' Her voice was soft.

'Looking for Matthew.' He wondered how the lady could see him; no one else ever did.

'Oh, my dear, he doesn't live there any more; you've missed him by only a month or so. He took his girls with him too, such lovely young ladies.'

'Do you know where they are, the kind people who lived here?' An emotion began to stir in him. He'd left it too late.

'I'm not quite sure if I should say. You do look like such a gentle man, and he did give me his new address, putting it through the letterbox for the post, you see, so I could send it to him. They were always such a private family.' The old lady felt pity for the young man; there was someone very lost behind the dirty clothes and broken shoes.

'Can I have it, the piece of paper? Can I see where they are, and I promise I will get it back to you?'

The old lady walked away from him after giving him a reassuring smile.

She was his only hope of finding his friend; she was walking away from him. As she closed her front door he breathed out hard and looked at number fifteen.

The old lady walked quickly out of her door again with something in her hands.

'Mean old thing in there. Here you are, dear, you go and find them.' The old lady placed a small bag into his hands filled with a few slices of bread and biscuits, and a valuable piece of paper.

Holding on to her hand a little longer than he needed to and looking into her eyes, he wished he had picked her to be his mother; she was kind.

'Thank you; you have saved me.' His voice was soft as he gave her the gentlest smile.

The old lady wiped a tear from her eye as she watched the tramp walking away from her.

Pushing the paper bag into his cardboard box, he looked up and watched the police car pass him.

# 20

Ruth sat at her school desk, feeling the old scattered blobs of chewing gum that had been stuck underneath touching her legs, praying it had gone hard enough not to stick to her skirt. Leaning on her hand, her elbow on the desk, she was lost as she doodled on the side of her schoolbook. Her desk was covered in old pen from other pupils who had sat there making their mark in previous years. Someone had used a compass edge to score the shape of a heart: *FD 4 CL*. She was trying to work out if the declaration of love might belong to anyone in her hot stuffy classroom.

She leant her body further to one side with her legs crossed, kicking one leg in and out, making her black school shoe flip on and off. Ruth could hear the mumbles from the teacher, with his large belly and brown suit, his tie shiny and his hair brushed over to avoid the attention from his balding head. His back was to the class as he drew a map on the large blackboard which took up most of the wall space at the front.

Taking a look at her black blazer, she saw the remains of the chalk the bully of the school had rubbed on her as she went into the classroom. She'd always been a horrible girl. The girls who sat close to the class bully would pretend to be her friend only so they wouldn't get a quick punch in the face or their lunch money stolen. They needed to tell her to get lost, just as Ruth wished she'd had the courage to for the last two years.

The girls behind Ruth sat chatting and giggling under their breath. She closed her eyes, hoping they wouldn't speak about her. Waiting in dread for them to pull her plait again the whole way through the boring lesson. They'd wait for the right time to tug at her hair just enough until she'd screech, making the whole class turn around and laugh. Why couldn't they all leave her alone?

She looked up at the clock. She only had to spend another twenty minutes enduring the teacher and the awaited threat. She never made an impact when she was there, not like the other pupils. There was nothing she could do to make herself heard in class. She was only another uniform sitting on a black plastic chair, always the unhappy confused girl who never fitted in.

Ruth looked into her stained pencil case; her fountain pen had leaked the week before and it still left its blue remains. Pushing the unsharpened pencils inside with her fingers, she immersed herself in thought until the teacher had finished chanting, thankful it was nearly time to go home, go home to another place where she had always been so very different from them all.

Ruth wanted to scream, stand on her desk and tell them all to go away. Looking around at the mass of black blazers, Ruth wondered if any of her so-called friends had ever been subjected to leaving school, only to go home to a mother who would dig her nails into their wrist while they ate their only dinner of the week. Taking one more look at them, she didn't think so.

Huffing out loud, she knew it didn't matter any more. Her mother was dead; she needn't worry about how she had never left her fear in the playground when she had walked from school to her mother's house. Even when they had moved away from her the fear and anticipation had still remained like the scars on her body. Ruth was constantly waiting for her to take them back from their father, to walk up to his door and simply pull them away from him. Their father wouldn't have been strong enough; he'd have let her do it.

She had a hold on his heart like she had a hold on them all, even though she wasn't alive. She went through their veins, all of them. And when they did go back she never failed to hurt them again, taking her life when they were waiting for her downstairs, waiting to begin something new. It was something she found easy, hurting them; she couldn't help it. A mad woman, that's what she was: a total fruitcake.

Ruth began to feel anger welling up in her stomach. She hadn't eaten school dinner that day; her belly was already full of emotions and dread, like it was every day as she walked around the large echoing corridors. She could still smell the cabbage from the kitchen in the air of the classroom; she was happy she had made the decision to eat when she got home.

The thought of their mother's memory box rushed through her like the scratching of the chalk on the board. Ruth had said she'd forgiven her father for what he had done, but the annoyance of his actions remained in her.

Zipping her pencil case up, she looked around. They all seemed like spoilt brats sitting around her pretending they cared what the teacher was saying; they had no idea about anything apart from the makeup covering their young faces. Ruth chose not to wear mascara to school; there was no reason why she'd want to make her eyes bigger so she could see the prettier girls, who'd cover their cheeks with blusher, suffocating their pores of their young skin. They needed the approval of the other spotty girls sitting next to them. It was all so messed up.

Ruth gazed around the class wondering which one of them was to grow up and beat their children, as her mother had once sat in a school blazer not knowing her future actions. If only they could all jump into their school bags with the hidden emotions and lives that lay ahead of them.

Ruth gave her attention to the brown-haired bully of the class, little Miss Charlotte Evans, who hadn't stopped staring at her. She wondered how many love bites Charlotte would have on her neck by Friday afternoon's hockey lesson. Ruth felt unsettled under the dirty looks, wishing she'd smile. Then again, she was the bully; it wasn't going to happen.

Ruth felt as though she was going to be sick, as she knew she was going to be bumping into Charlotte after school as usual. She wished she could jump into her own school satchel away from her, hide until she was home.

Each day when she got in Ruth wanted to tell Glenn the things she endured every day, but she knew Glenn would have Charlotte by the neck at the school gate in front of everyone, and then Ruth's fear of entering the dark brick building the next day surely was to double.

She watched the teacher's mouth move, not hearing what he was saying as he paraded past her, placing a marked test sheet into her hands. Ruth sighed, suddenly realising how much she hated geography. As usual the sweaty oversized teacher had written a *D* in red pen in the top left-hand corner.

The bell echoed through the classroom and the tops of the desks were lifted and slammed down again, the noise blending in with chatting and laughing. Ruth lifted her desk to place her workbook back. The sickness in her stomach doubled as she saw a cigarette had been placed inside her desk; she knew if she was caught with it she was going to get the detention of her life.

She wasn't sure how it had got in there or who it belonged to, but as she lowered the top of her desk the wonderful Charlotte was smiling and raising her eyebrows; the deep-rooted feeling in her stomach was confirmed.

The panic filled Ruth as she dashed through the busy corridor. Pupils were shouting at each other, shoving past her. Praying she could make it out of the school gates before she was seen, she headed for the sunlight coming from the open large oak doors.

Suddenly she felt the three familiar taps on her shoulder. Her stomach became tense. She had nearly made it, having only a few steps to go before being amongst the teachers in the playground.

'Where is it? Give it back.'

Crossing her fingers in her blazer pocket, Ruth turned around slowly to see good old bully Charlotte standing with her two pretend friends at each side of her.

'I don't know what you're talking about.' Ruth wanted to be sick. If she admitted to seeing the cigarette in her desk, she was going to be grassed up by Charlotte. She couldn't let it happen.

'You know what I'm talking about, Ruth Hopkins. Give it back or I shall take you into the toilet and show you exactly what happens to dishonest people.'

Ruth felt Charlotte's breath on her face, having to move her face to one side a little. The anticipation and awareness of what was going to happen next heightened her energy.

'Right, you were warned.'

Ruth felt the grip from Charlotte's fingers digging into her arm as she was pulled into the toilets. Her body was shoved against the cold white-tiled wall. The sting from banging her head bought tears to her eyes. With Charlotte's hand pushing hard onto her chest, she took the biggest breaths she could: one to hold her tears back and the other because the pressure from the pushing on her lungs made her feel as though she was going to faint.

'Let's see how big your tits are, Ruth, shall we? If you have bigger tits than us you can go; if not then looks like you're going to get a slap on that pretty face of yours.' The school bully pushed her finger into Ruth's cheek and stood back and waited.

Ruth stood breathless, looking at the three smirking girls standing in front of her with their arms folded. The brown tiles on the floor and the dingy white-tiled walls echoed her fear.

'I'm not going to do it; you can't make me!' Ruth's voice was shaking, her hair ruffled at the front. Glancing at the door, she wondered if she could run past them. She realised too late they had caught her eye movements and knew what she was thinking. One of the girls went and stood in front of the door, beginning to laugh.

'I think you're going to.'

Ruth felt Charlotte's breath in her face again; her nostrils were flaring and she meant what she was saying. Ruth wasn't going to be getting out of the girls' grotesque toilets until she did what they said.

Ruth placed her satchel at the side of her feet, her body shaking; she could feel the burning sensation at the back of her throat, holding back her tears with all of her strength. Pulling out her blouse tucked into her skirt, she rolled it up slowly, revealing her white bra. Her nerves and fear entwined, her body sweating with embarrassment.

'All the way, Ruth. There's a good girl.' She chuckled and snarled at her prey.

Ruth grabbed the edge of her bra with her fingers and pulled the bra from her small breasts, her chest moving in and out as her breathing was heavy, and her nipples out in the open, the cold air from the toilets rushing over her bare skin. She wanted to cry; she wanted to rip Charlotte's long brown hair out.

The laughter filled the toilets as all three girls roared out loud together, pointing at her.

They all rushed from Ruth's sight, leaving her watching the white door swing back and forward.

Ruth rolled her blouse down again and picked up her bag, her body shaking and cold. She closed her eyes for only a moment and scrunched up her face, unsure of how she was going to face them the following day.

# 21

---

They all sat together around the wonderful table handing the serving bowls to each other, filled with carrots and roast potatoes. They didn't speak while they filled their plates, only smiling in acknowledgment as each china bowl was passed. Sunday dinner was always the time when they'd sit and discuss the week they'd had, exchanging conversation and laughter between them all. Natty was to be home soon; her plate remained in its normal space, waiting to be immersed in hot flavoured food. The house felt warm and peaceful, the tunes from the radio in the kitchen only softening the atmosphere, as they sat in the wonderful dining room.

This Sunday felt a little different for them all. It had been a couple of months since Glenn had met the stranger at the station; he went through her mind as she poured the smooth hot gravy onto a small selection of dinner, gently rubbing her stomach with her other hand. A couple of months since having amazing sex with him in the grungy claustrophobic toilet on the train. Sex was something she'd always been scared of, but it had happened and she yearned to experience her body being touched like that again and again. After work she'd run to meet him in happiness; he'd always be waiting for her. He'd hold his arms open and as she ran into them they would kiss passionately, Stanley picking her up and spinning her around, ignoring the commuters' stares. To them it seemed like it was only them getting on the train, the only ones going home in the world. Sitting as close as they could, holding hands, laughing and speaking of how wonderful their married life was going to be. Before she got off at her station each and every night, he'd pull her head to his, holding the back of her neck gently, and kiss her lips with intensity; they'd be so absorbed in the moment, one day she had nearly missed her stop. He had informed her that the next time she got off the train he was going to go with her, determined to meet her father and ask for her hand in marriage.

Glenn sat moving her potato around with her knife, knowing it had been on Friday that he'd said such a thing. Tomorrow was going to be the day when she'd be accompanied home by a man she fell in love with on the train. Glenn's palms became sweaty; she felt the knife slipping from her hand a little. She had to warn her father, give him some kind of clue before she simply strolled in with a stranger.

Glenn watched her father scooping a spoonful of peas onto his plate. He seemed lost in his own thoughts as he always did. A few peas dropped from his heaped spoon; she could see his hand shaking. The words were in her mouth to speak; she couldn't let them go. Each time her father looked at her and smiled, the words she desperately longed to share with him remained hidden in her sickening stomach.

'That's not enough for you, Glenn; surely you want a little more?' he said, frowning, as Glenn was always the one with the biggest helping and even managed the leftovers from the serving dishes on a Sunday; she loved a roast dinner.

'Not feeling very hungry, Dad, sorry. The beef is really yummy though.' The thought of putting the brown meat near her lips made her stomach churn. Pushing her fork into the beef, she began twiddling her cutlery between her fingers. She wanted to hide it under her plate or throw it onto Ruth's when she wasn't looking. The slamming of the front door disturbed her thoughts.

Natty rushed through the door, throwing her coat under the coat rack, and headed straight into the kitchen to thoroughly wash her hands. Glenn saw her chance, pushing the soft gravy-immersed meat from her fork with her knife onto Ruth's plate as Ruth was busy gazing at the door of the dining room. Glenn felt a huge sense of relief to be free from the brown slice.

'Hi, everyone; sorry I'm late.' Natty sat in her uniform, grubby stains on the front, her hair ruffled. Catching her breath she stretched over to reach the large platter of brown meat. Their father always cooked too much; Natty was pleased to know she'd be having beef and mustard sandwiches at work the next day.

Glancing at Glenn, Natty smiled; she had been found out in entering Glenn's room. Glenn had been happy to tie the cord of Natty's dressing gown tightly around the handle of her bedroom door. The knots still remained in parts of the soft pink towelling.

'What's wrong with everyone?' Natty filled her plate with extra roast potatoes and then pinched another with her fingers, biting into it before placing the other half on her full china. She could feel a tension in the air. Frowning and pouting her lips, she was hoping one of her family members could at least smile as she sat.

'Please don't eat with your fingers, Natty; it's not ladylike.'

'Sorry, Dad.' Natty picked up her knife and fork, lowered her head and concentrated on finishing her dinner as quickly as possible.

Their father placed his cutlery at the edge of his plate and drank a mouthful of red wine, sensing his girls were lost as he in their own thoughts as they ate quietly. To take his mind from himself he was hoping one of his pretty daughters could share what a wonderful week she'd had. Fixing his attention on the chair that remained empty, he sighed; he only wished he'd gone up the stairs earlier, before his Eve, their mother, had put her head on the pillow and begun to dream a dream only she herself felt a comfort from. Glancing out of the window, he knew she was out there all alone as they all sat together; it simply wasn't fair. He'd yet again have to push his thoughts of anguish and pain further into the pit of his stomach until he made up his makeshift bed on the sofa. He hadn't found the courage to lie in the bed where she had slept so peacefully, the place he had seen her body and beauty for the very last time.

With his elbows on the table, leaning his chin on his hands, their father could see the sadness in his girls as they pretended they all wanted to eat together, only hearing the clanging of the metal on the fine china as they ate slowly.

'Do you girls have to tell me something?' He didn't make eye contact with them as he spoke, becoming upset from his thoughts; his voice was high as he attempted to change the heavy energy around him.

'No!' Glenn and Ruth answered in unison, as they quickly took their attention onto him.

Natty continued to eat her dinner, listening carefully to what was

108

happening at the Sunday dinner gathering, consciously chewing slowly so as not to miss anything. She nearly jumped out of her chair at the noise from Ruth's knife and fork cracking down onto the plate; she had thrown them down hard, nearly smashing the china.

Ruth ran from the table with her shaking hands covering her face. The thudding from her feet on the stairs vibrated through the white Artex ceiling of the dining room.

Sitting in shock, Natty, Glenn and their father looked at each other, hoping someone knew what was going on.

Glenn sighed, throwing her napkin onto her full plate, and followed her sister up the stairs.

Nervous and needing to know before anyone else, Glenn tapped gently on the bedroom door, where she could hear Ruth sobbing. Pushing the door open slowly she saw her small sister curled up in the corner, holding her legs up near her chin, crying like her life depended on it.

Glenn wanted to cry, remembering the only time she had seen Ruth as sad was after the discovery she had never belonged to their father.

'Hey, Ruth. What's the matter?' Glenn walked to her sister, speaking softly. She knelt down at Ruth's side and pulled her to her chest, feeling the dampness from her tears on her baggy yellow T-shirt. Holding Ruth's face with her hands at each side of her head, Glenn could see how lost she seemed. Ruth's tears and runny nose were soaking away her beauty. Wrapping her arms around her neck, Glenn rocked her to and fro.

'Ruth, tell me. It's all going to be OK.' Glenn felt uncomfortable in the affection she was attempting to show.

'Glenn, they hate me, all of them; all of them really hate me and want to hurt me all the time.' Ruth's heart felt like it was burning, her crying and breathing out of control.

'Hate you, Ruth? Who could possibly? Who could hate you apart from me?' Glenn spoke nervously, trying to make her sister laugh, and knew it was a stupid idea, the sensation of Ruth's breath on her neck reminding her of the awful lift ordeal at work. Moving her body away, Glenn sat next to her heartbroken sister. They both leant against the flowery wallpaper; Glenn placed her arm gently around Ruth's shaking shoulders.

'Glenn, is everything OK up there?' their father shouted from the bottom of the stairs, worry whirling in his stomach.

'Yes, Dad!' Glenn raised her voice and went back to giving Ruth her full attention. 'Ruth, tell me.' She pulled her yellow T-shirt over her knees.

'The girls at school, all of them, they always hurt me, call me names. I have never done anything to hurt them; I only want to be left alone. I can never get away from them. Doesn't matter how hard I try, Glenn. Why does everyone want to hurt me, my whole life, Glenn? I just want to run away from it all, to be left alone. Where's my prince now? Too wrapped up in his goddamn life, that's where. I wanted to tell you, Glenn, I did.' Ruth's voice sounded broken as her heart; she spoke through each sob.

'Who are they?' Glenn felt anger rushing through her as she had to watch Ruth speaking through her tears full of pain and confusion. She felt her comment about their father was a little harsh.

'See, this is why I never said; you'd only go and do something and make it worse. I wish they'd just kill me and be done with it.' Ruth's pain filled every inch of her young shaking body.

'Ruth, you have to stop speaking like that; you have to toughen up a little. Have you told the teachers, Ruth? They have to know. You could have told us.' Glenn pulled Ruth to her a little more. Making sure she felt protected finally.

'What's the point? They won't listen or do anything; they're just silly smelly fag-breath idiots who wear too much brown.' Ruth chuckled a little through her tears.

'They are a bit, aren't they?' Glenn smiled as she pulled away from Ruth, wishing she could be in her shoes for one day, walk into the school and smash those nasty girls' heads against the concrete in the playground.

'Yeah, they smell of cheap perfume and fags from the staffroom, surely sleeping with each other, all of them, thinking they're spending their day with a bunch of misfit kids to pass the time until they end up in the nearest pub. They wouldn't help me, Glenn. I can imagine them saying "oh, poor little rich Hopkins girl"; that's all I am to them. We've always been the little rich kids with nothing. Glenn, I really can't go back tomorrow; I can't. They wanted me to show them my tits; I did, Glenn, I did. They keep

110

hurting me. Look at my shoulder, Glenn, look!' Ruth pulled the side of her red jumper down and stared at Glenn. Pain and relief at telling fought in her stomach.

'What the hell is that?' Glenn sat back on her knees to look further.

'A compass. They kept going, wouldn't stop.' Ruth had walked home that day with her blouse soaked in blood; the girls had held her tight as they stabbed her again and again with the point of the compass they had stolen from her pencil case. Her screwed-up bloodstained school shirt still remained under the bed.

'No way, that's it. I'm coming in to school with you tomorrow; I'm not going to work.' They were only words; Glenn felt immense anger and pity for Ruth, but knew she wasn't going to miss her journey home from work for anything. 'Look, Ruth, we will go and tell Dad right now.'

'No way!' Ruth shook her head, wiping her wet snotty face with the back of her hand.

'Look, if you tell him this I will tell him my secret.'

'Don't kid me, Glenn! I'm not telling him, so no way; I'm going to have to deal with it myself.'

'Ruth, we will go down together and say; what do you think? I need to talk to Dad as much as you.' Glenn spoke with eagerness. It was her chance to tell him as his full attention wouldn't be on her; if she got Ruth to speak first then whatever Glenn said could be diluted a little.

'What do you need to tell him, Glenn, that is so important?' Ruth sniffed hard and wiped her face once more, her stomach still full of pain, aching as she needed to get it out.

'I've lost my virginity; I'm marrying him too.' Glenn squealed and clapped her hands together as she knelt on Ruth's soft carpet. She felt such happiness and excitement for everything that was happening in her young life.

'Oh, OK, Glenn, yeah, 'course! Never mind, Glenn, you take it all again. Did you hear the doorbell?' Ruth wished her sister would leave her alone to cry in peace. It was typical of Glenn to say such ridiculous things at such a time, confirming Ruth's belief she only ever thought of herself. What was the point in all of it? She looked at her dressing-table drawer; she was going to take the cigarette she

111

had hidden inside and smoke it, whenever she could hide from them all and rebel against the whole charade of family life, school life and life itself.

'Come on, Ruth; we will get your school stuff sorted too, eh?' Moving her head from one side to the other in a persuasive gesture, Glenn put out her hand for Ruth to grab.

Taking a deep breath, Ruth reluctantly took her selfish sister's hand and followed her out of the warm bedroom.

As they stood together at the top of the bannisters, they glanced at each other, both feeling they recognised something about the man standing at the bottom of the stairs in the hallway. The aroma around them becoming stale as he held a cardboard box, wearing dirty clothes.

# 22

'Let me take that heavy box for you, Lucas; I will put it over here.' Matthew gently took the box from the nervous guest, as he felt an overwhelming comfort at being in the presence of his curly-haired friend once more. He had recognised Lucas instantly as he opened the front door to him; his gentle smile had always reassured Matthew when Matthew had gone to visit him, a visit he'd make for both of their satisfaction.

'Girls, come downstairs; this young man spent time with your mother. Come on, girls.'

Their father's request had to be followed. Glenn and Ruth began walking down the stairs to the stale odour which remained in the hall.

'Sit, please, Lucas.' Pulling the spare chair out for his guest, their father hadn't stopped smiling. Part of Eve's life was with him, around the table of their family home, someone she knew, someone who had witnessed her beauty.

Natty sat dumbfounded as the dirty stranger sat opposite her. Her stomach filled with an unexplained emotion; there was someone rather interesting underneath his dirty stubbly face.

'This is Lucas, girls. Come in; don't stand in the doorway.'

'Hello, Lucas; I'm Natty. Nice to meet you.' She began to sense her cheeks burning.

'Hello, Miss Natty; it's a pleasure to meet you.' Lucas's voice was soft, overwhelmed with the elegance and beauty which surrounded him, the welcome and honesty from his friend, who had kept his word to welcome him into his home.

'That's Glenn.' Their father's voice sounded uplifted: something which hadn't been heard in a very long time.

'Hi.' Glenn smirked from the dining-room door, slightly lifting

113

her arm to wave, not believing there was a tramp at their dinner table. Such a thing could only happen in the Hopkins family.

'Hello, Miss Glenn; it's a pleasure to meet you.'

'And Ruth.'

Ruth smiled at the young man. It was something wonderful finally which had come to their home: freedom, a sense of living. Ruth was mesmerised by how he sat humble and proud at the glorious table.

'You are the pretty little blonde girl, all very much grown up now. I have never forgotten seeing you all those years ago. You are still as pretty; I can sense prettiness in your heart too. Hello, Miss Ruth; it is very much a pleasure to finally meet you again.'

'Aaah!' Natty felt her heart melting for the gentleman hidden behind his own mask.

Glenn felt fed up with the attention Ruth had been given from their father's tramp friend, but knew the attention was to be going back to her very shortly.

'Ruth, do you feel OK now?' Their father walked slowly up to Ruth and held her arm, squeezing it gently.

'Yes, thank you, Dad.' Looking into his eyes she felt bad for what she had said about him.

'Come on, let us finish this dinner; it's most probably cold now. Lucas, please have food with us all.'

Lucas's bottom lip began to wobble as he could feel himself wanting to cry. To be part of a family again was something he had never believed possible.

The energy had lifted around the table of cold food, each of them trying to ignore the smell coming from the humble young man, who ate with perfect table manners.

'You can clean up, Lucas, after you eat; I have some spare clothes for you to try. We have so much to talk about. I'm very happy you have come to see us all.'

'Matthew, I have never forgotten you from your first visit. I knew our lives would somehow link again in another time and place.' He spoke softly, looking straight at Natty, who was gently blushing at his glances.

'That link thing is fine with me, Lucas!' Their father was certain Eve had sent him back to them. She wanted to be with them all; she was his guardian angel, and they were to look after him.

Glenn knew it was her time, staring at Ruth, who was looking into the air, and then Natty, who couldn't keep her eyes from the flea-infested tramp for some crazy reason, and then her father, who was engrossed in pouring a little more cold lumpy gravy onto his cold vegetables. It had to be done now or it'd be when she and Stanley were standing next to each other, hand in hand, at the front door the following evening.

'Dad, I'm getting married!' Glenn's voice was raised, almost sounding squeaky.

Natty nearly choked with laughter as she heard her sister speak in such a way. Her thoughts quickly went back to the stained mirror in her sister's bedroom. It had all made sense. She needn't have asked her anything; that evening, when Glenn had come home, the smile and glow on her face had said it all. Natty had a feeling her sister really was telling the truth, as she sat still at the dinner table with her family and new acquaintance all staring in disbelief.

'Glenn, thank you for that little joke; not sure where it fits.'

'Dad, it's really true. I know I'm young; I really love him.' Glenn inhaled a deep breath. 'He's coming to see you tomorrow to ask you; bit old-fashioned in my eyes, but he's loads older than me so I can understand. He's so lovely, Dad. Please don't be cross with me; I've never felt anything like this before.' Her voice quickened as she felt their stares on her. 'It's a shock, I know, but look how life goes, and he's only fifty. You know what they say: nifty fifty.' Glenn began chuckling nervously, not believing she had told them all. She finally felt as though she was going to be sick and leapt up from the table before any of them could speak to her. Before she hastily left the dining room, she had one more thing to say.

'Dad, Ruth's being bullied.' With that she rushed up the stairs.

'Natty, will you get Lucas some towels, please? I think Ruth and I have to chat.' Matthew's head felt like it was going to explode. He shook his head gently, seeing his daughter sobbing at the end of the table. He had to help her; she needed him to.

He suddenly realised his daughters knew almost nothing about anything, the birds and the bees; they'd never been told anything. How scared and confused they must all have been, working it out for themselves; how were they to know if the choices put in front of them were the right ones? He was meant to guide them all in such a way that whatever was put in front of them they could handle, with no regret. They'd make decisions which they felt from the core of their beings, knowing who and what they all truly wanted from their wonderful futures. He knew they were all going to make mistakes, all experience something further in their lives they had never understood; he needed their mother more than ever before. If they were to fall in love, how would they know that they had, and if they had the right to feel it at all? He loved them more than life, but he was a man and only a mother knew how to deal with such things. Who was he to tell Glenn she couldn't follow her own feelings? He knew he had all his life. It had always been such a mess, and it still remained such.

He gazed out of the window in his quickening thoughts. He needed his Eve, their mother, to guide them, as she always had truly wanted to. It was her chance to be the sky, watching and protecting them in each and every moment.

# 23

'Thank you so much for your time, Mr Kenneth.' Matthew felt the sweaty palm of the headmaster's hand in his as they shook on their agreement for the school to take responsibility in the protection of Ruth. She only had one more week in their care before the school holidays commenced; Matthew hoped it wouldn't be too much of a feat.

The headmaster stood nodding his head and smiling in his tweed suit and chequered shirt, his shiny brown tie fraying only a little at the bottom. Matthew looked deep into his eyes, wanting him to understand the importance of his visit; Ruth's suffering had been a failing on the school for not protecting her and a failing on himself as a father. He needed to make it right, and hoped the balding sweaty man in charge was going to understand the greatness of his desire.

'Any time, Mr Hopkins.'

'I hope not, Mr Kenneth. I take it you will be speaking to the girls involved in such torment of my daughter?' He spoke assertively, knowing Ruth was waiting in anticipation behind the dark wooden door.

Sitting on the black plastic chair outside alone Ruth heard the muffled voices which were going to release her from her dread each and every day, feeling terrified her secret was being unravelled to the old man in charge of the mess and the smelly staff room and, of course, smelly-breathed incompetent teachers. Sitting in her school uniform, her hands in her blazer pockets, she desperately wanted to get off the sticky plastic chair and listen through the keyhole. She gazed into thin air, the lights flickering above her head. The walls were cream with thick painted brown picture rails, the old pictures of previous pupils in black and white hanging on the walls around her;

surely one of the boys in their grey shorts and little black caps had once been a bully. It had always been a very posh boys' school. Ruth thought they should never have changed it, then she wouldn't be there and those horrible girls wouldn't be either.

Imagining her father being one of the boys in the pictures made her think of her Uncle Harry; he must be in the picture further along the hall as he was only a little younger. She wondered how he'd have dealt with such treatment and how he'd have helped her in her time of despair, and even if he had been one of the bullies himself; she was never to know. She never dared ask about him, even though his blood flowed through her veins and heart. A feeling overwhelmed her as she wanted to let him know of her pain, the man she only remembered from a very long time ago. Who had never existed, who she'd never get the chance to bring to life again.

Huffing to herself she stood to take a closer look at the old pictures. Stretching her body up, she straightened one of the frames; it hadn't been hung properly and to her it showed how little the school cared about their pupils, past and present.

Ruth waited in relief for her father to come out of the stuffy office and take her home. Surely he wasn't going to leave her there, especially after speaking to her the night before around the quiet dinner table. She had sat with her shoulders slouched, crying in fear, releasing her raw memories of what she had endured. She hoped she could forget about it. Her shoulder stung as she attempted to rub the pain away with her hand. The new guest sat listening, taking it upon himself to place his grimy hand on her arm, his dirty bitten nails touching her soft jumper. He was kind; he didn't have to. She wondered if he'd wisely spent the money she'd secretly left him that day.

Her father had poured wine as she spoke, emptying the bottle by the time she kissed him on the cheek and went to rest her breaking heart, her body tired and shaking. She had taken each step up to her bedroom slowly; she'd left them together in the dining room, knowing deep in her young body and mind she still had to face the torment in the morning, the girls who were happy to destroy her young soul piece by piece. What were her school days trying to teach her? Had she learnt anything apart from fear and dread? She believed she was weak for not standing up to them, not hurting their young skin with her fists or nails. They'd wait by the school gate each morning so as not to waste any precious time in beginning their destruction of her. She had curled up on her soft bed and looked at her school satchel and known she'd hold it tightly as she walked into the playground. It had begun to look tatty as they'd throw it across the playground before the bell even went. She'd be scurrying on the concrete, picking up her books and pencil case.

The door of the headmaster's office was opened, and he and her father stepped into her echoing hall together.

'Are you OK, Ruth?' Her father's voice was soft and reassuring; he smiled at her as she turned around.

'Fine, Dad.' Ruth wondered how the fifteen-minute conversation behind the closed door could possibly have resolved the last two years of pain. Taking a deep breath and grabbing her bag from near the leg of the chair, she waited to leave with him.

'You can go back to class now, Ruth,' the headmaster said. 'You should have brought it to our attention earlier than this. You must never go through such things alone. Oh, and please tie your hair back before you get to your classroom; we like to keep up certain standards.'

Ruth stood in shock at the words she had never expected to hear; there was no way he could send her back to them. Also, not plaiting her hair that morning so they couldn't pull her pigtail while she sat fearful in class seemed to have been completely pointless. When she got her smack in the mouth, maybe he could take one for her and be loyal to his word.

'Do I really have to go back to class, Dad?' Ruth's voice was crackly as she held back her tears, praying her father had the strength to go against the orders of the man who stood with his arms folded next to him. The strength to stand by her, like she knew he wanted to.

'You must do as the headmaster says, Ruth. It's going to be all right now, and you haven't got to worry. The headmaster said it's going to be dealt with; isn't that right, Mr Kenneth?' He rubbed Ruth's arm, looking at the foul-breathed man for reassurance.

'Of course, Mr Hopkins, they'll be dealt with accordingly. Now off you go, Ruth; don't allow them to prevent your education.'

'Thank you.' Her father stopped rubbing Ruth's arm and gently guided her away from the attention of the headmaster.

As she walked slowly next to him Ruth knew the headmaster was speaking a pile of rubbish. She was so in trouble with the girls. There was only five more days to go.

'Bye, Ruth; see you when you come home.' Standing with his arms on her shoulders, Matthew wondered what was making Ruth cringe in pain. Taking his hands away, he quickly kissed her warm cheek and left down the long, echoing corridor. The echo of his footsteps moving further away from her, he didn't want to look back, sensing she was standing alone watching him, her eyes watching his every move. Leaving her in such turmoil was something he'd hopefully understand by the time he'd arrived home. He had to trust the school, with as much belief as he struggled to find in himself. It was the right way to deal with her problem. He didn't want her running away from anything in her life, not like he had, and she'd have to face it sooner or later.

If his brother Harry had been with him he'd have gone in and taken her from the loneliness, and let her stay at home until the bullies were thrown out from school by their ties. If it wasn't done he'd surely have taken it into his own hands. Looking down at the white-lined concrete in the large playground, Matthew wished he could be more like him, and for some unknown reason prayed Harry was right by his side at that very moment. He needed his brother, as much as he didn't want to admit it; his brother's daughter was being hurt again, and he didn't know how to help her. It was wrong of him to not let Harry know.

The truth in his mind began mixing emotions in his stomach. He wasn't Ruth's father, whether he had pretended all those years or not.

He was suddenly overcome with pain from leaving Ruth and from the reality of the loss of his fatherly rights over her. It wasn't sorted; the problem was still there. He had abandoned her in the echoing halls, vulnerable and scared. She was probably still standing alone, breathing in panic, longing for him to grab her from the classroom, for him to be her prince and rescue her like she had always believed he would.

Glenn was going to bring a man home, an old man who surely was wrong for her. Matthew knew he wasn't in a position to judge;

who was he to say anything? Deep in his heart he knew if his own father had been alive to meet his beautiful Eve he'd have shaken his head in disapproval right in front of her face. It wouldn't have mattered what his father thought; he was going to be with her anyway. He was determined not to be like his own father, aware he'd have to accept Glenn's decision whether he truly liked it or not. If Glenn felt the love and the passion for this man, then what Matthew said would have no impact, and why should it? It was to be Glenn's choice, her life; he would allow her to make it the way she believed it should be. All his girls had pieces of clay in their hands and it was up to them to mould them in any way they chose. He'd had his chance; he had never made much of what was handed to him, simply squashing it to make no sense or shape at all.

Inhaling a deep breath, Matthew made his way toward the gate knowing his vulnerable daughter was inside the school, having to tie her hair back and become part of such an escapade. Walking away from her became too much for him. He sat on the small wall that imprisoned the pupils, leaning his back against the wire mesh fence, realising how vast the playground was, the white lines painted and netball posts at each end, the red netting ripped and the metal poles rusty, overflowing bins nailed to the walls. It seemed disorganised inside and out. He never recalled the school being so disrespected when he attended with his brother Harry.

Feeling powerless, he tried to push the recurring thought of his brother to the back of his mind, hoping to overshadow it with thoughts of his happy friend Lucas, and how they had both sat chatting through the night. Lucas had spoken to him of how the hot water in the bath had pierced his dirty blocked pores to breathe life inside him again, how the bubbles had swished around him. He had begun to weep as he spoke of being in the bath as a small boy, when his father would push his head under for a while to release the devil from him. Lucas had known the devil was in his father; he had tried to tell him. Watching the young man at the dinner table had brought Matthew comfort from the loss of Eve and the anguish he knew his girls were feeling. The thought of Natty walking in and out of the room as they passed conversation made him chuckle. The young man was very handsome and his eldest daughter seemed to have taken note of the point instantly; Matthew remembered how she had stood wide-mouthed as he walked clean-shaven into the kitchen.

The wind had begun to pick up. Lost in his thoughts alone in the playground, he watched the leaves and old empty crisp packets swirl in circles; nature was something amazing without even knowing, to make patterns and mini-whirlwinds. His body shuddered as the wind became cold. The chill bit into him; he sat there in his thin black jumper, knowing his chest was bare underneath, his vest still on the bed at home. Home was where he was heading, to be greeted by his friend. The sense of company made him smile.

Pushing himself from the damp wall he stared at the glorious architecture of the school, nodding his head. He knew she was going to be all right; she was a Hopkins girl, after all. Hearing the squeaking from the heavy black gate echo through the ghostly playground, he walked away from her and didn't look back.

'Been shooting your mouth off, Ruth?'

Ruth sat nervously in the stuffy classroom, hearing the voice coming from behind her. Closing her eyes in dread as she pushed her finger hard onto the sharp tip of her pencil.

# 24

Absorbing his wonderful new surroundings, the warmth and the array of shapes and colours around him, Lucas looked at the clock and waited in eagerness for Matthew to come home. He was immersed in thought of the young blonde girl who he'd never forgotten, only to meet her and see her subjected to the cruelty of others.

It was something he could never have envisioned a pure beautiful child having to experience. The mean girls at school were envious of her beauty and her wealth. They wanted to take the devil from her also, and the devil wasn't in her; it was in them. He interpreted quickly as he stood in the quiet kitchen: they were the devil's messengers, the devil's advocates helping to create pain in the beauty of the world.

Walking slowing, embracing the relief of being home, Matthew gazed into the kitchen to see a young man in contemplation, holding pots and pans in his hands; he had pushed the food packets into piles covering every work surface, utensils and tea towels in every found space. A simple happy harmless man smiling in his own world in wonder at all of the items around him. Matthew had been unsure of how the young man was going to fill his day while he wasn't there to keep him company and could see by the mess in the kitchen he had filled it satisfactorily. He took a moment to hope he hadn't started emptying cupboards in any of the other rooms.

'Hello, Matthew! Would you like some beans on toast?' Lucas spoke excitedly while attempting to search for the beans amongst other tins of peas, carrots and soup, his eyes scouring them.

'Oh, yes, Lucas, that will be fine.' Matthew quietly sat at the table and pushed the boxes away so he could lean his elbows on the wood. The kitchen reflected the disorganisation he felt in his own mind. It was only 10.30 and he knew Ruth was alone. If he had been honest with his friend he really didn't feel like beans on toast, only another bottle of red wine, which was now hidden in the mess.

'How is your precious child, Matthew? Is she happy now?' As Lucas lifted tins and pans he spoke gently, not making eye contact with the man who sat with his hands on his face.

'Oh, yes, Lucas, she will be fine.' Matthew felt he was being dishonest with himself and the man who filled his home with excitement. The feeling in his alcohol-empty stomach was heavy and telling him something he knew he should listen to. When was he going to learn to follow his own instincts and heart and do what he felt was right, instead of how the world saw it? His own father had drummed into him again and again that that was how life itself was meant to be lived.

'I'm happy to hear, Matthew. She is a very beautiful girl, something quite different about her. Look at all this, Matthew; amazing, don't you think? All the different materials and textures. Do you know this box which holds this rice must have been thought of by one person? Who'd have thought four pieces of simple card could be transformed to hold and do so much? Who invented such a thing? Look, Matthew, look at this saucepan; some very clear-minded person invented a material which could stand the point of heat, the most amazing thing. Do you ever look at it, Matthew, this pot which I am going to cook your beans in? Once I find them, that is.' Lucas held the saucepan in one hand and chuckled, turning each labelled tin around with the other.

'I don't know, Lucas. I have never really thought of such things; they've always just been there. Haven't taken the time to really notice.' Matthew thought how exquisite it was for someone to think in such a way. He prayed he could jump into his friend's faded, damaged shoes and be so simple and grateful in life.

'You see, Matthew, everything starts with an idea; it doesn't matter what it is. The way you think and feel and how you dress in the morning, all the amazing buildings which surround us, the cars, the roads, all from an idea. It's marvellous, Matthew; one thing always leads to another, and it's your choice, Matthew, all up to you.' Lucas leant his body forward as the adrenaline for life rushed

124

through him. At the sight of his friend's pale face, fretfulness halted his feelings of wonder suddenly. He longed to take the pain from him, his friend who still remained in an argument with life.

'Matthew, you seem sad. You know deep in your heart you can change what's in your mind in a split second. Take her, Matthew, go and take your child away from such wretchedness. She doesn't have to be there; there isn't anyone in this world who says. Allow her to be free like she was born to be. You never brought her into this world for such things to happen to her; it isn't how it's meant to be. Take the idea, Matthew, make it grow and do whatever you want to, change the plans, scribble them out, rewrite them. Do what you need, Matthew, for you and your family. Do you know I thank you, Matthew? You are the kindest man, a man who I see as I stand in your kitchen with you, and a man who needs to stop fighting with himself. I will tidy up before I leave, Matthew, after I have cooked you a wonderful thank-you meal.'

'You can stay, Lucas, as long as you wish to, until you find somewhere warm and safe at least.' Matthew knew the young man was right. He could have taken his daughter away; he could have saved his Eve and his own life all at the same time. The thing was he never had the idea of even how to begin. Pushing himself up from the table, he walked past Lucas, smiling. Wanting to thank him for such words of kindness, he left the young man standing with a tin of rice pudding and a saucepan in his hands.

'The beans were in the bottom cupboard, Lucas.' Matthew peered around the door and smiled.

'Great, great, I must get on. Thank you, Matthew, for letting . . .' Lucas could hear Matthew going up the stairs. He wanted to make the meal perfect for him.

Clapping his hands together, Lucas jumped for joy as he stood in the glorious kitchen of inventions. The sink was full of bubbles, the bubbles sitting on the draining board. It was a spectacular thing. He was keen to pour cold water onto them and watch them disappear as simply and as beautifully as they had evolved into soft white cascades of colours with the demands of the hot water.

Matthew heard his friend thank him as he walked up the stairs. He stopped outside his beautiful Eve's hiding place, the bedroom where she'd remain alone understanding her own feelings, surely crying on the soft pillow each night while they weren't with her. He had no right to leave her so alone in her confusion and crazy misshaped world.

He needed only a moment alone, staring into the untouched perfect room, absorbing the idea of sleeping on the pillows and on the soft mattress where her fragile porcelain-like body had once lain, just as the small doll lay on her pillow. His friend was going to stay; Matthew's own hiding place, his makeshift bed on the sofa, now belonged to him.

Matthew closed his eyes, breathing heavy, sadness enveloping his body. He remembered how he'd hold Eve's hand while she slept, staying awake a little longer so he could absorb her beauty, watching her breathe in and out as she slept so peacefully. Not wanting to miss anything, not for one second; if only he could have stayed awake forever. How could something so wonderful go so wrong? Get broken beyond repair? He remembered how their bodies, when they used to lie side by side, would blend together as they held each other tight; their bodies had stopped merging into one without any warning at all. Shaking his head, Matthew sighed, pushing his hands through his black hair, and made his way down to Lucas.

Matthew was handed a full plate of beans and toast, feeling happy he hadn't been given rice pudding. 'Thank you, Lucas; it looks very nice.'

'Are you happy with it, Matthew? Those colours are rather glorious, aren't they? Thank you; I shall not get in your way. You won't even notice I'm here.' Lucas picked up his fork and smiled.

Looking around at the mess in the kitchen and the sink full of bubbles, Matthew rolled his eyes good-naturedly. Lucas had surely made his mark on the usually organised Hopkins home. 'I am very happy, Lucas; it's been a long time since I've been cooked a meal, especially as well as this.'

Matthew watched as his dinner guest picked up one bean at a time and moved them to different sides of his plate, placing them each side of his much-burnt toast. Feeling warmer in his black jumper and happy to be sitting with him, he realised how much better Lucas looked in his old green jumper, grey shirt and black

126

slacks. He had offered Lucas his black shoes also; Lucas had taken them in grace but still came down in his own shoes with the black leather at the front flapping up and down.

'Really, Lucas, it isn't a problem; really, it's wonderful to have you.' Matthew felt the tears which he'd managed to hold in his stomach all morning beating him, pushing their way up his throat, soon to be out. Swallowing hard and determined not to give in to them, he knew it was he who needed the young man to stay. It was he who should be thanking Lucas for knocking on his door, bringing simplicity to their lives.

'She was very beautiful, Lucas, wasn't she, the woman who sat in the chair alone?' Matthew began to eat his food, finding it hard to swallow.

Placing his fork on the table, Lucas spoke gently and reassuringly to the man who seemed to be sad and struggling to eat his offering of thanks. 'All of your daughters, Matthew, are very much like her, gentle and hiding a beauty and innocence only they aren't quite aware of. I remember how your wife engulfed the room with her tenderness and sculpted features, unenlightened in her impact on them all. Her smile, Matthew, was like an electric jolt running through my body when it hit me. I will never forget the feeling and I can only imagine how sharing a complete journey with her would impact your mind and heart in such an uncontrollable way. I can sense her presence now, Matthew.' Lucas picked up his fork and continued separating the soft orange ovals on his plate.

Matthew felt overwhelmed by such kind words from him, resting his tears in his stomach again, to stay there until he went to bed to be alone, pushing his head into the pillow and allowing them to flow. He frowned a little, bewildered by Lucas's table manners. 'Why are you doing that, Lucas? With your beans, I mean?'

'Dear Matthew, it's quite simple; the ones with the most sauce on go this side, and the others this side, then your meal is much nicer, juicer.' Lucas chuckled at Matthew's innocence, feeling he had a lot to teach him.

'Madness; I've never really thought of that.' Matthew bit into his toast, trying not to laugh out loud.

'Matthew, can I ask you a very personal question?'

'You can ask me anything, Lucas, yes.' Matthew spoke while chewing, and then placed his knife and fork on his empty orange-stained plate.

'I see you don't wear your wedding ring, Matthew; is there a reason for that?'

There was a short silence.

'Come with me, Lucas!' Matthew gestured with his head for Lucas to follow, pushing the chair backward, hearing the scraping of the wooden legs on the tiled floor. He leapt from the chair, rushed forward and opened the garden door. Walking quickly, he made his way up the garden to the display of apple trees.

Lucas took a slice of toast from his plate and followed him promptly. The fresh air hit him as he ate his toast; the hot sun was beginning to dry away the earlier chill.

'This is why, Lucas; this is where my Eve sleeps. I placed the ring near her; it must be long gone now. It will be a year in a few months.' Matthew gently stepped next to the grave, seeing the multi-coloured flowers and fallen leaves, the scent from the flowers remaining, protecting his true love.

'She is in there, Matthew? The woman who sat alone so gloriously beautiful, in there? But why?' Lucas found it hard to gain saliva in his mouth to swallow his toast. He was a little out of breath also. He glanced at the flowers on the soft grass. Matthew was hiding her away from the spectators of the world; surely it couldn't be true, he thought.

'Her ashes, Lucas, like small grains of stardust, that's all. Took herself away from us all, Lucas; she simply couldn't do another day.' Matthew's throat began to burn, and the tears fell from his eyes. Gently falling to his knees he lay his hand on the soft dirt, yearning from deep inside to feel her near him, only touch her beauty and watch her breathe all over again. Suddenly the pain and the tears overwhelmed his already hurting body; clawing at the dirt, he cried, 'Where is it, Lucas? Please help me!' He lifted his head in despair, pleading with his friend to help.

'Matthew, you must find it. She took herself away from you; why do you have to take yourself away from her? She is your wife, still this day as always; your love, Matthew. You must display it to the crazy world, kiss your ring every night and tell her, Matthew, let

128

her know how much you love and adore her. Keep her breathing, Matthew, in your heart and in everything you say and do; breathe her, Matthew, for your girls, like the breath a baby bird takes in its nest for the very first time. Give her a new breath of flight every day.' Lucas spoke while kneeling next to him, rushing his words and feeling a nervousness overtake him, grabbing Matthew's muddy shaking hand and staring deep into his eyes.

'God damn it, Lucas, I need to find it.' Yanking his hand away from his friend's grasp he continued clawing at the dirt.

'I know, Matthew. You must be gentle, be calm and it will reveal itself. Trust me.'

Stopping to take a breath, Matthew sat back on his bottom, pulling his legs up a little.

'Let me do it, Matthew; allow me to help you.' Lucas rolled the sleeves of Matthew's jumper up and began to move a handful of dirt, slowly making a small pile at the side of the grave.

'Lucas!'

'Shh, Matthew, just wait.' Lucas pushed through the dirt and moved the flowers and the small white apple blossoms away with respect and ease.

Looking up into the sky, Matthew wanted to scream. He began to feel cold again, wrapping his arms around his stomach, rocking backward and forward, feeling despair in witnessing Lucas leaning over his Eve.

Holding a ball of damp dirt in his hand Lucas smiled, his eyes glistening. 'I think this belongs to you, Matthew!' Handing over the moulded ball of dirt, Lucas stood and breathed hard in relief.

Matthew stared and began pulling the dark mud from the shining gold, finally holding in his shaking hand his wedding ring. He spat on it, rubbed it between his hands and promptly wiped it clean on his jumper, then placed the band of gold back where it belonged, holding his hand up into the air, seeing the outline of his ringed finger in the sky. 'Hello, Eve! I am never going to let myself be without any part of you again.' Pulling his hand back to his face, he kissed the ring on his dirty hand, holding it to his lips for a few seconds, breathing out in relief as he had feared it was gone forever.

Lucas touched Matthew's shoulder with a reassuring look, and held his hand out to help him from the grass. 'I am very happy you have taken her back again, so very happy. Let me make you a warm drink.'

'Do you think we will find the kettle?' Matthew laughed in gratitude and an overwhelming sense of comfort fuelled his body. As he wiped his face dry with his sleeve he held Lucas around the shoulder with one arm and walked inside. Taking a look back at his Eve's grave, he smiled a little, praying she'd understand them having to mess her flowers up a little, declaring how much he still truly loved her.

'Thank you, Lucas!' He smiled in gratitude to the new member of his family.

# 25

'Can you lock up tonight for me, lovey? I'm out with Harry, if he gets here on time, that is.' Suzy raised her voice across the small bookshop at her colleague, feeling tired from a busy day. Her muscles began to ache from the weight of the heavy leather books balancing on her arms.

She was thinking forward to her date as she had a bone to pick with him; she would have to pull him up finally on his habitual lateness. For the last couple of months she'd always been the one left waiting, in the pub, at home or outside the shop. The annoying feeling welling up inside her brought a realisation he'd be getting double points for being late again that very evening. *He'd better not dare,* she thought.

She already felt unhappy with his dating skills; he'd never taken her out to dinner or the theatre, which was something she adored. He'd normally get her a drink in the local pub and then take her back to his for a takeaway or a bacon sandwich and, of course, great sex. She knew deep in her heart she deserved to be treated differently. Her ex-boyfriend would never have got away with such failings, of course; he was now her ex, after all.

'What time you out with sweetie?' Her colleague's voice was high-pitched and full of excitement.

'Five. He knows I don't finish till six, so why he said that time I don't know; suppose I could have told him to shove it.' Suzy sighed to herself and felt he was becoming a pain-in-the-arse sex god. The shop felt warm, which made her feel a sudden overwhelming tiredness that surged through every muscle in her body.

'My dear, it's nearly five!' Her colleague walked quickly with little steps, shaking his head, to take the books from her. He could see how unprepared she looked for her date.

Feeling a huge relief at having the books taken off her hands, Suzy smiled at him. 'I know. Really, do I look like I'm in the mood?' Blowing away small strands of hair which had fallen onto her face, she was happy she'd chosen to clip it back at the sides.

'Oh, darling, go and make yourself look ravishingly divine. My arms are going to crack if you don't get your pretty bottom out of the way so I can finish up for you.' Pointing for her to move and get ready, her colleague chuckled.

'Huh! I did this morning; I just feel like going home and getting in a hot bubble bath.'

'You can get in the tub with him, dear. Are you going like that?' Her colleague scrunched his face up in disbelief, shaking his head and tutting. It really wasn't the thing to do, going out in your work clothes. It simply wasn't fashionable, he thought.

'No, definitely getting in on my own. Really not up to being all sexy and gorgeous for him.'

'Now, Suzy, darling, you don't mean such a thing; he's absolutely super and if he liked a bit of Willy I'd be the one getting ready to rub soap onto his muscly chest.' Her colleague roared with laughter and heard Suzy follow in his happiness.

'OK, that's fab.' Suzy spoke through her laughter, happy the shop was finally empty of customers; they had kept her on her feet all day. She really did like Harry, but there was something inside her which felt there was something missing within him, a void of some sort.

As they both leant on the counter finishing their giggles, Suzy kicked her shiny high heels off; her feet were throbbing just like Harry's head would if he was late. 'Is your name really Wilfred?'

'Why, yes, darling, it is, or if you like I can be anything you want me to be.' The laughing continued.

'Fuck off!' Suzy giggled, slapping his winged-collar flowery purple shirt in jest. She'd have jumped into bed with him if he wasn't so queer.

'He's here. Oh, he's such a wonder.' Standing up straight and moving from one side to the other, her colleague continued in his admiration. 'Oh, Suzy, look at that frame; he's such a peach.' Wilfred leant a little further over the counter, smiling, his blue eyes twinkling, as he touched the front of his waxed blond hair.

132

'Shh, he will hear you.' With a gentle punch to Wilfred's arm, Suzy poised herself, pulling her jumper down a little over her waist and then flicking her hair back from her shoulders.

'Hi, Harry; a little early for you!' Suzy smiled, trying to find her shoe with her foot.

'Been so busy, Suzy, haven't had a minute. Can't complain; now I can take you out.' Harry walked slowly up to the counter, his hands in his brown corduroy jacket, his jeans flared and his shirt cream. Smelling of his musky aftershave and looking very pleased with himself.

Suzy hoped he'd booked the posh restaurant in town. As he was so smart she hesitantly glanced down at her clothes. Her red trousers and white woollen polo neck really weren't a match for his efforts. They would have to do. Give it an hour or so and her clothes could be on his bedroom floor.

Harry kept his hands in his pockets and smiled. He glanced at his girlfriend's colleague, who gave him a small smile which he felt uncomfortable with.

Suzy felt downhearted but found it in herself to smirk at Wilfred, who was still leaning forward on the counter wide-eyed, checking her boyfriend out. She thought a hello from Harry would have been a good start, and her choice was certainly not to be sitting around old Chinese cartons that evening. The thought of her bath alone at home became instantly more tempting. Secretly and successfully finding her shoe, she grabbed her small red bag from under the cluttered wooden counter and went reluctantly over to kiss Harry on the cheek. Smelling his aftershave on her lips and tasting the cologne in her mouth.

'See you, mate.' Harry nodded at Wilfred and took Suzy's hand.

'Goodbye, darling.'

Suzy rolled her eyes at Wilfred, already knowing how her night was going to be.

'Such a peach, mm mm ... I could bite into that bottom,' Wilfred said to himself as they left the shop.

# 26

---

Lucas moved the saucepans through the hot bubbles, embracing the hot water and the softness of the white balls of foam, reflections of colour rushing through them like small rainbows in his hands. He clenched his fingers together so the white frothy foam squeezed through them. Placing his palms onto the bottom of the white butler sink, the cuffs of the green jumper getting wet as the bubbles rose over the edge of the sink and the water landed on his dirty shoes, he kicked his leg out to let the bubbles fall to the floor.

Lost in his thoughts, he gazed for a moment out of the small netted window in front of him, then took the small potted plants from the tiled window sill and watered them from the cold tap, soaking the dry earth. The bubbles dripped down the edge of the tiles; mesmerised and wide-eyed, he watched the race, wondering which stream of bubbles would reach the work surface first. He embraced each and every moment at the hot sink, everything he touched only to leave remnants of the soft white miracle he always longed to understand.

Wiping his hand on the side of his black trousers, Lucas reached for the almost-empty white bottle of gooey green liquid and squeezed it, tipping it up high in front of him so he could thoroughly see the green magic pour into the sink.

'Just one more squeeze for luck.' Lucas felt happy and as if nothing else in the world existed, swishing the bubbles with his hands, imagining the bubbles bursting like a pure white volcano, scented lava exploding around him, falling at his feet. Hearing the squeaking from the bottle as he completely emptied its contents.

Lucas placed the bottle on the soaked work surface next to the sink and began to hunt for another full bottle of green magical fluid, knowing it was something a household couldn't possibly be without. Glancing at the messy worktops and table, Lucas felt disheartened and scrunched his handsome face, sensing that all his merriment was soon to be over. Huffing and blowing out his cheeks, he began to pick up all the small boxes and tins around him, while simultaneously glancing over at the overflowing foam.

With a full bottle of red wine under his arm, Lucas filled his hands with small cardboard boxes. Moving from one side of the kitchen to the other, he looked around hastily to see where they could be placed. He knew the cupboards were empty, but he had no real desire to hide such inventions; it was sacrilege to dismiss something so clever, so formed and so purposeful, to shut it away in the dark. Feeling a little panic, Lucas tipped the boxes from his hands and gently set the wine down as he was sure it was going to tumble onto the tiled floor and smash into a thousand pieces. A sense of relief filled him as all the items were finally safe.

'Right, now what? Do the cold water thing? No, not yet, not ready, leave them for a minute,' Lucas muttered to himself as he became fidgety. Beginning to hum, he placed his arms behind his back and walked slowly around the kitchen; his humming turned into a small whistle and before long he was moving his feet, stepping from one side to the other and wiggling his hips, the wet brown tiles under his feet helping him slide along the floor with ease. Looking up to the ceiling, he wondered if Matthew would like to join him; such glorious happiness had to be shared.

'I have an idea. Oh, yes, Mr Hopkins, you're going to dance on the table by the time I've finished with you!' Lucas excitedly dashed over to grab the bottle of wine and two glasses.

'Right, now where are you, little opening-bottle thingy?' Scouring over the mess, Lucas knew he'd seen the small corkscrew with a brown bone handle somewhere. 'Hey, alakazam!' He held the corkscrew in his hand and smiled.

Pulling the cork and hearing the pop enthralled him. He placed the bottle on the side to allow it to breathe, just like he had when he had knocked on Matthew Hopkins's door only two days ago, released just as the aroma of the rich red fluid was now, realising he had also been accepted for what was inside.

Wiping his finger around the edge of the opened green bottle,

Lucas tasted the wine. The taste made him shudder, squeezing his eyes together, the sharp sensation clinging to the side of his mouth, making his mouth water unpleasantly.

'Oh, my, that isn't good!' Sticking out his tongue, Lucas wiped it with the back of his hand.

He poured a glass and held it in front of him, gently twirling it around by the engraved rim to admire the rich colour.

'Now what colour is that? Deep burgundy? Red? Blue? Surely a colour which has been named by someone, but really was it this colour?' As he continued to speak out loud to himself Lucas longed to meet the man who had introduced the colour alphabet to the world. Looking up to the white ceiling again, Lucas suddenly realised his new dance partner had been away from him for some time.

Matthew sat on the edge of Eve's bed, leaning slightly, unknowingly pressing on the small legs of the porcelain doll, inhaling a long breath as he rubbed his hands gently over the elegant red cover. A feeling of sentiment surged through him; he prayed for only a moment to hold her again, even have a chance to lie back-to-back once more, demanding to watch her breathe as she slept, needing to see her again, longing to smell her perfume on her soft unblemished skin.

Gently placing his fingers around the delicate carved handle of the small cabinet next to the bed, he opened it and took a cautious look inside. Instantly everything he saw inside reminded him of each and every moment he had been in her presence: the nail varnish, scented creams and glistening bracelets. The tears fell from his eyes as the lump in his throat that had been holding his emotions finally released. He took a tissue from the drawer and held it tightly between his fingers, her lip marks on the edge. Imagining her pushing the folded white sheet between her soft shapely lips, his hands shook as he kissed the lipstick stain, his tears falling onto the soft white paper. She was kissing him goodbye; it was to be their last kiss, her lips masking his lips with her beauty.

Folding the tissue Matthew placed it in the pocket of his trousers and continued to look at her belongings. As he sobbed for her he felt as though his heart had finally come to an end; it had broken into too many pieces, impossible to mend. Laying the small pots and bottles on the bed surrounded by her image, he pushed his fingers into the white creamy mush, his nostrils absorbing the fragrance. Rubbing the cream into his hands, he saw his nails stained from earlier, the dirt which altered the reality he had momentarily attempted to live. She wasn't there any more; in front of him was all there was of her. When was he going to stop pretending?

Standing slowly and taking the pretty items in his hands, he went to place them on the dressing table; she wasn't going to be invisible any more. With the thought in him he looked at the china doll; it had been secretly hidden under the bed for years, away from the world, away from the magnificence of the sun. He had to keep her alive, pretend he wasn't pretending. He knew it was the only thing to do.

Stepping back from the dressing table, feeling content in seeing Eve's belongings neatly displayed, he began to cry as he pulled the covers back on the bed. He was to sleep again where her beauty had once lain.

He heard a soft knocking.

Lucas stood in the doorway with two filled wine glasses, one containing fresh orange juice.

'Please come in, Lucas.' Matthew spoke softly, his voice a little hoarse. Rubbing his face, he sat on the bottom of the bed.

Lucas sat next to him and handed him the glass of orange juice. Quickly pulling it back again, he began to laugh. 'Only joking; I think this one is yours. It's a glorious room, Matthew.'

'Thank you, Lucas. Yes, it is. I'm not sure if Eve ever really liked it very much. I kind of told her how it was going to be, like I always told her how everything was meant to be; even her, in a funny way. She'd never have said anything to me. I am surprised she never changed it when I wasn't here; probably still felt like I was going to give her a hard time over the whole thing if she did. Oh dear, Lucas, if only I had my time again, I am sure I'd have been different. I am sure of it.' Matthew felt as though he was going to cry again; his stomach felt heavy as the seed of self-hatred began to grow inside him.

'Matthew, my dear friend with no idea, you do have your time again, each and every moment.' Lucas looked at Matthew's sad and flushed face, hoping he'd listen properly to his words.

'I meant with her, Lucas, my Eve. I want to buy her coffee again, buy her life again for her.'

'Yes, Matthew, that is exactly what I meant, my dear fellow. It is up to you how you keep her in your life and in your daughters' lives. Keep her alive, like I said, and allow the love you know she had for them to be part of them. Share it, Matthew; stop keeping it to yourself. Tell them everything they need to know about the woman who brought them into this crazy world. You will be safe, Matthew, I promise you.'

'It is easier said than done, Lucas.' Matthew felt a little stirring of anger as his friend's comment hadn't appealed to him at all. He was sure he'd never kept her to himself; he was certain.

'Oh, I see, Matthew; it's all about saying, is it? There is no one in this world who is telling you it is difficult, I'm afraid; only the man sitting next to me with teary eyes and a glass of red wine.' Lucas chuckled a little as he felt a protectiveness for Matthew stirring inside his rumbling belly. Nudging Matthew with his arm, he smiled.

'Oh, damn.' Matthew raised his voice a little as red wine splashed onto the cream carpet, spilling over the edge of the glass. 'I need a cloth. Lucas, quickly, hold this.' Handing the glass to Lucas, he moved to clean the moisture soaking into the threads of the carpet.

'Leave it, Matthew, leave the stain, and each time you look at it you will remember our very short and effective conversation. It is meant to be there, to remind you, like her room, all of it, Matthew. The sky she stood under, the sun which kept her warm and the bed where she slept, which protected her.' Lucas sat smiling, holding two glasses. He took a sip of orange juice, the sharp juice filling his mouth with pleasure.

'Lucas, you have a really sensible crazy way about you,' Matthew said while he watched the stain becoming more permanent.

Lucas began to roar with laughter as he could see Matthew was nearly bursting, desperately wanting to scrub away at the red residue.

'Matthew, what is the colour of the roses on the wall?'

'Red, of course.'

'See, you're happy to have those in your home.' Lucas stood and tapped Matthew on the arm before gulping down his orange juice, leaving Matthew to stare at the carpet alone, forgetting to ask him to come and dance.

Walking down the stairs, Lucas continued chuckling. His thoughts of Matthew were broken as he watched Ruth walking in the front door.

# 27

Natty felt uncomfortable lying on her stomach on her bed, her green covers scrunched under her body. Tapping her pen on the clean page of her diary and sipping from the straw in her can of cola, she let out a huge burp, the sensation of the fizzy bubbles going up her nose making her eyes water a little. Wondering why she hadn't noticed the missing handle on her drawer, she placed her cola on the side and pushed her body forward to take a closer look. As she hung over the edge of the untidy bed looking to see if it had rolled underneath, her long hair dangled touching the carpet; her pink dressing gown rolled over her bare bottom as she stretched out over the bed as far as she could, her half-naked body now creasing the pages of her diary. As she stretched out her hand to see if she could find the handle's whereabouts, she could feel the blood rushing to her head and her drink coming back into her throat. Being upside-down became too much for her; pushing on her hand, she managed to get her body back onto her bed, which was now messier than ever. Sweating and out of breath, thinking what a waste of energy it all was, she grabbed the cola from the side and finally became lost in her own thoughts.

*Thursday 3rd July 1975*

Dear Diary,
I really have no idea where to start, this week has been the craziest ever. With Dad's friend turning up only four days ago I can't seem to get my head around anything, let alone how goddamn gorgeous he is. He is a bit mad, but aren't we all in this house? I need to stop making it so obvious, need to stop staring at him, must definitely work on it. Can't get over

breaking my locket Monday. If only I had gone straight in to meet Glenn's old bloke and not worried if my frizzy hair was out of place before I saw Lucas then I would still have it around my skinny neck. Just makes me realise how much I really miss Mum; at least I had that. It was the most amazing gift anyone could have. Mum and Dad enclosed in a heart protected and together forever, and now it's gone and broken. Have to find the time to get it fixed. God knows when. Never seem to have time to do anything lately, crazy hospital. I know I made a complete fool of myself screaming so loud when my pretty chain snapped, think they all thought I was being murdered. I had to change, though. I couldn't let Lucas see me in such a mess. Trust Glenn to pull such a stunt, standing in the kitchen like she was deeply in love. Never thought she'd go for someone like that, he's soooo old, sex should be fun!!!!! Oh my God, feel so confused with it all. Lucas does something to me, kind of turns me inside out, I like what I see, and I'd so love to get to know him a little more. If he left Dad's side long enough to see me, that is.

Bit worried about Ruth, she really has been having a

'You have got to be joking!'

All of a sudden the room had gone dark; Natty could see a reflection of colour from the light earlier in front of her eyes. Throwing her pen down and still holding on to her drink she worked her way carefully to her door; after opening it she realised every room in the house was in complete darkness.

'Glenn, Glenn, get the candles!' Natty raised her voice as she held tight to the bannisters, walking steadily down the stairs.

'Bloody power cut.' Glenn leapt up from the sofa and made her way to the kitchen, fearful and cautious, dreading the feeling of having to move around freely in the dark. She wished she could hide under the cushions until the lights went back on. Letting out a huge sigh, she made her way to the kitchen, holding her hand out in front of her, reaching for the cupboard where the candles were always stored.

'Where the hell are they?' she muttered as she felt inside, her hand patting at the wood. The thought of staying in the dark longer gave her a sinking sensation in her very full stomach; she had been sitting eating chocolate and salted popcorn for most of the evening.

'Glenn, come on, I was in the middle of something.'

Glenn heard her sister's voice in the dark and, if she had been able to see her face properly, could have quite happily punched her between the eyes. 'I was also in the middle of something, Natty; it's not all about you.'

Natty sighed, moving forward to help. 'Glenn, they are always in there.' She squeezed a tin can hard in frustration.

'Someone has moved them. Maybe we can use your bright personality to light up the room, Nat.' Glenn shook her head in annoyance.

Ruth walked into the kitchen, sharing the darkness with her sisters. 'Natty hasn't a bright personality.'

'Ruth, have you seen them? Very comical, by the way; thought you lost your voice this week. Glenn, will you look, for goodness' sake? Ruth, help out, will you?' Natty started giggling and Glenn followed. Glenn's laughing became out of control as she bent her body forward trying not to wet herself.

'At least I haven't got to see your ugly face now.' Glenn was nearly on the floor through laughter.

'Just find them, could you?' Natty tried to speak through her giggling.

'I saw them in the drawer. How come you're not looking, bossy boots?' Ruth's voice was soft; it had been submerged into the dark background as all she could hear was her sisters laughing.

'Did you hear something, Nat?' Glenn asked in jest, now in the standing position with her legs crossed.

'Just look in the drawer, you. Or move out the way; I will do it!' Natty took a deep breath, hoping to push the laughter away. Opening the drawer, she touched the candles and a small box of matches.

'Hey, bingo! How did you know, Ruth?' Natty shook the matches, then took a handful of candles from the box.

Ruth stood with two fingers up at them both, thinking they couldn't see her, so what did it matter? Idiots, laughing like everything was always so wonderful.

She recalled seeing the matches the night of the big visit; their father had placed them in there after he'd lit the oven. That very moment, with the cigarette that she had taken from her bedroom drawer in her blazer pocket, she had known what she'd be trying before 'bring a pensioner home for tea' night was happily over. The last thing she wanted to do was to abide by the rules. The whole thing was an absolute joke. Why couldn't their father say he was too old for her, too grey and wrinkly for such a beautiful young girl? She was only eighteen, after all. Ruth had felt convinced that if Glenn was allowed to take part in such an escapade then a little puff on a cigarette wouldn't cause too much concern.

The thought had quickly come back to her as she made her excuse to leave the house. Sitting under the bus shelter nearest home, she had pulled her blazer around her white shirt to keep warm. Match after match she would light only for it to be blown out by the opposing wind. The cigarette hung from her mouth and the glances from the old lady who tapped her long umbrella on the concrete made her more determined to drag the poison down the back of her clean young throat. To say 'go to hell' to the lot of them: to her family, the girls at school and her own confusion and misery. Her attempt at blowing hoops with the smoke was a waste of time; the girls from school who always hung around the park entrance always made it look so easy.

Giving up finally after choking profusely and disturbing the old lady's solitude even more she went back home, having to face it all once more whether she wanted to or not. Absorbed by the odour of stale cigarette on her clothes she saw another new member of the family standing in the kitchen, shaking her father's hand. The poor man couldn't get a word in edgeways as Glenn did most of the talking as usual.

The small conversation was disturbed by Natty's screams echoing through the floorboards; another older sister was making a scene in Ruth's miserable life. Natty rushed down the stairs with her broken necklace in her hand. She came to a sudden halt when they all stared at her, especially Lucas; it was so funny to see her blush like she did. Their father tried with every fibre of understanding to keep everyone in the kitchen uplifted, he wanted to make a good impression, and it was all crap the whole evening.

Feeling the anger well up in her stomach, Ruth's mind continued to wander as she stood in the dark hearing her sisters' smug laughter. Quickly recalling how their father hadn't cared too much when she had come in from school that day, just gripped her shoulder and gave her one of those reassuring smiles that meant he didn't know what words to use. Their good old father who had spent most of his life smiling reassuringly at them all. She didn't want to tell him she had spent most of that day sitting in the smelly school toilet alone and scared, huddled up on the floor in the small cubicle, smelling the urine from the black stained toilet seat.

'Get a couple of saucers, Ruth, will you?' Natty finally lit a candle, dripped the wax onto the slowly retrieved plate and pushed the candle onto it, allowing it to stand. Another and another she lit and successfully placed them around the kitchen; the candlelight shone an orange glow onto her face.

Seeing the outline of her sisters coming into view, then their own reflections of beauty coming through the small lights, Natty sat at the table, placing a candle in the middle. Glenn and Ruth both pulled out a chair and joined her.

'Well, this is cosy,' Ruth said sarcastically.

'Yes, it is. I was just in the middle of writing.' Natty tucked her hair into the back of her dressing gown to keep a little warmer.

'No, Nat, I mean a brick-in-the-head kind of cosy!' Ruth had an urge in the back of her throat to inhale another dose of toxins; she hoped the girls at school could be kind enough to leave another one in her desk. Ruth knew she was going to sit with her sisters and pretend she cared. She had survived four days at school and only had one more; sitting like a little Victorian girl with her sisters around a candle shouldn't be too hard.

All three sisters stayed around the softly lit table. Their father and Lucas had been out for ages; their father had taken Lucas shopping and they still hadn't arrived home.

'How is it going, Ruth? Those girls leaving you alone now? At least Dad got it sorted for you, eh?' Glenn spoke gently as she sat with her knickers damp and the waistband of her chequered trousers digging into her hips.

'I am surprised you asked, Glenn, being so busy clearing out the old people's home and everything.' Ruth chuckled to herself even though she didn't really want to; she wanted to stay miserable until the bell went the next day after school.

'Oh, stuff you, then; thought I'd ask. Sorry, girls, have to undo my trousers!' Glenn knew it was going to be the last time she'd ask; after all, she was only trying to help.

'Ruth, don't be like that. Glenn was only asking.'

'Sorry, Glenn, didn't mean to hurt your feelings!' Of course Ruth knew she wasn't sorry at all.

Natty wanted to change the atmosphere around the table and needed to dig deeper with them; she hadn't had a proper chat with them for ages. 'So, Glenn, how do you think Dad took your newfound husband Monday? Looked like he was going to burst a blood vessel if you ask me, and I noticed he is wearing his wedding ring; kind of nice, I think. Wasn't Lucas funny when he got up and said, "I like your coat," to Stanley?'

'No, it wasn't funny; how was it? He's just a tramp in Dad's clothes. God, Natty, you haven't got the hots for him, have you? I do think Dad took it OK. I actually can't believe I am moving out of here next weekend. Dad seems too cool about it all. I think he's finally flipped.'

'It's because he's hanging around Lucas too much, that's why,' Ruth muttered resentfully. Glenn was moving out and all she was doing was spending her days getting a beating at school.

'Hey, you two, don't speak about Lucas like that!' Natty frowned.

'Oh, sorry, Nat, forgot you're also in love.' Ruth tapped the table with her fingers and began to whistle; she knew she'd pushed it with them.

'No, Ruth, it isn't like that at all; he's just really good for Dad. Nice for Dad to have some company.' Natty attempted to hide her true feelings for their father's friend.

'Of course, Nat, whatever you say! Anyone for a drink?' Ruth needed to move from the table for a moment; an unexpected anger surged through her.

Glenn laughed. 'No electricity, clever!'

'Juice, then. Sorry, can't remember everything; my memory's a bit shot. You need to get used to people around you losing their memory anyway.' Ruth chuckled to herself again.

'Any cake with that so-called joke, Ruth?' Glenn felt too happy to fall into the trap of her sister's wrath.

145

'Eating again, Glenn? You don't stop! Anyone would think you were pregnant.' Natty giggled, then all a sudden inhaled a sharp breath, her eyes wide and her mouth open.

The atmosphere in the candlelit kitchen changed.

'So very funny! Lost for words, me!' All of a sudden Glenn had an overwhelming sense of reality crash down on her; the thought buried deep in the back of her mind was finally being spoken of. It was becoming real; she needn't lie on her bed at night any more and wonder. Fear and adrenaline overtook her happiness instantly.

'You're so not, are you, Glenn?' Ruth sat down holding three glasses of orange juice. It was the most amazing thing that had ever happened, her sister having a baby. Her mood had changed in a second; there was finally something to look forward to in the lives of the Hopkins family.

'Have you two gone completely stark raving bonkers? Of course I'm not pregnant.' Glenn wanted to go and stick her head in the garden lawn, her body numb as she didn't know what to think, do or say. The only thing she could do was grab her orange juice and gulp the whole lot down, as she attempted to ignore the interrogation from across the table.

'What a classic, Glenn having a baby!' Natty roared with laughter.

'*Will you get off my case?*' Glenn prayed the lights would go on finally so she could run into the bedroom and look at herself in her mirror. As though if she looked at herself in the glass she'd find the right answers, the way to go around the whole ordeal. She was soon to be leaving her mother's home and her family; it all seemed to be a dream.

'Dad's blood vessel will certainly burst now. Do you know something, Glenn? I hope you are, and I hope you are happy with your old man; I really mean it!' Ruth was flooded with excitement, the same feeling she'd had when Lucas had come through the door and she had seen how he had lived so freely. She was aware she had put her own pain in front of them all, masking the happiness they all wanted to find. For the moment, she accepted that her family really weren't too bad after all. She promised herself for the sake of all the goodness to come not to give in to the girls at school, not to give them any more power over who she was and who she was going to become. The moment of strength burned in her.

'Do you mean that, Ruth, or are you being your lovely self like you have been all week?' Glenn touched Ruth's hand, feeling a sense of warmth and permission from her.

'I do truly, and if you like I don't even mind buying you a wedding present out of Dad's Green Shield stamps.' Ruth grabbed Glenn's hand a little harder and smiled.

'Thanks, Ruth; very thoughtful.' Glenn smiled back.

'Listen, you lot, what do you think Dad is going to say when you tell him?' Natty felt as though she was going to be sick, praying she was going to be at the hospital when Glenn broke the news to him.

'Anyway, we don't know yet.' Glenn did know in that very second; she felt it.

Ruth laughed. 'When did you have old man sex, Glenn?'

'So much for the caring thing, Ruth; that didn't last long. Some very wonderful crazy day in June.'

'Oh, help, you've got to be at least four weeks. Hold on, Sept, Oct . . .' Natty counted on her hands while trying not to laugh with nerves for her sister.

'Nat!' Glenn slapped Natty's arm and then joined her in her laughter.

'March. Have I worked that out right? Oh, let me have your blue trousers, then,' Natty shouted excitedly.

'Oh, my, I'm going to get some cake.' Glenn walked slowly to the work surface and took some soft chocolate sponge from the plate. Opening her mouth wide, she stuffed the whole piece in, her mouth completely full as the crumbs fell onto her brown blouse.

Natty calmed her laughter down and spoke gently. 'It's a shame about Mum, though, isn't it?'

'Trust you to ruin such a moment, Natty!' Ruth couldn't understand why Natty had to mention their mother when she felt so determined to feel better.

'Leave it out, Nat!' Glenn spoke while trying to pull the remains of the cake from the side of her mouth with her finger, the dry chocolate sponge sticking to her teeth.

'I was only thinking when I broke my locket that my birthday wishes did come true. I wished she would disappear, remember, Glenn, when I turned fifteen? You were there. It's my entire fault. And look how wonderful this is, and she isn't going to be here to share it. Do you think I could wish to bring her back?' Natty felt immersed in guilt at their unpredicted happiness.

'Don't think so, Nat!' Glenn rubbed her stomach and squeezed her fingers into another piece of chocolate cake.

'Well, I wished on my fifteenth birthday that I'd have bigger tits, but look, it hasn't happened, so it's nothing to do with your wish, Natty!' Ruth roared with laughter, not giving Natty the path to take Glenn's moment away, not that evening anyway.

'Fuck, I am going to have a baby!' Glenn exclaimed suddenly, staring at her sisters. Realising she was going to be a mother and she was only eighteen.

Desperate for the toilet, Glenn prayed for the electricity to go back on; she didn't want to walk alone in the dark. Looking around, she wished Natty had lit more candles.

'Yes, Glenn, that is exactly what's happening! You'd think the old boy would know better at his age. Oh, yes, Glenn is going to have a little grey baby in a mac!' Ruth winked at Glenn; it had been the first time she hadn't worried about school in a long while, and the feeling was brilliant.

As they sat around the candle, its flickering orange flame lit up their happiness, their beauty and their unity; hysterical laughter filled the atmosphere of the kitchen. Glenn was nearly wetting her knickers again as the tears of joy rolled down her face, Ruth was banging on the table with each roar of excitement and Natty was pulling her dressing-gown cord tight, trying to keep her laughter in as her stomach ached from the sense of freeness and joy they all shared.

# 28

'Good morning, Suzy, sweetie. Did you have a wonderful evening in those bubbles?'

'*Don't ask.*' Suzy threw her bag on the counter and sighed.

# 29

Ruth put one foot in front of the other, feeling a surge of determination as she walked through the narrow alley to school. The strap of her satchel over the front of her body was creasing her school shirt. She didn't care; it had been the first time she'd grabbed her school bag with eagerness to begin her school day. For a July morning the sun was taking its time to wake and hid behind the white mask of protection. The excitement filled her, to even think Glenn was going to have a baby. The whole thing seemed incredible. Finally there was something to look forward to, something to devote her attention to.

It was the final day at school before the holidays. From that moment she knew she wasn't to hide in the school toilets any more; she was going to hold her head up high, be strong and not ever allow them to diminish her life again. She was going to look at what she truly had in her life. What she had was beautiful; she knew it and felt it through every fibre of her young body. People did want her; they were happy for her to be in their lives, however crazy it was, and even if sometimes they had a funny way of showing it. She had always buried her true beliefs under her sadness, but eventually they were to emerge, just like the sun had been attempting to push its way through the thickening clouds to be glorious and take full command of the sky. She was going to do exactly that; she was going to become the sunshine in her own life.

Pupils ran past her, shoving her out of the way. Girls walked close together, speaking about the other girls in front of them; the boys strolled next to them, absorbing their attention and giggles. All fighting for acceptance, all fighting for approval and not to be the one who was walking alone, to be missing out. No one wanted to be like her.

Pushing her way to her classroom, Ruth saw them waiting for her. She held on to the strap of her bag tightly as they stared and smirked from the corner of the classroom. They were determined to make her last day hell; Ruth could feel it. The fear began to sting her stomach as she attempted not to make any more eye contact; she continued to walk with her head held high. She began thinking of the sun, her sisters and her father, and how unaware she was of the lives the cruel girls led when they arrived in the places they called home, their own dysfunctional four walls. Her head was spinning with thoughts.

'Hey, come here, you.'

Ruth's thoughts were running out of control.

*Just walk past, keep going, don't stop, Ruth; just think of the sunshine, the sunshine, sunshine.*

Ruth felt a tug on her thin black jacket and held her breath.

'See you after school then, Ruth.'

'Don't think so; need to get home.' Ruth felt like she wanted to cry instantly. She had to stand up for herself; she simply had to. In the back of her mind all she kept saying was *the sunshine, sunshine*.

'You don't seem to be understanding me, little rich girl: see you after school.'

Ruth forced a smirk and pulled her arm away from Charlotte's rough grasp. She felt as if her heart was going to stop. Looking up at the clock in the hall she told herself she only had to ignore them, suppress the fear for another six hours, think of the sunshine; until then that was all she had to do, think of the sunshine.

The mumbling and chatter in the classroom absorbed her mind and her gradually weakening body. Girls conversed as they sat on the desks with their feet on the black chairs; others giggled, removing the pencils from the teacher's desk, placing them on the cream window sill behind the brown curtains. Looking out of the heavy-framed windows she gazed into the sky.

She was nearly there; only one more hour to go. Sitting on the toilet seat, tears began to fill her eyes; she had been thinking all day about having to go into the changing rooms. It was her dreaded day, Friday. All the girls changing in front of each other, looking

151

at each other's underwear, checking their breast size, jumping around in their knickers. She would have to be amongst the cattle of puberty; they didn't have any dignity, parading around the small busy tiled room like they owned the place. Ruth knew there was absolutely no way she was going to get away from it as she kicked the blue PE bag at her feet.

'Goddamn sunshine!' Ruth opened the door quickly and breathed hard, her head thumping, her legs feeling weak.

The shouting from the girls echoed through the changing room; they were running around as Ruth had anticipated. She moved into the corner to change as far away from them as she could. If she kept quiet enough she could pretend she wasn't there, then they could all carry on in their own little way.

'Ouch!' Ruth felt the sting of her bra strap as someone pulled at it so its elastic would snap back onto her shoulder.

'Hey, Ruth, got your mother's bloomers on?'

Ruth heard the torment begin, keeping her head down and pulling on her grey shorts.

Someone grabbed her school shoe from in front of her and threw it on top of the highest locker.

'Go get it back, Ruth.' Charlotte stood tapping her foot with her arms folded, looking smug.

Ruth tucked her red PE top into her shorts, feeling anguished and humiliated; she knew if she attempted to move from her belongings they would throw them in the shower, soaking them, or something as cruel. Once again Ruth tried to move her thought pattern from them and over and over in her head began chanting *sunshine, sunshine*.

She was done with them all. Pulling her shoulders back, she walked over to the locker, pulled over a small chair and stood on it, towering over them all. It was where they all belonged, simply beneath her.

As she stretched over the locker she could hear them laughing and taunting her. Suddenly she felt her shorts being pulled down roughly; Charlotte had pulled her knickers down with them and her bare bottom was revealed to them all. The sting from their hands slapping her bare skin echoed through every part of her ridiculed body.

Suddenly it all went quiet; they all picked up their hockey sticks and left her standing unprotected and tormented.

'Don't let them beat you, Ruth; don't let them, Ruth,' Ruth said to herself as she stepped from the chair with her shoe in her shaking hand. Pulling her knickers and shorts up, she knew she wasn't going to cry; she was going to face them all, walk out into the playground and do the last forty-five minutes of the day.

She threw her shoe into the corner; it landed on her belongings. She pulled her hair tighter at the back and inhaled a deep breath; she wrapped her hand around a hockey stick and went out into the fresh air. The sun was still hidden behind the clouds, but it was nearly winning its battle to escape; it wouldn't be long and it'd be shining brightly above.

Walking onto the playground, she could hear the banging of sticks on the concrete and the laughter from the girls who huddled in little groups. The teacher blew the whistle and they followed the command like a flock of sheep, gathering in a circle. The teacher began calling names, assigning each girl to a group, asking them to pick a coloured ribbon to tie around their waist.

Ruth stood at the back of the circle, speaking under her breath, her bottom sore and her heart racing. 'Please, God, not white; please, not white.'

'Ruth Hopkins, white, please!'

Ruth couldn't believe what she had just heard. Did the stupid teachers have no idea at all what was going on? The headmaster hadn't told any of them; they were still being the ignorant allies to the bullies they'd always been before her father had gone to see them. Ruth picked the white ribbon from the pile of multi-coloured strands and tied it around her waist, walking to her assigned group.

'Hello, princess. Did you find your shoe?' Charlotte roared with laughter.

'Yes, thanks.' Ruth tightened her lips, overcome with emotions. She had to do this, ignore them.

'Don't get too near me out there, will you, Ruth?'

The whistle went again and the game began; the banging of sticks echoed through the playground. Ruth was pushed and shunted away by the girls on her team.

'Wait till later, Ruth.'

'Hey, Ruth, how's your arse?' Charlotte pulled Ruth's pigtail and nearly spat on her shoulder; the saliva which left her mouth only just missed her.

Ruth began to drag her stick behind her as the girls rushed back and forth pushing the hard ball around their feet. She didn't have the strength to fight them with her mind any more. How come the teacher never saw what they did to her? Did anyone really care if they hurt her or was the whole school out to get the little rich girl?

'Ruth, play the game, will you? Pull yourself together! This is a team sport; support the girls!' the teacher bellowed from the side of the playground, shaking her head.

Ruth felt like wrapping the string to her whistle around her neck at that very moment, thinking how much she looked like a lesbian with hairy armpits. Anger began to stir in Ruth's body; she felt as if her blood was beginning to boil. Huffing and blowing her cheeks out, she began to run a little to support her team.

'Hope your tits have grown bigger like your arse.'

Ruth heard the voice again echoing through her head; again Charlotte's voice become part of her being. Ruth's body began to feel heavy as though she couldn't hold herself up another minute; her vision became fuzzy; she pushed her hands tightly around her hockey stick, gripping onto the wood without being able to imagine ever wanting to let go. Taking her arms into the air, the hockey stick above her head, she slammed the stick with all her strength onto Charlotte's shoulder; again she held the stick high and brought it down through the screams from the faint vision in front of her. Again and again she hit her body with all her force. She felt like a robot; she wasn't going to stop. The screaming bellowed through the playground like the bashing of sticks and laughter earlier.

Everyone began screaming; the teacher ran forward, pulling Charlotte along the floor out of the way of the coming blow. The teacher couldn't get near Ruth as she continued bringing the stick down onto the concrete, again and again. Ruth thought she could hear crying and screaming around her; everything was a blur.

Suddenly Ruth stopped. Sweating, her breathing heavy, the palms of her hands burning from her grip, her body contaminated with adrenaline and shock. She couldn't stand; her arms and legs felt too heavy. She dropped to her knees; they smashed against the bloodstained concrete. Ruth's body naturally curled itself into a ball, just as she had once lain in her cot abandoned and full of fear. The concrete and the circle of girls around her witnessing the tears she had never had the strength to release before her father had leant forward, taking her from her soiled cot. She needed him to hold her now, to pull her into his arms and protect her again. The only reality was the warmth of the breaking sun on her back.

# 30

---

Harry sat alone on the sofa feeling disgruntled. Suzy had left in a mood that morning and she couldn't even find the kindness to kiss him goodbye. His coffee sat untouched, becoming lukewarm as he stared into space. His bare chest leaning against the soft cushion gave him a sense of comfort as he wondered what he could have done to upset her in some way, or if it was simply something she'd do: throw a tantrum now and then for no good reason. Did women do that sort of thing? Inadequacy rushed through him as, never having had a relationship longer than an evening, he felt unable to deal with such characteristics of the opposite sex.

The radio filled the background with a sense of false company; it was quiet, not like the evening before. He had never planned for them to knock on his door, his friends with a crate of beer. Card night was always Friday. They all barged past him, pushing out the chairs, and set up the card game for the evening. They were polite to her and asked her if she wanted to join in. She just chose to sit on the sofa, smoking one cigarette after the other, adding to the cloud of smoke building in his small home, in the company of loud drunken men. The only time she had dismissed herself from glaring at him and moved from the soft chair had been to take the order for the Chinese takeaway from the back of the phone book; he could see where she had torn the page in half.

Shaking his head, he pushed himself up from his comfortable position and despondently walked into the kitchen to grab a bag; he had to tidy before he went to work just in case Suzy decided to pay him a visit after work and give him oral sex for being so rude to him. A hard-done-by feeling came over him as he pulled the black sack from the cluttered cupboard under the sink, his bare feet cold on the blue lino. Shaking the bag out and having no enthusiasm for cleaning his friends' mess, he looked at the bedroom door and thought about getting back into bed. His bed where they had both slept without touching each other once; she had her back to him all night, with her arms folded. It was unfair, he thought; when he had played cards and laughed and drunk beer happily he had made sure his back wasn't to her, keeping her in view on the sofa.

Pushing the dirty Chinese cartons into the bag and picking up the beer cans, he was gradually convincing himself it was all her fault. Picking up the filled ashtray he tipped it into the bag; the ash and aroma overwhelmed him. It was such a disgusting thing to do; he could always taste the cigarettes on her mouth when she kissed him.

The table was finally clean and he pulled the last fragments off with his hand, pushing the four metal chairs in around the edges. Picking up a fifty-pence piece from the floor, he smiled in satisfaction. 'Gotcha.'

Harry felt gaining some money finally from the game of cards rather amusing; at least he had managed to win something from his newly married friend. His cheating friend, with his cheating wife; his friend who had been speaking loudly, blowing smoke into the air, radiating cockiness as he sat with Harry's money in front of him. He wouldn't be so relaxed if he knew the drunken lady with the bad breath who had stolen money from Harry's wallet was his loveable Samantha. The fifty pence was his first payment back from the £30 she had stolen. Harry chuckled as he placed the coin into the pocket of his jeans, knowing his friend had probably paid for his own champagne at the wedding and wishing he had drunk more.

Walking over to his cold coffee, Harry gulped the whole cupful back into his dry throat. Looking at the ripped telephone book again, he sighed and thought he had been an arse after all. He could make it up to her for such an evening, and at least she wouldn't want to turn her back on him any more.

Throwing the bag into the kitchen, Harry went into the bathroom and turned on the shower. Stripping off his jeans, which smelt of smoke, he stood in front of the mirror and looked at his naked body. His hair was beginning to show grey flecks at the front but his chest was still toned and firm. His age was showing on his skin and he knew he was still taking the whole dating thing for granted. Standing on his crumpled jeans, breathing in the steam, hearing the shower thrusting onto the empty bath, he closed his eyes and remembered his time with Eve.

# 31

Natty was folding washing on the bed, taking the items one by one from the clean laundry basket, placing her and Ruth's and her father's in small piles. Lucas seemed unable to allow his clothes to be washed; she was happy as it made her sorting a lot easier.

She held on to Ruth's red jumper tightly, squeezing the soft wool between her fingers. She had never realised her sister was in such torment, such pain and loneliness as she left the house every day for school. She wondered why Ruth couldn't have said anything to her, why she kept the affliction to herself.

Pushing down the jumper on Ruth's small pile softly and rubbing it affectionately with her hand, she turned her head and saw Ruth's bedroom door closed again. Natty wanted to go into her bedroom and check if she was all right. Ruth had spent nearly four weeks hidden behind her four walls. Natty had tried to go in before a couple of times as she could hear her crying through the night; when Natty woke up in the heat and went to open her bedroom window a little, she would hear her young sister's heart breaking. She had to get back into her warm bed as Ruth didn't want anyone to be near her.

Ruth sometimes came out of her bedroom to share food with them all over the silent dinner table; their father would spend most of the meal with his hand pressed on Ruth's arm as she attempted to swallow her food, her head lowered in shame, not making eye contact with anyone. Each and every night their father would gently knock on Ruth's bedroom door and ask her if she was ready for him to come in; he was going to continue until she'd one day open the door for him, so he could hold her in his arms and let her know they all loved her very much. It wasn't her fault; she had been pushed to it, and he had felt it from the moment he had seen the policemen standing each side of his broken child. She hadn't looked at him. He had asked her to go up the stairs and wait for him until he had spoken to them. Lucas had placed his hand into hers and taken her up the stairs, laying her on her bed and covering her with her pretty covers.

Ruth was to attend some kind of meeting for disruptive and uncontrollable children in the coming week. Their father said she wasn't going to attend; he wasn't going to stand by and watch his daughter being labelled in such a way like his Eve. She was hurting, that was all, and he didn't want them to mess with her head, to start making her ill, giving her tablets and all sorts of stuff to make her someone she wasn't. He had asked for her to be reprieved from going and they had refused. Natty had seen him screw the letter up and put it in the bin. He said he was never going to let her go back to school again; he just wanted her to come out of her bedroom for longer than a meal so he could talk to her.

Lucas had made her a plate of beans and toast one evening and left it outside her bedroom door. He had made a small flower out of paper and placed it next to the plate on the tray. It had remained outside all evening. Apart from the small paper flower; she had taken that.

It was such a kind thing for him to do. He filled their home with an energy and compassion which exhilarated Natty. Through all of the continued confusion he always smiled and whistled as he walked freely and happily around his new home. He was simply wonderful. Their father had bought him some new clothes so he easily represented the gorgeous man he was.

Rolling up her black tights, Natty heard the bathroom door opening. The steam filled the hall and walking toward her was Lucas, the bottom half of him wrapped in a large white towel; she could see his willy flapping back and forward as he happily strolled to her, though unfortunately hidden under the white covering. The water dripping from his shoulders showed off his tanned muscly body, the lucky moisture gathering in the ripples on his chest. The feeling of sexual arousal overwhelmed her; her heart felt like it was going to stop. He had simply walked straight into her room holding a bottle of shampoo; his confidence and innocence in his half-naked appearance sourced even more adrenaline from her nervous body.

'Miss Natty, do you mind if I ask you something? Why would anyone want to put this on their hair? It says "for dry frizzy hair"; who could want to make their hair go like that?' Lucas stood near her, looking confused.

Natty knew it was something she'd had to deal with her whole life, dry frizzy hair, and of course no one could want to have such a thing. Shaking her head in amusement and in happiness at his question, she laughed and took the shampoo from him as though she'd never heard of such a thing as frizzy hair.

'No, Lucas, it means *for* dry frizzy hair, not to get dry frizzy hair.' She smelt the open bottle; she had always liked the apple fragrance.

'Yes, that's what I am saying: it's for dry frizzy hair!' Lucas watched the pretty young woman in front of him; she seemed not to be taking his question seriously. He saw a very innocent lady who he realised he liked to be in the company of.

'Now, Lucas, let me put it this way: if you have dry frizzy hair like me, then you will buy a shampoo that says it's for poor unlucky-haired people like me. You see, it's meant to make it not so dry and frizzy. As you can see, it doesn't do much, as wonderful as the apples smell. You are so funny.' Natty liked him very much; she could feel it in her mind and her heart.

'Oh, I see. So I need to get one for brown curly soft hair, do I?' Lucas scrunched his handsome face up, still bemused by the lettering on the black and green bottle.

'No, this will do just fine, Lucas.' Natty smiled at him as she handed back the wet bottle of shampoo.

'That's good, then. Thank you for your help, Miss Natty. Your hair suits you, Miss Natty; dry and frizzy serves you very well.' Lucas smiled and went back into the bathroom.

'Thanks so much for that.' Natty laughed, feeling flattered in a funny kind of way, transfixed by his bottom as the tight towel revealed its pert shape beautifully.

Chuckling, she balanced a small amount of matching underwear on her hand and went to place it in her drawer. Quickly glancing at her dressing table, she moved aside a bottle of perfume and her diary, thinking she would have to stick her secret words back into her bag.

161

'Where the hell has it gone?' She instantly tossed the underwear back onto her bed, her knickers falling on the floor, and hastily moved her belongings from the cluttered side, bending over and checking under her bed and the small space under the dressing table. Her locket was gone. She knew she had put it on her dressing table; she'd placed it around a bottle of perfume. Frantically she began pulling open the small drawers, seeing the drawer with the missing handle again.

'Oh, for God's sake, where is my necklace? Please, God, where is it?' Fear tore through her stomach; it built greater and stronger inside her. A sweat overcame her; she was overwhelmed with panic, a sensation she remembered she had felt in the school playground waiting for her father to arrive to pick her up when she was a small child.

'God damn it!' Pushing her shaking hands through the front of her hair and pulling hard at the strands, she became frozen with fear.

'Miss Natty, what is wrong?' Lucas came into her bedroom again, the towel barely around his waist this time and his curly locks full of white soft bubbles.

'Lucas, my locket has gone; I think I've lost it.'

'Was it very important, Miss Natty? There are so many lovely things to wear.'

'Yes, Lucas, it was one of the most important things I've ever had and I could never replace it. Oh my God, why didn't I get it fixed? Why do I have to be so stupid?' Speaking quickly, Natty smelt the aroma of apple surrounding her.

'Miss Natty, please don't fret. We will find it, I promise; we will not stop until we have. We shall remain on the search of it, and until you have it back around your pretty neck we will not give up.'

'It's got to be here, Lucas; I left it right there. Thank you so much, though.' Natty picked up the long bottle of perfume she had wrapped the pretty gold chain around.

'Miss Natty, we will find it, but now I have to go and rinse these stinging bubbles out of my very sore eyes.' Lucas smiled while squinting, his eyes nearly closed.

'OK, Lucas. Thank you.' He made her chuckle, holding the perfume in her shaking hands.

\*

Ruth lay on her bed in a curled position; she had begun to feel hungry and was going to attempt to go down the stairs and hide her head in shame as she ate a quick sandwich. Her father wasn't in and Natty was too busy to notice her, and it didn't matter if Lucas saw her; he wouldn't judge. Her gripping hand became sweaty, her knuckles nearly white. Moving from her bed she went to open her wardrobe. Seeing her black school blazer hanging there, she opened her hand and let the necklace fall into the small pocket.

# 32

Driving through the busy traffic, Matthew gently leant over with his hand on the passenger seat, looking at the row of shops, the windows open as the warm fresh air touched his face to his approval. Trying to keep his eyes on the road, he could see the glorious department store in view; he knew he was near. It was between a laundrette and a hardware shop; he was certain of it.

Full of excitement and anticipation as though he was going on his very first date with her, he felt the nerves stirring in his stomach, recalling her sitting with her friends. The thought embraced his body. He was going to imagine it as though it was real when he entered the same place, pretend he was again waiting for her as he sat in the same seat, admire her beauty when he heard the bell of the door ring and she walked in. He chuckled to himself as he remembered her tripping over in front of him; she did look so sweet in a panic and trying to gain her poise.

'It must be here.' Pulling over and parking, he checked himself in the mirror and began walking down the road.

Standing outside the small shop, he felt a little warm in his cream jacket and old brown jumper, as the sun began to beat down onto the day. The noise of drying machines and the smell of hot linen came from the open door of the laundrette; the hardware shop was now closed with posters stuck all over the window, and mail had built up in the empty shop doorway. It was the only laundrette in town, so he knew he was in the right place.

'What the hell? Why would they do this?' Feeling downhearted he opened the wooden-framed glass door slowly, waiting for the bell to ring as he entered. The coffee shop was gone.

The dusty dim place felt almost suffocating after the fresh air on his face. He now absorbed the new surroundings with sadness.

Taking a slow walk around the shop he tried to remember where the chairs and little cosy booth had been. He knew they had sat at the table where a picture was hung: a picture of a tormented sea and a crew hanging on for their lives as the waves crashed against their boat, breaking the vessel slowly into pieces. Just like his heart. The picture was gone, and the memory he yearned to relive had gone down deep into the depths of the sea also.

'Excuse me, young lady, am I right in saying this used to be the old coffee shop?' Matthew stood next to the cluttered counter, hoping to get the attention of the young lady behind it; books were in neat piles in front of her. He continued looking around in disbelief.

'Hello, sir. Yes, you are right; the coffee shop went a little while ago now, and we've been here at least a year. Was there anything you were looking for?'

'Um, well, crazy as it seems, I was looking for something. Looks like it really isn't here after all.' Matthew thought the young lady behind the counter seemed pleasant. She had a sadness to her face which Matthew recognised.

'Why don't you have a look around? You never know; you may find something.'

'OK, I will do. Thank you so much.' Matthew smiled at her and was thankful for her gentle smile back at him. He began to browse around the multi-coloured bindings, his thoughts deepening. The coffee shop may have been taken away; it didn't matter. She had been in there with him a very long time ago. Whether it was a stuffy old bookshop or even an empty building, her gentle voice had once echoed through the walls.

Matthew closed his eyes for a moment and embraced every moment of his time with her there. He could almost hear her giggles echo through the shop and smell her perfume.

The array of books displayed in perfect size and colour took his attention. Putting his finger on each one, he found himself reading each and every title. Slowly pulling one from its place he opened it with interest, smelling the old pages, a dry smell he recognised from Lucas's cardboard box of belongings. He began to read. Looking behind him, he saw a small chair next to the window; he began to walk while he filled his mind with the words and his imagination began to flourish.

'Suzy, darling, who is that next to the window?'

'I don't know. He's been there nearly all day now. We're going to have to lock up soon. I haven't got the heart to tell him; he looks so peaceful.'

'Oh, sweetie, my darling, I will tell him. You know how easy it is for me to approach fine dark-haired men.'

Matthew was barely aware of footsteps approaching him.

'Excuse me, dear sir, we are closing in five minutes; you will have to leave now. We are open the same time tomorrow.'

Matthew looked up to see the brightly dressed man, instantly engulfed by his aftershave and hairspray.

'Oh, please excuse me; I am truly sorry.' Matthew closed the book hastily and rushed to the counter, taking money from his jean pocket and throwing it quickly on the side; the coins fell onto the blue carpet. 'Can I take this one?'

Standing outside the shop he breathed in the fresh air, holding the book close to his chest. It had been the first time he had lived in another world and someone else's life for such a long time; it enthralled him. He had left all the books he once owned at his old home, hoping the new occupants would enjoy them; he giggled as he had never bothered to read any of them. His escape had been right in front of his very eyes all along.

There was something about the shop that filled him with comfort. He was determined to get home quickly and finish the journey of the written words, return to his own image of the characters and discover how it was going to end for them. A whole life in one small book; it was something quite inspirational.

Walking with a quick pace back to his car, he took the yellow parking ticket from under the wiper and stuffed it quickly into the glove box, shaking his head. Placing the book carefully on the passenger seat, thrilled and thirsty with a fine to pay, Matthew smiled and started his engine.

'We get all sorts in here, Suzy.'

'Yes, I know what you mean.' Suzy looked Wilfred up and down, raising her eyebrows, and began to laugh. The thought of the quiet reader quickly entered her mind; he had seemed sad, and she had felt a pulling to him which she couldn't quite understand as she had watched him most of the day with his legs crossed and his head down, buried in his own company.

'Well, you know who your friends are.' Wilfred laughed along with her as he went to leave, gently throwing her the large set of keys to lock up.

# 33

He stood in front of her, making her cringe, the collar of his shirt stained with old sweat and dirt. His beard was yellowing under his nose and his yellow fingers and dirty nails needed half an hour under a hot tap. He held the glistening gold within his dirty fingers, moving it around. The roll-up was so small it nearly fell from his mouth as he attempted to hold it tight between his dirty teeth and drying lips.

'I will give you £10 for it; that's your lot.'

'But it's beautiful. I think I need a little bit more for it,' Ruth said, almost in shock. She moved her body back a little as the shop owner leant forward over the glass counter, his stale breath too near her for her liking, making her belly churn with sickness and nerves.

'We get things like this in here all day long! £10.50; it's all I am prepared to pay. Either put it back round your neck or leave it.'

Ruth knew it never had belonged around her neck. Gazing around the cluttered shop, she saw gold necklaces and bracelets, gold and silver, lined up and pinned tight to small squares of purple velvet gathering dust. She knew at that moment she wasn't the only one who had stolen something that didn't belong to them, stolen something from someone important.

'I really don't think you will find one like that.' Ruth's stomach filled with emotion as she watched the repulsive man throw the gold chain into a small plastic box, mixing with rings and bracelets; the locket hung over the edge. Ruth felt the money go into her hand while keeping her eyes on the soon-to-be-abandoned piece which could never be replaced.

Pushing the tears to the back of her throat, Ruth squashed the money into the pocket of her brown corduroys, looking up into the sky; it was the clearest blue she had seen for ages. She couldn't go home; she had to stay out for as long as she could.

There wasn't anywhere for her to go. She strolled around the busy town and looked slowly into the shop windows. She could have anything she wanted from the colourful displays. She was sick of buying things to pretend she was OK, to replace something inside her that was truly missing. Pulling the money from her pocket again and taking the rest of her notes and coins from the other, she held it in her hands, her eyes still fixed on all of the new fashions, all the windows of temptation. The only temptation she had was to run as far as she could without looking.

'Oh, sorry.' Feeling her body against the shoulder of an old lady, Ruth felt the emotions almost being shaken inside her, her tears rattling to come out; she wasn't going to let them.

The old lady sighed as she continued to walk past Ruth without accepting or acknowledging her apology.

'Silly old cow!' Ruth wanted to shove the old lady's umbrella in her eyes for walking past her as though she didn't exist.

She gazed around. She didn't feel comfortable standing in the wrong part of town; she was surely going to get into more trouble for being there than anything else. For some reason her father had always told her never to go there, said something about how the people around there weren't very nice, they'd hurt you if they had the chance. He would ground her for her whole life if he knew. She could never let her family know, under any circumstances.

Ruth aimlessly continued walking through the busy streets, observing the groups of girls from afar as they lounged on the benches successfully blowing hoops with their cigarettes. They laughed and joked together. She wondered to herself if they would give her a lug of the toxin she still yearned for. Her loneliness was confirmed with no friends to walk through the town with and the sight of her reflection in the shop window.

Out of the corner of her eye she saw him, another person alone. He sat with his head down by a bundle of newspapers, his clothes dark and dirty. The thought crossed her mind that she could always invite him to her house; her mother's house had always been too big and there was plenty of room for all of the lonely people, except for her. Ruth walked over to him slowly and placed all her money in his small grey hat. The only thing inside was a large stone. At first Ruth couldn't understand why it was there, but as she felt the gentle breeze she quickly realised the unpredictable wind would have taken the empty hat away if the man hadn't protected it.

'Thank you.' The man slightly raised his head and smiled.

'Can I join you?' Ruth happily sat next to him with her legs up; she felt the sensation of the warm concrete going through her trousers onto her bottom. From where she sat the world looked so big.

'Nice here?' Ruth asked softly as she watched the grateful man roll a cigarette; his hands were dirty and shaking. His kindness overwhelmed her as he held the thin cigarette out to her. She took the offered gift from him and leant forward so he could light it for her. Inhaling the dirty roll-up to the back of her throat, she blew out the smoke in satisfaction.

Leaning their backs on the wall and not speaking, they both blew smoke into the other world outside their own existence.

# 34

'Hello, Lucas; have you seen my father?' The sun was beaming from the sky as Natty walked out to speak to him. He was kneeling on the cool grass, his muscly chest uncovered. She had spent most of the day gaining the courage to walk out and ask him, pacing up and down in the kitchen, inhaling huge breaths with anticipation, the sense of excitement rushing through her.

She stepped closer to him, looking down at him, aware her finally chosen grey vest top was showing her small shapely breasts. She had checked in the mirror more than once, hoping it'd have the desired effect on him. Hoping he'd find her appealing and maybe want to touch her finally.

Lucas stopped digging around the small weeds in the flowerbeds and gazed at her, his handsome face a little dirty. Natty could see the glistening of sweat on his forehead, his bare gloriously shaped back showing redness from being exposed to the sun all day. The thought of getting the chance to rub after-sun on him later caused a stirring in her stomach; he'd only have to ask her to and she'd oblige. Her silent thought caused her to giggle a little to herself, imagining him wrapping his tanned muscly arms around her pale slim body.

It had only been two weeks since she had discovered the disappearance of her locket. It had felt like eternity. Every time she washed and saw it wasn't around her neck it caused a pang to build in her, a constant feeling of heaviness in her heart and an unsettling which could only be erased from her when she was in Lucas's company. Even if she watched him from afar, the young man had a magic way of making her feel better without even knowing it.

He had helped her search every part of the house and the locket couldn't be found. It had simply vanished; no one knew where it was and it felt to Natty like no one cared. Her father and Ruth had shaken their heads; her father had held her for a while doing his normal reassuring talk when he didn't know what else to do, assuring her it'd turn up when she wasn't looking. She tried to work out what he meant, how she was ever to find anything without looking for it, but then again she hadn't looked for Lucas and he had simply turned up in her life.

It wasn't the first time Natty hadn't been able to find her father. In the past he'd always tell them before he left the house. Now whenever he finally came home he'd shout hello to them all and head straight for his bedroom and close the door. He'd made himself invisible to them all, as though he had vanished with her necklace.

'Lucas, did you hear me?' Natty asked softly as she focused intensely on the sweat trickling down his back.

'Hello, Miss Natty. Isn't this amazing, this soil and the soft blades of the grass? It's so hot and they seem to stay cool somehow; rather amazing if you think about it. Come here and feel the grass, Miss Natty, feel the softness of each blade touch the tips of your fingers.' Lucas held his hand out for her to hold so he could help her down to kneel next to him.

His words stirred excitement in her stomach, even more than any sign of sexual intent would have. The simple words he used did something to her and she hoped he'd never stop talking, each word chained together with such meaning and care. She'd listen to his soft gentle voice around her all day and every day. Her thoughts overtook her as she knelt next to him and touched the grass, rubbing her hands around to feel the green soft wonder which Lucas had made into a new discovery.

'Yes, Lucas, it is cool and soft.' Natty tried not to giggle, feeling daft.

'Glorious, Natty, isn't it? Simplistically simple.'

'Yes; it's a bit like you.' Natty wanted to jump in the dirt at that minute for her stupidity.

'Sorry, Miss Natty, I appear simple to you?'

'No, Lucas, on the contrary. Anyway, have you seen my father?' Natty didn't want to interrupt the unusual grass-rubbing session with him by asking where their father was. At that moment she didn't care.

172

'Miss Natty, I haven't seen him today. He seems very busy lately, and I said I'd be more than happy to keep your garden pretty just like you, Miss Natty, just like all of you.' Lucas gently smiled.

'Oh, yeah, thanks, Lucas.' Natty felt flattered for only a few seconds until the man she felt strong emotions toward gave his thoughts to her sisters also.

'I feel your loving mother liked it a certain way; it has been very well kept. I know how important it is for your father to keep her alive and growing around him, like the seasons, Miss Natty.'

'Yes, she did like everything a certain way. Not sure what the seasons have to do with her, though.'

'Like everything changes in life, Miss Natty, but the seasons. It's quite simple to understand, like me.' Lucas began to laugh.

'I didn't mean you were, Lucas. Anyway, it's very hot out here; do you fancy an orange juice?'

'You see, Miss Natty, it is like this: you have to treat people like nature. If they are left untouched and not damaged they will grow to their natural beauty; a little kindness here and there and the nature will do exactly what it's meant to, just like your mother, Miss Natty. You have to allow people to be themselves and you must always be yourself. I sense your mother wasn't allowed to grow the way she was meant to from the emotions which run through your dear father still, my dear friend.'

'You're probably right, Lucas. Anyway, I am going to get us a drink.' Natty pushed herself up from the grass, feeling emotional with the thought of her mother and how she really could have been someone so incredible in her own life and theirs.

'Miss Natty, I really wouldn't mind making you a fresh orange juice; you do look a little flustered and it's very kind of you to make me something.' Lucas smiled innocently, not realising his words and manner had caused Natty to feel an array of mixed emotions.

'No, thank you; I will get you one.' Natty knew the flushing of her face was solely due to the adrenaline pumping through her body while she was attempting to hold back her sad emotions. She watched him stand up with her, his hands muddy and holding on to a small garden fork. As he wiped his muddy hands on the back of his jeans, his firm buttocks, she thought maybe if she rummaged through the cool dirt a little he'd allow her to clean her hands in exactly the same place.

The garden did look fabulous. He was right: only a little bit here and there and it all naturally grew where it was meant to. The multi-coloured array of flowers, the shining leaves and petals with the beautiful July sky's accompaniment were simply breathtaking to see.

Natty looked over at her mother's stone and knew she was with her own father. Natty quickly wondered if her mother would have liked her ashes to flow with the wind and be free to wrap themselves around the corners of the garden. Her ashes were confined in a vase; yet again she couldn't be free.

'I will go and make us a drink, eh?'

'Thank you, Miss Natty; you are very kind.' Lucas looked at her bare neck and felt extremely sad for her to have lost such a treasure. He felt a rush of excitement as he could see her nipples protruding through her small top.

'Lucas, you haven't got to slave over us all. You're not our servant; you are our guest and we love having you here.' Natty folded her arms, suddenly feeling paranoid about her small breasts showing, not that he'd ever notice anyway.

'I have to pay my way, Miss Natty. You have all been so kind to me and if I cannot pay for my living, I can help out in other ways, and I've used nearly all of your apple shampoo.'

'That's OK, Lucas; maybe we can get some more.' Natty walked away and thought how him being there had served her more than he thought; she hadn't stopped masturbating when she went to bed since he had come through the front door, imagining him with her, imagining his muscly innocent self on her.

Natty stepped back into the kitchen, finding the warm tiles comforting on her bare feet, putting one foot on top of the other and rubbing them up and down as she leant on the side.

'Ruth, what are you up to today?' Natty saw her younger sister sitting at the large wooden table, looking at a magazine. The memory of her mother rushed through her already tense body: the way on the dreaded day she had sat and flicked through the magazine with no care of the effect she'd had cutting up Natty's beautiful blue dress, the silk shreds Natty had held on to as long as she could. Natty wondered if her mother falling down the stairs had been an accident after all or if she had really wanted to hurt her after doing such a terrible thing. The thought made her shudder and even more goose pimples covered her arms as her small hairs stood on end.

'Not sure, Natty. I may go for a walk or something; lots of interesting people in town.' Ruth thought of how she wanted to run away, become a cartoon character and then she'd be able to run at the speed of light, just like the bird on the television. She began to feel cross as she'd had enough questioning from Natty over the last couple of weeks, and also felt the less she said, the better. She held the corner of the page, glancing at the rich people in the world, the music and film stars and the pretence of their smiles as they were photographed with expensive champagne. They had no depth; they wouldn't roll a cigarette for her from their nearly empty packet of tobacco.

Ruth had stayed quiet since taking Natty's locket. She had wanted to tell her when she had heard her crying about it to their father. Ruth dreaded the moment when Natty would finally come across what she'd done; it was only a matter of time. Ruth was sure she'd get a slap to her face for doing such a thing. At least this time it'd be for a reason, not like from their mother.

'Ruth, would you like a juice? I'm making Lucas one.' Natty felt like she wanted to cry as she sensed her sister's pain.

'No, Natty, you go ahead and look desperate.'

'What's that meant to mean?'

'Means nothing, dear Miss Natty; go and make your stupid juice.'

'Ruth, I'm not sure why you're being so rude. It isn't my fault you have to go to the meetings with Dad. You hurt your school friend really badly.'

'One, she isn't my school friend, and two, I suppose you mean a stupid place for stupid sisters. You don't have to say how ashamed you are of me, Natty; I already know.'

'Look, Ruth, they only have you there for a couple of meetings. You have to sort your anger out; you can't go round hurting people like that.'

'I am not angry,' Ruth said abruptly, almost speaking through her

175

teeth. 'It's everyone in this mad house that gets me like it, and if you really knew what she did to me for the last two years then I'm sure you could find the strength to do the same thing. I didn't even know what I was doing, but now that I do I would go back and hit her a lot harder, make sure she never got up. Dear Charlotte was coddled and spoilt by all the other kids and teachers. Looks like I gave Charlotte exactly what she wanted: a lot more attention. So stop bothering me and go and make your favourite person in the house a goddamn juice.' She looked down to see she had scrunched the page up in her hand; the crumpled magazine didn't look so glamorous suddenly. Soon she would have to attend a small group of other unhappy fifteen-year-old kids dealing with the same confusion. It didn't make sense to her; why would they put more of the same pain together?

Ruth had an urge to go and speak to her newfound friend; she also needed a cigarette. Her father had left some pocket money on the table for her to spend yet again. Since the day she had finally come out of her bedroom for longer than two hours he had been on the attack, showering her with money to spend, giving her extra attention. It hadn't lasted; he was now the one who wanted to get away from them all. He never sat at the dinner table for very long; as soon as he'd finished eating, he'd be back up the stairs and closing his bedroom door behind him.

'I'm going out. See you all never!' Ruth closed the destroyed magazine, sighed and made her way out of the front door.

'Bye, Ruth; be careful.' Natty poured two glasses of juice, full of concern.

'Miss Natty, is Ruth happy on this fine day? I would like very much to speak to her if she'd only allow it.'

Natty heard Lucas speaking as he came in from the garden. Turning around to see his figure outlined in the sun, she handed him his orange juice.

'Lucas, I'm not sure what to do with her, or where she's going at the minute,' Natty said softly as she stared at him gulping down his cold juice, watching his Adam's apple moving up and down as the juice went smoothly down the back of his throat, quenching his thirst. Her thoughts were confirmed by his sigh of relief as he placed the empty glass on the side.

'Thank you. Miss Natty, I am sure it will only be a hiccup for her and all she has to do is take a glass of water and it will all be gone.' Turning away from Natty he walked back into the sunshine, taking the small garden fork from his dirty jean pocket.

'Lucas, I was thinking maybe we could see if we could get you a little job. You know, you might actually stop working your fingers to the bone around here.' Natty raised her voice, hoping to gain his attention once again.

'That, Miss Natty, is a very kind thing to do for me, and I'm sure I can assist you in finding your necklace.' Lucas winked and finally left Natty alone.

As she touched her bare neck, the sheer reality of her loss struck a nerve. Leaving her full glass of juice on the side she made her way to her bedroom, feeling the tears beginning to stir from earlier thoughts of her mother in the garden. She couldn't hold them back as she fell onto her bed and sobbed into her pillow. As her tears fell she reached for her diary. She needed to write what she felt; it had to come out some way or another. Sniffing and wiping her eyes, she grabbed her pen from the side and began to flick through to the clean pages.

Natty felt like she was going to throw up as she read the words scribbled across the page.

'I CANNOT BELIEVE IT! WHY, RUTH?' Natty yelled out in disbelief as her sorrow evolved to anger while she read the words again and again.

PAWNED YOUR LOCKET BY THE WAY, ONLY THING IS CAN'T REMEMBER WHERE. YOUR LOVING SISTER RUTH. XXX

# 35

Harry paced up and down his disorganised office, the drawers of the grey filing cabinets open and the pinboard full of delayed jobs. The calendar of topless women could barely be seen through all the papers stuck one on top of the other, greasy old chip paper on the floor around the already overflowing bin. Brown tape stuck down on the arm of his black chair, holding the whole thing together, his knuckles almost red from his grip on the black phone receiver.

'Come on, Suzy, pick up.' He hadn't heard from her for a couple of weeks, since the day his so-called friends had made an unwelcome approach on his home. He wasn't sure why he hadn't gone to the bookshop to see her, walk in and say hello. It wasn't a cool thing to do. He believed if he played hard-to-get enough she'd be waiting for him on his porch when he arrived home one day. The only thing there when he arrived home was the newspaper and a very warm bottle of milk.

The more he thought about it and looked at the wrinkles on his hands, the more he recognised that the desirable impact he had on women seemed to be diminishing a little. This awful revelation surged through him, making his attempt to gain her attention even more desperate. Suzy was probably his last chance to have something finally right in his life. He had to gain the courage to go to the shop and see her.

The thought lay within him still that it was her who was being rude and difficult. God, there was no reason why people couldn't have friends. It may have disturbed their evening, but he was available now and she was being pompous in not choosing to share any time with him. He also felt the urge for some gratifying sex. He surely was done with picking up women from the local bar.

Taking a quick glance at the small white clock, he was convinced the bookshop was open. She was being stubborn. Did she really want him to walk in with a huge bouquet of flowers and say he'd accepted her behaviour and he was to blame?

As he walked quicker up and down his small office, the yearning to be acknowledged became too much for him. While he began to unzip his dark blue oil-stained overalls, he thought of how buying flowers was something he had promised himself he'd never do again. He couldn't turn up empty-handed, had to have something to take the attention from him. The thought of even walking into the flower shop in town gave him a dreaded feeling of unwanted memories he'd tried to forget about. The last time he had bought flowers had been for Eve, the beautiful white roses which were not accepted. He had promised himself he'd never go in there for anyone else again.

Slamming the black phone receiver down and then pushing his overalls to the floor, leaving them in a heap, he searched for his keys under the old oily paperwork and invoices. He had to think of something. He was determined not to go to the bar that evening; it was Suzy he'd have in his bed and she did give the best blow jobs ever.

'Bloody women.' Harry slammed the door behind him; the loose papers on the desk fell to the floor.

'Suzy, sweetie, that fellow is back again,' Wilfred whispered into Suzy's ear as she served another customer.

'Oh, yes, so he is. Leave him be, Wilfred; he's doing no one any harm.' Suzy didn't notice the paying customer trying to place money into her hand as her attention was on watching the avid reader choose a book and quietly sit at the window again. He instantly became immersed in another book. Suzy wondered to herself as she placed the money in the till if she'd seem over-the-top if she offered him a hot drink. There was something about him which bought a comfort to the shop in his arrival every other day.

Matthew placed a bag of books at the side of the chair, rolled up his sleeves of his green chequered shirt and with sheer delight began to read, overtaken again by the escape and feeling the words gave him, thrilled at each sentence helping to take him out of his own existence.

'Oh, darling Suzy, this phone has been off the hook most of the day.' Wilfred sighed and shook his head as he placed the phone back in its rightful place.

'I know; I wanted to make sure.' Suzy pulled her blonde ponytail tighter as her attention was taken away from the silent reader.

'Suzy, my dear, make sure he doesn't call? Now, why wouldn't you want him to? He's fabulous.'

'I don't want him to call. I've been checking for the last two weeks every time someone comes in; it's never him, so he can go and stuff himself.' Suzy tightened her lips in annoyance as she piled more books onto the counter.

Suzy kept to her word most of the day; she continued checking customers who came through the door. She had taken the phone back off the hook when Wilfred wasn't looking.

'Hello, madam. Can I bring these back, please?' Matthew placed the blue bag full of intently read books on the counter.

'Sir, you don't have to bring them back. You bought them; they belong to you.' Suzy was impressed with his well-spoken manner.

'I would like to purchase these, too, while I am here.' Matthew took some money from his wallet and concentrated on flicking through pound notes.

'Sir, you don't have to bring the ones you bought back; they belong to you. You are more than welcome to buy these ones. It will cost you a fortune if you bring them back like you have.'

Matthew held a selection of notes in his hand and pushed his wallet back into the back of his black trousers. 'No, really, madam, nothing really belongs to anyone, so I really have to return them. Have I enough money for these ones?' Matthew spoke gently, feeling a little confused as to why the pretty young lady felt what he was doing was wrong. He had to give them back; he couldn't bear having something taken from him again.

'OK, sir, if it's your wish.' Suzy held her hand out for the money and quickly checked to see who was coming into the shop. She again felt downtrodden as an old lady walked in, placing her large black umbrella in the empty stand.

'Thank you; you are very helpful. I did seem to notice – I don't mean to sound rude – it's only you seem a little sad today. Are you all right?'

180

'Oh, don't worry, just men.' Pushing the pile of newly bought books into the blue bag, Suzy smiled, grateful someone seemed to care about how she was feeling.

'Men? What, you mean us?' Matthew took the bag from the counter and smiled, his tone uplifted.

'Yes, I mean you. Well, not *you*. All you do is read.'

They both laughed out loud together.

'And what am I missing?' Wilfred rushed forward from the small stockroom which was in full view of the counter.

'Nothing, Wilfred.' Suzy laughed at her excited colleague.

'That's a bright shirt he's got on. So there's nothing I can help you with, then?' Matthew raised his eyebrows and even though he could feel a slight unease rush through him as it was the first time he'd ever spoken to another woman since his perfect beautiful Eve, he was happy to be in her company. She seemed gentle and caring, and surely only portrayed a tough exterior to keep the men from her door; she was a very pretty thing, and a fresh-faced beauty.

'You don't have to worry yourself, thank you. Anyway, I am sure you have other things to be worrying about, instead of silly old me, who's only been waiting for nearly two weeks now for him to come and say sorry for being a selfish fool and to finally take me out for something that isn't goddamn beer and takeaway. But no, hasn't bothered, has he? Doesn't care, does he? I've been losing my mind, not sure if I should call him, but I can't now, can I? I was always taught not to show desperation to the opposite sex. Oh! Sorry, I've got lost in myself there.' Suzy placed her hand over her mouth.

They began to laugh again. Matthew placed the heavy bag onto the floor and leant forward over the counter a little more.

'I'm sure he does, this gentleman. Care, I mean. There is no reason for him not to. Only speaking to you for this time, I can see you have a lot to share with someone. You remind me somehow of my three daughters; they are as pretty and also have so much to do and give in their young lives. It's just a matter of believing it for yourself. He'll call or come to see you soon, and if he doesn't I couldn't imagine what kind of man he is.'

'Thank you; your words are very kind. Shame he hasn't got the same outlook on life as you.'

'I will be back in a couple of days; you can let me know how it goes if you like.' Matthew picked up the bag again and tapped his hand on the counter as he left the stuffy bookshop, where he could smell the young lady's perfume. As he made his way to his car he suddenly felt guilty for speaking to her and smelling her perfume in the air. Closing his eyes in disbelief at his freeness, he made a promise not to speak to her so openly again.

'Now, sweetie, what are we going to do with you? Shall I take these books back to the shelf?' Wilfred looked over the top of his white spectacles at his worrying colleague.

'I will put them back; it'd be nice to see what he's been reading.' Suzy took the books from the bag and began to place them in order on the shelves. The thought of him and his kind words stayed with her.

Harry strolled almost aimlessly around town, not knowing what to do for the best, or what his next move could be to get the attention of Suzy without looking like he was chasing her. He had no choice but to make his way reluctantly to the florist. Burying the thoughts at the back of his mind, he'd never allow himself the pain and turmoil of going back to the memory of buying the most beautiful roses for someone who didn't exist any more. It also happened to be the first time he'd ever bought flowers as a grown man. He remembered how he and Matthew had bought an array of blossoms for their mother's grave, which was another wasted action; they were never forgiven for selling the pretty butterfly broach to pay for them.

Holding tightly on to his car keys, he quickly glanced into the shop window displaying rows and rows of gold and diamonds. The shop appeared old and tatty; the jewellery glistening in the sun beckoned him to go inside and take a closer look. The stale stench of old tobacco made him feel sick as he saw the grimy man behind the counter lighting a small roll-up, nearly burning his lips.

'You looking for anything special?' The unacceptable man spoke with a husky voice. He began to cough and splutter over the glass cabinet which protected more gold chains.

'I think I am only looking, mate.' Harry's attention was taken away from the vulgar man. He leant forward a little to see a charming little necklace with a heart-shaped pendant. 'Can I look at that one?' he asked, pointing through the glass.

'Haven't even got around to pricing it up. Gave the girl just over a tenner for it, not sure if it was even worth that much, and got to make my money back; say twenty quid on a good day.'

'Yeah, OK, can I look?' Harry knew how much Suzy would love it, and was relieved not to have to go into the florist. Thank goodness for small mercies, he thought.

Holding the necklace, he pulled the small heart open with his oil-stained hands and instantly became numb inside; every part of his body froze in shock and nerves. His insides felt like they were rattling and his breathing became heavy; his abdomen became tight. The two small pictures side by side stared back at him; they were allowing him to remember what he had broken, how he'd damaged so much. Could they ever give him absolution? Eve's long black hair shone and her brown eyes twinkled even in the small picture. It wasn't happening; it had to be a dream and he was still pacing up and down in his dreary office. Her elegant features overcame him as yet again the desire and passion he had always held for her returned.

Why were they haunting him in such a way? He wasn't allowed to forget what he had done to the most important people in his life. They were clasped side by side in the picture; it was the way his dear brother Matthew had always attempted to live, with her by his side. Harry wondered whether, if he hadn't intervened in the already broken pieces, it could have been glued back together for them.

Standing numb in the shop with his past life displayed on his shaking palm, he thought of his daughter, his little Ruth, who he'd dismissed as though she was to end up in a heart-shaped picture one day also reminding him of his mistakes. He had to do something about it. He had to bring her into his life some way or another. He had never kissed her small cheek or even held her while she slept. His brother Matthew had her; he also still had a part of Eve.

'Mate, hey, do you want to buy it or not? It isn't a museum in here, you know.'

'Oh, yeah, OK, I will take it. Don't worry about a bag.' Closing the locket and pushing it gently into the side pocket of his flared jeans, he threw the money on the counter and left.

Quietly standing outside the unwelcoming shop, Harry looked up to the sky and shook his head. Softly touching his pocket he blew out his cheeks in despair, then removed the necklace again from his pocket and quickly went back into the shop.

# 36

Tapping his Sunday newspaper on his leg, he cupped his other hand near the side of his face, peering through the window, the nets slightly diminishing the desired view of her outline. A tenderness for her overpowered him as he rubbed his hands against his chin, feeling the soft greying stubble. Observing her prancing around his living room, he thought of how she had filled every space since she had chosen to share her life with him from their meeting on the train. Each day when he woke up with her by his side in the bed he'd never shared with anyone before, a sense of miraculous dreaming began his day. Thirty-two years' difference, and how she enhanced emotions within him.

Experiencing life with another human being was something he'd never thought possible. He always had lived alone and had never married; he had no children and had made himself a boiled egg each and every morning for the last twenty years. For the last two weeks his kitchen had finally felt warm and lived-in; the only thing was that a woman at the stove gave him all sorts of trouble as he now had to sit and eat bacon and eggs. He didn't have the heart to tell her a simple egg and a couple of slices of toast were all he ever needed. She was remarkable, and she showered his home with the presence of a new beginning and a love he'd never believed he'd have the chance to experience.

Suddenly he had a heavy feeling in his stomach and wondered if what he was asking from her was unfair. She was so young, and did she really know what she was doing? She was carrying his child and he couldn't help feeling he'd trapped her in a false life. He could only offer her as much as his fifty-one-year-old body and mind allowed, and she, the young energetic lady dancing around the living room, was eighteen. These thoughts had begun entering his mind on the way back from the corner shop; everyone knew him and the man behind the counter had commented on how happy he'd seemed lately, and as he had walked back to his home he had known it was all simply down to her. Even with the sudden concern he couldn't help but chuckle watching her take things from boxes, gliding around to the music he could hear vibrating on the window pane, her bottom wiggling to the beat, her mouth moving as she sang along with the tune.

Glenn bellowed over the music and turned to shuffle again across the brown corded carpet, the rough fibres hurting her feet as she slid along.

'*Shit!*' Glenn instantly froze as she caught sight of the shadow at the window, then broke into giggles; she'd end up having the heart attack before him if he carried on doing such ridiculous things. The thought that he'd seen her dancing and using his red dustpan as a guitar caused her to feel a little embarrassed, and she'd have to cook the Sunday roast hot-faced and trying to be all serene and adult-like. Happiness filled her as she went to let him in, taking a quick look at the round wooden table where his lace doilies no longer sat under the fruit bowl. She'd had to throw them away; they'd reminded her of something her nan would have. Nerves at the thought of his response sat in her suddenly sickening stomach as she rushed to open the door, thinking she'd be getting rid of the nets which covered the pretty glass when she got the chance.

'Hello. What are you standing out there for? Didn't you take your key?' Glenn's happiness in seeing him showed in her wide smile; she spoke in delight even though her stomach was beginning to churn even stronger.

'Hello, Glenn. Before I come in, can I ask you something? It's really important to answer honestly. Are you sure you truly want to share your life with old me?' Stanley squeezed the rolled-up newspaper tighter in his hand, waiting to hear from the young lady who stood at his front door wearing a brown baggy T-shirt and beige flared trousers, her boyishly-cut hair shining and her grey eyes sparkling, her red lipstick covering her plump young lips.

'Hold on, Stanley!' Glenn's mouth began to water and she rushed up the stairs to be sick at last. It had been building up from the moment she had woken and she felt relief it had finally left her

186

body. Until the evening came, and then the morning, and of course the afternoon, and it'd be happening all over again.

Looking in the mirror, she saw small tears had welled in her eyes from her retching. She wet her face, enjoying the coolness of the water. Taking a small towel she softly dabbed it onto her forehead. She looked at herself in the mirror and smiled, noticing how tired she looked and how flushed from the dancing. Rubbing her cheek gently with her hand she thought of her family, how they had been in the last two weeks and how surreal it was to be away from them for such a long time. Glenn chuckled to herself as she thought of all of the arguments she and her sisters had had over something as silly as who was going to put the kettle on, and of how Natty would be so pleased to have the largest bedroom in the house finally. The day Glenn had left with Stanley she had asked them to allow her to settle into her new home until she came to see them; the time had gone so quickly, though.

Seeing the reflection of the brown bath behind her in the mirror, she shook her head and wondered how the hell she was ever going to make it gleam. She'd give anything only to have to keep her room clean and make a fresh brew every now and then. Brown, of all colours; what was he thinking? Her beloved Stanley certainly needed a woman's touch around the house.

'Oh, God, Stanley!' Throwing the burgundy towel into the bath she rushed back downstairs.

She found the whole situation comical as he'd actually waited outside for her to return. She held back her giggles as she approached him again. He was walking up and down the black cobbled path with his white chequered shirt and green cardigan on; she would have to remind him it was summer the next time he decided to leave the house.

'Stanley, are you coming in?'

'Glenn, I cannot until you tell me. Before we begin to fall in love even more and we get to know each other, before I change my blue slippers for some huge pair of boots, you have to tell me, Glenn: tell me why and if you really do want me so much. You have so much to offer someone much younger than me, and I could never forgive myself if it was me who prevented you from doing such a thing.'

187

Glenn stepped out onto the step and placed her hands on his cheeks, holding his face gently, looking straight into his dark grey eyes.

'Well, Mr Stanley, my stranger on the train, one: it's too late because I, as you know, am carrying your child, and even if I weren't I'd never want to share a moment with anyone in this crazy world but you. I'd share my train carriage with you every day for the rest of my life. I am so very happy to be getting to know you and learning all about why you have doilies and army pictures hanging around your home. I want to know everything about you and I am with you, Stanley; I love you. Now get yourself indoors and let's begin our life. Can you just promise me one thing: no more doilies?' Glenn's emotions stirred within her; how she loved this man. She couldn't have believed she'd ever be able to say such wonderful things about anyone in her life.

'Do you know, Glenn, when I step inside our home, I promise I will never leave alone. You will always be in my heart.' Stanley smiled and kissed her on the lips.

'I know, you crazy man. I need to go in now, though, and I think I am going to be sick again.' Glenn smiled and rushed back upstairs to begin the same ordeal she'd been enduring over the last eight weeks.

Stanley finally walked into his tidy home and placed the paper on the arm of the brown suede sofa. A sense of contentment had filled him on hearing her words; he thought deeply about what she'd said as he took the vinyl record from the record player and gently placed it back into the cover. Holding the thin cardboard in his hand he glanced at the pop star on the front with orange-and-blue hair, silver and black stars drawn on his cheeks and around his eyes.

Shaking his head, Stanley took his soft brown shoes off and retrieved his slippers from where Glenn had kindly placed them next to the fire. He happily relaxed in his favourite armchair and began to complete his regular Sunday crossword.

# 37

'Miss Natty, are you ready to begin searching?'

Lucas waited at the front door for her, taking in the vast space where he now lived. For the first time he properly absorbed the beauty of the crystal chandelier that hung in the hall. He'd never have believed he'd ever be lucky enough to be in such a spectacular home. From sleeping rough under bridges and in shop doorways to now be standing amongst luxury: it was as though he was dreaming and if he dared pinch himself hard enough he'd surely wake up. He wasn't going to take himself out of his dream if he could help it.

Another appreciation of beauty fuelled his already humbled self as he watched Natty walking slowly down the stairs, dressed elegantly for the hot weather. A white gypsy blouse sat perfectly on the edge of her shoulders, showing her soft pale skin, and a long cotton skirt flowed around her legs. He knew he was surrounded by beautiful company. Laughter began to stir in him as he thought in a kind way she looked like a big fluffy cloud, all puffy and white; he wanted to tell her and knew she'd be happy with how he saw her.

'I'm ready now, Lucas. I really am grateful for your help. I am not sure where we are going to start; there's so many pawnshops. It may even be gone now.' Natty touched her neck with dread that her locket might never be found again.

'We have to start, Miss Natty, by going out of the front door, and may I say how lovely you look with your frizzy hair tied back and seeming to look like a fluffy cloud this fine day?'

'Oh, well, thank you, Lucas; I do my best.' Natty's heart wanted to sink as she'd spent most of the morning picking her outfit to go out with him, and after two hours of taking clothes from her wardrobe, checking herself in the mirror, the gorgeous innocent man she had attempted to impress might as well have been looking into the sky. How the hell did she look like a cloud? And as for the frizzy hair comment, he wasn't going to have permission to use any more of her apple shampoo. If she had the guts she'd also ask him to swap rooms with her. Glenn wasn't even there and she still hadn't had the chance to sleep in her room. Natty sighed, looked down at her long skirt and frowned.

'You do really look marvellous.'

'OK, Lucas, yes, you said. Thank you, really.'

'Now shall we begin our mission, Miss Natty? You see, the sooner we find your treasured locket then the quicker you shall be able to forgive Ruth, and of course begin speaking to her again. It's a terrible thing to not have communication with each other.'

'Forgive her? How can I ever do that? When she does something awful? Lucas, I really do understand what it is you're trying to say; I really do. The thing is how can anyone be so cruel?' Natty spoke calmly but could feel a frustration building inside.

'She is your beautiful sister, Miss Natty.' Lucas placed both his hands together as though he was praying.

Natty hadn't spoken to Ruth since she had found the scribbled words in her diary. The crazy thing was that Ruth hadn't spoken to her either. She knew she had been found out; she behaved around Natty as if she couldn't care less, didn't care one bit. All Ruth did was hide in her bedroom and come down now and then for something to eat, sit at the kitchen table and flick through another glossy magazine, and she always smelt of stale smoke. One day Natty had seen her leaving the house quietly with a plastic carrier bag of tinned fruit. As Natty went forward to question her about taking food from the house she remembered she had promised herself she was never going to speak to her again; not until she apologised, anyway.

'Miss Natty, she is very sad and I can show you.' Lucas pulled the paper flower from his brown corduroy trousers. It had been ripped in half. He raised his eyebrows at Natty to show her she must finally understand how her younger sister was feeling. It was simply that she needed someone to listen, someone to help her and let her know it was all going to be all right. He had always needed someone to tell him the same thing when he was a young boy.

The small damaged paper flower fell to the floor and Natty hastily bent down to pick it up. As she did, yet again she saw Lucas's black shoes, faded and broken and only frayed string keeping the leather together.

Natty handed back the white paper to Lucas, who wore a tight red T-shirt. He looked so very handsome; she just needed to sort the shoe situation out for him, and decided to make a gesture she hoped he'd happily accept.

'I think I will get you some shoes while we are out, Lucas; what do you think?'

There was a pause. Lucas stared at Natty.

'It's really a nice and generous thing to do for me, Miss Natty; I am not sure if new shoes are my thing.' Lucas sounded as though he was going to cry, his voice soft and croaky.

'Hello, you two. Are you going out somewhere nice?' Her father walked past them, heading for the stairs, holding a cup of tea and a book.

'Just going to find my necklace, Dad. You know, the one dear Ruth pawned.'

'Look, Natty, I know what she did was unkind but she has a lot to be dealing with at the moment. She has her meeting tomorrow and I feel she's a little apprehensive about what they are going to say.'

'Oh, she's apprehensive? Well, so am I, hoping to find my locket. You can't agree with what she did, Dad; it was ludicrous.' Natty raised her voice slightly as the resurfacing of frustration now became stirred with anger.

'Of course I don't, Natty. I have no way of changing it for you now. I can help Ruth tomorrow, though; that is the only thing I can change.' He touched Natty's shoulder reassuringly, smiled and went up the stairs.

'Punish her, God damn it.'

'Miss Natty, I think she is already being punished inside her young body.'

Natty looked at Lucas in complete disbelief. She began to huff and shake her head, feeling her lips tightening, hoping to prevent words coming out she might regret later. Natty's annoyance was portrayed in her body language as she grabbed her car keys from the telephone table. As she rushed out of the front door her white flip-flop fell from her foot; while she stepped forward hastily she tried to put it back on. The more she pushed her foot forward, the more loss of control she had on the sole-shaped piece of rubber. She was angry, yes, but she knew she certainly couldn't make a fool out of herself, not in front of Lucas.

'Oh, for goodness' sake! Fluffy bloody cloud.' Picking up her flip-flop she hurried her pace, speaking under her breath with her car keys in one hand and her flip-flop in the other. Tripping on the edge of her skirt as she did so. It was the last straw; she hurled her flip-flop at her car, becoming gobsmacked as she saw it bounce off the bonnet onto the pavement.

'Miss Natty, did I say something to upset you?' Lucas asked softly as he wondered if she'd like to go another day.

# 38

Harry waited next to the counter in anticipation for Suzy to turn around; she was leaning on the doorframe of the stockroom, speaking to her very overdressed colleague. Harry tried to understand how he had the guts to even leave his house (or a pink palace, come to think of it) wearing his pink-and-white shirt with white slacks.

The time seemed to pass by for Harry with his thoughts of Eve. Going to see Suzy and gain her attention again had taken a little longer than necessary. The day he entered the jewellery shop he'd planned to have Suzy in his bed; instead he had spent the evenings since then looking at the small heart-shaped picture of Eve, while he placed his thumb over the picture of Matthew. Each night swigging from his beer bottles and wishing it could all have been so different.

The memory came flooding back to him as he looked at her, thinking of when he had held her bleeding weak body on the stairs, yearning for her to be OK, to stay alive for him to witness from afar for the rest of his life; it was the only way it was ever going to be, his feelings mirrored by his brother, her husband, the man who should have been holding her in his arms, his dear weak brother Matthew.

As he sat drunk each night, holding the locket in his hands, it simply reminded him of how crazy their lives had become. He recalled taking the picture of them both. Harry thought of how Matthew had run up to him with his camera the day he had brought her round to meet him for the very first time; he was so excited, introducing her to him like a child with a new toy. Harry's guilt rushed through his drunken numbness as he was meant to be part of them always; instead he had only destroyed Matthew's trust with the woman he had focused on longer than needed through the lens, as they chuckled next to his fireplace. When Harry clicked the button a negative of them appeared in Matthew's camera and a picture of her remained inside his heart.

Harry knew he'd blown it with her, the woman with her back to him, her long blonde hair shining in the sun's reflection through the windows. He placed the necklace in his pocket, aware he'd be giving it to her some time soon.

'Hi, Suzy.'

'Hi, I know that voice!' As Suzy turned around she felt a little downhearted to see Harry leaning on the counter; she had finally stopped checking the shop door for him.

'I am pleased you haven't forgotten me, Suzy.'

'Um ... yes. No. I mean I haven't.' Suzy shook her head, stumbling over her words. The thing was she felt she was beginning to forget him; deep down she didn't want to, but there had been far more interesting things to keep her mind occupied in the last four weeks. Shaking her head again she looked at Harry and could see he reminded her of someone, but she couldn't put her finger on it. 'Are you going to explain, then, Harry, or have you simply come in here to gloat?'

'No, I haven't; I've come to see if you'd like to kind of forgive me, and let me actually take you out for dinner. You know, with proper serviettes and candles, and a waiter and all that jazz. What do you say?' Harry moved his head from one side to the other as he smiled gently in his perfected persuasive look.

'I'm not sure, Harry. It has been quite a long time. I've kind of been getting on with things.' Suzy's heart was beating hard; she desperately wanted to jump over the counter and into his arms, but she had to hold some control for as long as she could. Before he left the shop she'd have him on his knees begging for her to go out again.

Wilfred walked up to her ear; she caught the softest of whispers as he made his way past her from the stockroom. 'Sweetie, just grab his balls.'

Suzy bit her inside lip, praying her laughter remained inside her, scrunching up her face and smiling as she watched Wilfred placing the silent reader's books back; he had only returned them an hour ago.

'Can I take you out, Suzy?' Harry began to feel nervous, his feeling showing in his body movements as he began to tap his hand on his leg. As he did so he felt the necklace in his pocket and swallowed hard; thoughts of Eve rushed through him as he attempted to entice another woman.

'No, Harry!' Suzy smiled smugly and turned her back on him, making her way back into the dusty stockroom where she wanted to bang her head on the heavy books, praying she could make him beg for her without blowing it. One minute, then she'd give in, she thought. Sensing him staring at her, she tried to make herself look busy and as though she didn't care.

'Suzy, I've booked a table now.' With his untruthful words dread overtook him; he would have to get to the restaurant fast and see if they had a table available. She'd do him a huge favour at that moment if she declined his invitation.

Suzy turned to speak to him. 'Oh, I see: you booked it and just assumed I'd be going with you?'

'Well, I thought . . .'

'Yes, Harry, you did, didn't you? How very presumptuous of you. Which restaurant were you planning to take me, anyway?' Suzy couldn't believe how self-righteous he was for actually believing he could walk into the shop after a month and click his fingers. The cheek of it, to book a table without asking her first.

'Um . . . the oriental one, you know, with the painted gold dragons on the window.' His heart sank. The need to gain an immediate booking was growing more desperate by the second as she hemmed and hawed.

'Well, at least I haven't got to order it for all your mates, I suppose.' Suzy loved the restaurant he had booked; it was one of her favourites. She'd spent nearly all her first dates in there, and despite the bad company she'd always devour the food.

'What do you say, Suzy? I will pick you up from yours at around eight?' Now Harry needed a booking at a specific time. Was he really that thick? he thought.

'Don't think I've forgiven you, Harry. I will come with you, though, considering you finally went to so much trouble sorting it all out.' Suzy gave him a gentle smile. Not too much, though; she didn't want him to see she was completely happy.

'OK, I will see you later.'

'Later.' Suzy waved and waited for him to leave so she could jump up and down and, if she was really brave, kiss Wilfred on the lips through sheer relief.

Harry closed the bookshop door behind him and closed his eyes in dread. How the hell was he going to pull this one off? Moving his head from one side to the other, not sure which direction the restaurant was, he decided to go left. Even if he had to pay double, he had to have a table.

# 39

Placing the locket on the table, Harry began to search for the yellow phone book, lifting the cushions and huffing in a panic. It had been a completely wasted effort walking hastily in the hot sunshine nearly half a mile from the bookshop. The restaurant wasn't even open and there was no way he was going to hang around outside for the two hours before opening time, to see a little Chinese lady come hobbling to the door and greet him. Throwing the cushions down hard, he felt angry and unsettled at his false plans and his lies to someone he had feelings for. Why did he keep hurting the people he truly cared for? He hoped one day he could understand.

'Where is it?' he muttered as he looked through the piles of clothes on the sofa.

Finally he remembered where he had placed it, the ripped yellow book which was used for the Chinese order. A relief came over him as he'd now be closer to gaining a table. Pushing his arm under the sofa as he was on his knees, he could feel it. 'There you are!'

Puffing a little and sitting on the sofa, he began flicking through the heavy book. 'Restaurants, restaurants, Chinese ones, hold on, here we go, bloody got you.' He gazed down the list, his finger touching the page as he checked each line. 'Bingo!'

Leaning forward a little with the open book on his lap, he grabbed the phone and placed it next to his side, the wire getting tangled a little around the table leg. He pulled it free and sat back for a moment, then pushed himself forward once more to retrieve the necklace, cupping it in his hand. The gold chain tapping onto the black phone as he dialled the number.

Hearing dialling in his ear, he pushed open the small clasp of the locket with the thumb of his free hand. He had become lost in his thoughts by the time he heard a voice on the other end.

'Hello, may I help you?'

'Oh, hello. Yes, could I please have a table for two tonight, say around 8.15pm?'

'Hold on one moment, please.'

The slight pause gave Harry a chance to bring the picture of Eve up to his lips and kiss it; adrenaline fuelled his body waiting for the answer.

'We have a table for 8.15 tomorrow evening. I am afraid we are fully booked.'

'You can't be!'

'Yes, sir; I'm very sorry. Would you like me to book tomorrow?'

'I need tonight. Isn't there anything you can do? Surely all your tables haven't gone.' Harry became abrupt with the gently spoken lady on the other end of the phone.

'No, sir, I cannot help you. You have to book early.'

'Shit restaurant anyway!' Harry slammed the phone down in anger and threw the heavy phone book across the room. 'Fuck it!' He leant back, breathing hard, holding tightly onto the necklace.

The restaurant was full as the old lady opened the door, hanging her cream woollen coat on the tall wooden stand. She was shown politely to her table with pretty cutlery and chopsticks. She placed her long black umbrella on the empty chair opposite. The waitress approached her wearing a red silk dress with an apple-blossom print, her elegant attire representing the elegance of the vibrant restaurant. The old lady smiled as she was ready to give her order.

# 40

'Dad, is it OK if we get the Christmas tree up this year?'

'Sorry, Ruth, what did you say? I didn't hear you.' Her father sat with his legs crossed, reading on the sofa, hesitantly taking his attention from his own existence to speak to Ruth. She had been standing behind him for some time, watching him absorbed and turning the pages slowly, yet another book taking his attentions away from her.

'The Christmas tree? Isn't it a little early, Ruth? It's only the beginning of December.' He stared at Ruth for longer than necessary as he spoke gently, knowing she'd be sixteen soon. All his beautiful daughters were going to be another year older, Natty twenty-one and Glenn, who had already made a spontaneous choice to begin her own life story, an innocent nineteen. He had prayed every night since he had shaken the hand of the man who was nearly his age in his kitchen that Glenn's story would have a happy ending.

His little Ruth was growing up so very fast and he could see by the expression on her face she was full of confusion and sadness. She hadn't wanted him coming in with her when he had taken her to the meeting only three months ago; he had dropped her off outside and yet again she had been left alone to sit with other angry children. As she gave him a small wave before entering the grim brick building he wondered where his little Ruth had gone, the vulnerable and gentle child he had promised to protect.

'Dad, can we, then?' Ruth sighed as she pushed her hands up onto the waistband of her jeans.

'Yes, Ruth, we can.' Her father smiled and quickly looked at Eve's chair, her soft grey blanket still neatly folded over the back.

A familiar intense loss instantly hit him; she loved the Christmas month. A memory came to his mind: when he and his perfect Eve first met they'd both sit laughing on his carpet wrapping each other's Christmas presents, trying not to let the other see. It was all part of the fun. She'd always guess and persuade him to allow her to open one before they went to bed and she laid her petite body next to him, her long shining dark hair falling around her beautiful features. When she fell asleep he'd push her hair behind her ear and fully absorb her beauty. She never knew how he lay awake staring, lost and enthralled with her. If only he'd told her.

'Dad?'

'Oh, sorry, Ruth.' Her father closed his book and placed it on the table. 'Right, the Christmas decoration, is it?' It was the first day of December; he felt ridiculous agreeing to such an event so early in the month, but as he looked into Ruth's eyes he knew he couldn't say no. He only hoped she wouldn't ask him to help. How could he even envision decorating the house with wondrous colours when his Eve had taken her life away from them all nearly a year ago?

'I thought it'd be nice to do it all together, you know, as Glenn and her old husband-to-be are coming over. Like we used to, Dad, do the tree together.' Ruth wanted him to see her, to understand she was also hurting; it wasn't just him their mother had left.

Placing a chair under the hatch in the ceiling, her father put the torch into the loft and began to pull himself up, his legs dangling as he swung backward and forward a little to bring the strength back into his arms before he hurled his body into the dark space. Hunching his back so as not to hurt himself on the beam, he made his way to retrieve the spindles and artificial branches.

His body became slow and heavy as he sat on an old crate. Placing his hands over his face he cried, the tears falling from his palms. His body ached, his heart still broken. As he sniffed and looked up to see the light coming from the hall through the hatch, his thoughts overwhelmed him and he longed to shut himself away, hide from everyone and allow his pain to leave his body. Before him was the large elegant box which held her dress, his beautiful Eve's gown which she had worn standing by his side gazing into his eyes and telling him she'd love him forever, she'd stand by his side and

200

love him until her own heart broke. He wrapped his arms around his waist to protect the pain of grief in his stomach, his sobs echoing through the small space, the torch on the soft beams of wood next to him giving him some light.

'No more, Matthew, God damn it. Get the tree. Get it. Pick that torch up and get it.' How could Ruth be so hurtful and cruel, asking him to go amongst Eve's belongings, her being and everything she had built up in a confused and precious life? Where had it all gone? All his plans and dreams of how he desperately longed to live, to share each and every moment with the woman he had bought a small cup of coffee. The thoughts filled his head as the tears filled his eyes.

Inhaling a deep breath and hoping to blow the pain out into the damp musky air, he continued to search. Pulling one small box from the top of another, he knew he was being punished; the soft pink blanket which had covered Ruth in her cot was folded in a small bag. He pulled it out and brought it to his lips, crying again onto the soft fabric; it felt like he was still taking her from her cot and holding her sore body close to his fast-beating heart. His little baby's sore skin and damaged mind in his strong grasp: the day had never left his mind, and now he could feel it in his hands, the blanket, the memories, the pain. Why couldn't it all simply go away? Be gone and destroyed with his dreams, the memories and the thoughts that tired his body, his books his only escape from the feeling inside him? He had never meant to do anything wrong; why was he still being so very tormented? Falling to his knees, he pleaded, 'Please, God, please take my pain away. I can't do it any more; I can't. I don't know how to make it all better for them. Please, God, take my pain away so I can be the man I'm meant to be, please!' The pink blanket rescued his tears as he yearned to surrender to his pain.

Ruth sat on the stairs with her elbows on her knees and her hands on her cheeks, fed up with waiting for him; she couldn't work out what was taking him so long. She heard the muffled voices of Lucas and Natty in the kitchen; for the last three months they had been each other's shadow. One day they might see her. She'd have to do something else to gain some kind of attention from them, even if it caused her sister anger. Where had everyone gone, why was everyone leaving her, why didn't anyone care? The man on the street seemed to be the only one giving her time, sharing laughter with her and looking out into the crazy world together.

'I know, Miss Natty, I know how important it is for you to find it. Maybe we can start again tomorrow as you have to be going to work.' Lucas walked out of the kitchen behind Natty, who unhappily wore her uniform.

Natty saw Ruth sitting on the stairs and her stomach felt like it was going to rip; her stupid sister made her feel this way, taking something so precious from her. She gave Ruth a filthy look.

Ruth remained in the same position, looking at them at the kitchen door, wishing Natty would have a reality check; it was only a piece of gold. Natty had spent far too long looking at that stupid little picture, pretending it was all OK for their mother and father. Ruth knew deep down she had done her a favour.

Hearing the boxes bash onto the carpet on the landing, Ruth turned.

'Oh dear, Matthew, let me help you.' Lucas raised his voice and gently pushed past Ruth on the stairs to help.

'Oh, thanks, Lucas. Hold on; I want to get one more thing.' Matthew peered through the hatch, his voice crackly.

Lucas picked up the box of glistening colours filled with tinsel and stars, hoping he could help them decorate their home with such beauty.

As Lucas walked down the stairs carrying the box he heard Matthew behind him.

Matthew inhaled a deep breath and attempted to speak, yet again having to pretend everything was fine. 'Lucas, I was thinking you've been sleeping in those flowery covers for too long now. I will go and get you something to replace them.'

Standing on the stairs and turning to speak to Matthew, Lucas could see he held a large cream box in his hands and wondered what glorious decoration must be inside. He saw the redness in Matthew's face, the aftermath of unsettled pain. Lucas knew Matthew had it in him to find the strength he needed; he only had to look around him and see how much he had.

'Oh, I'm fine, Matthew; I don't mind. I like to be amongst the flowers.' Lucas's voice was soft as he turned around to look over the bannisters at Natty.

202

Natty put her coat on and waved them all goodbye without saying a word.

She bumped into her sister on the garden path. 'Oh, hi, Glenn. You're looking knackered!'

'Yes, I am.' Glenn leant over and kissed Natty on the cheek.

'That's a bit weird.'

'What, Natty?'

'You kissing me.'

'That's what these old folks do when they greet each other,' Glenn whispered, and giggled slightly before making her way to the front door.

*Oh my God,* Natty thought as she waited for the cheek kiss from Stanley. 'Hi, Stan. I mean Stanley.'

Natty hurried off wiping her cheek, feeling as though she had just been kissed by her granddad. Their father was older than Stanley, but even at his age he'd still be able to give a woman a run for her money. Stanley was simply old in his ways and his manner. The thought quickly left her mind, driven out by the question of how her gorgeous sister could even do such things with him between the sheets. Getting into the car, Natty shuddered at the unpleasant image.

A sense of comfort overtook Glenn as she put her old door key in the lock.

'Hello, Glenn; you're looking fat!' Ruth remained in the same position, not attempting to move for Lucas or their father as they carried boxes past her.

'Oh, well, thanks, Ruth, and you're looking miserable.' Glenn felt the normal welcome from her sisters. It was almost thrilling for her to be amongst the insults and normality she had grown so accustomed to. Glenn had attempted to wear the pink-and-blue floral dress with style; she felt comfortable in it at home with Stanley, but around her sisters she resembled an old frumpy lady.

'Hello, Ruth. How have you been since your school problem?' Stanley took his mac off and hung it in the hall with Glenn's coat, which he had taken from her shoulders.

'Hello, Stanley. I haven't got a school problem any more because I don't go.'

'You're not going to go back to school?' Stanley frowned.

'No, Stanley, I am not.' Ruth looked at him and knew he was definitely one of the boys in the school picture; he had worn the small black cap, the same as her father and her uncle Harry. Her uncle Harry who she longed to see; she wanted to understand why he had chosen to abscond and pretend she wasn't alive, not even humour her in some way, as though she didn't matter.

'Right, let me get rid of this box and I will go and put the kettle on.' Matthew kissed Glenn and nodded at Stanley before going into the kitchen; he knew his face revealed what had happened in the loft and wanted to wash his face under the cool tap.

'What are you doing on the stairs, Ruth?' Glenn asked. 'How come all the decorations are out so early?'

'I am only sitting here. It's a free country, isn't it? And anyway, I thought I'd put the decorations out because you never know; you may actually get me a card this year.'

Glenn moved forward and rubbed Ruth's hair, messing it up a little, as she realised she never had been one for cards and finally understood why her sisters thought she was a tightarse.

'Ruth, may I help you fill your home with these treats?'

'Lucas, they're decorations, not treats,' Ruth said abruptly, pushing herself from the stairs, though she felt grateful someone in the Hopkins house seemed to care.

'Oh, OK. May I help? May I help?' Lucas spoke like an excited child.

'Hi, Lucas.' Glenn smiled at Lucas as she held Stanley's hand and led him into the kitchen to speak to her father.

'May I say, Glenn, you are looking rather vibrant in your pretty frock? Lots of flowers; you look like a meadow of pure nature, and a very warm welcome to you too, Stanley.' Lucas gave them a huge smile, tapping his heels together with excitement.

Glenn scrunched her face up, knowing she looked nothing like a pretty meadow. All she felt was fat: fat and frumpy and completely unattractive.

Lucas gave his full attention back to Ruth and held out his hand also for the pretty blonde girl to hold. 'Just us left, eh, Ruth? Let's go and do something spectacular.' He smiled as Ruth took his hand and they went into the dining room.

It was the first time Lucas had been alone with Ruth since she had taken the locket and he knew he finally had a chance to speak to her. As he watched her pulling the individual branches from the box he knew it was time.

He knelt next to the box of tinsel and before he could begin speaking he came across the most spectacular snow globe; he thought it was magnificently magical. Shaking the glass dome gently he became mesmerised as he saw the small white specks glistening, swaying and moving freely in the trapped space; they settled to the bottom as though they were resting until being woken with the gentle movement of his hand, happily shaking the dome to wake them up again to fall freely and elegantly around the moulded plastic figures. Lucas imagined himself pushing the red sleigh with Natty inside, gliding through the soft white blanket of snow, the cold crisp breeze on their faces, swaying around the trees feeling free and alive.

'Ruth, come and have a look at this, come and be one of the little people inside here; it's incredible. Come, Ruth,' Lucas said, not taking his eyes from the falling white particles.

'Lucas, really, are you that mad?' Ruth gently threw the branch onto the carpet and went to sit next to him.

'Look inside, Ruth.'

'OK, Lucas, what am I meant to be looking at?' Ruth leant forward; all she could smell was an apple fragrance.

'Which one are you, Ruth?'

Ruth took a moment and looked at the globe.

'The snowman.'

'What makes you choose the snowman?' Lucas looked at her and frowned.

'One day, with any luck, Lucas, I will melt away.'

'Oh dear, Ruth, you haven't got to melt away into nothing; you have so much wonder and love around you. You must not allow your mother to see you so sad. You see, Ruth, life can be like this globe; it's really calm and settled and then someone comes along and shakes away and everything goes a little bit up in the air, like the little robin floating in the water. He's all over the place. The little broken bird, Ruth, he's floating in the glistening water and there is no way he can be glued back, because sometimes, Ruth, if we spend so much time worrying and trying to fix every little thing then the whole thing gets broken.' Lucas spoke gently and steadily, feeling Ruth's knee touching his as they sat side by side. 'We'd have to damage the whole fantastic snowy creation for one small thing. You have to let things float around you sometimes.'

'Lucas, I do find it difficult letting things simply float around me when they cause so much worry, and how can I not allow her to see me so sad? I've spent long enough doing it.' Ruth was unsure of her honesty with Lucas and wondered why he assumed it was because of her mother she was so miserable. Had he not realised she had been subjected to pain and torment at school? He wasn't aware she didn't belong to the man who had invited him into their home.

'I do understand everything you feel, the way you want to hurt everyone to be here and to be noticed. You haven't got to do that; you haven't got to be heard by anyone. You know how you feel and you're so very wonderful. We mere humans must not allow others to cause us any harm, even if we appear a little different to them or feel different.' Lucas recalled for himself how everyone thought he was mad only because he wanted to be a little different; why couldn't they all have left him alone? He longed to help Ruth understand before they locked her away for feeling. A sense of aloneness began to stir in him.

'Lucas, I didn't do anything wrong. I've been hurt for such a long time and I don't know how else to be; it's like I'm always walking in the rain on a sunny day. It never goes away, Lucas, never.' Ruth began to sob gently; her tears began rolling onto her cheeks.

Lucas pulled his grey cuff over his hand and wiped her face.

Feeling the soft wool on her cheek, Ruth embraced the comfort and attention she was getting from him.

'I promise you, Ruth, the very pretty thing you are, you really can allow the pain to leave you, and I promise you will be safe. The thought of living past pain forever is as crazy as me wanting to understand why green's green.' Lucas smiled and giggled slightly. His own tears deep inside him, allowing it to be Ruth's moment only.

'Thank you, Lucas. Not sure of the point of the conversation; I do feel a bit better, though. And I also wonder why green's green.' Ruth laughed with him.

'Shall we do this?' Lucas squeezed Ruth's shoulder and then got up to place the globe on the mantelpiece.

'Looks crap there, Lucas.' Ruth laughed louder and knew by the time they had finished sharing the decorations she'd be feeling better. It was really lovely to be in his company and she could finally understand how Natty felt.

She needed him to forgive her. 'The locket, Lucas.'

'No more, Ruth; you haven't got to explain.' Lucas knew the pretty little blonde girl who he had embraced in his thoughts all those years ago, as she stood close to her father's legs in the mental home. He had sensed then and still did that she had a pretty heart too. He pulled streams of gold and silver tinsel from the box and smiled. He understood and she needn't be forgiven for displaying the pain that was hidden inside her actions, not to him, ever.

'Wow, looking good, you two. Has anyone seen the can opener?' Glenn stood and admired their efforts as she rubbed her large belly, aware of how huge she looked.

'Why?' Ruth jumped from the chair as she grabbed another star from the box; they were their mother's favourite.

'Need to saw some wood with it. What do you think?'

'Nice to see you haven't lost your humour, Glenn, along with your figure.'

'Oh, get stuffed.' Glenn huffed and walked back into the kitchen where she and Stanley were helping prepare dinner.

As Ruth hung the star in perfect harmony with the others she smiled; she knew the whereabouts of the can opener. After she had taken the bag of tinned fruit to her homeless friend they had both sat laughing on the pavement as they held the cans in their hands; it was the only thing she'd forgotten. She knew it was safe under her mattress.

She nearly fell off the chair as she heard the screams coming from the kitchen.

'Aaaaaaah! Oh my God! Thank you, Dad!'

Walking slowly to the kitchen door in apprehension, she peered around the doorframe. She saw Glenn holding their mother's wedding dress over her arm, as she held tightly to their father; he was smiling and happy to be in the private moment with her.

Ruth stepped back from the door, hoping they hadn't seen her.

As she turned she looked at Lucas, who was standing in the hallway with a half-hearted smile, attempting to reassure her with his expression.

Placing the white star on the stair, Ruth walked slowly up to her bedroom.

# 41

## 1976

'Miss Natty, your dear father looks like he is finally making peace.' Lucas wiped the condensation from the kitchen window as he saw Matthew standing in the garden; the snow was falling hard.

'Oh my God, he must be frozen.' Natty went quickly to open the garden door and ask him to come in.

'Miss Natty, allow him to be.' Lucas grabbed Natty's arm gently.

'But he has no shoes on, Lucas!' Natty looked at his hand on her arm and shook her head. Uncertain of what to do, she smiled at Lucas and took his hand gently away.

'I am sorry to have touched you in such a way, Miss Natty. He knows what he's doing; trust him.'

'What are you two looking at?' Ruth came into the kitchen, taking off her purple woolly hat and matching gloves.

'Dad!'

'Sorry, did you just speak to me, Natty?' Ruth left her brown duffel coat on and walked to the back door.

'No.' Natty scrunched her face up in disbelief as she had promised herself she wasn't going to.

Ruth opened the garden door. The freezing air rushed over her face; the warmth of the kitchen began to dispel.

'It's freezing out there, Lucas; I have to get him.' Natty paced up and down the draughty kitchen.

'Please, Miss Natty, leave him be; allow him to be at the grave of your mother alone.' Lucas put his hand into his brown cardigan pocket and felt the ripped paper flower.

'Lucas, stop being so crazy!'

'Miss Natty, it's been over a year now and I am sure he has a lot of things he needs to say to your beautiful mother.'

'Yes, Lucas, I do know it's been that long; she is our mother.' Natty felt frustrated with the confusion she had, knowing she wanted to get him in and also understanding what Lucas was saying; she did have to allow her father to be left alone with her mother.

'I didn't mean to insult you in any way, Miss Natty.'

'You didn't, but he's hurting so much. I know Christmas was hard for him, sitting around the tree and everything, but look at him, Lucas.'

The thought of her necklace came back to her again as she and Lucas had spent so much time searching to no avail. She wasn't going to give up, though. If only she could look at it now and see them both smiling together, when they were happy, when all the confusion and mess hadn't got caught up between them. Ruth had no idea how it felt to have such a thing taken away from her; it had been the only real thing in her life, knowing her parents did love each other once and she had been born into the world because of it.

Looking at Ruth standing at the open door in her warm coat, Natty wanted to go and pull her blonde pigtail out; she should be at school instead of busybodying around the kitchen and flitting in and out of the house, pinching groceries. Natty had heard their father asking her where she had pawned the necklace; she wouldn't answer. For some strange reason she had totally forgotten.

'Oh my goodness, Miss Natty, we have to change the calendar!'

'Lucas, it really doesn't matter right now.'

'Yes, Miss Natty, very much so. It says December 1975. And it is now January 1976. You are all another year older, Christmas has been and gone, and I feel, Miss Natty, it is going to be the year of great things. There is no possible way you can leave it up there, otherwise, Miss Natty, we are all living in the past.'

Ruth smiled at him from the door. Her cheeks red and her body warm, she hoped their father would come in soon.

'We will get the new one out in a minute,' Natty said. 'Oh dear, you do choose your times, Lucas.'

'It's OK, Miss Natty. We cannot spend another minute living in the past.' Finally moving away from the view of Matthew at the window, he let the small net fall and went to find the calendar.

Natty stood unhappily next to Ruth at the open door.

Feeling the soft snow on his face and seeing his breath in the cold air as he exhaled, their father could see Eve's grave had been covered with the soft white flakes; only a small piece of the stone had managed to escape. In his black T-shirt and black trousers the snow covered his shoulders slowly, his tears feeling warm on his cold cheeks. He had to feel it, feel the pain, desperately longing for it to release itself from his tired body; he had to give himself permission for it to happen right at that very moment.

As he lowered his head, glancing at his bare feet in the snow, he could feel the burning sensation going through his heels and moving down into the arch of his soles like blades. His toes were red and numb but he knew he had to suffer; he had to embrace it. Looking up into the grey sky with his eyes open he could see the flakes falling onto him; as they touched his eye he blinked so they'd melt onto his face. Opening his mouth, he wanted to feel the soft touch of them on his lips. His body began to shake; he was determined not to move until the pain from the crushed snow under his feet became unbearable.

'Lucas, please go and get him in, please; he is so cold.' Natty held her hands on her head, pleading with Lucas as she watched him throw the old calendar in the bin. He then joined them at the door.

'Miss Natty, he is allowing nature to take him, to help him understand; that is pure freedom. He wants it to speak to him, to help him find his own answer. Just remain here. You must not prevent him from feeling his pain; protection isn't the way. Please don't go and help him, Miss Natty; do this for your father. Ruth, he is OK, I promise you,' Lucas whispered to them as they stood frightened and concerned.

Matthew closed his eyes and began to feel a tightening sensation in his stomach, the pain in his feet shooting through his legs. He had to bring it all into his stomach to get it out; he was going to get it out.

To Ruth he looked like the snowman in the Christmas globe, frozen and alone with his arms out. She prayed he wouldn't melt;

she didn't want him to. It didn't matter how angry she was with him for everything: for the stupid pen set on her sixteenth birthday, for not being her father, for her mother and for even giving Glenn the stupid wedding dress. She didn't want him to disappear into the soft white ground. She was OK with it all; she only wanted him to come into the warmth.

'Why won't he come in, Natty?' Ruth asked with desperation in her voice.

'I don't know, Ruth.' Natty held out her hand for Ruth to hold. Feeling her sister's fingers wrapping around hers, Natty became comforted instantly; her younger sister had been away for far too long.

The freezing wind picked up and swirled the already settled snow around Matthew's cold and shocked body. He closed his eyes hard as the wind beat at his face; the soft snow now seemed to be like small pieces of glass shattering his skin. The cold air cut into his lungs; it seemed his throat was on fire. His tears rolled into his mouth, falling from his lips; his nose began to run, his breathing heavy and his heart beating hard. His hurt and grief wanting to leave him, thrusting their way up from his stomach through every muscle and cell in his body. Gritting his teeth at the unbearable wrenching of pain he fell to his knees, the cold biting into his legs. Taking the snow from Eve's grave and holding it to his face, his body finally erupted with agony.

'Aaaaaahhhhhhhhhh! Aaaaaaaaaaaaaaah! TAKE MY PAIN, GOD; TAKE IT! I GIVE IT TO YOU!'

'OH MY GOD, DAD!' Natty yelled out in fear, the tears welling up in her eyes as his screams shook her.

Ruth's hand in hers had become sweaty; she could feel her body shaking as the tears rolled down her cheeks also.

'Miss Natty, one more minute, give him one more minute.' Lucas spoke with an assertive gentleness, touching both of their shoulders.

'Eve! My beautiful Eve, please, with all of your beauty, please forgive me. I love you, I love you, I love you.'

Holding the snow from her grave against his face, Matthew inhaled the deepest of breaths; a feeling of peace flowed through his body and mind as pure as the persecuting snow.

# 42

'He's a really nice fellow; he comes in the shop all the time. There is something very gentle and unassuming about him; you don't meet men like that these days. I really feel for him. It must be costing him a fortune; every book he reads he brings back. Honestly, Harry, I can't work it out. I'm actually thinking of giving him a discount, but knowing the kind of man he is I can imagine he'll refuse. He hasn't been in since before Christmas, so he may have finished his reading.' Suzy spoke with her mouth full of chocolate chip ice cream and a cushion on her lap, not making eye contact with Harry. She began swirling the mushy ice cream around her spoon in deep thought. She hoped the reader would come in again; she liked to see him and enjoyed their brief exchange of conversation. A small blob of chocolate ice cream fell onto her black polo neck, just over her chest. After quickly jumping up and trying to shake it away to no avail, she licked her finger and rubbed the small brown stain away.

'Would you like me to do that?'

'You can't get in my knickers that easily any more; you're still being punished.'

'What, still? It's been nearly five months, Suzy, and I told you how very sorry I was for lying to you. I was so desperate to see you again I only said the first thing that came to mind just so I would have at least a chance of picking you up, so we could actually speak to each other. And, of course, so I could explain myself to you. Now come here and let me get the ice cream off your jumper.'

Harry lay on the other sofa with his jeans a little undone at the top and with his chest bare. His body wasn't bad for a fifty-four-year-old, really, and he hoped to make the most of it. For her to even be in his presence was a bit of luck after his performance about the restaurant. When he had humbly picked her up she had walked out of her front door in a tight black dress, high heels and a small red jacket; she had looked adorable. The nearer she got to the car, the more he waited for the slap in the face he assumed she'd subject him to.

As he'd sat in the driver's seat looking sad and let down about the whole restaurant idea, he could see he was winning her over. She sat with her arms folded while he grovelled for another chance. He would have bet all his Friday-night card money she'd have got out of the car. With the heavens on his side she said she was determined to go somewhere, anywhere, even if it was his house with cold beer and a pizza; she hadn't spent all evening getting ready for nothing.

The only punishment she had directly put to him was not having any sex until she had completely accepted his bullshit.

'So he comes in your shop to chat you up, does he?' Harry rubbed his groin; he could feel the hardness as the thought of touching her soft round breast stirred anticipation and excitement.

'What is it about you men who say such stupid things? No, Harry. He's so nice; shame you're not a bit more like him.' Suzy knew he could shove his offer to wipe the stain from her jumper up his arse. As she picked up the cushion and threw it at him she hoped it'd hit him straight in the brain area.

The cushion landed hard on his lap.

'Ouch! You seem to know a lot about him.' Harry spoke through his cough.

'Of course I'm going to chat with him when he comes into the shop. I think you'd like him. He spends most of his time in the corner reading anyway; he likes to be where he met his love. Honestly, it's like a true-life love story; his dearest love dies and he embraces her in his heart forever. Ahh!'

'Oh, I see. Sounds more than a quick chat, Suzy.' Harry's thoughts went back to the locket.

'He tells me of his family and how he loved his wife so much he'd never allow himself to love another, and reading helps him sit away from real life for a while. I think it's so romantic.' Looking at Harry, she tutted, knowing he could never understand such

214

romance. She was sure the silent reader would never serve burnt pizza and beer to woo a woman either.

'Sounds like a real fruitcake to me.' Harry tapped his groin area, and all he wanted at that moment was for Suzy to lift her green miniskirt up a little and sit on his firm willy.

Suzy threw another cushion at him and shook her head. She saw how tempting he looked, and she hadn't felt him for the last five months; maybe she was also hurting herself by leaving her knickers on longer than necessary.

'Come here, Suzy, let me smell that perfume I bought you for Christmas.' Harry waited for her to come over, beckoning her with his hand. An unusual thought went through his mind as neither of them had ever asked each other about their families, and he suddenly wondered if Suzy had something to hide.

Harry felt unusually jealous when she spoke of this man. It was an emotion he had never experienced with any other woman but Eve, the wonderful beauty who had slipped in and out of his life.

'What, after that "fruitcake" comment? Listen, buddy, if it wasn't for Wilfred making you out to be such a charming catch then I may not have listened to your desperate attempt at licking my arse.' Suzy raised her voice a little, giving him a smug look.

'What's going on with him anyway?'

'I've told you, he's a real gentleman. He seems sad, though, some days more than others, but it's so good to have him enjoying our books so much.'

'I didn't mean him; I meant Wilf or whatever he wants to call himself.' Harry was certain the customer was also enjoying his girlfriend.

'Oh, nothing; just likes men, that's all. Thinks you're a bit of all right.'

'Well, that's made me want to be sick.'

They both laughed and Harry raised and lowered his eyebrows, widening his eyes in his attempt to persuade her with only gestures to sit on his lap.

'I am going to leave now; I've got lots to do.' Suzy placed the empty bowl on the table and stared at Harry. Thoughts rushed through her mind as a gentle throbbing arose between her legs.

'I've got something to do tomorrow, but let's not worry about that now, eh?'

Harry watched as Suzy pushed her hand slowly into her knickers, her miniskirt scrunched up a little around her slim waist. She pushed her own fingers inside herself as she stood smiling at him; he could see her pink lace knickers over her hand. She pushed her fingers in and out of herself as she teased him.

Jumping up, Harry hurried to her, unzipping his jeans, pushing her down hard onto the sofa. Moving her hand away and wrapping her bare slim legs around his waist, he pushed himself firm and hard inside her wet opening, thrusting into her with force, gripping her blonde hair, his movements rough and dominating, bringing her to groan in gratifying pleasure.

# 43

Natty ran up the stairs, bursting for the toilet. Before she went to work she hoped to write something in her diary; she had been meaning to most of the morning, as with working and spending most of her time with Lucas she'd only get a chance when she tucked herself into her covers at night. She wanted to do it before another morning she'd wake up with her diary on her lap and her pen lost within the covers.

Grabbing her diary from her brown leather bag and then kneeling across her perfectly made bed to reach for a pen in her drawer, moving her fingers through the papers and old makeup, Natty scrunched her face as she had nearly wet her knickers from the delay. She couldn't hold her yearning to get to the toilet another minute and rushed to the bathroom.

'Ahh.' Sitting on the toilet seat finally in sheer relief, Natty opened her diary and flicked through the pages near the back of the book, noticing she only had a few more pages left.

'Oh, damn it.' Natty spoke out loud with her red knickers and black tights around her ankles and began to write.

*Feb 1976*

Natty Hopkins, Natty Dunstable, Mrs Natty Dunstable. Why am I even kidding myself? I mean, how obvious does it have to be that I find him completely adorable? Oh my, he's such an amazing man. He's been so kind to spend so much time with me trying to find my locket. I really have a terrible feeling it isn't going to be found ever, but he keeps insisting it will be, he says he will do anything to find it even if it means travelling to the other side of the world. He has to think of himself a little. I mean he still hasn't got his job and the last one he did get only lasted a week, far too generous with the scoops of ice cream he gave in the small shop, they just couldn't afford to keep him there. 'One more scoop for luck,' he'd say; the manager said 'one more day and you can collect your wages for luck' and my dear Lucas had to leave. He did look rather gorgeous, though, in his small white paper hat. He dances all the time when no one is looking in his bedroom, I'm sure of it.

I have to get myself a reality check and realise he only wants to help find my locket. Wish it hadn't gone missing and then the time we spent together would really be because he wanted to be with me, the future Mrs Natty Dunstable, ha ha!!

How can I not be drawn to him for being so kind and understanding? He knows how important it is for me to find my locket and promised he wouldn't stop. He seems to be the only one who understands the meaning of it, All I want is for it to be found, for Lucas to really see me, for Glenn to have a healthy baby next month – goodness, she looks fat!! – and maybe I could search in my heart to be a little kinder to Ruth. I know she's finding it all hard. She won't speak to anyone, not that I've asked her if she's OK. And as for Dad it would be nice to see him a little more; he seems to have his head inside yet another book most of the time and I'm actually amazed he's making us all lunch today, instead of being hidden away in his bedroom and the dining room. He does seem a little better lately. I really hope it lasts. It's so hard to see him in so much pain. Not only that, we can never show our own if he's so consumed with his. If he's hurting then how have we got time to let him know how we really feel about Mother?

Cannot believe it's been over a year now, feels like yesterday when we saw her for the last time so peaceful. Not going to go there; I cannot cry before work. I miss what she could have been. I hate not knowing how it'd all have been the day we all went home. She never gave us the chance to find out, she never gave anyone a choice in anything. I know Glenn is hurting having her first child and Mother not being there to be part of something so very incredible.

PLEASE, GOD, PLEASE DON'T LET IT SNOW AGAIN THIS YEAR, I COULDN'T BEAR WATCHING SUCH AN ESCAPADE WITH DAD.

I've got to go now and have a family lunch, corned beef sarnie. I am so happy I have Lucas who is so wonderful to be around, so real and honest, so caring and innocent; I really want to kiss him, to touch him in some way and get him to notice me. Here I go again talking about Mr Lucas magical Dunstable. I think it goes with my name, though. Natty Dunstable, of Grand Manor Palace, swimming pool and a chauffeur-driven car, with butlers and cleaners and all that great stuff. Sounds like a dream to me, really. I just want to get my locket back, that's all. At least I can trust Lucas with my feelings and he is gorgeously crazy.

xxx Mrs Natty Dunstable, ha ha!!!!

'Oh my God, no loo roll.' Natty dropped her diary onto the floor and walked slowly, resembling a penguin, to retrieve some toilet roll unhappily from the bottom of the sink cupboard.

'Natty, lunch!'

Natty could hear her father's voice from the bottom of the stairs.

'OK, give me a chance. What's a girl meant to do around here, huh?'

Flushing the chain and washing her hands, Natty left the bathroom and quickly threw her diary and pen on her bed from the doorway.

'Miss Natty, are you looking forward to working today!'

'No, Lucas, definitely not, like a punch in the eye.'

'Why would you want a punch in the eye? Maybe we can skip that idea and continue our search tomorrow. I am yet to buy you a small birthday gift.' Lucas took the corned beef and tomato slices from his sandwich and placed them on the side of his plate.

'Why, Lucas, do you continue to separate your food?'

'I relish every flavour, Miss Natty.' Lucas smiled and bit into his buttered bread.

'Anyway, going back to my small gift, my birthday was ages ago now and the sort of thing I am looking for your measly £15 wouldn't cover.' Natty laughed in jest, bashing him on the arm, seeing him glum and taking the whole thing personally.

Natty left the table, leaving one half of her sandwich. She took her favourite grey cardigan from the coat hook and went to leave for work. 'Bye, all.'

Natty could see their father pushing some paperwork into his leather case to go and collect some work from his office. He'd worked from home for so many years now, and he promised he would continue until his eyesight went and he could no longer see all the numbers. Maybe if Lucas gave him his £15 he could help him invest it in some way.

Ruth hadn't eaten her sandwich; she wrapped it up in foil and took a packet of biscuits from the cupboard before leaving the house. Not saying goodbye to anyone was a usual occurrence for her.

Natty chuckled as she put her key into the ignition. 'Small gift? Oh, Lucas, you have a lot to learn.' She shook her head as she drove away.

'Bye, Lucas. Try not to do anything crazy today.' Matthew tapped Lucas on the shoulder as he walked past him.

Lucas stood alone in the house, the hallway finally peaceful.

Rubbing his hands together and tapping his feet he began to move his body slowly, making his way into the kitchen.

'Pancakes, I think; yes, lots of pancakes.'

Cracking the eggs into the large bowl of flour, the white residue going over the edge, Lucas sang to himself and tapped his feet in happiness. The clouds of white flour enthralled him; he closed his eyes and felt the texture with his fingers.

'Best get a wooden spoon.' Lucas took the spoon from the cutlery drawer and began tapping it on his thigh, feeling the slight sting on his leg through his blue cords, his tight red T-shirt covered in white stains.

Through his singing Lucas was sure he could hear a knock at the door. He shook his head, thinking it was only in his imagination as everyone hadn't been out for even half an hour. He continued stirring the cream-coloured gooey mixture; he only hoped there was some milk. As he opened the fridge he finally became sure the knocking was real and he closed the fridge door in wonder, lowering his eyebrows as he placed the glass bottle of milk next to the mixing bowl.

As the front door was finally opened Harry could see a young man covered in white powder with a wooden spoon in his hand, his mass of brown curls almost white.

'Hello, sir; can I help you?' Lucas grinned at the stranger who seemed nervous at the front door.

'Hi, I take it Matthew lives here still?' Harry spoke gently, his stomach filled with nerves, as he squeezed the necklace in his pocket through his jeans. His heart had been beating hard and he had felt as though he wanted to be sick all the way to his brother's house as he drove steadily in his van. The fear and doubt had overtaken him as he knocked on the door, his palms sweating and his body shaking with dread at the idea of being greeted at the door by his daughter Ruth. Thankfully only a messy smiling stranger stood before him.

'Oh, yes, indeed he does, and what a wonderful fellow he is too. I am afraid you have missed him; he is at work, you see, and sometimes doesn't come home straight away, normally goes to the b—'

'What time?' Harry rudely interrupted, the anticipation and adrenaline getting the better of him.

'Can I ask you something, dear sir? Why is it, do you think, that when you put hot water onto bubbles they get wonderfully bigger, and when you put cold on they disappear somewhat?' Lucas smiled. He felt the man looked almost upset.

'Sorry, mate, I really only came to see Matthew, and I'm not too bothered about stuff like that: a bubble theory boy, eh?' Harry began to walk away from the front door, his heart beating hard as the thought of coming back again and having to go through the same emotions was too much for him; he might not be as lucky next time. He longed to get it over with; having the locket had been haunting him since he had left the grimy pawnshop.

'Well, sir, I take it you are a man without a theory,' Lucas said in a high-pitched voice, frowning.

Harry turned to him and laughed. 'I think you're right there. Listen, I have something to give to Matthew and as I haven't seen him for some time I was thinking maybe you could do it for me; you know, give it to him.'

'Well, yes, sir, you are more than welcome to come in and wait for him. I am making pancakes if you would like one.'

'Actually, I'm not too sure if that's a good idea.'

'Sir, do you not like pancakes?'

Harry paused for a moment.

'OK, I'll come in then.'

Harry closed the door slowly, taking in the surroundings he remembered so clearly. As though he'd been taken back in time he closed his eyes, his heart wanting to be there but his mind telling him it was completely the wrong thing to be doing. What was he thinking? What was going through his stupid empty head?

Opening his eyes he began looking at the stairs and recalled the time he had sat with Eve over his lap. The pain from the memory shot through his abdomen; it was too much for him, the dining room only a few feet away where he had made forbidden love to her, where she had conceived his child he'd never known.

The thoughts overcame him, aware if Matthew knew he had been in his home, if he knew he'd seen his life again, it'd finally kill him. Harry missed his brother terribly and knew he'd never be forgiven for behaving so inexcusably.

'Come through, sir; come, the kitchen is right here.'

'Yes, I know, theory boy,' Harry said under his breath as the excited young man who Matthew had in his home grabbed his arm gently to lead him into the kitchen.

'Right, let me put the frying pan on the stove, then I can make you a magnificent delight, sir.' Lucas was like an excited child, flitting from one side of the kitchen to the other almost in a panic.

'Harry, my name is Harry.' Standing near the table Harry was amazed at how messy the kitchen was, how disorganised everything seemed. No way this home belonged to the one and only Matthew Hopkins.

Lucas came to a standstill as he held the frying pan in his hand.

'You are Harry, my kind friend's brother? The man who I have heard about in brief conversation? You don't resemble Matthew at all. Why are you here? I do believe if you have tried everything you can do, kind sir, then there is no more to be done, so if you have

222

come to hurt him once again, I do apologise, but I don't think I will be making you any pancakes today.' Lucas placed the pan on the lit gas ring and walked to the front door.

'I haven't come to hurt him; I've come to give him something I think he will be happy to have back.'

'Please, sir, if you allow me to take it from you I may be able to protect him from you.' Lucas spoke with his back to Harry.

Harry knew he deserved such treatment even from the young man covered in flour.

Lucas opened the front door and Harry stood next to him.

'Excuse me, sir, I think I can smell burning.' Lucas rushed from Harry's presence.

Harry looked up at the ceiling and sighed; the whole thing seemed like a waste of time. Taking the locket from his pocket he looked at the small telephone table; a thought rushed through him, knowing he was unhappy with being parted from the small chain which gave him a connection to his life. Closing his eyes, he knew it didn't belong to him. Gazing at the table once more and then the locket, he left the burning aroma in the hallway.

As Lucas rushed around the kitchen with the frying pan full of black smoke he could hear the door slam. Throwing the pan into the sink full of bubbly water he ran into the hall.

'Well, I should think so, too.' Lucas walked slowly over to the small telephone table.

Outside, Harry slammed the door to his van, the impact rattling through his vulnerable body. His hands still shook from being in his brother's home, a place he was once welcome, as he embraced the image of Eve once more, bringing it to his lips, his heavy breath on the small heart-shaped beauty.

# 44

Glenn had been cleaning all day as though her young life depended on it. Pulling the heavy blankets onto the burgundy carpet. The sweat trickling down her temple, her short black hair wet at the sides. She felt old and frumpy and had had enough of carrying the weight of a bag of spuds around with her for the last week. Rubbing her stomach, she breathed in hard. Even Stanley had become quicker than her on the stairs; he always managed to pass her on the way to the bedroom at night, holding two cups of hot cocoa. Some nights, as he did, Glenn wished he could instead bring a dirty magazine up with him and then they could look at it together and see what sorts of things could happen between them, maybe spice things up a little; after all, she was only nineteen and she had only really begun to discover her own proclivities. Or, with Stanley in his stripy pyjamas, maybe not. The source of confusion for her was that he was only a few years younger than her father, and she'd never seen him taking a hot cup of cocoa to bed.

Glenn still had always felt safe with Stanley in the last nine months with whatever he took to bed. Even from the moment she had lived her life on the edge and had amazing sex with him on the train, there had been a sense of security and acceptance with him she couldn't quite understand, but for some reason he seemed like a different man now; she knew all he wanted to do was protect her and it began to drive a girl crazy after a while. She hoped he'd become spontaneous again once their baby was born.

Wiping her brow on the blanket she sat on the edge of the bed, breathing hard. Her back began to ache but she was determined to continue even if her hands were to bleed; she needed to get organised. Everything around her seemed old and it didn't matter how hard she tried; it still looked old. Glenn promised herself once the baby was born she was going to give the brown and dingy cream walls a good paint. Chuckling to herself, she wondered if Stanley wouldn't be too dismissive of a little pink and lemon here and there.

Picking the green blankets up from the bedroom floor, Glenn yanked at the white flannelette stripy sheet still on the bed, tugging with all her might.

'Get off. Why is all this so hard, honestly?'

Finally the sheet was in her hand. Glenn smiled in satisfaction. 'See, smelly old sheet, you're not going to beat a Hopkins.'

Making her way to the stairs, Glenn couldn't see in front of her, the blankets becoming heavy in her tired arms. She felt each step with her foot before making her way down to the small hallway.

'Stanley, could you help me with these?' Glenn called, to no avail.

She could hear his snoring coming from the living room, where he had been resting in his favourite armchair for most of the day. Dropping the blankets where she stood, Glenn shook her head, becoming fuelled with annoyance.

'Right, the music's going on.' She paced to the record player, huffing as she did so. Finding her favourite record, she blew the small specks of dust from the black shiny vinyl. As she turned the volume up she looked at the back of his chair. Feeling pleased with herself and also sensing anger stirring inside, she waited a moment for him to move. Nothing. Feeling defeated, she went back upstairs to begin the menial task of cleaning the brown bathroom suite.

Her lips tight and still angry, she grabbed the toilet roll holder. The plastic smiling doll with a woollen pink-and-blue crocheted dress protecting the roll of paper had sat on the toilet cistern smiling at her for far too long while she did her private business. Taking it by its little plastic head she opened the window and threw it hard out into the air; the blonde-wigged doll could go to hell, just as Stanley could at that very moment.

Hearing the beats coming through the floorboards, Glenn shook the cleaning powder into the bath, smiling as she turned to look at the final resting place of the doll. Feeling certain at any moment the music would be turned down and her goal of getting the love of her life out of his comfy chair would have been accomplished.

225

'Glenn, you OK up there? Glenn, honey, you OK?' Stanley called from the hall, standing on the pile of blankets. Shrugging his shoulders, he decided to make a drink. He was desperate to turn the music down. Confusion set in as Glenn had known he was resting, and to put the music on while he slept was a little inconsiderate. He reminded himself she was young, and she'd obviously taken him at his word about how they were to get to know each other. Still, as much as he hated the beating of the music she had chosen, he was finding it difficult to understand why in God's name it had to be blaring through the wall to the neighbours also.

Glenn scrubbed hastily at the bath, making faces with her finger as the white marks swirled under the cloth. She hadn't heard Stanley and became lost in her own rhythm.

Stanley opened the kitchen door and the cleaning fumes began to sting his eyes. Everything was polished, cleaned and ironed. He shook his head in pride.

'Ouch, oh, that hurts, ah!' Standing up straight, Glenn felt a stabbing pain in her stomach.

She continued to clean, and this time felt a surge of cramp.

'Oh, shit, this doesn't feel good.' The feelings came hard and intense, barely giving her a chance to take a breath.

Throwing the clammy white cloth into the bath and leaning forward on the rim, Glenn began to breathe in and out, hoping she could take control of the unwelcome pain and it would subside so she could wipe the smiling faces from the bath.

'What are you smiling at? Fuck, shit. You really have to be joking. Not now!' Glenn had a sudden realisation her baby was on its way and all she wanted was for her mother to take care of her, to rush into the bathroom and tell her what to do, let her know it was all going to be all right, she wasn't going to die with the pain overcoming her body. Tears fell from her eyes as she raised her voice for someone to help; she was alone and scared.

'STANLEY! STANLEY!' The vibrations from the music seemed to drown her voice out more the louder she called.

Stanley placed the woolly tea cosy over the teapot and began to tap his hands on the side, actually enjoying what he was hearing. Smiling to himself, he thought maybe he could get used to it after all.

Glenn began to rock to and fro as the pain became so intense she wanted to rip the orange tiles from the bathroom wall.

'STANLEY, YOU DEAF ARSE!' Glenn felt the warmth of water trickle down inside her legs, her flared jean dress now a dark blue at the front.

Stanley took two cups slowly from the cupboard and happily placed a sugar in each. Waiting for the tea to brew, he poured the milk and wondered if Glenn would like to join him. Tapping his hands on the sideboard, he moved his head back and forth slowly, embracing his newfound enjoyment.

'IF HE DOESN'T TURN THAT SHIT DOWN—'

Stanley slowly poured the tea and placed the two flowery cups on a wicker-edged tray and held it in his hands, moving his body from side to side, stepping backward and forward gently as he made his way into the noisy living room.

Feeling a small sense of guilt for having to turn the music down so they could enjoy their tea in peace, Stanley looked up at the ceiling and hoped Glenn wouldn't mind; he knew how much she loved this particular song. Anxious at not really knowing what to do for the best, Stanley walked over to the whirling record.

His fingers nearly touched the off button and then he hesitated again, moving them away. Wiggling his fingers in thought, he looked at the ceiling once more.

'Oh, I will turn it off this once.' A sense of peace came over him.

'STANLEY, WHAT THE FUCK ARE YOU DOING DOWN THERE, YOU FUCK?'

Stanley felt as though his heart was going to jump out of his chest as he heard Glenn's desperate screams.

# 45

A s Natty walked around the market she bent over to each box of flowers, smelling the mixture of fragrances blending into one amazing sensation. Touching the soft, delicately formed petals with the tips of her fingers, she remembered how much her mother loved white roses especially and how flowers had always been a huge part of her life.

'Miss Natty, look how they grow so perfectly formed, each soft vibrant petal in the right place. Do you think, Miss Natty, if people were left alone their petals would perfectly form in the right places?'

'I have no idea.' Natty shook her head as she looked down at Lucas's shoes. 'Lucas, as wonderful as these flowers seem, if we are going to get you a job you really need to do something about those.'

Natty pulled her jean jacket together at the front as the breeze began to pick up a little, her small grey sleeveless top her other only form of warmth. Black flared corduroy trousers and purple and white pumps completed her chosen outfit to spend a day with him; she hoped he liked it. In his soft grey jumper and jeans he really looked rather handsome. She wanted to compliment him on his dress sense but couldn't receive such honesty about how she appeared to him in return, so she rejected her thought. She began to search in her bag for a hair bobble as her wiry brown hair blew around her face.

'My shoes aren't doing the job, Miss Natty.' Lucas pulled a long-stemmed red rose from the plastic vase and held it out to Natty. He grinned.

'Lucas, you're not taking me seriously at all, are you?' Natty raised her eyebrows, wanting to smile at the handsome man whose eyes sparkled with the reflection of the gentle March sun.

'Do you like, Miss Natty?' Lucas chuckled, tapping his feet.

'Yes, I like, Mr Lucas. My mother would have too, and she loved roses.' Natty smelt the rose in his hand and gazed into his eyes a little longer than necessary.

'Do you know we have to look at everything, all the beauty around us, all the wonderful things nature has given us to live with? You know, like your mother, Miss Natty. I hope she took the time to see all the miracles around her, because now she shall never see another leaf fall, never smell another bonfire or hear the crunching of pure white snow under her feet, Miss Natty, and never eat another piece of sponge.'

'Right, that's it; you're coming with me.' Natty took the long-stemmed rose from him and shoved it back amongst the bunches. A small red petal fell to the cobbled ground.

'Hello. It's lovely to see you again; you haven't been in for months.' Suzy opened the glass door for her mysterious reader as he stood outside with a pile of books in his arms.

'Hello. It's really nice to be in here again. You're looking very well, young lady, and I was thinking I haven't even asked your name all this time. I do apologise for being so rude as you have always been so very kind.'

'My name is Suzy,' she said, smiling at the silent reader who wore a dark blue shirt and black trousers. He appeared more attractive in some way. Her thoughts made her blush slightly, and she was flattered that he wanted to know her name. Moving forward she happily took some of the books from him.

Placing the rest of his books on the counter, Matthew rubbed down his shirt and looked around the bookshop, inhaling a lingering breath. 'Thank you for your help, Suzy. That's a pretty necklace you're wearing.'

'Thank you.' Suzy touched the gold chain on her neck as she spoke in admiration for her gift.

'May I say you seem happy? I take it everything is going as planned with your young man.'

'It is. Well, I still haven't been wined and dined, but at least he's trying.' Suzy felt comfort at being in the company of the interesting and compassionate man again. She had missed him being around the shop and hoped he wouldn't choose to stay away as long again.

'He is very lucky, Suzy, to have a pretty lady like you by his side.'

'Well, you're very charming today. I do hope he realises too.' Suzy began to giggle.

'Well, I would if you were by my side.' Matthew took a deep breath, pausing in his conversation as he thought his comment was a little forward and unnecessary.

'Um.' Suzy looked away as she could feel herself blushing again. She was lost for words for the first time in her life.

'I am very sorry; it was a little forward of me to make such a forthcoming statement, as true as it might be. Well, you know what I mean. I only love another and, as I have said, I promised myself to always have her in my heart.' Matthew bashed his head with his palm and knew he hadn't changed; the more he spoke the more like a fool he was acting, and he doubted the pretty young lady cared much about his love for Eve. The thought of ever contemplating becoming involved with another woman was something Matthew found unbearable.

'It's OK, honestly, you haven't offended me at all. It's so inspiring to see such love really does exist. All of the romantic novels in here surely couldn't compete.'

'Actually I have read a couple and they really aren't too good.' Matthew chuckled, hoping to gain some sense of dignity back with her.

'And, returning your kindness, I am so very certain the love of your life was also very lucky to have you by her side.' Suzy gave him a heart-warming smile.

'I'm also not too sure about that. Anyway, I will leave you to get on.' Matthew felt an instant longing for his Eve to be waiting for him when he arrived home as he turned his back to the pretty young lady and went to browse over the bookshelves.

'Your name: I didn't ask you either.' Suzy raised her voice a little.

'Matthew, my name is Matthew.' He gave her a gentle smile.

'Oh, hi, darling!' Wilfred walked quickly from the back of the stockroom and interrupted the energy which was building between them.

'Hello, nice to see you again. Still wearing those bright shirts, I see?' Matthew put his hand up in acknowledgment and continued his search for another story, another life to lose himself within, hoping to ignore the stares from Suzy.

'He's back, then?'

'And?' Suzy punched Wilfred on the arm.

'Oh, darling, I do like a bit of rough!' Wilfred pushed his glasses onto his head and went back into the stockroom laughing.


'Right, Lucas, I'm buying. Which ones would you like?'

Lucas felt dumbfounded as he looked at the rows and rows of different shoes. Picking up a brown pair of platforms, he scrunched his face, feeling disgruntled, and wondered why such things were invented.

'What is the purpose of these very large heels, Miss Natty? Why does anyone need to be so tall?' Placing the unappealing shoe back on the rack, Lucas looked down at his feet, seeing his blue sock sticking out of the front of the fading black leather.

'It's the fashion, Lucas.' Natty moved further into the shop, the smell of leather surrounding her. Sitting on the soft cushioned chair and placing her brown bag on her lap, she waited for Lucas to decide.

'Can I help you, sir?' The gently speaking salesman approached Lucas with his hands cupped together.

'No, thank you, kind sir.'

'Lucas!' Natty frowned.

'Natty, I have been in these shoes for a long time now, and they brought me to you. If I get more then all the things I have experienced in them will be diminished forever. How can I simply throw them away, as though all this doesn't matter? What if my new shoes take me somewhere I don't want to be?'

Natty got up and went to speak to him, speaking softly as she could see the expression of fear on his face. 'Lucas, you are in charge of the steps you make, no one else. You brought yourself to us. Did you have those shoes when you were a child? No!'

Lucas instantly remembered having to place his sore beaten feet into his school shoes, and how he'd lace those black shiny shoes up, attempting to pull his small grey socks further up his legs, hiding the bruises: the aftermath of his parents' punishment. As he hobbled to school he knew he wouldn't be dancing that day.

'I was happy to throw those shoes away, Miss Natty; my steps in them were very painful.'

'Look, Lucas, how are you going to dance in those old things any more? I've heard you; you're incredible. Why don't you dance?'

'Dance? I haven't danced for many years, Miss Natty. I told you I threw those shoes away.'

'Lucas, how about making your new ones your dancing shoes?'

'Do you think so, Miss Natty? Do you think I could make my steps again?'

'Yes. Now go and pick some. Maybe those platforms will do great.' Natty rubbed his arm and sensed his body shaking; she chuckled at her comment and went to sit back down.

'Sir?' The salesman hadn't moved, standing next to them with his hands still cupped.

'Yes.'

'Do you need help?'

Lucas looked at Natty and back again at his feet. Rubbing his hands through his brown curly hair, Lucas became unsettled.

'No, thank you, kind sir.'

Natty placed her hands onto her face in disbelief, beginning to feel frustrated. 'Lucas, get rid of your fear; they are only a pair of shoes.'

'Fear, Miss Natty: what a funny word. Do you not think it is a created feeling, Miss Natty?'

'Well, not really, Lucas, considering you're full of fear in simply picking something everyone uses every day of their lives.' Natty spoke with a harsh tone.

'Do you think, Miss Natty, if the word "fear" wasn't in our vocabulary then people wouldn't feel it? I mean, if it was "happy" and I was standing in this place feeling as I do, then wouldn't you see me as feeling happy in not buying a pair of shoes?'

'If you were happy then you'd buy them.'

Lucas frowned. 'Why?'

'Because you would; you'd be jumping all over the place singing for joy and buying a pair of goddamn shoes!'

232

'Excuse me, sir, I have another customer to serve; I do hope you make your mind up soon.' The salesman walked off shaking his head.

'Miss Natty, I feel I am choosing to be happy in not buying any of these shoes today.'

'It's like trying to put a square peg in a round hole with you, Lucas.' Natty jumped from the chair, squeezing her leather bag between her fingers.

'Does that not depend how big the hole is, Miss Natty?'

Natty stormed out of the shop and felt thankful to be in the fresh air again.

Lucas followed her, also feeling happy to be out of the display of moulded leather. 'Isn't that your father, Miss Natty?'

'Oh, yes. Maybe he can talk some sense into you.'

'Sense!' Lucas followed Natty as she sped off toward her father. 'Hi, Dad. DAD!'

'Oh, sorry, Natty, lost in my thoughts there. How are you two?'

'Been getting more books, Dad, then?'

'Yes, I know.' Matthew looked at the huge pile in his arms, feeling almost embarrassed.

'What's going on, Dad? Why are you in the bookshop so much?'

'I like reading, Natty, of course.'

'Dad?' Natty felt there was more to it. Feeling as if she had lost him to the bookshop concerned her a little.

Her father dropped his shoulders as he spoke, the books also becoming heavy in his arms. 'Oh, Natty, I began going there to feel her presence, your mother's presence, and her soul, where she has been. Her voice once echoed through the spaces. I like to be within the walls of where she once was.'

'Dad, she's never been to the bookshop and home is where she spent most of her time, and anyway you're certainly not going to find what you're looking for reading about tropical rainstorms.' Natty chuckled as she took the top book from the pile.

'And how would you know that, my little Miss Cocky Pants?'

'Miss Cocky Pants!' Lucas giggled.

'Dad, Mother isn't in the bookshop; she's gone. I know you have to accept it like we all do. Please don't make yourself suffer any more.'

233

'I know, Natty. I realise every day she has gone.' Her father lowered his head.

'Dad, you cannot keep hiding behind everyone else's words; honestly, it's no good for you. Have you ever thought about writing your own book?'

'Me, write a book?' Her father lifted his head at Natty's comment, roaring with laughter.

'Yes, Dad, and why not?' Natty spoke with enthusiasm for her father's new venture.

'All a man wants to do, Natty, is read a few words.'

'Dad, I'm being serious. I bet you could.'

'Young lady, I have never brought you up to be a gambler.' His thoughts went back to realising their whole lives had been a gamble, and the thought of putting pen to paper was something even more unpredictable.

'Tropical rainstorms, Dad, really? I think you have been around Lucas too long.' Natty laughed as she looked at Lucas and smiled, placing the book back on top of the pile.

'Yes, but he does make a grand pancake.'

'Yes, he does, Dad.'

'Well, thank you to you both for such a wonderful compliment; I shall make some more this evening. You would make a marvellous writer, Matthew, all those feelings, all those thoughts all just waiting to erupt from your body onto a page; oh, how exciting. Glorious.' Lucas spoke with excitement.

'So enough about me; what have you two been up to? Still searching, Natty?'

'Shoe shopping, Dad.'

'Did you get anything nice?'

'Please don't ask, Dad.' Natty turned to Lucas and rubbed his arm, giving him a gentle smile.

'Oh, OK, right. Well, I will see you both at dinner; pancakes for pudding it is, then.' Matthew left them both standing together. The thought of writing his own book had become more appealing by the time he got to his car.

'Let's forget about the whole shoe thing and go and buy something for Glenn's baby.'

'Oh, that would be wonderful. What shall we buy?'

'Shoes.' Natty grinned as she walked off slowly.

'Oh dear!' Lucas frowned as he caught up with Natty.

They were both back in the busy market. The hustle and bustle of sellers and smells enthralled Lucas, helping him embrace the day even more. A cluttered stall of brass and porcelain plates took his attention.

'Miss Natty, look how pretty this is.' Lucas held a small brass trinket box in his hand, decorated with hand-painted butterflies and leaves, the colours glistening as he moved it to and fro.

'Oh, wow, how beautiful; it is lovely, Lucas.' Natty looked in his hand and touched the purple butterfly delicately.

'Please allow me to buy it for you. Please, Miss Natty, I haven't bought you anything for your special day and you were going to buy my shoes.'

Natty took the trinket box from Lucas and turned it over to see a small sticker with a price of £15 on the bottom.

'Oh, no way, Lucas; it's all your wages.' Natty placed the box back on the brown velvet table, wishing it was a little cheaper as it was something rather pretty; she had never seen anything like it before, a little bit like her locket.

'Oh, please, Miss Natty.' Lucas put his hands together as though he was praying.

'No, Lucas.'

'I shall, Miss Natty.'

Natty slapped his hand gently as he went to pick up the small box.

'Lucas, if you dare buy that for me I shall never speak to you again. I mean it. I don't want it. I will be really cross with you and our friendship shall be banished for ever.' Natty walked away, leaving Lucas at the stall. She felt her words were a little harsh as she knew he took everything literally.

Feeling the soft scarves and woollen cardigans at another multi-coloured stall, Natty waited for Lucas to catch up.

'These scarves are nice. What took you so long?'

'It doesn't matter.' Lucas rubbed his hand on his front jean pocket, shuffling back and forward, seeming nervous.

'Can I have this one, please?'

Natty wrapped the red scarf around Lucas's neck and smiled, looking into his eyes. 'This is for you, Lucas, for being so crazy.'

'Miss Natty, thank you; how can I ever thank you?' Lucas squeezed the soft wool between his hands with delight.

'You don't have to, but it will help if you pull the price tag off.' Natty knew how he could repay her for her kindness; all he had to do was place his lips onto hers.

'Oh, yes.'

'I am going to get something for Glenn while I am here.' Natty gazed over the small knitted cardigans, picking one up and touching the small white buttons.

'That isn't going to fit her, Miss Natty,' Lucas said with a laugh, tugging at the string of the price tag.

'For her baby.'

'I don't mean to sound rude, Miss Natty, but do you think Glenn's baby looks like a monkey?'

Natty began to chuckle as she paid for the blue knitted cardigan and matching mittens.

As they walked home, happily laughing and chatting together, Natty saw a small advert in the theatre window. *JANITOR WANTED. NO QUALIFICATIONS NEEDED. APPLY WITHIN.*

# 46

Glenn cautiously leant over the small wooden crib so as not to wake him, admiring his beauty and flawless skin. Glenn had only been out of hospital a few days and she had finally been left alone with him, as Stanley felt happy to collect some groceries.

Looking at her watch, feeling the anticipation and excitement of seeing her family again, she knew she'd be with them all soon; it had been so long since she'd had time to really sit and chat. The hospital had only allowed her five minutes with each of them and as they had left the burning had set in again in her stomach, feeling alone and vulnerable with her newborn baby lying in a crib next to her. This day was different; they were all coming and they could spend as long as they liked with her.

'Hello, little man. What do I do with you now? Are you going to do something or simply sleep all day?' Glenn placed her hands on her hips. 'So are you telling me I went through all of that panic and getting fat so you could do nothing? And I didn't even finish cleaning the bath,' she said gently as she rubbed her hand softly on the crocheted blue-and-white blanket.

Stanley had managed to be there for her when she needed him most, calling the ambulance promptly. He had stayed by her side all the way to the hospital as she yelled incoherently at him, digging her nails into his shaking hands.

As she looked with sheer pride at her baby with masses of black hair lying on his side, his small closed pink hand just showing over the blankets, she knew it was worth it, every single terrifying and unpredictable minute.

Looking down at her floral dress, Glenn wrapped the shiny material around herself tightly to see her wobbly stomach. She knew she'd be back in her favourite flared jeans in no time at all and the thought of pulling the soft blue fabric onto her legs made her smile.

Finally hearing a knock at the door, Glenn checked her baby once more, placing her hand onto the blanket softly. 'Mummy won't be long; be back in a minute to watch you doing nothing.' She smiled with pride as she went to open the door.

'Hello, hi, everyone come in!' Glenn screeched with excitement, opening her arms to greet them all; her father, Ruth, Natty and Lucas all huddled together on her small doorstep, each one carrying gifts. Ruth held a huge bunch of flowers which covered nearly half of her body; Glenn scrunched her face as she knew she didn't have a vase big enough to carry so many colourful stems. After each of her visitors gave her a cuddle, apart from Ruth, who walked slowly past her into the kitchen, they all went straight into the living room, gathering around the crib to admire the new family member.

'Have you got a vase, Glenn?' Ruth shouted from the kitchen as she happily placed the flowers into the sink.

'Hi, Ruth, thank you. I have only a little one.' Glenn went to join her and opened the cupboard, taking the small brown vase in her hands. Ruth looked at it and then met her eyes. They both began to laugh.

'I said to Dad you didn't deserve so many. Maybe we should have got you a plant; you know, old people like plants, don't they?' Ruth took the vase from Glenn, who raised her eyebrows, not looking too impressed with her joke.

'Very funny, Ruth. Oh, my, how lovely to see you.' Glenn finally smiled, pulling Ruth forward by her neck and giving her the big cuddle which she had missed out on earlier at the door.

'Glenn, you're strangling me.'

'Just getting you back.' Glenn finally let Ruth go and laughed as she watched her flattening her hair at the top.

'Glenn, what the hell is that on the stove?'

'Nappies, Ruth.'

'Nappies? Why are they on the stove?'

'Going to boil them later.' Glenn pulled the large aluminium pot forward a little and began moving the nappies around, pushing them further into the cold water with her finger.

Ruth looked over Glenn's shoulder and laughed. 'Oh, my. I've seen bad cooking skills, Glenn . . .'

'It's the way you get the nappies clean; it's something to do with the towelling.'

'Oh, boiling little poo stains out, eh, Glenn? Who'd have thought?'

'Thanks for doing the flowers, Ruth.' Glenn tapped Ruth on the head and left her in the kitchen.

As Glenn walked back into the living room she felt a sense of life and energy she hadn't had for a very long time, seeing her family finally around her. All her family together; she wanted Stanley to hurry.

'Sorry, Glenn, simply not happening; too many flowers. You will have to do them.' Ruth walked past Glenn and tapped her on the head, laughing, heading straight for the crib. She stood next to Lucas, who was almost transfixed by the little bundle.

Lucas whispered to Ruth as she stood at his side. 'Can you see what I mean, Ruth?'

'Actually, yes, he does look a bit like a monkey,' Ruth whispered back, chuckling quietly under her breath.

'Hey, you two, what are you saying about my little Billy Bear?' Glenn stepped forward protectively.

'Billy Bear?' Ruth frowned, not understanding why her sister spoke as though her baby was stupid.

'Oh, let me hold him, Glenn.' Natty threw her bags down and hovered over the crib again, smiling.

'I'm not sure, Natty; they say if you pick them up it will throw their feeding times out,' Glenn said, gently rubbing her forehead with her hand in uncertainty.

'Glenn, he's yours; you can pick him up whenever you like.' Natty put her arms out near the sleeping baby.

'Oh, go on, then. I've been busting to for the last hour.' Glenn felt a little worried about him being picked up and hoped it wouldn't cause him to feel distress in any way.

'Glenn, he's beautiful. You had exactly the same hair when you were born.' Their father sat and admired his grandson being picked up by Natty.

'I can see your hair hasn't changed much, Glenn.' Ruth roared with laughter, slapping her hands on her brown tartan skirt. She could see by the way Glenn's short hair was sticking up she hadn't styled it that day. When she lived at home she wouldn't have left the bedroom until each hair was perfectly styled with nearly a whole bottle of hairspray.

'Glenn, he really is such a gorgeous thing, really he is. So what name have you decided on?' Natty paced up and down in pride as she gently rubbed his little soft pink cheeks with her finger, feeling immense happiness.

Their father decided to go and make a drink for everyone and thought of holding his new grandson a little later, allowing his daughters to do the things women do when they are all around a newborn.

He walked back from the kitchen and leant around the doorframe. 'Have you got a vase?'

'No, Dad, sorry, only that one.' Glenn smirked at Ruth, who followed their father back into the kitchen.

'Dad, this house is a bit brown, isn't it?' Ruth stuck her fingers in the water of the towelling nappies.

'A little, I think, but I am sure your sister will have it to her taste soon.' Her father hunted for the cups and pulled the tea cosy from the pot, looking at Ruth, grinning.

'Sooner than later, Dad, I hope.' Ruth smiled back at her father.

'Um, yes, Ruth. At least the baby has a woolly hat.' Her father began to laugh with Ruth, pulling the tea cosy onto his head as he began prancing around the kitchen.

'Lucas, would you like to hold him?' Natty looked at Lucas, who stood with his hands in the back pockets of his jeans next to the empty crib.

'May I, Glenn? May I hold your precious gift of life?' Lucas moved forward, shaking a little.

Glenn could hear Stanley opening the front door, the rattling of his keys helping her to relax more, knowing he was at last at home; she breathed heavily, happy, sensing the empty feeling had gone.

Stanley placed the shopping bags in the hall, walked in and kissed Glenn on the cheek, then greeted Natty with the same gesture. Natty rubbed her cheek as the wet from his lips remained

240

on her face, wondering what was wrong with a handshake like the one Lucas was lucky enough to receive.

Stanley walked into the kitchen to help and stepped back in shock as he saw Glenn's father jumping around the kitchen with his own mother's tea cosy on his head. 'Hello, Matthew.'

'Oh, hello, Stanley. Good show.' Matthew shook Stanley's hand with eagerness, leaning forward to cuddle him and patting him on the back.

'Dad, Dad,' Ruth called, trying to hold back her laughter.

'Yes, Ruth?'

Ruth moved her eyes up and down, concentrating on the top of his head.

'Oh, yes.' Her father slowly pulled the tea cosy from his head and smiled awkwardly as he placed it back onto the brown teapot. He felt an overwhelming happiness for the man who was taking care of his daughter better than he could have himself. He was extremely pleased they were getting married in a few months, knowing he'd be more than honoured to give his daughter's hand away in marriage as she stood by his side in her mother's wedding dress.

Lucas held out his arms, feeling apprehensive, looking at Glenn once more to make sure it really was OK. Feeling the warmth of her baby in his arms and knowing he was the little baby's protection, the immense feeling engulfed his body; a tear fell from his eye.

'Glenn, he is remarkable. You've allowed me to hold him in his first few weeks of life; thank you so much for such an amazing moment.' Lucas gazed at the perfection of the baby, the thought of him looking like a monkey suddenly disappearing.

'That's fine, Lucas, really.' Glenn sat on the sofa next to Natty, thinking how much she liked her sister's jeans. Looking at her own dress she rolled her eyes, promising herself she was going to stop eating Black Forest gateau after dinner for the next month.

'Humans are like pebbles on the beach, but if you look closely enough they are all completely different. You see, when you look from afar every one blends together; you cannot tell the difference. Just a mass of circular shapes. Get a little nearer, you can see the unique patterns and colours they have, some with rough edges and some without. I have this pebble in my arms and one day he will be amongst the mass of different stones, blending in like he isn't any different. But he will be the only one who is loved the way we love him, the only one who is protected how we'll protect him and truly accepted just for being born. I have in my arms the most perfect pebble on the beach of life.' Lucas began to sob, and the small bundle of perfection began to cry with him.

'Feeding time!' Glenn jumped from the sofa and gently took her baby from Lucas. 'Lucas, there are some tissues on the side.' She smiled reassuringly as she held her crying baby in her arms.

'Oh, thank you, Glenn.'

Sitting back on the sofa Glenn pulled down the front of her dress, gently pushing her nipple into her baby's mouth, his crying comforted.

As her baby brought nourishment and warmth to his hungry body, contentment absorbed him, hearing his mother's heartbeat and feeling the protection of her already tired body.

'Oh, please, Glenn, that's the last thing I ever thought I would see you doing, popping your breast out for us all to see.' Ruth covered her eyes in jest and everyone began laughing.

Their father walked in carrying tea on a wicker-edged tray, placing it on the glass coffee table.

'Glenn, I think I will go and have a look around your garden while you see to my grandson.' Trying not to make any eye contact with his daughter their father left swiftly, followed by Stanley. Lucas stood for only a moment before realising he was the only man in the room.

'OK, Dad. And they say men are the stronger species.' Glenn chuckled as she watched them all leave with embarrassment.

'Right, while you're sitting down for a bit, it's present time.' Natty pushed the small bag onto Glenn's lap.

'Could you do it for me, Natty? I seem to have my hands full.' Glenn huffed as she began to feel a little tired.

'Well, your breasts aren't going to be for long if he keeps sucking them to near draining point.' Ruth giggled. Glenn and Natty joined in; they hadn't been together for such a long time.

'That's really nice. I'm going to shrink it, though.' Glenn admired the blue knitted cardigan and matching mittens from Natty.

Natty smiled. 'If you shrink it, I will shrink your head.'

'It's so nice to have you here. I've missed you.' Glenn touched Natty's knee.

'Natty, did Glenn just say she actually missed us?' Ruth shuffled on her knees.

'Yeah, you know, like a really bad spot on your first date, or athlete's foot.' Glenn laughed but deep down felt how much she really had missed all the banter with her sisters and even the borrowing of her clothes.

'Oh, nice to see Glenn's no different now she's got a baby on her breast and she's living in a lot of brown and, of course, suffering a really bad case of no fashion sense whatsoever.'

'Ruth, shut your face. You're taking him after; you can wind him for me. I've read in so many books babies who suckle don't need to be winded, but you can never be too careful, and he really has drunk quickly; my nipple feels like a hot poker.'

Ruth became instantly quiet. The thought of holding a newborn seemed rather scary, but the vision of her sister's nipple being hot and red made her want to run into the garden with the blushing men.

'You OK, though, Glenn?' Natty gave a sincere smile to Glenn, hoping she wasn't pretending everything was all right.

'Yeah, I'm good; well, apart from feeling like I am sitting on a bed of drawing pins, and of course I feel so wonderfully attractive. I think so, Natty.' Glenn dropped her voice to a whisper, pointing out to the garden. 'I do feel a little needy with Stanley.'

'What she means is, Natty, a bit like you with Lucas.' Ruth smirked, feeling pins and needles building up in her feet from kneeling on the carpet for so long.

'Right, you take this little Billy Bear from me and all you have to do is put him over your shoulder and gently rub his back.'

'You have to be mad; as lovely as he is, Glenn, how can I do that?'

Glenn smirked. 'Take him, Ruth. You can do this.'

Ruth felt an immense sense of comfort as her baby nephew was placed gently onto her shoulder. Moving her arms underneath his small bottom so he lay completely comfortable, she began rubbing his back.

'Oh my God, he feels so beautiful. Oh my God, I think I have actually got him to go to sleep. Who needs to wear a flowery old lady's frock to do this, eh? He smells so yummy.' Ruth spoke with eagerness and excitement and continued smelling his neck and feeling the softness of his cheek with her lips.

'Keep going, Ruth, he really likes it.' Glenn held on to the small cardigan and mittens, her voice soft.

Glenn and Natty looked at each other, each knowing what the other was thinking. They both tried not to chuckle.

'Oh, he's adorable; I could eat him. What's that smell? Oh, he's sicked up a blob of your breast, Glenn, which has to be the worst nightmare, the inside of your breast on my shoulder.' Ruth closed her eyes in disbelief. They all began laughing together at Ruth's repeated requests for someone to wipe the small white oval stain from her shoulder.

'Is it OK to come in now?' Their father tapped on the dark wooden door with an envelope in his hand. 'Here you are, Glenn, a little something for my beautiful grandson; once you have chosen his name then all you have to do is fill it in, and the bank will take care of the rest. Good to have some savings for him now and then. I am sure your mother would have agreed; she always put rainy day money away.'

'I hope, Glenn, your baby has no rainy days, only sunny ones, so can we agree your father has been kind enough to give your beautiful son a savings account to put away for sunny days?' Lucas gazed at them all.

They all agreed and smiled at the wonderful idea. The conversation became steady and the day moved into the evening wonderfully, everyone embracing each other's company; they all ate and laughed, and Ruth spent most of the evening smelling the shoulder of her green flared-collar blouse.

As they left they all waved through the car window to Glenn and Stanley. Matthew honked his horn a couple of times as he drove away, feeling immense pride and a desperate wish Eve could have held her grandson, little George Matthew Jefferson.

# 47

Suzy lay on her sofa, her eyes closed, immersed in the soft background music from the radio. Her feet were sore and aching and she was glad to be home at last. She had kicked her white stilettos off at the front door as soon as she got in. Pulling the brown throw over her legs and grabbing a cushion, she had slumped onto her small three-seater sofa in relief, smiling to herself as her evening was going to plan. From when she had locked up the bookshop she had dreamt of running herself a hot bubble bath and lying in the hot scented water until the steam penetrated her pores, massaging soft moisturising cream into her whole body and huddling on the sofa wrapped in a soft blanket, ravaging a whole tub of strawberry ice cream.

Hearing the soft music vibrate around her small organised living room, Suzy's thoughts went onto the silent reader. She had been thinking about him most of the day, hoping he'd come back into the shop so she could hear more about his life. She found him fascinating and thought there was something almost admirable about feeling such love for another human being. This woman was no longer alive and he still carried the love he had for her from the first day they met.

Rubbing the back of her neck, Suzy felt distant from the man in her life, aware she was simply another one on his long list of conquests. A pang grew in her stomach as she knew he'd never hold such love and admiration for her, not like the silent reader had for another.

Suzy covered her body more with the throw, moving further down the sofa; as she wriggled down her black miniskirt ruffled under her bum slightly and her pink blouse pulled across her large chest. She felt comfortable as she began to savour the experience of her last meeting with the man she'd watch in the corner of her shop with interest. Her imagination ran away with her as her visions seemed real, the soft music helping her to relax as she became lost in her visualisation. He'd come into the bookshop walking handsomely and slowly to her, his body appearing strong and in control. Taking the books from her hands, throwing them onto the floor, he'd hold the sides of her face, placing his lips on hers. He'd move his hands away from her face, pushing them up the front of her blouse, feeling her firm breasts. Their kissing would become more intense, his tongue moving quicker and harder inside her mouth, their sexual desire for each other becoming too much for them as he ripped the front of her blouse open, pushing her hard up against the counter. Abruptly he'd push her skirt up around her waist, tearing at her knickers with his strong grasp. Turning her body around, pushing her body forward on the counter, her face slamming against the surface, her fingers gripping the edge as he'd thrust himself into her hard, pounding her body with pure dominance, his fingers pushing into her breasts as he filled her with his . . .

'Oh, for fuck's sake.' Suzy opened her eyes unhappily as she wanted to touch herself, feeling the wetness building between her legs, the throbbing and desire for her need to be fulfilled, but now the phone was ringing. Feeling downhearted and instantly bored at coming out of her thoughts, she threw the orange cushion at her small ginger cat who was happily curled up on the armchair opposite. Huffing and pulling her creased skirt down a little, Suzy went to the phone.

'Hello.' Suzy's tone was harsh as she snarled at the cat in frustration. Pushing her hair from her face, she waited for a response on the other end of the phone.

'Hi, Suzy, it's me.'

'Oh, hi, Harry.' Suzy knew at that very moment she'd not be getting in a hot bath alone; her plan was soon to be thwarted.

'Fancy coming over? I've missed you.'

Suzy gritted her teeth as she heard his gentle tone. 'Harry, I was kind of going to have a quiet night in tonight.'

'Well, we can have a quiet night together; you know, we don't have to do too much talking.'

'Yeah, I can imagine what you've missed.' Suzy looked at the ruffled throw on the floor and where she had just been lying. If he hadn't disturbed her, she'd have been on the verge of an orgasm.

'If you'd rather stay in alone than spend time with me—'

'No, it's not that. I love spending time with you, you know that, but not tonight.' Suzy shook her head, thinking all a girl wanted was to masturbate and eat a tub of ice cream alone once in a while.

'I think I understand. It's OK; I will just sit alone too. Really miss you, though. It'd have been nice to get something to eat and be together.'

'OK, OK, I will be over. Give us half an hour or so.' Suzy sighed as she placed the phone receiver down. Picking up another orange cushion, she hurled it at the cat, who scurried out to the hall.

Patting her shirt down and pinching her cheeks for a little colour, Suzy reluctantly pushed her stilettos back onto her sore feet. Slamming the front door behind her and feeling the cold breeze whirl around her body, she rushed to her car, her thoughts consumed with the silent reader named Matthew.

# 48

'Lucas, come on, you're going to be late.' Natty took a glance at the small watch pinned to her uniform as she leant on the bannisters, her voice raised.

Lucas heard her bellowing from the bottom of the stairs and in a panic crammed the blue plastic bag into the drawer. Sitting on Glenn's old flowery covers he sighed, placing his hand over his heart and feeling the pulse in his throat. He became warm in fear, clenching his hands, trying to hide his palms becoming sweaty. The adrenaline surged through him as he knew the bag wasn't safe hidden in the small wooden drawer; she'd find it, and it would all be over. Pushing himself from the bed he rushed to open the drawer, retrieving it again into the safety of his clammy hands. Hastily lifting the mattress Lucas placed the bag underneath, pushing it as far as he could, praying the contents of the bag wouldn't become damaged as the heavy mattress fell back onto it. Puffing out his cheeks, Lucas patted the covers down, keeping his hand on the soft cotton a little longer than necessary.

'He's starting today, then, Natty?' Matthew's head was lowered as he scoured over paperwork that had been due back in the office for the last week; he was forcing himself to sit at the table and finish it that morning. The distractions become more intense around him as Natty paced up and down the kitchen waiting impatiently for Lucas, who still hadn't come down the stairs. The idea of writing his own book sat dormant in the back of Matthew's mind, only coming to the forefront now and then. He pushed it away like the work he had piling up which he had reluctantly brought home. The writing for him was only a matter of time, like everything else in his life.

'Yes, Dad. I think I'm more nervous than he is. Oh, my, I have to be going to work soon; I wish he'd stop faffing about up there.' Natty felt hot, looking under her armpits, small sweat stains developing under her arms. She knew how unattractive she was going to feel all day.

'Yes, Natty, I can see that. I'd really appreciate it if you stood still while waiting.' Her father twiddled his blue pen between his fingers and smiled, shaking his head gently.

'He must know the job like the back of his hand; I mean, it took them three months to teach him. I can't see why; he's only got to do a bit of sweeping and clean smelly old dressing rooms. You know, Dad, how hard can it be to fix a few things?'

'Natty.' Her father raised his eyebrows at her harsh comment.

'I am only saying, Dad; I'm not being rude.'

'Now the other janitor has left he can do it the way he wants to, and you know Lucas; he'll manage it quite brilliantly.' Her father began to add the long row of numbers scribbled on the paperwork.

'I suppose you're right. I am really going to miss spending time with him searching for my locket. He really hasn't stopped looking, Dad. It's so kind, don't you think?' Natty's emotions were mixed; she was glad that Lucas would have something for himself finally, but the thought of not being with him as much caused a heavy sensation to build in her chest. As she touched her bare neck she knew her locket would never be found. Ruth only had to say where it was; she simply refused to remember. Now Lucas had better things to do. She wished she had never seen the vacancy in the window.

'Four thousand makes that ...' Matthew tried to count as he heard Natty speaking in the background. Having lost his count he placed his pen on the table and wiped his hands down the front of his black trousers in frustration. 'Are you saying you like him, Natty?' He smirked.

'Of course not! What, me liking Lucas? No way, Dad ...'

'Hello, Lucas; you look like you're ready for work.' Raising his voice, her father addressed the happy young man standing in the kitchen doorway wearing a pair of faded blue jeans and a casual blue chequered shirt, and of course his old faded leather shoes.

Pulling the cuffs around at his wrists, Lucas wished he hadn't

249

overheard Natty's comment. He had known she couldn't possibly like him in such a way. It was confirmation that the only way was for him to remain in her company as long as he could. Get her to finally see him. He was more than the tramp who had stood desolate and dirty in their hall in the pretty month of June only a year ago. If he spent enough time with her their feelings could be mutual.

'Do you think it is a little too smart?' Lucas's voice was a little unsettled as he attempted to bury the disappointment he felt in his stomach. He had to pretend he hadn't heard. She'd fall for him eventually, in the end.

Matthew and Natty looked at each other and laughed.

'Lucas, you look wonderfully ready, apart from the shoes.' Natty walked up to him, brushing his shoulder with her hand with a reassuring smile. A sense of dread beating at her as she was certain he had heard what she said. If only he knew how she felt. Natty wondered what she had to do to get him to notice her, to see her wanting him.

'Thank you, Natty. I am off, then. I feel I have the sweeping to a fine art now. It's so amazing being amongst the smells and colours. The atmosphere, Natty, it's simply breathtakingly full of depth. Do you know even when I am the only one there I feel like there is some sort of presence? The theatre is alive with energy every single second. It has its own voice, Natty; it has its own heartbeat.' Lucas stared intently into Natty's glistening light brown eyes as he shared his joy.

'I can imagine it does.' Natty watched his lips move and felt the longing to kiss them.

'It's about more than simply imagining it's real, Natty; it is. I wanted to say goodbye to Ruth before I left.'

'She's gone out, Dad, hasn't she?' Natty turned her attention onto her father, feeling jealous Lucas's thoughts had gone to Ruth.

'Yes, I caught her yet again cleaning out the biscuit tin before she went. I give her money for lunch, so I am not sure why she has to take food out with her, wherever it is that she goes.' Matthew worried for Ruth; he didn't want to question her about her whereabouts, feeling she was already feeling pressure at not attending school any more. He had finally made a decision she wasn't going back and she could sort herself out; she'd be leaving in a month anyway. It would be time for her to do something with her life, get a small job and begin her journey, entwine herself into the big world. He felt he should have taken her back to the second meeting for so-called angry children.

Glancing over at the morning's post he recognised the large brown envelope which was to make him aware of her absence, yet again asking him what he intended to do about it. He knew he'd open it later, throw it in the bin like he had the others. In his core he knew he was yet again showing a weakness in his actions, burying his head in the sand like he always did.

Pushing the small blue lid back onto the pen and placing it at the side of his paperwork, he rubbed his face up and down with his hands and sighed. He wanted to forget about his work and get back to the last few chapters of the war book he'd intently read. Then he could go back to the bookshop; he needed desperately to get lost again within the museum of words. A rush of energy suddenly surged through him as an unexpected thought came to him.

'Yeah, why not?' he said aloud to himself.

'Sorry, Dad?' Natty turned to him.

'Lucas, I will give you a lift.' With his voice raised with enthusiasm Matthew walked past them and grabbed his black jacket from the coat hook.

'Oh, thank you so much, Matthew; that is a very kind thing for you to do.'

Picking his car keys up hastily, Matthew opened the front door and made his way energetically to his car, walking with a bounce in his step. 'Lucas, are you coming?' he called.

'See you, then, Natty.'

'Bye, Lucas. Good luck.' Natty puckered her lips, yearning to move forward a little.

Lucas squeezed her nose and smiled. He could see her cheeks flushing as she stood in front of him. Making his way out of the kitchen, he began to chuckle.

'Ouch!' Natty stood alone in the kitchen feeling dumbfounded, rubbing her nose in disbelief.

# 49

Matthew eagerly paced up and down outside the door; as he passed it again and again he could see the fingerprints smudged on the darkened glass. He was sure some of the prints belonged to him and felt happy he had made his mark on the shop, as his Eve once had. He could almost imagine he could see the outline of her fingerprints overlapping his as he stared at the multitude of individual identities.

Tugging down the elasticated waistband of his black jacket, Matthew began brushing the fluff from the arms. He gently moved his fingers again and again through his soft dark hair, setting himself up with enough courage to do what he had come to do. Holding his breath and puffing out his cheeks he let out a long sigh. He knew there wasn't any harm in asking. She could always say no.

Firmly gripping the tarnished brass handle, Matthew slowly stepped inside. The smell of the old pages enthralled him each and every time.

Wilfred and Suzy were busy in the stockroom when they heard someone coming in the door. They both began glaring, hoping the other would want to go and serve.

Suzy gazed at Wilfred with a heart-meltingly sad expression.

'Oh, Suzy, you really are a dreary dream sometimes. I'll go and help, shall I?' Wilfred handed Suzy the books and walked swiftly to the counter, then quickly turned back, giggling as he hurried back into the stockroom.

'Suzy, sweetie, I think you should serve this customer.' Wilfred put on his glasses, which were hanging by a long chain around his neck.

'Oh, Wilfred, do I have to?' Suzy spoke in a soft voice, dropping her shoulders forward, hoping her puppy eyes would work the second time.

'Look, it's an absolute must; it's the wonderful man who sits at the window,' Wilfred whispered hastily, shaking his head.

'Oh, no, it's OK. You serve.' Suzy felt instantly embarrassed at seeing him again after her thoughts had run away with her. He'd somehow know he had been in her fantasy.

'Darling, he won't bite, unfortunately.' Wilfred raised his eyebrows and tightened his lips as he glared at her, thinking she must be crazy to avoid him; if he had the chance himself he'd have him in his one-bedroom flat in no time at all.

'OK, I will go.' Suzy held herself upright and brushed the front of her hair, and then quickly looked down at her white cotton polo neck and blue corduroys. She knew they would have to do.

Suzy stood behind the counter and watched the silent reader. He seemed lost in thought, looking through a small pile of books on the mahogany table. His head was down as he immersed himself with interest, one hand in his pocket as he gently flicked the pages open with the other.

'Hello, Matthew; it's nice to see you again.' Suzy felt awkward as she could feel herself blushing. She prayed he couldn't read her mind as he glanced at her gently and smiled.

Matthew closed the book as he suddenly noticed how pretty the young lady was, his thoughts confirming to him that she deserved such an invitation.

'Hello, Suzy. May I say you look very lovely today?' Matthew spoke gently, feeling relaxed and calm as he approached the counter.

'Thank you, Matthew, it's very kind of you to say.' Suzy could hear Wilfred giggling in the stockroom just behind her. She turned and glared at him, opening her eyes wide, her eyes bulging as she non-verbally warned him. He'd be getting a firm punch in his skinny arm when they were left alone in the shop again.

'Suzy, I haven't come to look for books today. I know you may find this a little forward of me, and perhaps it's not even my place to ask. I was wondering if you would like me to take you out to dinner. I know how much you have been waiting to be in wonderful

253

surroundings.' Matthew had never felt so relaxed in the presence of a woman, especially one he was asking out for dinner.

He suddenly became overwhelmed as his emotions of happiness and guilt began their internal battle. The image came to him of Eve's perfect soft smile as she'd walked up to him when the very same building was once a coffee bar, the day his life had started and finished all at the same time twenty-six years ago. Eve remained as strong in his heart and mind as she had been that very day. If only he had his chance again to ask his perfect Eve for dinner, to treat her only how she truly deserved.

Suzy stood in silence as she watched him asking her. She needn't have wonderful surroundings to be fulfilled; the shop counter was perfectly acceptable. Her thoughts rushed through her mind to her fantasy from the night before; her stomach began to churn with nerves.

'Matthew, it really sounds like a lovely idea.' Suzy spoke with a high-pitched voice, her nerves began to show.

'Oh, I see, Suzy. I take it it's a no, then?' Matthew felt downhearted and ridiculous at the same time.

'Well, no, not really. I mean I'd love to; I just feel my boyfriend wouldn't like it very much.'

'OK, Suzy, I completely understand. I thought it'd be nice for you. Bye, Suzy; your boyfriend is a very lucky man.' Matthew gently winked and turned away to leave.

As Suzy watched him leaving she felt annoyed at herself, knowing if she waited for Harry to take her, it would be never. What was she doing? It really was only dinner.

'Matthew, I think I will, actually. Yes, I'll take you up on your offer!'

'That's great, Suzy.' Matthew smiled.

'Thank God,' Wilfred said out loud in the stockroom.

'The only thing is I am not sure when I am free, but I will let you know, if that is all right? Or you could let me know and I will work around it.' Suzy spoke in eagerness.

'Suzy, that's perfect for me.' Matthew waved gently as he left the shop.

'Oh my God, Wilfred, he's taking me out for dinner,' Suzy said, keeping her attention on the doors.

'Well, my little sugar, I should hope so too. I would have simply died if you had refused. I wonder what he's offering for dessert.' Wilfred pushed his glasses further onto his face and chuckled.

Suzy rushed into the cluttered stockroom and punched Wilfred's arm as they giggled excitedly together.

'What all the laughter about in there?'

'Oh, shit.' Suzy held her breath as she punched Wilfred once more and left the stockroom again.

'Ouch!' Wilfred laughed.

'Hi, Harry.' Looking at the large glass window, relieved at not seeing the silent reader anywhere outside, Suzy leant forward over the counter to kiss Harry on his cheek.

'Hello. I enjoyed the other night, Suzy. I was hoping you would like to come over later.' Harry stood smiling in his dirty overalls, holding a small bag from the bakery.

'Um, OK, yes, that's OK, I will, yes, Harry. What have you got there?' Feeling in a flap, Suzy touched her face, hoping to take the attention away from her guilty expression.

'Oh, just lunch, ham and cucumber roll. Are you OK, Suzy? You seem a little flushed.'

'No, I am absolutely fine, just been a busy day.' As her nerves began to show, all she wished he'd do was leave the shop and take his lunch with him.

'Don't I get a kiss?'

'I just gave you one; don't want to spoil you until tonight.' Suzy leant across the counter again, kissing his stubbly face; she could smell petrol on his face, her thoughts instantly going back to her invitation to the restaurant.

'See you later, then. Did you fancy picking up some fish and chips on your way over?' Harry scrunched his face.

'Yes, that's OK, I will do that.' Suzy sighed with sheer relief as he finally left the shop.

'Suzy, my darling, I think you're going to get yourself into a little bit of trouble, you know, two fine men at your pleasure.'

'Shut your face, Wilfred.' Suzy felt agitated as she emptied the books from the boxes. *Bloody fish and chips,* she thought.

*

255

Matthew walked slowly around the shops as his thoughts were on his actions and the feelings emerging in his stomach: the adrenaline and excitement of doing such a brave spontaneous thing, sitting with the guilt for his perfect Eve. Shaking his head, he couldn't understand why he could contemplate doing such a thing to her.

'You have got to be kidding!' Matthew came to a sudden standstill outside the second-hand shop. An old typewriter had been displayed in the window, surrounded by old pots and pans. As he moved closer with his hands in his pockets he knew something had led him there. If he hadn't chosen to go to the bookshop in the first place then he never would have seen it.

'That is quite unbelievable,' Matthew said out loud to himself as he looked up at the clear blue sky, biting his bottom lip in anticipation, for even contemplating putting paper in the small white dusty machine and beginning to write was something he had never thought he'd ever have the capacity to do.

Matthew's thoughts were disturbed by the thud from a large cardboard box being placed next to his feet. The shop owner stood next to him for a moment, rubbing the dust from his hands.

'Do you like it, mate?' The untidy-looking man spoke with a husky voice.

'Um, yes, it looks like a good one.' Matthew took his hands from his pockets, folding his arms.

'It is, only got it in this morning. I don't think it will be there long, little beauty.' The shop owner pushed the heavy cardboard box with his foot.

'How much is it?'

'I was gonna stick a fiver on it. I think one of the letters is stuck. Only needs a warm-up.'

'OK, yes, I can do a fiver on that. I will take it.' Matthew felt excited for his cheap purchase.

'OK, mate, let's go and do the business. I know it has black ribbon but the red isn't that clear. It might need changing. Then again, it depends how much you're gonna use it.' The man walked away into the shop as he spoke, his voice becoming muffled.

Matthew followed the man into the cluttered shop. Old chairs and tables were stacked amongst old clocks and racks of musty-smelling clothes hung around each wall. Fake furs and sheepskin coats, elegant dresses: they had been hanging for some time, by the look of the dust that lay on the shoulders of the black leather jackets.

Matthew gazed to the back of the shop as he took his wallet from his back pocket. 'How much for that bike?'

'God, that old thing? Stick another fiver on your bill.'

Matthew knew how much Lucas would love it; he could make his own way to work and it'd certainly give him a sense of freedom.

As the man moved the bike forward Matthew could hear the wheels squeaking. The brown leather on the seat had been torn, showing the soft foam underneath.

'Just needs a warm-up, that's all.'

Matthew chuckled at the man's comment and happily placed a £10 note on the side.

'Anything else I can do you for, mate?'

'The only thing is I'm not sure how I am going to get the bike home.'

'Can get it delivered for you, not too much.'

'How much?' The mouldy aroma in the shop was starting to irritate the back of Matthew's throat as he reached for his wallet again.

'Make it a fiver.' The man smiled while tearing a small piece of cardboard and holding on to a pen.

'You don't happen to get jewellery in here, do you?' Matthew placed the £5 note on the side.

'No, mate, only those beads over there.'

Matthew could see a small basket of colourful beads and bangles, plastic and dusty.

'Not to worry; thanks for your help anyway.' Feeling sadness in his stomach, Matthew so wished Natty could be reunited with her necklace; he only wished Ruth could remember which shop she had pawned it in.

'Any time. Stick your address down and we'll get it to you later today.'

'Only the bike; I can take the typewriter.'

Matthew took in a long breath outside the shop as he relieved his throat of the dust, holding on to the small machine. Adrenaline rushed through him as he wanted to get home quickly and place it in the cupboard under the stairs before anyone questioned him.

Turning quickly, he bumped into an old lady.

'Oh, I'm so sorry. Hold on, let me get that for you. Are you all right?' Matthew picked up her umbrella and placed it gently back into her hand, desperately trying to hold on to his typewriter at the same time.

The old lady didn't say a word and continued on her way.

Shocked by her manner, Matthew frowned.

The night drew in; sitting alone at the kitchen table, Matthew's thoughts were on the small cupboard as hidden inside was his new beginning. Now it was in his home there was no reason for him not to attempt writing.

As he sat he could gently hear Lucas and Natty's voices coming from the dining room. Getting up from his seat, he decided to give the writing idea a little more time. Looking up at the ceiling, he knew Ruth was yet again alone upstairs and on the side was her untouched dinner.

A knock at the door disturbed his thoughts. Placing his cup into the sink, Matthew went to answer.

The soft evening air surrounded him as he opened the door and smiled.

'Lucas, you have a delivery!' Matthew raised his voice in excitement.

# 50

An unpleasant aroma from the greasy chips began to irritate her. Holding them carefully so as not to rip the white paper bag, Suzy waited for Harry to eventually answer the door. As she glanced up to the sky she could see it was going to rain, sighing in relief as she knew she had missed the oncoming downpour.

Tapping her foot and tightening her lips, the annoyance consumed her body still from when she had had the brief encounter with him at the bookshop. She was irritated with herself for even bothering to make the effort of grabbing dinner, having to hastily find the nearest parking space outside the shop before running in and standing at the back of the long queue. The thought of being downtrodden had gone through her mind as she kept her eyes on her car parked on double yellow lines. The image of Harry sitting with the large cod and chips on his head once she was finally served had made her chuckle, as the thought of chucking the hot food at him became more tempting. The invitation to dinner was something she had to hold on to, knowing it was the only thing which could keep her sane at that very moment. All wasn't lost; she had been noticed as a beautiful woman who deserved to be treated once in a while. Harry couldn't even be bothered to go to the chip shop with her.

At long last the door opened. Harry stood handsome with a green hand towel wrapped around his waist, his bare chest slightly wet.

'Hi, Suzy, will be with you in two seconds, jumping back in the shower.' Harry smiled and rushed away from Suzy, who still held on to the hot greasy bag.

'Oh, OK, Harry. Nice to see you too.' Suzy went in and closed the door, thinking how lovely it must be to have the time to wash after work, instead of standing in the chip shop for nearly thirty minutes.

'Stick mine in the oven, will you, to keep warm? There's some cash in my wallet,' Harry said with his back to Suzy as he hurried back into the steamy bathroom.

Throwing the slightly ripped bag on the work surface and huffing, Suzy knew exactly where she would like to put his chips. Blowing out her cheeks and pushing her hair behind her ears, she turned the oven on to the highest setting, placed Harry's bag on the rack inside and slammed the door.

Suzy got herself a plate and placed her lukewarm dinner in front of her. Banging the bottom of the glass sauce bottle, she watched the small remains splatter over her sausage in batter, then threw the remains of the salt in her hand over her left shoulder for luck. If she had any, it'd be the silent reader walking back out of the bathroom.

Sitting on the sofa with her dinner on her lap, Suzy leant forward to grab Harry's wallet. As she looked through the notes she caught sight of a blob of red sauce on her jumper.

'Oh, for heaven's sake.' She licked her finger and wiped at the small blob, then sucked her finger clean.

She wouldn't normally take the money. It was only fish and chips, but she felt he was being a little too cheeky, so he was damn well going to pay for his useless efforts.

'What the hell?' Suzy felt a pang in her stomach as amongst the notes a small picture had been hidden safe. Taking the picture out and holding it between her damp fingers, she could see a beautiful woman with long dark hair. The woman in the picture was so perfect and petite she almost didn't seem real. Her lips were a bright red and her brown eyes shone with happiness.

The brown cladding on the walls seemed to close in on Suzy, as her thoughts were mixed, not understanding or wanting to understand why her boyfriend singing in the shower had such a thing and, more to the point, who it was. Forgetting the money and placing the picture back amongst the notes, Suzy threw the wallet back on the messy table.

As she leant back onto the soft cushions she looked down to see the stain on her jumper from earlier. She felt scruffy and harassed and completely uncomfortable sitting in the living room alone, eating chips on a stranger's sofa, hearing the rain thrashing on the windows. Sighing, Suzy knew she was all ready to leave, do something simple like kick her shoes off in her hall and get into soft sheets. She wasn't going to ask him as, the mood she was in, the fish and chips would certainly go over his freshly cleaned head.

Her thoughts were disturbed by the sound of the oven door slamming.

Blowing the chip bag and his fingers, Harry sat down hard next to her, moving back and forward to get comfortable, his actions bringing more annoyance to Suzy as he made her body jolt.

'Hi, Suzy, I'm back. You have sauce on your top.' Placing an old newspaper on his lap Harry opened the hot paper bag, a clean towel wrapped around his waist, his chest bare and smelling wonderful.

As he opened the bag Harry frowned, not understanding why she had put the oven up so high; it surely was common sense not to do such a thing.

Attempting to wipe the stain from her jumper, Suzy couldn't look at him; she felt unhappy with his flippancy with her, and of course the photo was going through her mind with intensity. She suddenly didn't feel hungry as anger swirled around in her empty stomach. She sat picking up her chips and dropping them again despondently. She'd find them too difficult to swallow as the words to ask him who the pretty lady in the hidden picture was were also stuck in her throat.

'Aren't you eating, Suzy?' Harry asked with his mouth full.

'No, I've suddenly gone off my dinner,' Suzy said sternly, as she glanced at her content boyfriend, her boyfriend who kept such a picture safe on him every day when he was meant to be thinking of her. She knew she had to ask him; the pretty lady could even be a long-lost relative, and she'd then feel silly for overreacting.

Seeing him rolling his chips up in small pieces of fish skin and dipping them in the small amount of sauce on the paper, she knew it was going to be a waste of time. She'd be getting a very bad headache within the next ten minutes and she'd be leaving.

# 51

'What you doing?' Ruth spoke with an aggressive tone, hovering over Natty as she searched through the cupboards in the kitchen.

'Well, if it's not a crime, I'm looking for paper.' Natty pushed her hands through the cluttered drawers also. She was beginning to feel irritated with Ruth as she stood next to her; she could almost feel her breath on her neck.

'You can tell Lucas isn't here. You look a mess.' Ruth raised her eyebrows as she could smell an odour of sweat coming from her sister, who was wrapped in her pink dressing gown with her hair frizzy and messy.

'It's quite obvious Lucas isn't here. I'm not even dressed yet.' Natty shook her head, wiping the sweat from her forehead with her dressing-gown sleeve. 'Honestly, Ruth, what's got into you? Aren't you meant to be doing something with yourself, like maybe looking for a job? You have left school, you know.'

Ruth could feel anger welling up in her belly; she knew she was in the mood for an argument, and deliberately began to wind Natty up. 'Sorry I'm not as perfect as you; got it all so sorted, haven't you?'

'Ruth, get lost, will you?' Natty slammed the drawer shut. Feeling harassed and sweaty, she pushed past Ruth, bashing her shoulder with hers.

'I do things.' Ruth raised her voice, clenching her fist as she wanted to throw her sister a punch in the face at that very moment.

Natty turned around quickly.

'Like what, Ruth? What do you do around here but mope about, thinking the whole goddamn world owes you a living? It's not all about you. Our mum's also dead, Ruth, Dad's wife too. So get a grip!' Natty screamed at the top of her voice.

'Has nothing to do with our mother, Natty, just get sick of watching you make such a fool of yourself with Lucas.' The emotions in Ruth's stomach confirmed to her how very much she missed their mother and deep in her heart wished she could be walking down the stairs to see her standing in the kitchen, whatever mood she was going to be in that day. It'd mean she was still there with them all. The unpredictability of their mother somehow kept them alive, gave them a purpose for surviving each and every day. Everything in Ruth's life seemed all too predictable as she stood at the kitchen drawer, not knowing what to do with her new existence.

'Well, it certainly has nothing to do with Lucas, so butt out.' Natty held tightly on to the small pad she had found and began hastily walking up the stairs, her dressing-gown cord coming undone with her quick movements.

'I will put it away for you, Natty, don't worry about it. Maybe if you pushed the stuff in properly you wouldn't have to slam it like a stupid kid.' Ruth became even more fuelled with anger as she squashed the still-open drawer's contents down with her hand. She didn't know what to do with her anger; she could always rush into Natty's room and smash her face in. Each push of her shaking hand made more junk overflow around her hand.

As she managed to close the drawer properly, she saw what looked like a piece of white paper protruding from under the bread bin. Ruth frowned as she wondered what it could be; the temptation to be nosy got the better of her. Glancing up at the door of the kitchen to make sure her smelly sweaty sister wasn't in sight, Ruth placed her finger slowly on the paper's edge and pulled it out carefully from its hideaway.

Ruth held the white envelope in her hand, seeing the writing on the front in blue pen was scruffy and somehow rushed. As each word came into clear vision, Ruth blinked again and again to make sure she wasn't seeing things. She wanted to scream. The thought of smashing things around her came to mind. *How dare he?* she thought. Who did he think he was, doing such a thing to her?

The hidden envelope was for her and only her. *Miss Ruth Hopkins*, scribbled on the front, confirmed it again and again to her. She read it over and over. *Miss Ruth Hopkins, Miss Ruth Hopkins.*

'It belongs to me. Goddamn *me*. How dare he?' Ruth tightened her lips, gazing around the tidy kitchen, feeling the walls closing in on her. She felt suffocated with betrayal from them all. They all knew she had it; they all planned to keep it from her.

Taking a deep breath and pushing the envelope back under the wooden bread bin, Ruth rushed to the food cupboard to take a couple of packets of biscuits and a tin of mandarins. Shaking out a blue bag from under the sink, Ruth placed them inside; scrunching up the edge of the plastic, she placed them under her arm. She knew she had to speak about it before she did something she might not regret.

Natty jumped as the slamming of the front door shocked her. She sat perched on her bed with only her feet covered by her green blanket. Her sheets were ruffled under her body, which irritated her; not feeling up to making her bed that morning, she made do with how uncomfortable she was.

Pushing her untidy hair behind her shoulders and seeing her dirty uniform on her bedroom floor, she sighed to herself as she had so much to do. Not having written for such a long time, it was important for her to put her feelings down; the rest of the world could wait. Being alone in the house overwhelmed her with sheer relief.

*October 1976*

Dear Diary,

My sister drives me stir crazy, I want to squeeze her head!!! She is so selfish. I can't believe it's always about little Ruth. Little Ruth, who just so happens not to have had her goddamn dad, beats someone up, but no, that's OK, nicks my precious locket, but that's OK too, all OK when it comes to little Ruth. How dare she say I am gagging after Lucas? She is a real pain. That's what she is. I'd swap her with Glenn any day and that's saying something. I feel so angry; I was in quite a good mood until now.

Anyway I am not going to waste my precious time worrying about her when I've got time to finally write. I would like to first apologise for writing to you on this awful lined pad, but

I am waiting for another diary. Hopefully I will get bought one for my 22nd birthday this year. I doubt Glenn will be getting me anything, nothing unusual there. She is so wrapped up in little George and Stanley. She hasn't had time to look at herself in the mirror to see she looks like a forty-year-old. I mean she's only nineteen. Does Stanley know he's turning her into an old woman? She is happy though; I can't take that away from her. Would like to help her lose some of her weight though, and so wouldn't want to borrow her big old jeans now; how funny. Conscious Glenn is a fatty.

George is rather beautiful. He's seven months old already, only seems like yesterday when she had him. I must go to see them more; with work and spending time with Lucas my days seem to blend into one. Will go over soon, will take Lucas with me.

Oh my, Lucas, how he's changed. Love to watch him pedalling down the road in the morning on his little bike. He must sort that squeak out though. He always comes in smiling. I feel a little worried as he mentioned the other day to Dad about finally standing on his own two feet and getting a little place. I feel this home won't be the same without him if he goes. I hope he keeps in touch, and he doesn't get too wrapped up in the glorified dancers he spends most of his days with. Wish I never saw the advert now, then instead of lying on my bed writing I'd be with him, maybe looking for my locket. Funny, really: if it hadn't gone I may not have spent as much time as I did with him. I have to be grateful to Ruth for such mishaps. She's been good for one thing.

Each time he speaks and talks about all the wonders of the world it's as though it's the first time he has ever said anything. He is so in love with life, so in love with the beauty which surrounds him. Surrounds us all. He keeps telling me I'm too rushed to see things; have no idea what he means. Then again, if I had the time to notice the butterflies with pretty little wings and the glistening cobwebs in the morning dew then I would. I am hopeful one day I can see through the same lens as him, share his eyes. Mmmmmm, and his bed! Only joking, not. Ha ha!

Dad, what can I say about him? He works, reads and then reads a little bit more, and for some reason stares at the cupboard under the stairs a lot.

It'd be nice to get together for dinner with them all, maybe get Glenn and George round too. Stanley could come if he could get out of his armchair.

I wish Dad wouldn't think so much. If only he could see it was all going to be OK without Mother here. Be nice if he could begin to walk in the garden again without becoming tearful. Not sure if he's ready. It will only be two years in December; it's like nothing when you've spent so long loving and sacrificing. I know she was unwell and I seem to not be able to forgive myself for not being able to help her, but what can a busy head like me do?

I was unfair throwing Mother in Ruth's face; I think it was my pain I was giving her, even though she is really getting on my nerves. She is barely in and when she is she gets everyone going, or she is in her room doing who knows what, maybe planning how to be even more miserable. I just want her to leave the biscuits alone; tea isn't the same without a custard cream to dip.

Yet again I am going to miss Lucas pedalling down the road, whistling and smiling in some crazy way all at the same time. Hope he's up when I get in, would love to see him. Time is of the essence if he wants to stand on his own feet and all. I mean, have you heard of anything so crazy? There is plenty of room here, and I really don't care that I still haven't got Glenn's room; he's welcome to stay in it as long as he needs to.

Look at my uniform on the floor, grubby old thing. Can't believe I will have to hang it on the line to air for a bit. Since Lucas isn't here I feel I've kind of lost my zap in it all, can't be bothered to even begin getting ready. Dr McKenzie is quite tasty at work, but then again Lucas does it for me each and every day. He's like a breath of fresh air in my lungs each time I inhale. All I want to do is absorb his body with mine and engulf myself in his conversation. Oh dear, may need to explore my body in a minute if I keep this kind of chat up, simply haven't got time for such pleasures. Work calls. I am going to visit him one day at work though, surprise him. I hope he brings me some more of that chocolate cake, so yummy.

I've had enough of writing on this paper, so going to put hints out for a new diary. Still remember like yesterday how Mother wrapped my old one in foil. Each time I make my sandwiches I think of her.

Bye, see you soon, on better paper. xxxxxxxxxxxxxx

Ruth rushed to the forbidden other side of town; thoughts of the hidden envelope and her irritating sister filled her mind. She was gagging to smoke a roll-up with the only man in her life who truly understood her. He would mostly sit and nod and pass her a grubby cigarette with his dirty hands. She would rant away about all her family and everything that bothered her. He'd listen; he'd be present through each and every word. The smelly blanket which covered their legs had always been more comforting than her flowery bedding at home; it was all real. She didn't have to hide behind small luxuries; she could be herself.

Standing on the busy kerb she wished she hadn't left the envelope under the bread bin; she had every right to take it and let them all know she had found it, open it and read it out loud. Make them listen to every word it said. Ruth prayed when she got home again the letter would still be there.

'You've got to be kidding. What the hell?' Ruth pushed her arm harder onto the already broken biscuits, the small tin of fruit pushing into her armpit as she watched her only friend in the world being moved along by a policeman. The man in uniform began to throw his only belongings away from him, pushing him to move along with them.

Ruth felt like she wanted to be sick. She wondered how her friend had been seen by him; it was the only way he had lived, away from the world. Why was he being made into everyone else? Ruth's fantasy of escaping from the world as she sat with him was dwindling as quickly as her friend had been pulled away from the wall they always leant against. She knew she had to stop it happening; it couldn't be allowed. Why couldn't he be left alone?

Ruth waited for the speeding cars to pass before dashing across the road, her tears building up inside as she witnessed the destruction of someone's existence.

'Leave him alone, leave him!' Ruth shouted at the top of her voice as she approached her fretful friend and the man in the black uniform who towered over her.

She finally reached him. Picking up his bags for him and rubbing her friend's arm, she began to cry.

'How did you see him? You're not meant to; you're meant to leave him alone, allow him to be as he wants. What is the matter with you people?' Ruth became hysterical, her tears falling down her face; she felt heartbroken for her friend.

'Move on now, young lady; there isn't anything here which concerns you.' The policeman spoke in a deep authoritative voice.

'There is; there is a man who wants to be left alone to live how he wants, and for some reason he isn't allowed to,' Ruth shouted through her tears.

'Young lady, please leave; I have this matter in hand.'

'No, you don't have anything in hand; all you have is your false life. Maybe you need to go and live next to a wall and start feeling something.'

Ruth felt the touch of her friend's hand on her arm. As she gazed at him, looking into his glistening blue eyes, she knew he wanted her to stop fighting for him.

Ruth picked another small bag up and stepped back from the policeman.

'Look inside yourself after you've left work, won't you?' Ruth wanted to say one more thing to the uniformed predator, his dark blue jacket a mask to the world; he couldn't be cruel enough to do such a thing, surely.

She followed her downtrodden friend up the road. His shoulders were lowered and his head down. It was the first time she had sensed desperation in him.

The policeman turned away from them and began walking in the opposite direction.

'Hey, wait!' Ruth cried out desperately.

Ruth's friend stopped and looked at her, taking his belongings from her grasp.

'It has been the first time someone has ever fought for me; thank you. And thank you for the can opener.' His voice was soft and gentle; as he smiled he leant over and kissed Ruth on her wet cheek.

'You can't leave. You can come and live with us; we have tramps in. You know what I mean.' Ruth felt at that very moment someone else leaving her. There was desperation in her voice, which mirrored the turmoil in her stomach.

'I cannot live inside; I cannot live with the world as it is. I have to be free. You never know, dear child, we may meet upon a wall somewhere.' As he gave her a reassuring smile he handed her a small roll-up.

Ruth saw him abandoning her. The biscuits and fruit she had taken from the cupboard were still under her arm. Placing the roll-up in her grey jacket pocket, she looked up to the sky.

'Mother, why can't you let me have anything?'

Tears began to well up in her eyes again as she squeezed the tobacco from the roll-up into her pocket, feeling it fall into small pieces just like her life in the October breeze.

Ruth decided to go home and read the hidden letter. Her tears falling as she attempted to place one foot in front of the other, her body trembling as the adrenaline from earlier surged through her young body. As she passed a bin, she gently placed the bag of food inside, hoping another temporarily invisible man who wanted to be free could find it.

'What's your problem?' Ruth raised her eyebrows, almost snarling at the old lady tapping her umbrella on the side of the metal bin and glaring at Ruth in disapproval. The old lady walked away shaking her head, wearing a long cream woollen coat.

'People in this world are going mad; I will give them something to moan about.' Ruth pulled the bag out from the bin again, not understanding why, and she began to walk home.

# 52

'Hey, mop boy, be treacle and remember my bin tonight.' The elegant beautiful lady leant around the white doorframe of her dressing room, wearing fishnet tights and a black sequinned leotard. Smiling, she went back in and closed the door.

'Of course I can; the pleasure is all mine.' Lucas wiped his hands on a cloth which hung from his leather belt and grinned, enthralled with the beauty and skill of the young lady who he'd watched intently from the side of the stage earlier: the way she floated around the stage, her feet barely touching its surface. After each performance came to an end he'd close his eyes, allowing the vibrations of the frantic cheering to pump through his body, blending every cell into his own fantasy. The gratitude from the audience made him happy; they recognised the sheer heavenliness. He needn't have tried to make them see; it was in them all for the rest of their lives, part of their souls witnessing such a spectacular moment.

He pushed the mop bucket with the handle; the force of the metal dirty-water container scraped along its small wheels. The sound of the squeaking reminded him of his gift from Matthew, making his smile brighter. Taking the mop from the water, Lucas listened to the slopping sound of the soft cotton fibres on the brown-tiled corridor. He loved putting water on the old tiles, making them shine like stones in a stream. They'd glisten almost instantly with the touch of the water, and once they dried to a dull orange again he'd happily begin cleaning the whole corridor in eagerness to see them shine all over again.

As he hummed to himself Lucas looked up to see the young lady leaving her dressing room. She was extremely attractive, fully dressed in a simple pair of flared jeans and a long-collared lemon blouse. He couldn't help but feel she blended in with all of the other people in the busy streets; he knew deep down she wasn't the same as she had magic feet. Just as he once did.

Lucas finished his evening shift to his sadness as he loved to be amongst the stimulating surroundings: the smells, the noise and of course the pretty young ladies rushing back and forth past him most of the evening. Beginning to sing and tapping his feet, he made his way to his small locker. Taking his blue jacket and red scarf from the hook, he took joy in moving his feet up and down, sliding them back and forward on newly cleaned tiles. He was excited to get home with the piece of chocolate cake he had wrapped in a serviette, knowing how much Natty loved it, and hoped one day he could take them all home a piece.

Making his way out of the back exit he breathed in the evening air. The chilly air on his face felt refreshing as he had been hot all evening in the theatre. Twirling around and around on the spot and moving his body with ease around the small back yard, he gazed at the stormy sky; the stars danced with him as he looked deep into the darkness. His pores absorbed the moisture in the air as he glided back and forth, the small light on the wall shining upon him; he was in the spotlight for the very first time in his life.

Giggling to himself, he stopped and gently pulled his scarf back around his neck. Alone under the soft light, breathing hard, he wondered if the coming month of December they would all be gifted with snow. He wanted to make Natty the biggest snowman she had ever seen, place flowers for button holes, crystals for eyes and a beautiful cherry for its nose. His unexpected thought of a snowman made him chuckle.

His thoughts came to a sudden halt and a feeling of despair consumed him as he checked again and again for his bike, behind the heap of black bin bags he had only piled around it earlier. Throwing each bag into the middle of the cobbled yard, he stood breathing hard, gripping his brown curly hair, confused and scared. His body shaking, uncertainty about how he was going to tell Matthew he had lost his very kind gift consumed him.

All of a sudden Lucas felt a soft tap on his shoulder.

'Boo!'

Lucas turned quickly, feeling anxious and out of breath from the adrenaline pumping through him.

271

'Miss Natty, you made me jump. Oh, what a wonderful surprise. I've had such a terrible situation approach me this evening. I also have a piece of cake for you here. I was very much looking forward to seeing you.' Lucas pulled the soft sponge from his pocket with his shaking hand, his belly churning still from the misfortune of his bike. Shrugging his shoulders, he smiled cheekily as with his dance he had squashed the cake into the serviette.

'Thanks, Lucas, looks very appetising.' Natty began to laugh as she held in her hand a small wet block of chocolate goo.

'It's still going to taste magnificent, all those sugars squashed together. You must be careful pulling the paper from it. You can't lose those small chocolate sprinkles; they're a must.' Lucas's nerves were hidden from her by his wonderful smile and deep-bellied laughter.

'You dance, Lucas? I've never seen anything like it before; you're amazing.' Natty felt enthralled with his hidden talent as she stood behind the wall, experiencing him in his own world. She knew the banging from his bedroom was him doing such things; she had been right all along.

'Simply moving about and being silly, Miss Natty. Thank you for saying; it was kind of you to compliment me so.'

'Lucas, you're brill. You must dance more.' Natty spoke enthusiastically, her voice filled with excitement.

'Miss Natty, please, I must tell you something before we speak of such crazy ideas for me. I can't seem to find my bike. I believe someone who is less fortunate than I may have taken it. They must need it more than me, so I suppose it's OK. They only had to ask and of course I would have given it to them, as beautiful a gift as it was.'

'Oh, Lucas, that's terrible, and it was such a lovely gift.'

'I know, Miss Natty. How shall I tell your father?' Lucas looked down at his feet with shame.

'Lucas, don't look so serious. I have it; I was only playing a joke on you. It's behind the wall. You are a silly thing sometimes.' Natty shook her head as she chuckled nervously; seeing Lucas so upset wasn't something she had planned.

'You have it? Do you need it, Miss Natty?'

'No, Lucas, it was a joke.'

Natty could see the relief on his face as the sparkle came back in his large brown eyes.

'I seem to have trouble understanding what is so funny about me placing my bike in its usual place and then having it be taken for no reason. I am not sure if that is a feeling I would ever like to have again, Miss Natty. I do hope that you don't repeat such a thing.'

'Lucas, I won't, promise. We have established the unfunny whereabouts of your bike now, so I was wondering if you would like to join me for something to eat? My treat.' Natty spoke softly as she looked at him with affection.

'Miss Natty, I would be very happy to join you. Wasn't your father making dinner this evening?'

'Not tonight, Lucas; he came home with another bag of books and went straight to his bedroom, so I feel we will all be fending for ourselves this evening.'

'What about Ruth? Isn't she going to join us?' Lucas felt confused as he worried for her.

'Burger and chips OK?' Pretending she hadn't heard, Natty began walking to the lost bike.

'Burger and chips sounds glorious. The thing is, Miss Natty, I can't seem to understand round food. I mean, how can it end up so, Miss Natty?'

Natty stood next to his bike, watching him chatting on to himself, shaking her head. All she hoped he would do was stop speaking and kiss her.

'Lucas, come on.' Natty knew he wouldn't stop until they reached the small café bar in the evening market.

Lucas dashed to get his bike in relief and walked along the road, pushing it with one hand. As he continuously spoke, all Natty could hear was the intermittent squeaks from its wheels.

The late-night market was bustling; the smells of various foods filled the air.

'Oh, Miss Natty, how glorious, absolutely breathtaking. This is such a wonderful surprise. Look how people carry about their business.' Lucas held firmly on to the handlebars of his bike and admired the busy market.

273

Natty hadn't heard him as she walked off hastily in front to sit at the pretty table.

A small candle was lit in the middle of the two-seated space with a red-and-white chequered tablecloth, and a small artificial flower. With the small lights hanging around the edge of the canopy it seemed the ideal place; it was a setting which seemed almost romantic in an unassuming kind of way.

'This will do perfectly, Lucas.' Natty looked around to see she was speaking to herself as she placed her soft leather bag on the wicker chair. Rushing forward quickly, she saw Lucas alone with his bike; his attention seemed to be on everything other than her.

'Lucas!' She raised her voice to get his attention.

Natty sat down alone and waited for him to join her; she was aware he was on his way by the sound of his wheels.

'Miss Natty, this table is wonderful. How quaint, I must say.' Lucas propped his bike at the edge of the canopy, pausing to take another lingering look around him.

'Yes, Lucas, it's not bad if you sit at it either; you'll get the real effect then,' Natty huffed, rolling her eyes, as she felt embarrassed to sit at the table alone any longer.

'Miss Natty, I'm putting my bike over here, in view. I'm not sure if I could cope with another fright.'

Lucas finally sat opposite Natty at the small table. He began gazing around again, squinting intermittently at the small bulbs above his head.

'Lucas, what are you doing?' Natty asked impatiently, her hands on her chin.

'Miss Natty, this is rather brilliant; you must try it. Squint your eyes, Miss Natty, and watch the lights stretch across the sky.'

'Lucas, you can stop doing that now.'

'Miss Natty, it's spectacular.' Lucas stopped squinting, to Natty's relief.

'Yes it is, Lucas; you do look much better not doing that with your eyes.'

'Do you think when you gaze around that people are happy, Miss Natty? I mean truly and sincerely happy. Under all of their fashion and bright red lips. I mean your lipstick does look rather wonderful; pink is your colour. Look deeper, Miss Natty, at them

274

all; look into their eyes and see if they really need such coverings of themselves.'

Natty listened to him and wondered if they were ever to get around to ordering food. She gently took the menu from the waitress and smiled.

'Right, Lucas, what are you having? Nothing round, I assume.' Natty peered over her menu at him.

'Or green or mushy; other than that, Miss Natty, I am easy.'

'I wish,' Natty mumbled under her breath.

'Sorry, did you say something?'

'No, Lucas. Then again, "easy" isn't a word which comes to mind when all I want to do is eat something. The waitress is really miserable.'

'We are not to judge what goes on in someone's life, or how they hold themselves up to the world. We mere mortals are not to know, when she takes her small white apron off and hangs it up at the end of the day, where her little white shoes will walk. Allow her to show what she needs to. I'm sure she isn't going to remember you in the morning.' Speaking softly, Lucas touched the tips of Natty's fingers.

'Thank you so much, Lucas.' Natty knew Lucas did have a point. She stared at his hands near hers and wished he'd place his hand on hers completely.

The pretty young waitress with two long brown plaits in her hair returned holding a small pad and pen. Her eyes seemed sad, her shoulders hunched as she stood next to them.

'Can I have a burger with relish and chips, please, and a piece of Black Forest gateau for pudding? I might go for lemonade. Yes, I will; lemonade it is.' Natty placed the menu at the side of her plate.

'Hello, I hope you are well. If I could ask you to be so kind, can I please have a burger roll without the burger, two helpings of chips and lots of sauce? And an ice water will be great. Thank you. May I say you have a very pretty smile?' Lucas held eye contact with the waitress the whole time. Watching her smile as she walked away gave him a sense of satisfaction, happy he had managed to witness her real expression of happiness.

Natty felt a slight jealousy churning in her rumbling stomach at the attempts of the man she shared her table with to help the pretty stranger feel better. His heroic over-politeness also bothered her. She couldn't understand why he was trying to make her look as though she didn't care about other people's feelings. Determined not to show her irritation building, she inhaled a deep breath and placed her red paper serviette on her black corduroy jeans.

Natty felt interested in Lucas's dancing and she definitely wanted to find out more. 'Lucas, you dance; why didn't you say?' She leant forward slightly in eagerness, pushing her arm across the table a little further, hoping he'd touch her hand with his.

Lucas looked into Natty's eyes for a moment. He knew he could tell her anything; he'd tell her everything about himself and she'd still allow him to bring her chocolate cake. He was going to trust her with something about him so glorious and painful.

'Miss Natty with apple-smelling hair, I think you must have been imagining it. I moved my feet; anyone can do such a thing. Tap your feet now underneath this table; you can do exactly as I did.'

'I saw you dancing, Lucas; you were doing more than tapping your feet, and it was truly amazing to see.'

Lucas sighed slightly, hoping Natty would stop speaking in such a way. 'Miss Natty, it isn't amazing, only something I am unable to do any more.'

'You can do it; I saw you, and why wouldn't you with such a talent? Honestly, it was magical.'

Lucas held Natty's hand and began to open himself to her, to reveal something he'd kept hidden for many years.

'You see, Miss Natty, I was somehow born with dancing legs, magical feet. I attended clubs and won competitions in small school halls and such. I gave it up; I grew out of it.' Lucas shrugged his shoulders.

'Lucas!' Natty raised her eyebrows, aware he had more to tell.

Lucas gripped her hand firmly; she wasn't going to let him get away with it.

'OK, Miss Natty, you win. My mother and father wanted to punish me. They'd tell me I was different to the other children; they weren't possessed by the devil like I was. The devil; I mean, how absurd to feel such a way about your child. They'd beat my legs until they were too sore to even walk on, a way of taking away my

276

one and only gift. I caused them too much turmoil in the way I perceived life; they believed I was punishing them and trying to embarrass them, especially in front of their friends. They did it simply to hurt me, to prevent me speaking of all the wonders in the world. Some days, Miss Natty, I would hobble to the small dance hall and grit my teeth through each and every move, crying the whole way home as the pain became unbearable. I'd have another beating once I was home in case I spoke to them. How was I going to help them to punish me, to say I was wrong feeling like I did? They only had to love me, Miss Natty. They finally stopped me, Miss Natty; each time I moved my body in such exhilaration it'd remind me of seeing them above my body with faces full of hatred, their misunderstanding for my love for life and everything in it. So the way you saw me moving today was only my feet wanting to feel the rhythm of my heart, my old heart.' Lucas's voice was shaky as he moved his hand from Natty's and pinched her nose.

'Ouch!' Natty sat in shock from his words; she could see his tears welling in his eyes. Before she could respond to him two plates were slammed down in front of them.

Standing as though he hadn't had the painful words leave his mouth, Lucas smiled at the waitress. Natty was in shock at his manner as he began to speak to her again, the miserable pretty young lady with bright red lips.

'Please allow me to serve for you; you look as though you could do with a little sit-down. Please help yourself to my food. It smells delightful.'

'But, sir!'

Lucas held his hand out as he could see the young lady looking confused at his request. 'Your apron, my pretty young thing; I shall wrap it around my waist for a while and step into your shoes, take the heartache I sense you carry. Please, may I?'

Frowning and nearly smiling at the same time, the young lady slowly undid her apron; handing it over to Lucas, she began to giggle. Lucas pulled out his chair further for her to sit opposite his huge plate of chips and buttered roll.

Lucas happily wrapped the apron around his waist and rubbed his hands together.

Mingling around the tables, Lucas welcomed everyone, asking

them politely if they needed anything further and explaining that he would be more than happy to help.

Natty closed her eyes in dread as she waited for him to get in trouble, wanting to laugh at his self-made predicament; he had no clue where the kitchen was and no idea how to serve. Opening her eyes, praying the whole moment was soon to be over, Natty watched the young lady sitting opposite her; she was hysterically laughing, holding one of his chips. Natty felt her lips tightening in outrage, believing the young lady was being far too comfortable with his food. Natty certainly wasn't planning to buy her dinner and wanted Lucas back in his seat, holding her hand again and looking into her eyes. Instead she was hearing laughter from around the small restaurant as the customers embraced him, shaking his hand as he passed them one at a time.

'He's a pretty good catch,' the young lady said briefly to Natty, before putting her attention back onto Lucas.

'Yes, he is, isn't he?' Natty squinted, filled with even more anger. A sense of jealousy began to burn through her; she wasn't happy with the emotion and wished she had waited at home for her soggy piece of cake.

To her relief Lucas was back at their table.

'Hello, young ladies, and how may I help you two on this very fine evening?' Lucas giggled.

Natty quickly looked at him. 'Lucas, your chips are getting cold.'

'And so I can see. The service around here is simply impeccable; I'm sure I can order more?' Lucas's eyes were fixed on the young lady in his seat.

Still laughing, the young lady stood and held out her hand for her apron.

'I hope I helped you be in different shoes for even a moment, my dear.'

'Thank you, I haven't laughed for such a long time. It was very kind of you. Your girlfriend is so lucky.'

Lucas looked at Natty, who had half a burger bun in her mouth; he liked what he had heard. 'And thank you too for allowing me to do your wonderful job.'

The young lady walked away smiling and continued to take a lady's order; her children were laughing and chatting at the table.

Lucas sat and began to dip his chips into an extra-large pot of sauce.

'My chips are very nice. They're better cold.' Lucas laughed aloud.

Natty began to laugh with him, nearly spitting out her lemonade.

'Lucas, I'm sorry for such a thing happening to you. You cannot let it beat you. You must continue your dancing. Like you said, you were born to do it.' Natty wiped her mouth with the paper serviette, tearing a hole in the middle. Sighing, she screwed it up and pushed it under her plate.

'Miss Natty, I think we should be worrying how you're going to eat the huge piece of Black Forest gateau when it comes along.'

'You can help me.'

'Mushy: can't do it, remember? This one is all yours.'

Lucas looked across the tables as he could hear someone speaking rudely to the waitress. Lowering his head and slowly placing his napkin at the side of his plate, he swallowed hard.

'Now where are you going?' Natty placed her empty glass on the table and looked into the air. Feeling fed up with not being the centre of attention, she leant back and folded her arms, sulking.

'Excuse me, sir.' Lucas stood next to the young lady and smiled at her reassuringly.

The large man looked up in disgust. 'Yeah, what do you want? All I want to do is order my dinner.' His voice was rough and he needed a shave.

'Yes, sir, and as you can see, all this pretty young lady wishes to do is take your order. Which, of course, will be given to her with respect and courtesy. Please, it is unnecessary to take advantage of people much younger than yourself.'

'Look, mate, I don't know what you're going on about. So bugger off.' The man's voice became deeper and more aggressive.

'I think you need to be clear in your actions. You will carry them always.'

Lucas could see the man becoming angry.

The man stood, pushing himself toward Lucas slightly.

'Oh, you're rather tall, aren't you?' Lucas swallowed hard, seeing the size of the muscly stocky man who towered over him. He composed himself, feeling a little shaky as he stood smaller than the stranger in his soft chequered shirt and cream work trousers and, of course, his broken black leather shoes. 'Sir, please let me explain before you throw a punch. You may miss my head; as you can see, I am very much smaller than you. It's clearly and simply like this: if someone offers you a bag of sweets, it doesn't mean you can plunge your big fingers into the bottom and take the whole lot.' Lucas felt in control and calm.

'Look, mate, you're crazy. Get lost.'

Lucas felt the man's body moving closer to his.

'Sir, this pretty young lady had no choice in serving you; she didn't ask to come to your table and be spoken to in such a way. Does she have to be abused? She is, of course, being kind enough to take your order. And by the size of you I can imagine you're having all that's on the menu. So what I mean is don't take advantage of kind gestures which are put in your way.' Lucas glanced over to Natty; he could see she had covered her face with her hand.

'Listen, mate, it's her crap job, not mine.'

'It's her belief she takes home about herself each night after having to be amongst the world. Each night counts. If people are taking all of her sweets, then what does she have left when she gets home? Only an empty crumpled bag, nothing left inside.'

The grumpy man stared at the young lady; her head was down as she focused on the lights' reflection on the grey cobbles.

Sighing, the man took his attention back onto Lucas for a moment and then back to the young lady, realising he had behaved inappropriately.

'Yeah, mate, I can kind of see your point. I'm sorry to take advantage of you, miss.'

The young lady smiled again at Lucas.

The man shook Lucas's hand and then the young lady's. Sitting back in his seat, he continued to give his order graciously and respectfully to her.

Natty's embarrassment and anxiety at Lucas's actions consumed her. Taking her hands from her face, she sat with her arms folded and wondered why they were there. He may as well have taken the waitress's phone number. He had spent most of the evening with her.

'What made you do something so crazy, Lucas? Look at the size of him!'

'Miss Natty, size is an illusion. People live like umbrellas, no choice; they choose to have no choice in how they behave and treat people. You see that umbrella at the side of the empty table? It's been simply forgotten, laid down on the cold damp stones, pushed away from sight by a boot or a black stiletto heel. Not needed until it suits.' Lucas held a chip in his sauce as he spoke. 'The umbrella may not want to get wet each time the miraculous rain falls from the sky, but it doesn't have a choice. Just pushed around and expected to get soaked. We humans have choice each day we wake to greet the sky, and we choose to be cruel and rude and selfish and judge. The very large man has chosen to be rude with his food this evening and there is nothing anyone can do about it. Choice, choice, Miss Natty, like you choosing to put your hair in a pretty clip this evening.' Lucas smiled cheekily.

'You do like to chat, don't you, Lucas?' Natty giggled at him, shaking her head. He had never had an off button; she was sure he'd go on talking forever. 'I kind of see your point; it is what umbrellas are made for. Like this large slice of cake which has been made for me to devour.' Natty smiled as she could see the waitress bringing over a larger-than-normal serving of pudding. All down to Lucas, of course.

'Because someone says that's how it is.'

'Here you go again, Lucas; you're not making sense.'

Lucas began to laugh with a mouth full of chips; a blob of sauce sat on the side of his lips.

'Oh well, Lucas, whatever you're talking about, look at the size of this cake.' Natty picked up her fork and began to move the cherries around on the top of the creamy chocolate-sprinkled slice.

They both began to laugh.

Placing a piece of cake in her mouth, Natty closed her eyes and savoured the soft flavours rolling around her tongue.

Lucas watched her in admiration at her pleasure. She was the prettiest and funniest thing. He felt an excitement and contentment at being in her company as he always did.

As Natty opened her eyes she sensed he'd been staring at her for a while. She cleaned the chocolate and cream from her teeth with her tongue before she continued to speak.

'Lucas, please consider dancing. And I promise, Brownie's honour, I will never mention it to you again.' Natty frowned, confused as to why Lucas was waving his finger across his mouth.

As Natty spoke Lucas chuckled, as the skin of a cherry had stuck to her front tooth. Feeling cheeky, he decided against letting Natty know of her leftover food and slowly placed his hand back on the edge of the table. Trying not to laugh, Lucas went back to finishing his cold chips.

Lucas wiped the sauce from his mouth and looked up to the sky. His thoughts returned to the small blue bag under his mattress. A heaviness and dread began to build in him. It was something he tried to push away when he saw her. He'd hurt her feelings, pretty Miss Natty who sat opposite him scraping around the edge of the bowl with old fruit skin on her tooth, taking the last helping of cream residue with her spoon. She was happy until he came along. If only he'd stayed in the shop doorway and then he wouldn't have to see her cry.

# 53

Wilfred sat on the small chair at the glass window of the bookshop with his legs crossed. Moving his leg up and down, happily showing off his white leather slip-on shoes and his pink socks. Mocking the silent reader named Matthew. Suzy glanced at him as she labelled books at the counter, giggling a little and shaking her head at his actions. Wilfred was pretending to flirt, holding three books on his lap at the same time.

'Oh, hello, you gorgeous woman, I am going to take you out to dinner. It's a thing I do, you see; I am such a hunk and I like to see if I get the attention, then I let them guess when it will be, which means *never*!' Wilfred giggled.

'You're not at all funny, Wilfred; he will remember, but I believe it was me who said I will let him know.' Suzy stopped and leant across the books on the counter, feeling a little let down; she had been looking forward to going out to eat with Matthew, to being spoilt by a man finally. She had even contemplated asking Wilfred if he'd mind being masculine for a day, then he could take her. Pulling the neck of her pink fluffy jumper, she wished she hadn't put it on, as she began to feel hot and harassed.

'I've so much money, you see, so I bring the books I've bought back so I can see you more and show you what you're missing.' Wilfred pushed his glasses down and closed the books balancing on his lap. Placing them back on the small table next to him, he began to speak in a serious tone. 'My little peachy Suzy, you can simply ask him, you know. I can see each time he comes in you get your little frillies in a twist. It's obvious enough even for me to know.'

'I'm not getting my frillies in a twist, Wilfred; I'm cool about the whole thing. It doesn't matter, does it? And I'm with Harry anyway.'

'Yes, but is Harry with you? Suzy, darling, it's been six months now. Really, you must stop looking like a little mushy puppy every time he comes into the shop.' Wilfred dusted his white slacks down and pushed himself from the chair.

'You're the one who looks like a mushy puppy panting around him, Wilfred.' Suzy slammed one pile of books on top of another.

'Oh, I simply give up with men; I can't seem to cope with the whole thing. I take them back to mine to wine and dine them on all sorts of expensive things, and, hey presto, I never get a call the next day. I wonder if I'm meant to only have sex with them. I do like to take, you know, for them to give me pleasure as much as allowing them to take complete control of my anal passage.'

'OK, a little too much detail there.'

'Sorry, dear, almost forgot you were in the room.' Wilfred sighed with delight and patted the sides of his heavily sprayed blond hair.

'Not good to hear such things, thank you.' Suzy thought about what Wilfred had said; was Harry really with her? Each time they went out for a drink, she'd watch him looking into his wallet which held the image of another, someone she needed to ask him about sooner rather than later before she completely dissolved.

'Well, Suzy, my glorious and messy sex antics aside, the next time he comes into the shop you make—'

All of a sudden the rattling from the door caught their attention. Smiling in his black coat stood Matthew, returning a bag of books, the handle stretched around his arm, bringing them back in eagerness to see Suzy once again.

'Hello, Suzy, how are you today? Your jumper is very pretty. Hello.' Acknowledging them both, Matthew sensed he had interrupted them.

Shunning Matthew, Wilfred turned his nose up and stormed off, wiggling his bottom, his skintight slacks showing the outline of his underpants.

'Is he OK, Suzy?'

'Um, yes. Really sorry, Matthew; he has to put the Christmas decorations up in the shop and he really doesn't like doing anything too manual.' Suzy began to blush, her sweating becoming more intense.

Matthew began to undo his coat, feeling hot instantly; the

heating in the shop seemed unusually high. 'I don't mind giving him a hand.' He flapped the front of his coat open and placed the bag of books down, leaning it against a bookshelf.

'We couldn't expect you to do such a thing; you're a customer. I'm sure he will get over his little stress session.' As Matthew leant over to set the books down in front of her, she smelt his soft musky aftershave. Being around him and his scent aroused her once again.

Laughing together, they held eye contact for a moment.

'Oh, please don't mind me. I can hear you two flowers speaking about me; I can hear you. Honestly, your sort, playing these silly games. Please, man, take her out to dinner; she is desperate!'

Suzy felt dumbfounded; the embarrassment engulfed her already hot body. She held on to the Sellotape with her mouth wide open.

'I'm really sorry about that. Wilfred, so uncalled for.' She squinted at him. He was going to get a punch in both his skinny arms, harder than ever before.

'You asked her six months ago; now what's a girl to do? Left to me, darling, I'd have you slapped into shape.' Wilfred waved his finger in the air.

'Oh, Suzy, it hasn't been so long, has it? I'm really sorry. I keep meaning to make a date; I've been so busy with everything.' Matthew was more than aware he'd had the time to take her. Since he had asked, the guilt had built inside him for his Eve. As much as he wanted to take Suzy out, the longing to keep Eve in his heart was greater. The fear of forgetting about her for even a moment was too much for him.

'It's not uncalled for to be annoyed, Suzy.' Wilfred placed his hands on his hips in an authoritative pose and looked harshly over his glasses.

'Suzy, your colleague is right.'

'Wilfred is my name, darling.'

'Sorry, Wilfred is right. Is that really your name?' Matthew began to laugh as he heard Suzy become hysterical at his question.

Wilfred huffed and raised his head in disgust. 'I feel I will be far better suited finding the Christmas balls; it looks like between you two, it's the only chance of anyone getting them in their hands around here.'

After absorbing what Wilfred had said, Matthew and Suzy gazed at each other and burst into laughter.

Suzy held her stomach and attempted to speak. 'Sorry once again.'

Matthew breathed in and out a couple of times and spoke intermittently through his chuckles.

'Suzy, please forgive me for treating you so dismissively. As soon as Christmas is over I shall take you wherever you like; if you'd still like to join me, that is? I'll understand if you have changed your mind.'

He realised as he spoke that the typewriter was also something which he'd denied himself. Still hidden under the stairs as though life after Eve didn't really exist. Her heart had stopped beating, not his. He wanted to breathe for her, smile for her and watch their daughters for her.

Wilfred's voice echoed from the back of the stockroom. 'Help is such a wonderful thing; it'd be nice, darlings.'

Matthew took his coat off quickly and threw it on the small chair he'd always sit in. 'I'll help him if he doesn't grab mine.' Matthew laughed before making his way into the stockroom at the back of the shop.

Suzy began to laugh again, smelling him as he passed her. Smiling, she felt happy and filled with relief; the anticipation for her dinner was finally over. It had been the only thing which had kept her sane, with Harry's wallet problem and all. It felt right, Matthew being in the shop: comforting and safe in some inexplicable way.

Her chuckles were still coming as she went to the shelves and placed the newly numbered books back. Grabbing his balls sounded like a good idea to her as she heard them laughing from the stockroom. Harry hadn't made her feel like this in a very long time, her belly full of adrenaline and fantasy, and all Matthew was doing was helping Wilfred decorate the shop in green and red baubles, green holly leaves and a few candy sticks here and there.

'Hi, Suzy. Come and give us a kiss.'

'Oh, God, Harry, you made me jump. What are you doing here?' Suzy looked instantly at the stockroom entrance, her body numb, praying they wouldn't come out. She knew the decorations were stored deep in the back behind the books. Closing her eyes quickly in dread, she paused to retain her composure.

'Fancy shopping, get some Christmas bits?' Harry moved closer to kiss her on the cheek, his overalls tied around his waist by the sleeves. His black T-shirt seemed grubby too.

'Um, Harry, I'm a little busy, have to decorate the shop and everything.'

'You can get fancy Nancy to do it.' Placing his hands on her hips, Harry moved a little closer. 'Well, if you can't shop with me, how about we see each other later? Let me have those lovely red lips of yours.'

Suzy pushed her mouth onto his, her stomach filled with dread, waiting to be caught by Matthew. It was ludicrous.

'Where is Nancy anyway? Extra quiet in here. Do you wanna?' Harry wiggled his eyebrows.

'Have no idea, and his name is Wilfred.' Suzy moved him off gently and pushed out a false chuckle; behind it all she was charged with nerves.

'I haven't got lots to get anyway, only yours.' Harry kissed her ear, hoping to tempt her to touch him.

'So you're not going to need me, then.' Suzy pushed him off again, blowing on the front of her fringe. She desperately needed the moment to be over, for him to leave the shop.

Putting his arms up into the air, Harry finally got the message from her body language. 'I suppose you're right.' He leant over and kissed her again on the cheek. Waited next to her longer than needed.

'Are you off, then?' Suzy touched his arm. 'I'll see you later.'

'OK, yes, see you later, at mine then.'

'At yours it is.' Suzy rubbed her forehead in desperation; at any minute Matthew would be walking out of the stockroom with Wilfred's balls in his hand. The thought and the difficult situation she found herself in almost made her want to become hysterical with laughter. Feeling the laughter building in her, she politely guided Harry to the door.

'See you later, Suzy.'

Suzy nodded.

The moment the door was closed, Suzy rushed back behind the

bookshelf and erupted into sheer belly laughter; tears came to her eyes. The image of Harry seeing another man walking from the stockroom was one thing, but one carrying Wilfred's balls was certainly another. Tapping her chest, she attempted to contain herself.

As Harry felt hurried from the shop by his girlfriend he became worried and deflated. The reality hit him that he only had one person in his life to buy presents for. What had made him create such a situation for himself? He had a family. It was his fault and he knew it. She was going to be seventeen soon, his little girl.

He watched the families across the street walking and embracing each other's company, how they held hands and laughed as they carried their gifts for each other in their Christmas bags. Children skipping along the street with their mothers, and the father who held his son on his shoulders. How and why had he chosen to miss out on such a thing?

Harry wondered how long the young couple kissing in the shop doorway had been together, seeing the way they held each other close with passion, not caring about the looks from others, wanting to share how they felt with the whole world.

'Here we go, a box of balls.' Matthew placed them on the counter, the sleeves rolled up on his red jumper, ready to get going.

'Righty, sugar puff, come and follow me.' Wilfred walked past him quickly and beckoned him with his finger.

'OK, Wilfred, whatever you say.' Matthew picked up the box again, winking at Suzy.

Harry leant on the lamp post only yards from the shop and wondered what gift to buy her; the way she had been lately, he thought a smile was an idea. She had changed over the last few months; she hadn't taken her knickers down in front of him as much as she used to. If he was to be honest with himself he only needed a cuddle now and then, for her to lie on his chest and hold his hand, for her to be peaceful and safe in his presence. They didn't have to speak or have sex; they only had to be still, to hear each other breathe and now and then look into each other's eyes.

Harry looked down at the concrete, believing such peace didn't exist. Pulling his wallet from the back pocket of his overalls he slowly opened it, feeling for the small picture with his oil-stained fingers. If only he could lie peacefully with her forever.

Gazing at the light coming from the window of the bookshop, Harry reluctantly pushed the picture inside his wallet again while walking away. He remembered how he had taken the pictures from the locket, placing them in the sink; as he had poured the water onto them a panic had shot through him. He had grabbed Eve's image, pressing it onto his lips; he couldn't wash her away. Looking down, he had seen his brother's small heart-shaped picture swirling around in the thrashing water; he had used a fork to push it further down into the plug hole.

He wanted his family back; he needed them. He was tired of pretending he was happy at Christmas. Like he'd done from the day his brother had closed the door on him, closing the door on his life.

# 54

---

Matthew paused for a moment, kneeling on the soft blue carpet in the hall, before leaning into the cupboard under the stairs. The small typewriter had sat safe amongst old paperwork from his office. A few old books were piled neatly in there, and the black boots Natty had been looking for for the last few months.

Feeling the keys under his fingertips, he promised himself he'd begin writing. The whole idea from Natty wasn't silly; anyone could do it, and they simply had to begin. He nodded his head in self-approval.

Hearing the thudding of footsteps on the stairs, Matthew shut the cupboard door, turning the small brass key in haste.

'What you doing on the floor, Dad?' Ruth plaited her wet blonde hair as she spoke to him.

'Hi, Ruth. I was sure I put Natty's birthday present in here; must be in the bedroom. Silly old me, eh?' Standing up, he brushed the carpet fluff from the front of his black trousers.

Ruth looked at him and thought how good he was at hiding stuff that didn't belong to him. She felt anxious being around him.

'What did you get her?' Pushing her finished plait over her shoulder, Ruth spoke sternly.

'Only a little something, Ruth.'

Ruth watched him walking up the stairs as he was speaking to her. Shrugging her shoulders and feeling no care for Natty's birthday, she went to her tartan rucksack and pulled out a card which had been more designed for a sixty-year-old. Peeling the price sticker from the back, Ruth sat and scribbled her greeting. *To Nat, Love Ruth. xx*

Sitting at the kitchen table alone, Ruth looked at the centre of the tiled floor. How they'd all stand in a row and be checked over and over by their mother; how the fear and dread consumed them each day. After everything, what made her miss her mother so? Tapping the pen on her teeth, she wondered how the rest of her family felt about her still and hoped one day her name would be mentioned so she'd be able to begin speaking of her.

Throwing the pen down on the table, Ruth went over to the side, seeing a quite large rectangular present. It was wrapped in floral paper; it reminded Ruth of something she'd seen before. Picking up the box, she shook it and tipped it back and forward and upside-down a couple of times, determined to sense what was inside.

Tossing it back on the side, Ruth's attention went onto the bread bin. It had been such a long time since she had found the letter addressed to her, and she intended to wait for it to be handed over. The longer the time went, the more threadbare the trust she had for her father became.

Ruth had been annoyed with herself ever since that day for not taking it. When she had got home from seeing her friend's life being controlled and hurried into the kitchen, all she had found was a pile of old stale crumbs, little pieces just like what she had left for her father and her family. It was up to her father to give her letter back to her. She'd wait until he did, even if it was forever, only to prove to herself her feelings mattered to him. The anger in her began to surge as she watched Natty coming into the kitchen.

'You all right, Ruth?' Natty went to the sink and filled the kettle with water.

'Yeah, I am, I suppose. Happy birthday, by the way.'

'Thanks. What's that?'

'A present, Natty, by the looks of it.' Ruth rolled her eyes and sat back at the kitchen table, tapping her fingers on the wood.

'Who's it from?' Natty hoped it'd be from Lucas. By the size of it, it certainly wasn't the diary she'd been longing for. She picked up the box and shook it a couple of times, squeezing the front and tipping it back and forward. 'This paper is nice. I recognise it from somewhere.' She saw Ruth sitting with raised eyebrows, with both hands on her cheeks and her elbows firmly on the table.

'It's from Lucas! How sweet he is.' Lucas knew; he had wrapped it and left it on the side for her before he had gone off to the theatre. It wasn't going to be opened until he came home. She'd wait for him even though the temptation engulfed her.

'I see you've dressed up for your birthday, Natty.' Ruth looked over Natty's choice of attire as she became twenty-two. The diamond burgundy tank top and chequered burgundy blouse certainly didn't go with her red jeans.

'What's wrong with it?' Natty looked herself up and down. She'd thought she'd make the effort too.

'Nothing, if you're colourblind and never go out.' Ruth smirked as she pushed her card over with her hand in the midst of abusing her.

'I see you've bought me a card; thanks, Ruth.' Natty opened her card and tried to ignore the antics of her sister, who obviously was in the mood for a row.

The card only took a few seconds to read. Natty smiled at Ruth and placed it next to the bread bin.

'I wouldn't leave your card there; you may lose it.'

Ruth's comment was almost interrupted.

'Hi, Dad!'

'Happy birthday, Natty. Here you go.'

'Thanks, Dad.' Natty was handed a small square box. It hadn't been wrapped with pretty paper or even a little bow; the black velvet case sat in her hand, and it simply had to be opened.

Inside was a thin gold chain which had clasped onto it a small pearl; it seemed almost too delicate to touch.

'Thank you, Dad; it's really pretty.' Natty leant up on her tiptoes slightly and kissed him on his soft cheek. She understood how he endeavoured to replace her locket. It was impossible to find any substitute for the sentiment her locket held. Natty prayed it was being taken care of.

Her father stood with his hands folded, sensing she liked it and he had made amends for her loss. Rubbing her arm and gazing at the beautiful young woman she'd become, he felt content. He made his way back upstairs to his bedroom.

Natty pointed at her sister and spoke a little aggressively. 'Don't even think about it, Ruth.'

'I won't. Natty, what do you think Mother would've bought you today?'

292

'Sorry, Ruth? Well, that's a silly question.' Natty closed her small box and placed it next to her card.

'Why is it silly? Only a question. If Lucas asked you then you'd answer.' Ruth heard the doorbell and went to answer it.

Natty thought about what her sister had asked her and felt certain she'd have got the diary she had been so desperate for. The emotions in Natty were still raw from the loss of their mother; she'd rather Ruth had not mentioned her, especially on her birthday.

The cold air instantly came into the hall.

'Oh, little George, come to me.' Ruth grabbed her little nephew from Glenn and rushed back into the warmth of the kitchen.

'Hi, Ruth, how you been? Well, I've been great, thanks.' Glenn placed her bags on the floor of the hall and pulled her pink scarf and sheepskin coat off, hanging them on the already-full coat hook, still in shock from Ruth snatching her son from her arm.

Ruth lifted her heavily clothed nephew up to smell his bottom. 'God, he stinks.'

'Well, off you go then, seeing as you were so eager,' Glenn said sarcastically, placing the nappy-changing bag into Ruth's hand. 'Hello, Natty; happy birthday. Is that the kettle on? I'm gagging, and not just for tea.' Glenn laughed as she gave Natty a card and a present wrapped in pretty yellow paper.

'Thanks, Glenn. You've changed: card and present all at the same time.' Natty opened her card and smiled. Pushing her fingers around the edges of the Sellotape, she felt as if this was what she had been waiting for; a relief came to her and an overwhelming gratitude.

'Oh, it's a makeup set.' Natty was confused by her sister's colour choices for her also and knew her last chance for the diary had to be Lucas.

'I loved the colours,' Glenn said. 'They'd so look good on me.'

'Take it if you still lived here I'd certainly have lost it, then?'

'Yep. You still might; I've nearly run out.'

Natty laughed with her and then set out four cups to make tea.

'Ruth, you having one?' Natty turned her head to get Ruth's attention.

Ruth's nose was scrunched up in disgust as she unpinned George's nappy. 'Oh my God, how do you do this?'

293

'Ruth, you can't change him on the kitchen table.' Glenn began to laugh.

'Yuck, this is making me feel sick.' Ruth held the nappy at her side, hoping one of her sisters who giggled uncontrollably would be kind enough to remove it from her promptly.

Natty and Glenn watched with pleasure at seeing Ruth in such a state of desperation over something so small.

'Take it, take it, oh God.' Holding his little legs up with her other hand, Ruth glanced down out of the corner of her eye again to see his poo-stained pink bottom.

'Give it over here.' Glenn went and retrieved the soiled nappy from her. Pulling the lining from the soft fabric, she placed it in the bin.

'Not in here, Glenn!' Natty raised her voice as she ran for a plastic bag so it could be thrown outside.

The awful aroma filled the kitchen.

'Oh, will someone open a window? How can something so small smell so badly?' Ruth gently wiped his little bum with one hand and held her nose with the other, her voice squeaky.

Their father came into the kitchen, wrapping his arms around his daughter who he'd not seen for some time. Glenn raised her eyebrows at his overwhelming affection.

'Hello, Glenn, it's so lovely to see you. Is that little George I can smell?' He let go of Glenn and watched Ruth at the kitchen table.

'Dad, the whole street can smell him; then again, it could be Glenn.' Ruth still held her nose, her voice making them all laugh. Finally she had finished and could breathe properly, to her relief.

'Be careful with the pin; he has a little bit to tuck in.' The spontaneous laughter in the kitchen even made Ruth giggle.

'I've got to tuck it in as well? Oh dear. Here we go, all finished. Easy!' Ruth picked George up in her hands, his little legs kicking back and forth and up and down. His nappy fell from his bottom and slid down his chubby legs, landing back on the kitchen table.

The noise of their laughter made George begin to cry.

'Glenn, I think you need to take him. Give him back when he's not doing his baby thing.' Ruth took him to Glenn, who seemed fatter than ever, wearing a pink knee-length frilly collared dress.

'Liking the outfit.' Ruth smirked as she went to frantically wash her hands.

Glenn paced up and down with George in the kitchen, her hand on his bare bum.

'Is that the time already?' Natty looked up at their mother's clock over the fireplace as they all sat comfortably in the dining room. Ruth sat with her legs up next to Glenn, who sat upright, moving her legs from side to side, with George on her lap. Their father sat on the floor with his legs out, one foot over the other.

Natty waited for Lucas to come pedalling down the road at any moment.

'He's here.' Natty sat up a little more, waiting for him to greet her on her special day.

'Have I missed something, Natty?' Glenn looked at her eager sister sitting in the armchair next to their mother's chair.

Lucas slowly looked around the doorframe, smiling at them all. The aura of happiness and love that surrounded him overwhelmed them all. The energy coming from him was surreal; he was sharing a part of himself with them without even being aware of the impact of his presence.

Lucas went straight over to Glenn.

'Welcome, little man, to another day of your wonderful life and of course your very first magical Christmas.' Lucas saw glistening stars reflected in George's big grey eyes. 'He's amazed by the sparkling Christmas lights; look at his eyes.' He gently touched George's cheek with his finger, savouring the softness of his pure skin.

'Hello, Glenn. It's very good to see you.' Lucas gently waved at her.

'Hello, Lucas. I hear you have a job now. You might get enough money to buy yourself some shoes. I'm only joking; you look really well.'

'And, Glenn, may I say you also look extremely well? Lovely and plump; you seem very content. Your dress is very pretty.'

'Thanks, Lucas; it covers my fat.' Glenn giggled at his constant innocence.

'Miss Natty, happy birthday. I do hope you liked your gift?' Lucas turned around Eve's chair and happily sat down.

Everyone in the room looked at each other, unsure of what to do. Their mother's chair hadn't been touched since she had passed away. Natty remembered how she cried as she dared to sit in it briefly, she knew they had all forgotten.

Matthew needed to break the silence, his tears building in his throat. His perfect Eve would've been upset if she had been aware someone else sat where she had lived out her own existence for so long, for too long.

'Lucas, what made you take a seat there?' Matthew spoke gently and politely, rubbing his hands up and down his legs, wiping the sweat from his palms.

'Matthew, it's the most beautiful chair; if I was allowed to pick any of them in here then I'm certain it'd be this one. There's uniqueness about this little piece of furniture which you don't normally see: gently and carefully made, delicate on the inside but with an outer strength that holds much weight.' Lucas cupped his hands together and smiled while pushing his hands through his soft curls.

Matthew felt a pride and an immense love overwhelm him suddenly, the tears in his throat calming.

'Do you know, Lucas, you enjoy the beautiful chair, and I'm truly thrilled you appreciate such perfection.' He smiled and without any warning Suzy came to his mind.

'Oh, yes, Matthew. You only have to see your daughters to see such a thing.'

'Oh, Lucas, that's so sweet I'll forgive you for your "plump" comment,' Glenn said while moving George's arms up and down in a game, hearing her son laugh making everything that had happened in her young life so far almost bearable.

'Oh, Glenn, your plumpness is a beautiful thing.'

'OK, Lucas, I'm not sure I could forgive you the second time.' Glenn smiled at him.

'Right, I'm going to get my gift.' Natty rushed to the kitchen.

Sitting back next to Lucas, she set the rectangular gift on her lap.

'Isn't that my wallpaper?' Glenn laughed and everyone joined in.

Lucas felt wonderful as he had managed to find a spare roll at the back of her wardrobe; it was such a shame to waste it.

'Wow, thanks, a huge box of chocolates.' Natty held in her hands a large purple box with a selection of treats.

'Shall we have one before dinner?' Glenn clapped George's hands together.

'Glenn, if you keep on, do you think you'll get into Mother's wedding dress?' Ruth put her feet down onto the soft red carpet, rubbing the tops of her feet as pins and needles had set in.

Glenn moved from the sofa, holding George in her arms. 'Look, I'm going to get in it; you watch me.' She could see their expressions of doubt.

'Anyway, let's open this box.' Natty pushed up the lid of the box and realised with her tossing and turning of the present the chocolates had fallen out of their little compartments.

Ruth put her head down as she saw how her curiosity had turned the chocolates upside-down.

Placing them back, Natty offered the box around.

'Glenn, here you go.' Natty held the box up and smiled.

'No, Natty, I'd better not. Ruth is right; I have to get into my dress.'

'You will get in it; it's five months away.' Natty raised her eyebrows to tempt her.

'Oh, go on, then; only one.' Glenn helped herself and bit a piece from the top, placing a small piece of chocolate in George's mouth with her finger.

Ruth laughed. 'See, those who indulge bulge.'

'Well, Ruth, you've got to get in your dress too, so think about that chocolate.' Glenn smirked.

'What dress?'

'Your bridesmaid's dress.'

'I don't have to wear a dress, do I? Oh, please, Glenn. What about Natty?' Ruth pushed the nutty chocolate into her mouth.

'Yep, Natty too.' Glenn licked her finger and wiped away the chocolate-coloured dribble around George's mouth.

Natty felt dread at having to wear a long gown. She prayed it wasn't going to be Glenn's favourite colour.

'We'll have to go shopping, OK, girls? Come on, George, let's go and lay you down for a sleep.' Glenn grinned. An excitement stirred in her stomach as she didn't have long before she became a young married woman.

'Dad?'

'Thank you, Natty, Turkish delight for me.'

'Lucas?'

'Thank you, Miss Natty.' Lucas took the box from Natty, placing it upon his lap. 'The smells are incredible, all mixed together, almost making one huge chocolate in themselves.' He glanced at the choices, seeming almost frozen with delight.

'Lucas, which one you having?' Natty spoke gently while sighing, aware her simple offering was going to take some time.

'Now let me see. We have a caramel softy, milk chocolate matched with its caramel sweetheart. A hazelnut swirl.'

'My favourite.' Ruth raised her voice.

'An orange truffle, the yummy chocolate, blend of chocolate with an orange twist; the choices are breathtaking. Perfect praline, encased in a chocolate gem.'

'Lucas, it will be my next birthday before you've picked.' Natty sat back on the sofa with her arms folded, wanting to pick hers.

'And, Miss Natty, I shall buy you another glorious box. We have exotic delight.'

'That's awful.' Ruth put out her tongue in disgust.

'Lucas, pick, will you?' Natty crossed her legs. He was going to read them the whole box; she simply knew it.

'I will have this one!' Lucas said excitedly.

'Thank God.' Natty leant forward to take the box.

'Actually, no, it's fudge. I feel this one will be it.'

'Hallelujah!'

Ruth and their father chuckled in the background.

'What about nutty heart? This is for me, wouldn't you say: roasted hazelnut smothered in thick caramel?'

'Yes, Lucas, the perfect choice for you.' Feeling relief as her birthday gift was handed back to her, Natty felt her father's hand in the box again.

'I'll have this one.' Her father put the chocolate in his mouth and went to begin dinner, turning around to smile at her.

The force of Ruth's hand went into the quickly emptying tray and she rushed out of the living room laughing, following their father.

'Hey, you lot.' Natty closed the box and placed it behind the pillow on the sofa.

'Happy birthday, Miss Natty. You look rather vibrant today, and a splendid choice of colours for your special day.' Lucas leant back in her mother's chair, savouring his final choice.

'Thank you, Lucas. I'm going to the shop; I'm going to need to write tonight after this.' Natty went out into the hall and grabbed her blue woollen coat from the hook.

'I'll come.' Ruth pulled on her brown duffel coat and waited for Natty to smile.

Ruth and Natty began walking to the small newsagent's.

'I had a nice day today, Natty; really glad I stayed in.'

'Why? Were you going out, then?'

'I was. Anywhere would have done.' Ruth happily walked by her sister's side.

'Well, after everything this year, I'm happy you stayed in too.' Natty touched her shoulder.

'You know Dad hid my letter, don't you?' Ruth stopped walking.

'What letter?' Natty stopped only a little further up the road.

'Natty, my letter.'

'Why?'

'You know why, Natty. Why? You can tell me what it is.'

'Listen, Ruth, how do you even know it was for you? If you were meant to have it, I'm sure Dad would've given it to you.'

'My name was on the front, so obviously it was for me.' Ruth felt confused at Natty's denial of knowing what had really happened to it.

'So then why didn't you open it? For all you know it may have been Dad's. From the meetings you used to go to, or even the school. Not exactly been the best-behaved at school, have you?'

'Oh, thanks. She had it coming to her.' Ruth had been having a good day up until then.

'Ruth, honestly, if it was for you, you'd have it. Now can I get to the shop?' Natty was beginning to feel harassed. They had a birthday dinner and chocolate sponge birthday cake to eat. Natty was aware she'd be eating Glenn's helping.

'You're probably right.' Ruth's thoughts were mixed; a sense of relief came over her, as she could have got it all wrong.

'Let's go, then?' Natty continued walking with Ruth by her side.

'Natty, I promise I won't touch your necklace.'

'I know, Ruth, or I will chop your fingers off. See, you have my

299

pink nail varnish on.' Natty smiled reassuringly, helping Ruth to understand she wasn't cross with her.

'The letter didn't look official.'

Natty sighed. 'Ruth, let it go.'

Walking into the shop, it seemed busier than normal. Natty walked over to the cluttered shelf of drawing pins and string and other stationery items. Picking up the selection of lined books, Natty knew she was being impatient and looking in completely the wrong shop.

'You getting it in here? They're not very good, are they? And what is that smell in here?' Ruth went around to the other side of the shop alone.

As Natty stood at the till, placing the black lined book down on the newspapers on the counter, she tipped her money into her hands. Amongst the copper and silver coins she could see a small pink bow, dirty and fading, part of the wrapping which had covered her locket. Natty's thoughts went back to her pearl necklace; she knew it'd never be the same, as kind a gesture as it was.

Wondering what Ruth was doing around the side of the packed shelves of biscuits and treats, Natty heard a group of Girl Guides laughing at the magazine stand as she sorted out the money to pay for her book. The shop assistant's attentions were fully focused on the group of uniformed young girls as they flicked through the choice of reading material. One of them grabbed an adult magazine from the top shelf, making her thoughts about it extremely clear through giggling and intrigue.

Natty put the money down and took her book.

'Ruth, I'm ready to go.'

'Let's go!' Ruth pushed past Natty at the shop doorway, nearly making her drop the book under her arm.

'Hey, stop, you!' the shop assistant shouted from the counter.

'Ruth, what the hell are you doing?' Natty blinked as everything felt confusing instantly.

'Run, Natty!' Ruth shouted with desperation in her voice.

Before Natty could move any further the shop assistant grabbed her shoulder.

'Hey, what are you doing?' Natty demanded.

'Get the little thief back.' The shop assistant's voice was deep and aggressive.

Natty pushed the man's hand from her shoulder and turned quickly. 'She isn't a thief; she has her own money.'

Thoughts flashed through her mind almost instantly. Her sister had the capacity to steal; there was no way she'd do a thing like this, though. She'd swear on her own life.

'Ruth, come here!' Natty demanded, beckoning her sister over with her finger, feeling the breath from the angry shop assistant behind her. Seeing Ruth pacing up and down the street, Natty hoped she'd come to them and have the whole incident cleared up so she'd get her birthday cake.

Ruth walked slowly to them with her head down.

'Tell this man he's made a mistake.' Natty tightened her lips and raised her eyebrows at her worried sister.

The shop assistant and Natty were pushed out of the way by the group of uniformed menaces rushing out of the entrance. As the girls walked up the road they turned around again and again, staring at Natty, giggling. Natty stared back at them suspiciously and believed the stroppy shop assistant needed to take a closer look at who was leaving his mixed-spice-smelling shop.

'Natty, can we go?' Ruth glanced up at her sister, nerves and adrenaline almost making her legs and arms feel numb.

'No, Ruth, we have to clear this mess up. You have to show this man you haven't taken anything from his shop.'

'I haven't, Brownie's honour.'

Natty looked up at the images of the girls in the distance and knew Brownie's honour was nothing much to go on either.

'Ruth, come on, I want to get home. Sir, I really think you've made a mistake here. She wouldn't steal from you, honestly; she has more than enough money.' Natty spoke while keeping her attention firmly on Ruth.

'Can't believe you, Natty.'

The man became impatient. 'I'm going to call the police.'

'Seriously, Ruth! Sir, please let her show you.' Natty began to shake with adrenaline also as the whole incident seemed ridiculous. She couldn't wait to give this man a piece of her mind when he realised he'd caused them unnecessary stress; she was going to demand he let her have her book for nothing, without a doubt.

Natty held out her hand to Ruth.

Ruth paused for a little and blew out her cheeks. Looking away from her sister, she pushed her hand up under her green polo neck and pulled out a small flat packet of ecru tights, handing them to Natty. Still not making eye contact with her sister, Ruth pushed her hand into the pocket of her cream flared slacks and opened it to reveal a handful of penny chews.

Natty stood frozen, shock and embarrassment overtaking her as she had been sure the man had made a mistake.

'Now I'm calling the police.' The man rushed back into the shop.

'Oh, Ruth!' Natty wanted to cry for the desperation she was sure was inside her sister at that very moment.

Ruth put her hands in her pockets, staring at the pavement.


'Dad, not too many for me, thanks.' Glenn sat at the kitchen table with her father, who was peeling potatoes for dinner. Glenn carefully wiped small smears of chocolate buttercream from the edge of Natty's birthday cake with her finger as she pushed the white candles into the sponge. George slept on a soft chequered blanket on the carpet in the dining room. Lucas sat beside him, tinkling a small bell from the Christmas tree and humming a beautiful lullaby.

# 55

The impact of the hot piercing water moved over his pores, helping him to relax, to forget the overwhelming emotions consuming him. He moved his neck from side to side, letting the water fall down the side of his body. Only a moment of relaxation fell over him before the room felt as though it was closing in; he found himself gasping for breath, the anxiety and guilt causing his limbs to become numb.

It was critical the emotions that overwhelmed him were to be washed away. The shower was his only place of comfort. Rubbing the shampoo onto his dark hair, he felt the soft bubbles rolling down his face. The panic became too much for him to bear as he collapsed onto the bath's surface. The hot water burning his back as the steam glided from his skin. The tears wrenched from his stomach for his Eve.

Kneeling in the bath, curled up like a small child, Matthew saw the tears from his eyes vanishing with the foamy fragrant water down the plug hole. He'd never get back the tears he cried for her, just as she'd never be with him, passing him a soft towel when he pulled the white shower curtain across.

Was there no way it could magically happen: she'd come back to him?

Pushing his eyes closed hard, he breathed in and out slowly, attempting to stand, gripping the edge of the bath with his weakening arms. He held his hands over his eyes as the heating water touched his pain- and desire-racked body, washing the bubbles from his chest.

As he pulled the curtain back he shook his head, knowing what he wished for could never come true. Taking a stripy blue-and-white towel from the rail, Matthew wiped over the steamy mirror, water drips racing down the glass.

In the clear space on the glass he could see who he'd become: an image of a lost soul who desperately needed to have one more chance with his perfect Eve. What had made him invite Suzy out for dinner? Where did the desire come from to take her out, to be at a place he never took his Eve? He did enjoy being in her company, and the new pile of books sitting on his bedroom floor confirmed how many times in the last couple of weeks he'd been there. How he felt for Eve was like a battle within himself, an empire falling into small pieces little by little. He wanted more than anything to take Suzy out. Closing his eyes and shaking his head he began to dry himself, the mixture of emotions fighting within his guilt.

The bubbles were high and soft around her body in the bath. Her long slim leg protruding out of the water as she shaved through the foamy cream, Suzy sang along to the music from her radio in the background.

An excitement she hadn't felt for a very long time stirred in her stomach. She chuckled as she thought of how he had eventually asked her. She still had the piece of paper which he had left in the front cover of a book he'd returned.

*Dinner Friday 7.00pm, your choice, Matthew. x*

The fun of writing on a small piece of paper herself and sliding it into one of the books he had chosen, with her choice of restaurant and of course a very easy written *yes*, was something she found endearing and almost romantic. The whole moment was exhilarating.

'Got to get myself all shaven and smooth; you never know, he may feel them. Why do I even bother talking to you, you stupid cat? You have no idea what the hell I'm going on about.' Suzy flicked some bubbles from the shaving cream on her leg at her cat perching on the side of the bath. With the sensation on his little ginger face he leapt off and dashed to safety.

Suzy glanced at the small round clock quickly before dipping her head under the water as the anticipation became too much for her. She only had an hour and a half to get herself looking simply gorgeous. Suddenly she realised she might even have time to masturbate before she went; with that she lifted her head, wiping the water from her face, placing her legs on each side of the bath. Closing her eyes she felt the warmth of herself as she moved her fingers on her tingling skin. She gripped the edge of the bath with her hand as the water swirled around her wet bubbly body, climaxing with intensity in the thought of Matthew inside her.

Finally ready to go, Matthew looked at himself in the mirror, happy with his crisp white shirt, black trousers and extremely smart tailored black blazer with gold buttons. His black shoes were polished and his hair neatly waxed back. His greying hairs at the side didn't look too bad either; at fifty-seven he still was pretty handsome. Pouring a small splash of aftershave gently into his shaking hand, Matthew finished his look with a smell to match.

Blowing out his cheeks, feeling confused about his forthcoming actions, Matthew sat on the edge of the bed, taking his wedding picture from the side. Touching Eve's face with his fingers, he brought it up to his lips and kissed the photo gently.

'Wow!' Natty nearly spat out her tea in shock.

'Oh my God, Dad's still got it in him!' Ruth nudged Natty on the shoulder.

Holding his car keys in his hand, he walked over to them and kissed them both on the cheek.

Natty and Ruth were completely lost for words in astonishment at his appearance; he stood with his shoulders back, looking damn hot.

'You can breathe again, girls; I'm only going out for a bit.' Seeing them finally quiet made him chuckle as he left them alone dumbfounded.

Ruth and Natty looked at each other, smirking.

Opening the glove box of his car, Matthew worked his hands around a pile of tapes. He pushed one into the cassette player; the song which his Eve had loved bellowed around him.

'Change that one, shall we?' Matthew pulled the tape out quickly and pushed it back into the glove box as he drove away, settling for the radio.

Natty poured the dregs of her tea into the sink and straightened up her uniform, ready for work.

'What do you reckon, Ruth?' Natty chuckled.

'Yep! So obvious.' They both giggled together.

She clasped her necklace with a pretty pearl hanging from the thin gold chain, silently complimenting herself on her look. Her simple black dress, the neckline across her shoulders fitting perfectly on her slim body, her black fishnet tights feeling wonderful on her freshly shaven legs, her cheeks still flushed from her delightful orgasm. Her long blonde hair down with simple curls around the side of her face, bright glossy red lipstick and thick black eyelashes bringing out the beauty of her blue eyes.

'That's me done.'

Harry hadn't come to her mind once until the phone rang.

'Don't answer it, don't answer it, then you won't have to lie.' As Suzy turned in a panic at hearing the phone she nearly tripped on her cat. 'For fuck's sake, animal, honestly. I told you you were a stupid cat.'

Pacing up and down the living room with the phone still ringing and tapping her gold sequinned handbag on the side of her leg, Suzy began checking out of the window again, pulling the nets to one side discreetly, in case he spotted her eagerness. The phone rang on and on.

With sheer relief Suzy saw the headlights outside. Picking the phone receiver up and then placing it down swiftly, Suzy made her way out of the front door.

Leaning in the open window of Matthew's car, Suzy was aware her cleavage was showing fully. The thought of him looking at her made the throbbing sensation in her knickers quite apparent to her.

'Hello, Matthew. Oh, my, you do look different.'

'Hello, Suzy; you look very pretty. Best get in; the February air isn't as warm as normal.' Matthew saw how very beautiful she was, the young lady who he'd have the pleasure of spending a wonderful evening with.

'Pretty' was far too innocent a comment for her liking, considering how aroused she felt sitting next to him. Suzy breathed in hard and began thinking about her cat to calm herself down a little; if she carried on at this rate she'd be going to the toilet to feel herself up after each course.

They both looked at each other and smiled.

Harry lay on his sofa with the phone receiver on his ear, letting it ring while he watched the football on the television. He wasn't going to give up until she answered.

'Oh, Matthew, it's amazing, isn't it?' Suzy walked in front of Matthew to the beautiful table, the surroundings and atmosphere nearly taking her breath away.

'It is, Suzy.' Matthew felt relaxed and happy with her choice of restaurant, a very beautiful place, somewhere he'd have loved to bring Eve. He loved Chinese food also.

Matthew pulled the chair out for Suzy, who looked at him in shock.

'Thank you, Matthew; that's the first time this has ever happened to me.'

The lights were dim and the candles and fragrance of food embraced them both as they sat in the corner, a discreet place where lovers surely sat.

The calming atmosphere helped Matthew to relax. He was going to enjoy the evening; he'd given himself permission from the minute he had sat and looked at her pretty face, the flicker from the candle shining onto her beauty.

Suzy attempted to get the fantasy of him out of her head as she placed her crisp white serviette on her lap. The orders hadn't taken long to come out and in front of them both was a selection of oriental temptations. Everything was absurd to her; she was constantly consumed by the thought of who Harry had in his wallet, and here she was sitting in the most incredible restaurant in town with another man.

'Suzy, are you comfortable being here?' Matthew placed his chopsticks on the side of his plate.

'Yes, Matthew, I am. It's such a beautiful place. It has been worth the long wait. Not very good at using these sticks, though.' Suzy was desperate to grab the shining cutlery beside her plate.

'Do you know I'm not very good with them either?' Matthew picked up his fork and spoon and continued to eat, knowing in a few seconds Suzy would be following.

'Oh, thank God; I'd never get anything in my mouth tonight otherwise.' Suzy chuckled to herself at her private joke.

'Sorry it took me such a long time to ask. Here now, aren't we?' Matthew smiled at the young lady chuckling away to herself, finding her endearing and innocent.

'That's really OK.' Suzy spoke with a mouthful of noodles. She was starving.

'It's the least I can do, with all of your help in the bookshop and your patience with me coming in and out.'

Suzy felt a little downhearted, not wanting it to be a thank-you dinner.

'Suzy, I also bought my daughter Natty the same necklace you are wearing. I liked it very much when I saw it on your neck in the shop, and as you are young and pretty I thought she'd like it too.'

Suzy became more uplifted with his comment, softly touching the necklace Harry had given to her.

'Suzy, I hope you don't mind me saying I feel you seem to have something else on your mind.' Matthew placed his cutlery aside and took a small sip of his intended one glass of the evening.

Wouldn't he like to know? She gulped her wine back and quickly poured herself another, hoping to give herself a bit of Dutch courage, then she could open up a little more.

'No, Matthew, I'm OK. Here really isn't the place for boring old me to go on. It's kind of you to be concerned.'

'Well, Suzy, where is the place? We're in a setting where two people can speak without being disturbed.' Matthew raised his eyebrows, prompting her honesty.

'Is everything good? Anything else I can get you?' the handsome dark-haired Chinese waiter asked them.

Looking at each other, they both laughed.

'No, thank you; we are fine,' Matthew said gently to the waiter, who left them in peace once again.

'I know, you're right. I really shouldn't be putting this on you. You haven't brought me out to hear about my personal life.'

'Oh, your boyfriend.' Matthew moved his head up and down,

cupping his lips. It was hard to believe a beautiful woman such as her could ever have man worries.

'Is it that obvious? There really is something not right about him. I do try to get close; well, I think I do. There seems to be a void in him. You see, I found a picture in his wallet of this, may I say, extremely beautiful woman. Honestly, I don't think I've ever seen such features.' Suzy gulped her wine as she spoke quickly. 'I feel he still holds a flame for her. Needs a good blowing out, that's what I say. I know it was a very long time ago; I can tell by the picture.' Suzy slumped her shoulders, wishing she hadn't said anything. Harry always seemed to be interrupting her day. And now he was at her dinner out.

Matthew poured her another glass of wine before he answered.

'Suzy, sometimes these burning flames refuse to go out; they keep flickering inside. Sometimes the flame's so strong you can almost sense it burning your mind and heart also. Trying to blow it out doesn't work; you have to accept the small flame ignited in yourself as part of who you are, so even though your boyfriend may hold this for someone very beautiful as you say, I am almost certain, as lovely as you are, you are a flame also in him. And you'll keep burning away also. Love is something we keep within our bodies for lots of people, and it's part of us in the end. I sense with the feelings you have for him you must not allow it to stop burning. My flame for my Eve burns each and every day, and she keeps me warm and alive, gets me up in the morning, so as much as it can torment your body with pain, it reminds me I am alive, if I can still feel such emotion.' Matthew had never realised the impact of his love for Eve kept him moving through the day; she wasn't even here any more, but she helped him breathe through each season. He was the luckiest man alive to have love inside himself for someone such as her.

'I feel like a fool now, making a goddamn fuss over it all. Sorry it didn't work out for you, Matthew, really I am. She sounds like a really wonderful person.' Suzy placed her fork and spoon down. A small acceptance came over her for Harry for the first time, and it was all thanks to a complete stranger who had walked into her shop and smiled.

'No, Suzy, you can't criticise yourself; feelings are feelings and the mind has a funny way of playing tricks on us. It played tricks on my Eve; she took herself away. The voices in her head, Suzy, were stronger than the people around who loved her.' Matthew's throat began to burn as he pushed down his tears with a cool glass of water.

'Do you have any other family, Matthew, apart from your beautiful daughters?' Suzy wished Harry could feel such a way about her as the man who sat smart and handsome, living for a woman called Eve. She couldn't comprehend why she'd take herself away from him.

Matthew contained himself, gently leaning back on the chair, breathing slowly.

'Well, you know I have my girls. Glenn has George now and he is the chubbiest thing you've ever seen. He's a wonderful joy to be around. Eve would have loved him completely. Stanley seems to be making them both happy. She is getting married in three months; it feels almost unreal.'

'Married? Wow, I bet you're so excited.'

'He's nearly my age, so I am still a little apprehensive for her, but as I've said, love is love.' Matthew spoke between each mouthful of chicken and rice, one of his favourite oriental dishes.

'Only age, isn't it?'

Matthew nodded as he swallowed his food. 'Then there's Natty; she doesn't speak much about her job as a nurse, but makes her feelings for Lucas very clear. If I dared mention the secret she's attempting to keep isn't one, then she'd deny it incessantly. He's the funniest thing, crazy in a very intelligent way; he lives with us. I feel you'd like him if you met him. Loves the world and every small piece of fluff in it. I know there is more to him.'

'He sounds nice.' Suzy smiled.

'Yes, he is, very. My life changed quite a bit when he arrived.'

Suzy knew exactly what Matthew meant.

'And, of course, my little Ruth. I know she's hurting, so I wish she'd come to me. She has got herself into a little trouble, taking things which don't belong to her.' Matthew paused, squeezing his napkin between his fingers. 'It was such a day, the police at the door with Natty's arm around her shoulders; she couldn't stop crying. I don't know what made her steal. She has to go to a place each week and help the community, painting and gardening for the aged. She's very lucky. One more thing and they are going to take her away for a little time. I couldn't let her be locked away in some room; I did it to Eve and I couldn't do it to her too.' Matthew's thoughts went onto Harry briefly and then, almost as if still in the day, his thoughts went back to when he asked the doctor to take his Eve away. Suddenly full of emotion, Matthew placed his cutlery in the middle of his plate, wiping his mouth on the serviette, and waited for the intense emotions to secretly float around his body.

'Oh, Matthew, you have so much going on, then.' Suzy poured herself another glass of white wine, shaking the bottle and checking its remains before placing it back into the ice bucket.

'What about you?'

'Only me, I'm afraid, and my stupid cat Norris.' Suzy chuckled.

Matthew knew it was time; for some unknown reason he felt safe in her company. In some strange way he sensed she'd understand. Most importantly, she'd want to listen.

'I do have a brother.' Matthew felt as though he was going to bring up the food he'd swallowed.

'Oh, wow! There are lots of presents at yours, then?' Suzy leant forward to hear more, wondering if his brother was as handsome as him.

'I haven't seen him for seventeen years now, may I add.' The burning sensation in Matthew's throat became more intense with each word. The more he spoke about him, the more he made him exist; he was out there alive.

'Why wouldn't you? That's the age of your daughter, isn't it?'

Matthew sighed and looked down to his half-eaten food.

'Sorry, Matthew. Should keep my big mouth shut.' Suzy gulped down the rest of her wine.

'He hurt me a lot, Suzy.'

'That's a shame. Do you miss him? See, I'm still doing it.'

'He hurt me too much for me to miss him. I do miss what we had, or I believe had.' Matthew paused.

'You don't have to say if you don't want to; we'll just get more wine.' Suzy giggled nervously.

'No, it's OK, Suzy, honestly.' Matthew gulped his water, quenching the back of his dry and burning throat. 'For some reason he took it upon himself to interfere in my marriage. Abused the love I had and still have for my Eve. He did, you know, he did something awful and probably still is doing a thing which comes very easily to him. Charming women upon women to sleep with him, whoever they were; he just couldn't leave my Eve out of it. Charming and getting away with everything, and being completely inconsiderate. Sorry, Suzy, let me order you some more.' Matthew's words left his mouth with ease; he was thankful to release them at last. Maybe he'd finally be able to put his brother to rest in his heart. Waving the waiter over, Matthew ordered another bottle of very expensive wine.

'Sounds like a real arsehole – oops! Bit posh in here for that?' Suzy smiled and felt for him with intensity. How could anyone do such a thing to someone so kind?

'I'd love to join you in this bottle, Suzy; I have to be driving you home, though.' Matthew poured another glass for Suzy and believed she'd be staggering back to his car.

'Good riddance to him, that's what I say. What kind of man does such a thing?' Suzy's voice began to rise, her words a little slower than normal.

'Well, my brother.'

'Needs a good punch in the face!' Suzy mimed a punch as her voice became more and more raised, still with a gentle tone.

'Probably.' Matthew chuckled at her actions, knowing she'd have a headache in the morning when he saw her again at the bookshop.

'Well, you, *you*, yes, you are so much better.' Suzy pointed at him.

'Thank you, Suzy, and it's a damn shame he isn't here to hear a pretty blonde woman say that about me and not him.'

'Well, you just let me see him and I will give him a talking-to.' Suzy suddenly lost most of her senses.

'I think it's time we got you home, young lady.' Matthew pulled out her chair, holding her arm, helping her to stand a little.

# 56

'Oh, my dear Suzy, darling, you look crap. Take it you went through the sheets? Tell me all the really gory details.'

'I've got a headache from hell. Think I made a complete donkey's bollock of myself. Do you know, didn't even get a midnight kiss; well, don't think I did. I thought I was seeing two of him.' Suzy threw her woven bag behind the counter. Kicking it underneath with her soft red pumps, she leant over the soft wood and placed her hands on her head.

'Oh, peachy, double sounds good to me. One at each end!' Wilfred grinned as he filled the till with cash.

'Really, Wilfred?' Looking out of the corner of her eye at her overly scented colleague, Suzy scrunched her face up.

'Oh, yes, so could do with that now!' Wilfred began to roar with laughter, closing the till and flicking his hair, going into the stockroom.

'Excuse me, I'm going to chuck!' Suzy dashed past him with her hand over her mouth.

'So need to teach her how to have a good time.' Wilfred shook his head and smiled.

# 57

---

'Hold on, George, I'm coming!' Glenn rushed out of her bedroom, attempting to put one shoe on as she hopped along the hall, holding under her arm her other shoe and a small pile of dirty washing. Her rushed attempt at her makeup only half-finished, the top of her short black pixie hairstyle still wet.

'Oh, no, makeup.' Glenn's mouth dropped open as she saw George pushing the remains of her favourite pink lipstick over the wall.

George looked up at her and smiled, his face a bright pink and the strands of his hair coloured to match.

'Of all the colours, Billy Bear, really?' Glenn bent over, feeling harassed, and grabbed a dirty T-shirt from the pile to wipe his face.

Rushing into her bathroom she looked at herself all flustered, the button to her undersized jeans pinching her waist. Lifting her brown chequered blouse she could see the marks where her skin had almost gone white with her blood circulation restricted. She was determined to look her best even if she spent the day with pinched skin and tight high heels; she hadn't been out with the girls for such a very long time.

Picking up George and kicking her clothes down the stairs while she held him in her arms, Glenn felt clammy and panicky; the nerves began to consume her at having to leave George for the day. It would be the very first time since he had been born. Her fearful thoughts consumed her as she placed him pink-stained in the toy-filled playpen.

She gained her breath and smiled at him briefly before dashing back into the hall to retrieve her other shoe. She felt happy without the left one on as it was always the one that gave her the biggest blisters.

On the way to the hall she paused to puff the cushions on the sofa. Stanley's cushion was scrunched up on his chair where he had spent most of the evening before. Grabbing it, Glenn began to punch it straight. Laughing to herself, she made her way into the hall and pushed on her white stiletto shoe, then glanced up the stairs. With a sigh, she rushed up to quickly make her bed.

Pulling the covers over and tucking in the edges, Glenn blew out a breath of desperation at how fast the time was moving. She needed to get ready and time was against her.

'Lipstick!' Taking a small cotton bud from the bedroom drawer, Glenn swirled it around the small opening in the gold lipstick tube, taking on the last pieces of pink saviour. Softly rubbing the cotton ball against her lips, she began to hear George cry. Huffing, she rushed down the stairs, feeling the back of her heel beginning to burn.

'Mummy will get you a drink; hold on.' She walked past the playpen with haste, going straight into the kitchen. She rolled her sleeves up and began to wash up, puffing, out of breath, checking the time on the clock in the kitchen. George would be due for his drink and nap shortly.

'Oh, goodness, drink. Hold on, George.' Tightening the lid of his cup with her bubbly hands and taking a biscuit from the tin, Glenn went back to calm him.

Placing his small bubbly cup and biscuit in front of him and tapping him on the head, Glenn felt relieved she could finally get on.

'Oh, snot.' Blowing out her cheeks, Glenn went and found a cloth to wipe his nose.

'There you go, Billy Bear, Mummy's feeling all lovely and attractive now.' Glenn could see him scrunching up his face in disapproval at his orange juice. 'There's nothing wrong with that; a few bubbles won't hurt you,' she said as she dried the cups on the sideboard, almost throwing them into the cupboard once they were dry.

A pile of ironing caught Glenn's attention and throwing the flowery tea towel down, she grabbed it. Standing next to the table with a pile of clothes in her hands and seeing she'd left the cupboard door open in the kitchen, she went forward to close it.

315

Somehow she managed to bang her head on the wood and catch her forehead on the metal handles. At that moment Glenn wished she had chosen the wooden ones, as she was sure she had a mark in the middle of her forehead, to match her blister and aching waist.

Hearing the doorbell, Glenn paced up and down the kitchen with the pile of laundry still in her arms, looking frantically to see where she could place it. Panic filled her as she wondered how she could justify going shopping, leaving the house in such a way, once Stanley came home from a busy day at the office.

'Oh, for God's sake!' She forcefully pushed her foot onto the small pedal of the bin; the silver lid sprang open. Glenn promptly, with a sense of sheer relief, pushed the clean clothes inside.

'That's you sorted for another week!' Glenn rubbed her hands together, feeling satisfaction overwhelm her.

Wiping her hands on the sides of her trousers, Glenn went to answer the door.

'Hello, let's go!' Grabbing her handbag, she rushed back to kiss George on his cheek. She could see his nose beginning to run again, the wet sticky gloop sitting on the edge of his lips.

'Oh, thank you, Glenn, so nice to see you.' Ruth stood at the door shaking her head at her sister's haste, seeing how tight her trousers were on her bum, and knew she'd be reminding her later of how fat she was getting, whether she liked it or not.

'Yeah, Ruth, that's cool. Thank you, Lucas, really kind of you to sit with him; all his snacks are in the fridge, and juice. He is due for a nap about half an hour ago; there is a change of clothes on his bed, as he may get dirty; try not to let him go out in the kitchen, he tends to play with the bin, and if you could read him a story later, hopefully we won't be long. Do you want me to put him asleep first before we go, then that way I know he's settled?'

Natty, Ruth and Lucas all stood dumbfounded as she hadn't even taken a breath.

'Dear Glenn, I can promise you I have it all under control. I am so happy you have allowed me to be with George for such a time; we are going to have so much fun. Now please go and have the most wonderful day with your sisters.' Lucas placed his hands on her shoulders, giving her a reassuring look.

'Remember, Lucas, he is only thirteen months. Come on, let's get this ordeal over with; last thing I am in the mood for today is trying on lots of different dresses.' Natty brushed the front of her pretty flowery blouse down, subconsciously comparing herself with Glenn, who was too near to Lucas for comfort. She began to feel agitated as Lucas looked into Glenn's grey eyes.

'Oh, no, I know exactly what dresses you're getting; you just have to try them on for size.' Glenn looked at her sisters standing in the doorway; they both looked very pretty. Glenn particularly liked Natty's blouse and blue corduroys. Ruth wore a simple red bomber jacket, a chequered shirt and green cords. Her long blonde hair fell soft on her shoulders. Seeing her family made her feel even more of a mess, an overweight stay-at-home lump of lard.

'Glenn, are we going?' Natty sighed.

'I can always nick them for you, Glenn, could save you some money, that way you could actually buy yourself some clothes that fit that big arse of yours.' Ruth ran down the garden path laughing, knowing she'd get a swift swipe from her sister's fist if she didn't.

'Oh, I see, you find it funny you've turned into a thief, do you?' Glenn hurried out onto the path, wanting to thump her.

'As much as you think it's funny looking like a beached whale, pretty sister.' Ruth held her stomach as she roared with laughter.

Finally all three of them were out the front, making their way out for the day.

'Blimey, Lucas's pockets were really full; what the hell did he have in them?' Glenn patted her hair down at the front, breathing in as she walked next to her slimmer sisters.

'Maybe he was pleased to see you!' Ruth giggled as she felt a slap to her arm from Natty.

'You could have a point.' Glenn began to accompany Ruth in her wind-up.

'What do you reckon, Glenn, oral sex?' Ruth smirked as she looked at Natty.

'I'd even swallow if he stayed and did my housework.' Glenn laughed aloud with Ruth.

'You two are outrageous.' Natty spoke in a harsh tone.

'Calm down, Natty, take it on the chin.' Ruth stopped and bent over with laughter at her unintended pun. Hearing Glenn laughing along with her made the situation even funnier.

317

'I will meet you two at the bus stop.' Natty rushed off in front of them, feeling furious at their jokes about Lucas and knowing that even if they had a willy put in their faces they wouldn't know what to do with it. Her thoughts rushed through her mind as she glanced at them once more; they still stood side by side in hysteria.

'Hello, George, you precious little thing, shall we have some fun? Honestly, the adults do panic, don't they? Now, how hard can it be to take care of someone so beautiful?' Lucas placed his blue thin jacket with chequered lining on the armchair.

'Shall we wipe your nose first, little fellow?' Lucas found a tissue in the kitchen and went to lift George out of the playpen, dabbing the soft white tissue onto his face and around his mouth as gently as he could.

'Oh, I have something for you, George; I nearly forgot.' Grabbing his jacket, Lucas emptied the pockets onto the chair: a selection of goodies which he had wanted to bring along to share with George to make their day together completely wonderful.

Pulling out a small Union Jack on a small plastic stick, Lucas began straightening out the paper edges. He frowned, unhappy it had crumpled in his pocket. Aware George was too young to understand the Queen's Jubilee, he hoped the damaged flag could help him know the events which happened while he was young. George would have something to share with his own children.

'Flag isn't doing much for you, is it, little fellow? You look tired. Shall we get you to sleep?' Lucas stopped waving the small flag and took a blanket from the table, placing it in the bottom of the cluttered playpen and laying George gently on top, the soft wool touching George's face as he pushed his bottom up into the air and his little legs under his chest. Lucas began rubbing George's soft brown hair, touching his small forehead, singing a lullaby as he leant over the netted frame. Briefly remembering Natty's mother singing the same song as she sat alone in the corner; her pretty innocent voice echoed around the mental hospital. A place Lucas knew neither of them should ever have been.

As he watched the small boy falling asleep in his own peace, Lucas was convinced he'd only gone into the home so he could now be sitting where he was; his life was linked to the pretty lady who sang so beautifully. Looking up at the ceiling, Lucas knew he was going to thank God before he went to sleep that evening. Thank him for the people who surrounded him with a feeling he understood to be love, an immensity of loveliness and safety.

'Natty, wait up.' Ruth and Glenn followed Natty.

'Go away, you two. Let's get this dress stuff done quickly so I can be around normal people.' Natty stood at the bus stop with her arms folded and her lips tight in disapproval.

'Oh my God, Natty, you are such a stick-in-the-mud. Glenn's only joking; I mean, she's getting married, so any chance of any swallowing is a no-go.' Ruth pushed Natty's arm gently, wishing she'd lighten up; they hadn't been out for so long, and she didn't want it spoilt for anything.

'Smile, Natty.' Glenn hit Natty's other arm.

'Oh, will you two get the hell off me?' Natty pushed their arms away, trying not to laugh.

'Bloody wish, Natty, that's all I can say.' Glenn took her purse from her bag, smirking.

'Suggest you think again on this bridesmaid shopping, then, if you want.' Natty began chuckling.

They all became hysterical as the bus pulled up in front of them; as they went onto the bus they all felt pains in their stomachs through laughing.

'What do you think, Natty; reckon I can have a go on my wedding night?' Glenn and Natty sat together on the chequered fabric, turning around as Ruth sat behind them so they could all be together in conversation.

'Not quite sure, Glenn; what if he brings his stripy pyjamas?'

'Won't be looking at his stripes.' Glenn began to blush.

'OK, you two, really, enough now. The thought of you and Old Boy really doesn't appeal, and I didn't think we had to go into complete detail about the whole strange thing.' Shaking her head, Ruth took her money from her pocket to pay.

'Tickets, please!'

Ruth handed her money over to the bus conductor, who turned the handle of his small silver machine and handed her a small white slip of paper. As she folded the paper into a small square she

319

watched her sisters in disapproval; unless she was doing the joking and winding up, she had never really been happy. As she sat behind them, her belief about herself was confirmed to her.

'What's wrong, Ruth? You like ladies?' Glenn's voice was almost squeaky as the mere mention of such a thing caused her embarrassment.

'Not sure! Who's the one getting married? You're both meant to be an example. Anyway, nothing wrong with a little bit of female tongue.' Ruth stuck her tongue out as she pressed the button on the white pole for the bus to stop, to her relief.

Without any thought they all took each other's arms and walked happily to the wedding shop in town.

Ruth was enthralled with all the beautiful gowns hung closely together, the elegantly sewn sequins and pearls. Surrounded by delicate lace and silk, Ruth felt as though she was finally in her princess castle. She could pick anyone she wanted to attend the coming ball, embracing the sensation of the expensive material touching her fingers as she slid her hand along the dresses, stepping slowly around the red carpet.

'Hello, little fellow, that was a quick nap. Guess what: shall we make you something to eat? I think it should be OK. I'm hungry too.' Lucas had watched George sleep in his playpen for the last hour; he hadn't moved from his side, seeing his small tucked-up body curled in comfort and his small chest moving in and out with each and every new breath. Lucas's voice was soft as he pulled George up over his arm and held him tightly. Wiping the boy's small nose with the cuff of his red jumper, Lucas made his way into the kitchen.

'Mummy!' George's voice was soft and slow.

'Hey, little fellow, Mummy won't be too long; she has lots of important things to do. She's marrying your daddy, you see. And it's going to be such a wonderful thing. Right, now where shall we put you?' Lucas held tightly on to the fretting young child as he searched for the small wooden highchair he had seen once before.

'Mummy.' George began to cry in his own searching.

'Oh dear, don't cry, George, Mummy won't be long.' Lucas felt a panic overwhelm him; he couldn't bear hearing such a thing.

'Mum, Mum!'

320

'Here we go; I can see your chair!' Lucas placed George into the wooden seat and began to pull the little brown leather strap around his waist, holding him in safely. Lucas began to sing a song to him as he grabbed a saucepan from the shelf and a wooden spoon from the drawer.

'Here we are, George; make some music.' Lucas's voice was calm; he wanted to cry for the young child who sat sobbing in his chair.

*Clang! Clang! Clang!* George began to giggle as the noise echoed through the kitchen.

Lucas took another saucepan from the shelf and another spoon from the drawer and sat on the floor next to him.

As Lucas beat the saucepan hard, it gave him an idea of what to cook for lunch.

'Beans, George, beans!' Lucas could hardly hear himself speak through all the noise and chuckles coming from his little friend.


'Please, Natty, do not say what I think you're going to.' Glenn's voice was full of worry.

'What, Glenn? They are lovely, really pretty.' Natty looked at Ruth and desperately attempted to hold her laughter back.

'Glenn, you have to be joking. You can't make us wear them.' Ruth stood with her hands on her hips, shaking her head.

'Look, you two, it's my wedding day.' Glenn held out two bridesmaids' dresses on metal hangers.

'But there are so many other lovely colours; there are so many frills.' Natty stepped forward and touched the cold silk.

'Looks like you will finally wear a dress after all, Natty. No scissors about, are there?' Ruth giggled and knew her comment was really uncalled for.

'Why don't you get lost, Ruth? Who wants you as a bridesmaid anyway?' Natty asked harshly.

'Can you two just take this seriously instead of always thinking of yourselves?' Glenn felt a little upset at her sisters' attitudes toward her dress choice for them, and the pangs in her stomach as she yearned to see George didn't help. She prayed Lucas would be all right with him and know what to do.

*

321

*Clang! Clang!*

'George, are you ready to eat?' Lucas raised his voice slightly as he placed a small plate on the highchair table, beans on one side and toast on another. With anticipation he pulled the music maker away from George, gently placing it on the floor.

'Mummy!'

'George, let me show you something; if you keep them separated you can really taste the juice.' Lucas leant over the small table, moving the beans around the small yellow plate.

Sitting at the table next to George, Lucas began to eat his lunch.

'No, George, you must not move your body so hard in your chair; it may fall over. Stay still and eat, little fellow. Look, beans, yum yum.'

Lucas attempted to eat as he heard the thudding of the wooden legs on the tiled flooring. George would move his body back and forward in the chair, holding on to his little table screwed to the wood.

'OK, little man, we are going to have to help you not tip that chair over.' Lucas quickly pushed his plate to the centre of the table. Going into the garden he began his search; he knew his idea was going to work and then they could both eat happily, make an orchestra of cutlery after their bellies were full. He just could not risk him tipping himself over.

Standing amongst Stanley's tools, Lucas pushed his hands through his curly hair.

'Here we go! This should do the job.'


'I'm not going out there, Natty; there is no way I am standing in the middle of the shop in this. No way!'

Natty sighed. 'I kind of get what you're saying, Ruth. What do you think we should do?'

'Is there a little window we could escape through? I can't believe she picked these; she seems to have the same taste in men, doesn't she?' Ruth giggled in desperation.

'What the hell was she thinking with these, Ruth?' Natty's giggles became more apparent as she stood next to Ruth in the long gleaming mirror, a soft white curtain draped behind them as they stood dumbfounded side by side. 'I think she's getting us back, you know, for all the horrible things we did to her. Oh my God, I cannot imagine what Lucas will say when he sees me in this.'

They both looked straight ahead at the dresses, aware they had no way of getting out of wearing them.

'Really, Natty, she has to shove these. I'm not wearing it and that's that. I don't care if she's getting married or swallowing on her wedding night; it's not happening. Purple, of all the flaming colours; why did this have to be her favourite? Doesn't she know there are other colours? And the style, oh dear; I look like a huge mound of material. Can't do it, simply can't. It's such an awful colour for a dress.' Ruth looked down at the mounds of material wrapped around her small figure, shaking her head with her lips tightened in complete disapproval.

Natty held her nose, trying not to burst into laughter; it seemed to be the funniest thing. Glenn was keeping herself busy in the glamorous shop.

'How is this funny, Natty?'

Glenn tapped on the curtain. 'Are you two done in there? Let me see; I can't wait.' She hovered outside in excitement, jumping on the spot and clapping her hands.

Natty looked at Ruth. 'You go out first.'

'Sod this; I'm going to tell her we are not wearing them.' Ruth pulled the curtain back quickly.

'You look amazing! How beautiful do they look? I knew it, knew they'd be the right colour. So got an eye for details, haven't I?' Glenn almost screamed with happiness, her voice high-pitched as she moved around the shop in glee.

Natty and Ruth stood side by side in full view of the other customers in the shop with their shoulders lowered, gritting their teeth.

'I can't wear it, Nat. We'll simply have to refuse,' Ruth whispered under her breath.

'You will have to tell her, then, 'cause I'm not,' Natty whispered back.

'So? What do you think?' Glenn rushed toward them. 'Well, cat got your tongue or something, Ruth?' She crossed her arms and began tapping her foot on the carpet, waiting for her sister's response.

'Um. Glenn, I really like it; yes, I do. Lovely, all of it.' Ruth spoke hesitantly, knowing she simply couldn't let her sister down. She'd have to get her back another day for subjecting her to such torment.

'Natty?' Glenn nodded her head as she waited for another gracious comment.

'Yeah, lovely, Glenn.' Natty smiled half-heartedly.

Glenn paused for a moment and began to rub her chin in contemplation.

'I was kind of thinking you two remind me of something I threw out of my bathroom window.' Glenn roared with laughter at her sisters. They all began to laugh together.

'Does this mean we're ditching the big fluffy purple idea, then, Glenn?' Natty could barely speak through laughter.

'No, Natty, we are so keeping them.' The shop was filled with laughter and adrenaline. They all held on to their stomachs as the laughter flooded from them.


'Now wasn't that lunch nice, little fellow? All safe and snug. Shall we go and blow some bubbles?'

Lucas took George into the back garden and happily sat with him on the cold paving slabs. George snuggled up on his lap as the wind and the warm air swept past them.

'Watch, little one, look at the colours in them. Some will give up against the wind and pop in the sky; the others will fight against the strength of the air, they won't give in, and they will swirl and bounce high above the clouds.'

'Bubble!' George giggled and smiled in awe. The small plastic tube he held was wet and bubbly.

'That's it, George, bubble: you said it. Now watch, George, watch them fly like the wind, just as you will one day. The sky will always be above you, protecting you and keeping you safe, and you shall float and glide like this wonderful creation we see before us.' Lucas took George's hand gently and blew another bubble onto it.

'You have your bubble now, George; simply let it go. Oh, it popped. Never mind; we can always blow another, but don't tell anyone.' Lucas smiled as he kissed George on his head, feeling surprised his hair didn't smell of apples.

*

'Tickets, please!'

'Thanks, you two; it's been nice.' Glenn placed her bags on the chair.

'Nice? We didn't even get lunch!' Ruth rubbed her stomach as she sat behind Glenn. 'Really, Glenn, on a serious note, is there any actual reason we have to go purple?'

'Oh, yeah, Stanley has his tie now.'

Natty and Ruth looked at each other and frowned.

'Oh, so we have to go with it because of him?' Natty looked for her change.

'I won't even nick it; I will buy him a pink one.' Ruth giggled.

'I'm sure Lucas has loved every minute of being with George.' Natty sat up straight as she spoke about the man she'd love to be dress shopping for, to become Mrs Dunstable.

'Lucas, oh lovely Lucas!' Ruth punched Natty's arm, smiling.

'It was a bit daring of me. I have pulled so much hair out trying to get George to listen, I will end up bald before Stanley. Oh my God, it's like I'm speaking a different language.'

'How sweet, two baldies together. Lucky his name isn't Gerry.' Natty and Ruth began laughing as they sat side by side on the red double-decker bus.

Not making eye contact with them, Glenn began to smirk at Ruth's joke, opening up a small bar of warm chocolate from her bag.

'Dress is going to be pulling in some skin.' Glenn undid the button of her jeans. 'My trousers have been sticking up my bum all day.' She quickly turned around, hoping she could eat the chocolate without her sisters seeing.

'Yes, we noticed your big cheeks.' Ruth nodded her head, happy with her comment, and then began to laugh with Natty once more.

Glenn turned around again, leaning on the metal chair frame. 'Do you know I took George to the beach the other day? I refused point blank to let him come out of his pram, and do you know when I took his little socks off he only had sand in the little buggers?' She sounded happy and relieved to be speaking of George.

Her sisters laughed. They could see she was really enjoying her day with them, and apart from the purple dress ordeal they were with her.

325

'Anyway, Natty, what about you and Lucas, then?' Glenn placed the last piece of chocolate into her mouth without offering her sisters any.

'What about it?' Natty's laughter came to a sudden halt; she leant on her handbag and began looking out of the window.

'Oh, come on, so obvious, really. You might as well wrap your knickers around his neck; not like you can give the game away any more.' Ruth's voice was raised.

'Not like that at all. He really is a nice fellow,' Natty said, still staring out of the dirty window.

'Bloody hot now he's not dressed like a tramp.' Glenn smiled.

'Oh, so you approve of him now?' Natty raised her eyebrows, making eye contact with Glenn finally.

'I'd grab him up, Natty, if I were you, honestly. You know, if you feel like it.' Glenn turned around while she pushed the empty wrapper into her bag.

'Ruth, Ruth.' Natty moved Ruth's arm back and forward as she could see her staring for far too long at another passenger.

Ruth found herself fixated on a pretty young lady reading a book in the next row of chairs; her hair was short and blonde and she wore a very smart black suit.

'Ruth!' Natty pushed her, feeling embarrassed.

'I'd like to kiss her.' Ruth spoke softly and almost in a daze.

'Is she joking?' Natty tapped Glenn on the shoulder. The two of them giggled nervously, praying the passenger wouldn't overhear.

Glenn turned around once again. 'Ruth, give it a rest.'

'I'd like to kiss her, the lady with the happy eyes.' Ruth continued to stare.

'You will end up with a black one in a minute if you don't stop staring at her,' Natty whispered in a stern tone. 'You're being silly. I mean, you like boys.'

'Now, Natty, how would you really know if I like boys?' Ruth raised her eyebrows with a snarky look.

'Well, it's pretty obvious.' Glenn couldn't help but get involved.

'Why is it so obvious, Glenn?'

'Well, because you do.'

Ruth could see the pretty young lady smiling at her and happily returned her gesture with a little wave.

'OK, Ruth, made your point.' Natty pinched Ruth's leg.

'Anyway, the other day I had to cut some funny tiger-shaped mask from the back of a cereal box for George. He loved it; he was roaring around the house getting under my feet all day.' Glenn spoke quickly, praying to change the subject, and longed for the pretty lady to leave the bus.

'I'm going to kiss her soon; I am.'

'Ruth, please. Anyway, you're not going to believe what happened the other day: I picked up one of George's many multi-coloured coated chocolate button things. I continued hoovering.'

'Continued hoovering? Oh, very posh.' Ruth spoke while smiling at the young lady.

'And you know what? By the time I got the whole living room done, it had melted in my hand. I thought, *Goodness, why does everything have to be so hard?* I mean, also, how do you explain to a one-year-old boy his sugar has melted on his cereal? Screams away, honestly, keeps insisting he hasn't got any. It's melted, boy, I keep saying, it's melted. Just like my head if you keep asking.'

'Did you put more on?' Natty leant forward more.

'Oh, certainly, yes. Not sure why it always has to be so confusing. So I stuck the whole sugar tub in front of him and he dug his little hand in. Think he's off sugar for life.' Glenn laughed and her sisters followed.

'So you don't cut off little Billy Bear's golden crust any more, either?' Ruth scrunched her face up.

'Not funny, Ruth; really, about as funny as your antics lately.'

'Couldn't tell you about my antics, but if you promise to shut the hell up for five seconds, I promise sincerely with my hand on my big girl-loving heart, Brownie's honour, I will wear that big mother of a dress.'

'Yeah, me too.' Natty smiled.

'Just be adult about it, you two. You're getting off soon; I will send Lucas home.' Glenn began to feel irritated; she had been away from George too long and knew Stanley was going to be home late from the office. Deep down she didn't want her day with her sisters to end.

'Adult? Oh, goodness, really? A little bit of stripy-pyjama sex and you're big now?' Ruth pulled her bag onto her shoulder, ready to get off at the next stop.

'I've had a baby, even bought my own furniture.' Glenn didn't look at her.

'That's a shame. Could have bought some bigger-arsed jeans.' Ruth pulled the cord and went to stand near the open entrance of the bus, holding on to the pole, waiting for the bus to stop so she could simply step off. She could smell the cigarettes from the upper deck and felt a sudden urge to inhale; the thought of her only friend rushed through her mind.

Natty and Ruth finally arrived home. Slumping into the armchairs in the dining room they looked at each other and laughed. Hearing the phone ringing, they both sat waiting for the other to get up again.

Ruth ignored the chimes and leant over, taking off her shoes.

'I will get it, Ruth, don't you move.' Natty huffed and stormed off.

'Hello? Oh, hello, Glenn. Right, OK! He had an orange face ... yes. He cut the legs off what?' Natty placed her hand gently over her mouth, praying she could hold back her laughter.

# 58

Her hair felt a tangled mess as her face felt the soft pillow, snuggling further into her minute of pure comfort. Pulling the white sheets up to her chin, gripping them with her fingers, she attempted to go back to sleep.

The thought of her dinner with him went over and over in her mind. It had been three months since she had spent most of the evening conscious with him, and she wished she could do it all over again. It had been lovely and exciting. She wished she hadn't drunk so much and ruined such an evening. She might even have got the goodnight kiss she was hoping for. It was such a waste of good underwear, she thought; her mind flitted from one thought to another. He hadn't been back to the shop since. She only wished there was some way of getting hold of him.

Aware she'd have to be getting up for work, she sighed. She could call and ask for forgiveness for not turning up. She didn't want to spend another day watching the door and praying each customer was him. The thoughts went over and over in her mind as she hoped it wasn't her inquisitiveness which had made him disappear, and of course her awful inability to stop at one bottle of white wine.

He must be busy, she thought; yes, that was it. She wondered what he was doing that morning. What if he went to the shop and she'd chosen to stay in bed all day?

The confusion and emotions which rushed through her were immense. Seeing her clothes scattered across the floor, she thought she was never going to find her knickers in all the mess.

Her thoughts were disrupted as she felt his strong arm coming over her slim waist.

As he kissed the back of her neck, her naked body tingled. As he pushed himself closer to her she felt his firm penis rub against her body.

'Morning, Suzy.'

'Morning, Harry.' Suzy spoke gently as she felt the sensation of his fingers between her legs, making her aroused instantly. Grabbing his hand, Suzy pushed his fingers further into her waiting wetness. She knew she'd be searching for her knickers later.

'I think the flowers are here.' Matthew spoke hastily, panicking at the top of the stairs as he tied his purple tie.

Ruth rushed to open the front door, clutching the front of her long dress on the way.

'Pink! Is she joking?' Ruth took the box of flowers from the lady, shaking her head in disbelief at the colour choice. As she went to close the door she could see an old lady standing at the front gate wearing a cream coat and holding an umbrella. Ruth popped her head out again quickly and looked at the sky; it definitely wasn't going to rain. 'Stupid old lady.'

'Ruth,' Matthew said, uncertainly, 'your dress is very nice.' He frowned a little, unsure of where his daughter was underneath the mounds of purple material.

'Not funny, Dad.' Ruth smiled and placed the box of flowers on the telephone table. The scent from the roses and fuchsias was beautiful. A selection of petite pink roses lay at the bottom of the box. Ruth carefully took them in her hands and then a larger pink rose for her father's button hole and attempted to walk up the stairs to him, her elasticated neckline falling slightly from her shoulders, the bottom of her dress getting caught underneath her sparkly silver heels.

'Here you go, Dad.' Ruth slipped his rose into his dark blue jacket and patted his chest.

'Thank you, Ruth. Are you sure you can make it back downstairs safely?' Her father chuckled.

'Can you give these to Glenn, Dad? You look dapper, by the way.' Ruth picked her dress up at the front and turned to make her way down again. She held her head high, pretending she was making her way down the stairs of a banquet.

Her father inhaled a deep breath as he was left holding the small roses in his shaking hand. Gently straightening the rose in his button hole, he slowly made his way to Glenn's old room. She had slept there for the evening, as Lucas was happy to sleep on the sofa, his blue plastic bag tucked safely under the cushion.

It had been a wonderful night, all of them home together again. Matthew had waited for them to all fall asleep before creeping into the kitchen and sneaking out the garden door. He wanted to sit with Eve for a while, speak to her about the morning's wonderful event. Sitting with her in the night sky under the stars, he asked her why she had to sacrifice herself, why she had to miss out on being with her daughter on her wedding day. And of course the answers from her never came. He had to let her know it was a waste of a wonderful life they all could have shared together. As he gazed up into the night sky he could see the moon playing hide-and-seek with him, blemished behind the trees. He closed his eyes and prayed in another life they would both have their time again.

Tapping gently on the bedroom door with his knuckle, he felt a weakness in all his limbs; his knees could barely hold his weight.

'Come in.'

Pushing the door open slowly he saw her, momentarily forgetting all else. Her silhouette at the window, she was simply flawless. His beautiful daughter was an image of perfection, just like her mother. The sun's reflection surrounded her. Her guardian angel sealing her with warmth and love, his Eve, her mother was there with them; he felt it with every cell in his body.

Glenn looked over her shoulder and smiled at him. Her father knew she was as precious as the wedding dress she wore. Immersed in the moment, his hand pushed harder onto the small petals.

'Hi, Dad. What do you think? I got in it after all.' Glenn's voice was shaky and soft; her eyes sparkled, her cheeks a little flushed. Tears overwhelmed her; she swallowed them back down into her emotionally full body as he walked toward her. She prayed he wouldn't notice the extra panel sewn into the back of the dress to make it fit.

'Glenn, my dear Glenn, was I meant to see you? You look exquisite.' Her father had an inability to find the words. In that moment he thought he'd never feel with such intensity again, filled with exhilaration and an overwhelming love for his life and his family. He pushed the lump to the back of his throat, a burning sensation hurting him as he was desperate to let his tears free. 'I cannot believe what I am seeing; your mother would have been so proud of you.'

They stood opposite each other.

'Dad, can you fix my flowers into my hair?' Glenn smiled softly at him. She could see he was shaking.

'Oh, let me call Natty.' Her father went to turn.

'No, Dad, please, could you do it?' Glenn grabbed his arm gently to stop him leaving; she gazed reassuringly at him.

Moving slowly behind her, he placed the small pink roses on her dressing table. His hands were clammy and shaking as he began sliding the gold flower pins into her hair to keep her pretty lace veil in place. It was completely divine as it touched her shoulders gracefully.

He hoped he wasn't hurting her as he spoke softly. 'I cannot believe you're all grown up now.' He reached carefully for another flower pin.

'Dad, I'm not all grown up. I only look like I am. I love him, Dad, with all of my heart. That's all I know. I love George. I love you all; I even love Lucas. I know I'm not all grown up. I'm so scared, Dad.' Glenn lowered her head a little.

'Love isn't anything to be scared of.' He felt Glenn move her head down and prayed she wasn't upset, finding the words hard as the emotions were fighting to come out of his body.

'Dad, how did you know you were ready to marry Mum?' Glenn stood poised once again, taking in a deep breath.

He paused for only a moment, holding the pin near her hair.

'I always knew. Glenn, there wasn't a time; it had been in me all along. The dream of marrying her was in me before we had even met.' He swallowed hard.

'That's very beautiful, Dad.'

'Yes, she was. I just wish ... anyway, let's not get into all my stuff.' He couldn't speak of the mistakes he had made. The thought was unbearable.

'Dad, it's why I'm here, it's why you're putting pins in my hair, why I'm standing in her wedding dress. Everything about this moment is because of her. So it's our stuff, Dad.' Glenn turned around slowly to look at him. Looking into his glassy eyes, she knew he missed her terribly.

'It should have been her putting your pins in; I'm not doing a very good job.' He was almost whispering, giving her a solemn look.

'Dad, I'm happy it's you.' Glenn touched his soft pink button hole with the tips of her fingers.

'Thank you, Glenn; I am happy you asked me.'

'I wish she was here, though, Dad, after everything. I really do.' Glenn's emotions surged to her throat. She was desperate to cry.

Putting the small pin on the dressing table, her father gently moved her veil at each side, moving his fingers carefully down the lace as he spoke to her. 'She is my angel, she's in your eyes and sees and feels everything for you. She's standing right here with you, wishing she could straighten your pins out.'

They chuckled together, holding back their tears.

'I love him so much, Dad.' Glenn's tears began to well in her pretty eyes.

'It would be impossible for the whole world not to notice today, Glenn. You're sparkling like the stars, every single one of them.'

'Does it show?' Glenn smiled; her eyes glistened, full of beauty and love.

'It certainly does. I remember looking into your eyes on the day you were born, as your innocence and love shone right through just like now.' Moving his face a little closer, he touched her nose with his finger.

'I'm scared, Dad; I'm scared I'm going to make a mess of it all.'

'Glenn, you don't know where today is going to take you; your innocence is an amazing advantage in all this. You don't know how it's going to end, but you can sure make it begin. Simply enjoy and embrace each and every moment, even the difficult ones; they have a funny way of making you a little wiser.' He wiped a soft tear from her eye away with his finger. 'The love you feel, don't ever push it away. Allow yourself to have it always. Your mother and I are so very proud of you. Believe in it, my beautiful child.'

'Dad, you're going to make me cry even more, then my mascara will run.' The tears began to roll down her cheeks.

As he pulled her to his chest his tears fell with hers, his hand touching the back of her veil. This was the moment when he had to let his daughter go finally. His loan on her young life was now over. She was free to take the steps she wanted to. He'd pray every night she'd remain as happy as she was right then in his arms.

Stanley sat on the edge of their bed holding his tie in his hands.

'Hello, George. I'm marrying Mummy today; do you think I should?'

# 59

---

It was tranquil, each corner echoed with the night's presence, a calmness settled within each room.

'Oh, hello, Matthew, you made me jump. Why are you sitting in the dark?' Lucas whispered as he went into the living room, holding on to a full cup of frothy cocoa. It was nearly midnight and he'd finished his shift at the theatre.

'Hello, Lucas. Don't worry about me; I was thinking to myself.' Matthew sat back in the armchair.

'Would you like me to make you a drink, Matthew? The kettle is still hot.'

'No, I'm fine.'

'If you don't mind me asking, what are you thinking about?' Lucas perched on the arm of the sofa, being careful not to spill his drink, speaking with innocence.

'Oh, nothing, honestly. I've been meaning to do something for a while now, that's all.' Matthew leant forward in his chair.

'Well, Matthew, I suggest you do it, whatever it may be.'

Lucas came slightly into view in the dark room. Matthew smiled at him.

The reflection of the moon came through the netted window; Matthew could see his daughter's wedding picture. He knew she was still being protected as the silver light shone upon them. Time seemed to have passed so quickly, three months and one day since they had shared their vows. A sense of sadness surrounded him, as he remembered sharing his as though it had been only yesterday.

'You go to bed, Lucas; you must be very tired. I will be fine.'

'Matthew, I hear a concern in your voice.'

Matthew rubbed the edge of the armchair with his hands, as they both sat in the dark.

'She's gone, Lucas; how can I justify doing anything good for myself?' Matthew's voice was crackly, on the verge of erupting into tears.

'Matthew, Glenn will be wonderfully happy. Stanley is a good man.' Lucas sensed how distressed Matthew was as he sat in the dark.

'No, Lucas, I mean my Eve. You remember her still?'

'Yes, Matthew, I do; she was the prettiest thing I'd ever seen, if you don't mind me saying, of course.' Lucas's thoughts went onto Natty quickly.

'What's the point of it all, Lucas? Really, is there any?'

'Matthew, if life wasn't so important then why would people fight for it? It's living people are scared of.' Lucas could hear Matthew's sniffing and gentle sobs.

'But she didn't fight, did she? She gave up.' Matthew's voice was deep and husky.

'Dear Matthew, I don't think she did. I believe ending her life was her only way. It was something very important to her. It was something she needed to do. I feel her fight was to live.' Lucas felt emotional as he sipped his warm drink.

Matthew sighed and sat back in his chair. 'I can imagine you're right, Lucas.'

'She only existed in the dark shadows she carried for so long.' Lucas spoke gently, almost whispering.

'Lucas, how do you know this?' Matthew wiped his eyes as he gazed at the moonlit window, his voice soft.

Lucas chuckled respectfully, taking another quick sip from his cup. 'I think you must remember where we met, Matthew.' He tipped the last dregs of chocolate into his mouth; the chocolate powder congealing at the bottom had always been his favourite. Pushing his finger into the base of the cup, he scooped up a blob of dark cocoa. As the damp cocoa burst into powder on his tongue he became curious about how it was made.

'I kind of see now. Thank you, Lucas.'

'Please, Matthew, you must do exactly what it is you were thinking. God bless you, Matthew. Goodnight.' Lucas squeezed Matthew's shoulder before making his way to bed.

Lucas placed his empty cup at the side of his bed. Cupping his hand over his mouth, he opened the drawer to see the blue plastic bag. Panic and guilt overwhelmed him for doing something so awful. She'd never speak to him again; she had already told him such. Jumping onto the bed and pulling up the dark blue covers, he pushed his finger further into the remnants of fine powder.

Matthew got up from his chair and turned on the light. Gazing again at Glenn's beautiful wedding picture in a silver frame on the window sill, blowing out a huge sigh, he made his way to the cupboard under the stairs. Kneeling down in the dark he reached in for the typewriter. As he balanced it on his lap, he softly rubbed his hands over the front, feeling the keys.

There was a silence to everything in his life at that minute, alone on the floor in the hall. The only sounds were the ticking of the clock and his breathing. Looking up at the ceiling at the elegant chandelier, he understood finally where he had gone wrong, why he couldn't just leave Eve be, to love as she wanted and to breathe each and every breath for everything she felt important. His precious daughters had suffered at her hands and his weakness. It had all been for nothing.

Pressing down a little harder on the typewriter, he knew he could do it. Eve would have wanted him to. She'd be with him through every word.

Placing the typewriter on the small table in the living room, he decided to make a drink. His eyes were sore and stinging through tiredness and tears which had been shed, but he wasn't going to stop until the first page was written, even if it took all night.

As he took a cup from the kitchen cupboard, tears began to fall from his eyes again; his stomach began to burn with a sadness he couldn't bear. Leaning up against the work surface, his arms out straight, he gripped the edge and cried hard, his tears falling onto the tiled floor.

'Eve, I miss you.' Breathing erratically, he attempted to contain himself as he took another cup from the cupboard. Placing a teabag in each cup, one with sugar and one with extra milk, he poured the water in, making the milky tea he knew she'd enjoy. Slowly he made his way back to the living room with the two cups, placing them on the mantelpiece.

337

He needed some paper; there was no time to waste. Dashing into the dining room to fetch some, he glanced at Eve's chair, her soft grey blanket still folded over the edge. Touching it with his hands, the softness on his fingertips, he took the green cushion which was originally for the sofa into his hands and placed it on his face, smelling her and remembering the day he placed it behind her back as she sat looking out into the garden.

Holding the faded cushion to his chest, he took the paper and pens from the mahogany drawer and frantically made his way back.

He was finally ready; it had been such a long time since he had bought the typewriter. Laying Eve's green cushion behind his back he pulled the small table across, leaning forward as it was the same height as his knees. Blowing the dust from the keys he placed the paper inside, rolling the handle at the edge as he watched the paper glide around the oval reel.

Holding his hands out, he clicked his fingers and moved them up and down, not knowing where to start. His fingers hovered over the letters. He could see one of them was a little lower than the others. He remembered the shop owner telling him one of them was a little stiff.

Again and again he pressed the letter; again and again he pushed his finger more firmly onto it.

*Y Y Y Y Y Y Y Y Y Y*

His tears welled up in his eyes once more. Sitting up straight, he coughed, hoping to prevent them from leaving his body. Looking up at the two cups, he rubbed both his hands over his face. Dried his eyes and yanked the piece of paper swiftly from the machine. Taking another piece, he rolled it through again and inhaled a deep breath, his fingers like magnets on the letters, creating meaning and bringing rhythm to his thoughts.

# 60

'One, two, three, turn, fall and glide, Come on, you can do this. OK, music off. Let's do this without any distractions. Again!'

Lucas stood at the side of the stage, embracing the intense rehearsals. The sweating flush-faced men in black trousers bare-chested, their muscles pulsating with enthusiasm and passion, the atmosphere exhilarating.

Gripping the wood of his mop handle, Lucas stood frozen with awe for the men. His stomach was filled with intense emotions at the beauty of the body's ability to move so; he was captured with disbelief.

'Come on, it's one, two, three, fall, use your arms, bring the energy through your soul,' Lucas said under his breath. He knew the dance routine; he understood it, felt it, and longed to be like the six agile men flying free with pure power.

'Imbeciles. Move again, again, again.' The choreographer's voice was full of aggression, as he became more and more impatient; the whole thing was intolerable for him as he became increasingly agitated with the young men who tore every muscle to its limits.

Lucas swallowed hard, becoming frightened at such harshness. Dance was and had always been the most beautiful spectacle in the entire world. How could anyone destroy it? Lucas felt himself moving forward onto the hot lit stage to ask the balding man why he had to be so unkind, but he knew it'd be his job. Stopping in his tracks, he felt desperate to throw the dirty mop down and show him the moves, show him he needn't be so rude to people following their dreams, his own dream. Lucas began to shake, feeling the tears welling up in his eyes.

'Again. This time the music; at least we can get that right. That's it, glide. Smile. Wonderful, we have it finally. Yes, we have it.'

Turning and whirling and prancing around every inch of the stage, the men were truly magnificent. Lucas's tears fell onto his cheeks as he lost himself with amazement at the side of the stage. Looking down at his feet, his old shoes and tatty baggy janitor trousers, he knew his magic feet were masked there somewhere.

Again they rehearsed; he became entrapped in the moment of a fascinating performance. He was engulfed, in a trance of pure delight.

'That's a call for today.'

Standing back a little, Lucas allowed the young men to pass him at the side of the stage, pushing the mop bucket across with his foot in case they fell into it. Smelling their sweat, he felt their energy pumping from their masculine strong bodies. He longed more than ever to be with them; it had been burning inside him for so many years, yearning to come out. He was born to dance, but he wouldn't allow himself to be free.

Pushing the full bucket of dirty water with the force of the mop he slowly walked behind them.

Laughing and hitting each other in jest, they were jubilant they had finally managed to get their steps right. They didn't turn around; they couldn't see him lingering behind, and he was of course only the broom boy.

Lucas leant the mop and bucket against the white-painted brick wall and took the broom. Pushing his grubby hands through his brown curls, he went to make his way back to the stage, to be alone once again.

The young men were hovering outside the dressing rooms as they spoke; Lucas could overhear them.

'You're not going for it, then?'

'No, it's a dump, wouldn't put my dog in it.'

'What you two on about?'

'Room going, not too dear either. Shame; could have done with the change.'

Gripping the broom, inhaling a deep breath and wondering whether they'd take interest in him if he was to talk to them, Lucas made his way toward the men.

'Excuse me. I hope you don't mind me asking, as I overheard you. Is the room you speak of still available?' Lucas's voice was soft.

'Oh, yeah. Not bad either,' the tall blond dancer said loudly, grinning at him.

The group of men chuckled between themselves.

'Could you possibly let me know where it is?' Lucas wiped his hands on the dirty rag hanging from his brown leather belt.

'Look, mate, it's a bit of a dump, but if you're looking, 45 Parkside. It'd probably be all right for you, thinking about it.' The young man looked Lucas up and down.

'I am looking, thank you. I'm very grateful for your help. And may I say how sincerely you move?'

'Yeah, OK.' They all began to laugh as they went into the dressing room, closing the door in his face.

Lucas took a pen from his shirt and wrote the address down on his hand, making his way back to the empty stage.

Lucas wiped his sweaty brow; his chores were done. As he stood at his locker the door from the men's dressing room was flung open. They were smartly dressed, still chatting and giggling.

'Here you go. Treat yourself.'

'Thank you, that's really kind.' Taking the paper plate of sandwiches and leftover cake, Lucas sat on the floor outside the dressing room. The slightly stale bread stuck to his teeth. He saved the jam tart for Natty, placing it on the edge.

Laying the crumpled plate at the side of his legs, he sat thinking of the dance rehearsal.

'Oh, mate, sorry.' A smart young man had come rushing out of the dressing room, accidently kicking the paper plate. His black hair was waxed back and he wore a black fitted suit, a crisp white shirt and a thin black tie; his shoes were polished to shine. They watched the jam tart roll across the floor.

The young man went to pick it up and began blowing dust residue from it.

'Uh, strawberry.' The jam stuck to his fingers. Making his way to the small sink in the corridor where Lucas kept his cleaning items, he quickly washed them.

Watching the young man hastily drying his hands, Lucas went to stand with him. 'How do you do it?' Folding the plate, Lucas pushed it into the bin.

341

'Do what? Stick my fingers in jam?' The young man laughed, pushing the paper towel on top of the already-full rubbish bin.

'Dance like you do.' The excitement stirred within his stomach.

'Just do. Always have, always will.' The young man smiled and went to pass him.

'How? I mean, how do you get in here to do it?' Lucas raised his voice, hoping to get the attention of the man once more.

The man turned quickly, pushing his hands into his trouser pockets. 'Can you dance?'

'I think so. To be on fire each and every time I move. Every inch of me pulsates with happiness and being free as the wind.' Emotions stirred in Lucas; he spoke with a passion he thought he'd buried long ago.

'Hey, you got it going. Just get the forms, only a few papers, fill them and let them see.' The helpful man began to walk away, stopping in his tracks once more. 'Oh, by the way, thanks for your comment earlier; nice to hear someone appreciates us.'

Lucas tied the blue bag up hastily and took his coat from his locker, holding his scarf in his hands, the collar to his coat sticking up as he made his way excitedly to the front desk.

A lady sat in small glitter-rimmed glasses, looking over them, smiling.

Wrapping the scarf around his hand again and again, Lucas waited nervously for the courage to ask for something he had never thought possible. Stepping forward to the edge of the shiny wooden desk, Lucas's hands became clammy; he wrapped his scarf tighter and tighter around his shaking hands.

'Excuse me, I was wondering if it would be possible for you to let me have a form?'

Peering over the top of her glasses, the busy lady seemed confused.

'Here, I mean. Like the young man said I have to fill it in; a few papers, he said, and then they can see.' Lucas swallowed hard, feeling the pulsating of his temples.

'You want to dance like all the others, do you?' Her voice was high-pitched, almost squeaky.

Opening a small file she handed him an application form. The elite dance school attached to the theatre.

Lucas took the form, his hands shaking with an anxious anticipation. Seeing the white paper near his fingertips, his thoughts went to his parents. How they'd punish him for doing such a thing. His legs began to ache with the memory of the torment he had been subjected to. Having the papers in his grasp, he could see the pen on the back of his hand.

Gritting his teeth he made his way out of the theatre. Breathing in the cold night air, he gently folded the form, placing it in his pocket, feeling the blue plastic bag scrunched up in the bottom. Gazing at the starry sky, pulling his soft scarf gently around his neck, he made his way to 45 Parkside, the wheels of his bike the only sound.

# 61

'**D**ad, have you seen my gloves?' Ruth raised her voice as she leant around the white doorframe.

Her father didn't look up at her. He pressed each letter with force on his typewriter, completely lost within his own world.

'Thanks.' Rushing up the stairs and dashing into her father's bedroom, Ruth glanced at the china doll propped up on the white pillows; it was as though the small blue piercing eyes in the porcelain face watched her with intent as she moved around the immaculate room, aware in no uncertain terms she had to be crazy to have even taken it upon herself to enter. She'd be in trouble.

Shrugging her shoulders and continuing her forbidden search, she carefully began to hunt through her father's chest of drawers. The November chill was really biting and she wasn't going to get cold hands for anyone.

'Here we go!' Ruth held a soft pair of grey woolly gloves, pushing her fingers into them with satisfaction, the warmth from the expensive wool piercing her hands instantly. Quickly a smile came to her as she recalled the day when she had held her mother's hand. Her small bare hand was wrapped and protected as she walked by her mother's side. A day she remembered ended so sadly.

Holding her hand up in front of her face, Ruth could see her hands were the same size as her mother's, her mother's beautifully manicured hands, which would come down hard, stinging her and her sisters' young skin. An overwhelming sense of comfort and sadness rushed through her. Looking over at her mother's doll, Ruth suddenly felt an unusual guilt for touching the gloves.

'What you looking at? They're gloves, for goodness' sake, not the crown jewels.' Ruth glared at the doll as she left the bedroom with her belly churning with emotions and her hands warm.

'Bye, Dad,' Ruth shouted from the hall, her hands in her coat pocket.

Her father pulled the sheet of paper from the typewriter and placed in another.

'Dad, I am going now. Anyone there?' Ruth became hot and sweaty waiting for her father's response.

Her father pressed more and more firmly on each letter, his imagination flowing, biting his lip as he couldn't write the words quickly enough. Fear entrapped him; he prayed he'd write as fluently as his thoughts, the printed letters seeming to pour onto the white sheet.

'Dad, I'm going to ask Glenn if I can go and live with her!' Ruth's voice bellowed.

Still he pressed each key.

'Yes, Ruth, I hear you.' Her father didn't look up.


'Billy Bear, Mummy has had enough of plastic sausage and cake, darling.' Glenn sighed as she attempted to balance the small plastic food on the toy plate.

'Mummy some.' George pushed the tiny plate closer to her mouth.

'Yum, yum. Mummy full now.' Glenn pretended to eat the food to keep him happy, rubbing her belly. The plastic sausage rolled from the plate onto the carpet. She leant over to pick it up and smiled as she placed it back again; it fell back onto the carpet.

'The stupid thing, for Christ's sake.' Glenn leant across, picking up the sausage again. Holding the plate as still as she could, she concentrated on balancing the fake food in the middle.

'Mummy!' George knocked the plate out of her hands and onto the floor.

'I've just managed to balance it! Oh, why bother?' Glenn tossed the plate into the playpen.

George began to cry.

Glenn pulled him to her lap. He kicked and screamed, his little legs stiff. He was hard to hold as her jean skirt became caught under his legs. He wanted to play with the plastic food and he was making enough noise for the whole neighbourhood to hear. Leaning over, Glenn quickly picked up a plastic corn-on-the-cob; with the force of his arms the food was flung into the air. Glenn felt harassed and hot as the strength of her son got the better of her. Gently pushing him to the floor, she pulled her skirt down.

'See, if Daddy wants to eat plastic, Mummy has to do dinner.' Glenn blew out a long breath and made her way thankfully to the kitchen, flapping the front of her stripy T-shirt as the sweat rolled from under her breasts.

'Darling, have you seen my favourite shirt?' Stanley walked into the kitchen, ignoring his son kicking and screaming on the carpet.

'No, I haven't.' Glenn raised her voice over the cries, thinking of where the sausage finally would be going if her dear husband hassled her for anything at that moment.

'Damn it.' Stanley stood solemnly as he tried to button up his next choice of attire.

'Oh, thinking about it . . ,' Glenn's thoughts went back to the ironing pile she had happily put in the bin. The idea of maybe not giving Stanley too many helpings of sticky toffee pudding and custard rushed through her, and then he might get into the shirts he had left.

'Thinking about what?' Stanley carefully picked up George through his screams and placed him still kicking into the playpen. Instantly the cries subsided as George happily held the plastic plate.

'Oh, nothing.' Glenn went back into the living room to join them, holding on to a tea towel. Picking up the other colourful food items, she placed them in the netted pen. 'Here you go, Billy Bear, eat some and it might shut you up.'

'Glenn,' Stanley said sharply as he gently rubbed his son's head.

'Oh my God, Stanley, he hasn't stopped all day. I'm doing dinner now anyway.' Glenn smiled reluctantly.

'What're we having?'

'Sausages.' Glenn laughed to herself as she went back into the kitchen, taking a pan from the shelf.

Stanley picked George up from the playpen and sat with him on the floor.

'Daddy, Daddy.'

Picking up the small toy abacus, Stanley began to move the coloured wooden beads along.

'Now, little man, how old are you? You're nearly two.' Stanley leant over and spoke softly, raising his head to inhale the smell of fresh onions being thrown into the pan from the kitchen. 'One-two.' He slid the red balls along.

George giggled.

Glenn drained the potatoes she'd been boiling and began to mash them. The relief of being left alone by her son made her happy.

'Mummy?' George pushed the beads along, wanting to hear more counting.

Stanley moved twenty coloured beads along. As he moved he became aware Glenn would only be twenty-one in the coming month. As he slowly pushed them along the metal, George pushed them back again.

Stanley paused in his interaction for a moment, hearing his young wife singing to a song on the radio from the kitchen as she mashed through the soft white potatoes, and knew she'd be adding lots of extra butter just for him.

'Daddy, Daddy.' George pushed the abacus into Stanley's chest.

'No, it's OK, George, Daddy has to get ready to go out after dinner.' Stanley placed the abacus next to the sofa and grabbed a small yellow train.

George began to cry once again.

Stanley sighed as he picked up the beaded toy and slowly moved fifty-three beads along. The vast amount proved to him the thought which had gone over and over in his mind only an hour before they were married. How could he be so unfair as to hold such a beauty back from her young life? There were surely so many wonderful things she could be doing. Instead she was looking after him, ironing his shirts and making his house finally into a home. There must have been other things she wanted, someone younger, anything bigger and better.

The wonderful aroma of sausages blending with the fresh onion filled the air. Stanley walked slowly into the kitchen and kissed Glenn on her cheek.

'What was that for?' Glenn pushed her head into her neck, chuckling.

'Does there have to be a reason?' Stanley smacked her bottom as he left the kitchen again.

'Hey, Stan, I think the shirt you have on makes you look extremely handsome.' Glenn blushed as she looked at her husband at the kitchen door, wiping her hands on a tea towel before she tapped his chest. She always liked him in light blue. How she loved him; he meant the world to her, and if only he really understood how her life began the day he came into it. He was always so kind and gentle to her and their son, Glenn felt like the luckiest woman alive, even if she had to balance plastic sausages and iron stripy pyjamas.

Scooping mash from the serving dish, Glenn glanced at George in his highchair, her son now unable to see over the edge of the dinner table, as Lucas had felt the crazy need to cut the chair's legs down. It hadn't been such a silly thing after all. She'd sit with Stanley on the floor, leaning on the sofa with a small shandy, while George ate in his chair.

As Glenn and Stanley sat at the small dinner table they heard a knock at the door.

'I will get it.' Glenn pushed a forkful of mash into her mouth quickly.

'Hi, Glenn. Can I move in?' Ruth walked straight past Glenn in the hall, pulling her coat undone.

'Oh, hi, Ruth, why don't you come in?' Glenn tutted, shaking her head. 'We're having dinner; did you want some?'

Heading for the spare chair at the table, Ruth sat wiping her nose as the cold air had made it run.

'Hi, Stanley, nice shirt. Hello, little man.' Ruth leant over to the side to see George clearly.

Glenn continued to eat.

'Actually think I will have something.' Ruth cheekily made her way to the kitchen cupboard, finding a box of chocolates. Placing the box of chocolates on the table, she took it upon herself to open it. 'Yuck, these are the sort that stay in the cupboard all year round.' Ruth pushed her tongue out in disgust at the melting chocolate.

Glenn and Stanley began to laugh.

'Think they have actually been there that long.' Glenn was happy Ruth had finally been taught a small lesson in simply helping herself.

'So, can I live with you?' Ruth asked with eagerness, as she pushed the box away from her.

'Are you joking? No way are you living with us!' Glenn looked quickly to Stanley for moral support; she knew he'd be extremely unhappy about it.

Stanley thought about the abacus and wanted Glenn to be honest; she didn't have to pretend her sister wasn't welcome just to please him.

'Why, Glenn? I can help you with, as you call him, Billy Bear, do stuff around the house for you, may even get a job. Please, Glenn, please let me?' Ruth gave Glenn a puppyish look as she pleaded.

'What's brought this on, Ruth?' Glenn could feel intense indigestion coming on.

'Well, what's the point of me at home? Dad's always writing, or reading. Natty has all loved-up eyes. Sick to death of hearing about her locket; yes, I know it's my fault.' Ruth grabbed a sausage from Glenn's plate. 'And Lucas will be going. It's not going to be the same without him, ever. Oh, please do this for your little sister? Nice sausages, by the way.' She giggled.

'Ruth, we've only been married for six months; you can't just turn up on the doorstep, taking chocolates and nicking my blessed sausages.' Glenn began to feel furious with her sister's impertinence.

'Oh, pretty please.'

'Will you tell her, Stanley?' Glenn stared at him with raised eyebrows.

Stanley paused for a moment, looking at each of them.

'I think it might be nice for you, Glenn, someone your age. Do girl things, you know,' Stanley said softly, hoping he pleased his young wife with his answer.

'I don't believe this.' Glenn folded her arms.

'Look, Glenn, George seems happy about it.' Stanley watched Ruth and George playing peek-a-boo, reassuringly touching Glenn's arm.

Glenn could see all three of them looking at her, waiting for her to say yes, waiting for her to make the biggest mistake ever.

'OK, OK. Just for a while, I might actually like being around you. Are they Mother's gloves?'

Ruth had placed the gloves next to her at the table.

'Oh, yeah. They're so warm.' Ruth picked them up and dropped them again.

'You'd best get them back, Ruth, before Dad sees.' Glenn felt a concern for Ruth.

'He doesn't see anything apart from that stupid typewriter; God knows what he's got to write about anyway.' Speaking with a slight hostility, Ruth took her coat off and hung it over the back of the chair.

'Let me hold them.'

Ruth flung the gloves across the table, the finger of the soft wool landing straight in Glenn's mash.

'Brilliant, Ruth. See, everything you touch.' Glenn felt an overwhelming dread for saying yes, looking at the gloves in her dinner. She hadn't even moved in yet and already she could see her fist going in her sister's face.

They all laughed, Glenn in desperation as she picked the soiled glove from her dinner and ran it under the sink.

As the steam moved in front of her she thought hard of the woman who had brought them into the world and wasn't with them any more to witness their lives. Squeezing the wool gently between her fingers, Glenn longed for their mother to have had the chance to hold George on her lap, hold him close and embrace the sensation of him sleeping on her body. Glenn looked over at her son's messy face, mash on the strands of his hair, and smiled. She was going to make his life wonderful. Not allow him to carry such pain as she and her sisters did. Stanley and she were always going to be there for him, always.

'Hi, Dad.'

'Oh, hello, Ruth. Where did you go? Did you have a nice time?' Her father stood in the hall with a small pile of clean paper, making his way back into the living room.

'It's cool with Glenn.' Ruth smiled as she knew the soggy glove was in her pocket.

'What's cool with Glenn? What are you talking about?' Her father took the pen from behind his ear and quickly wrote on the paper.

'Moving in with Glenn, she's OK with it.' Touching the side of her brown duffel coat, Ruth could feel a wet patch.

Her father frowned.

'I did say, Dad.' Ruth made her way upstairs.

'No, you didn't, Ruth. I'm not sure if it's OK.' Rushing into the living room, he frantically pushed the paper into the typewriter, panicking he'd forget what he wanted to write. Again he absorbed himself in his words.

Holding on to the bannister Ruth stood on the stairs, shaking her head. Annoyance and sadness overcame her cold body as she waited for him to insist she wasn't going anywhere. Where had he gone behind the letters within his own existence?

'Night, Dad!' Her voice was soft as the typewriter echoed through the house.

# 62

'Sorry it took so long mate, to get you in; couldn't have you living with those mice.' The fat man gave Lucas a piece of paper. Lucas could smell stale cigarettes on his breath.

'That's really kind of you. The wait has suited me very much. I've been staying with a wonderful family. You'd love to meet them; they are the most sincere people you could ever meet. To think about it, I'm not really sure why I am leaving.'

'Yeah, I bet.' The fat man frowned, not caring much for his new tenant's feelings.

Lucas took the receipt for his very first payment of rent. His new home, 45 Parkside, was now where he was finally going to become independent. He had burdened the Hopkins family, his only family, for too long; he couldn't bear to outstay his welcome. How he'd miss them. In his hands a small piece of paper written on in pen revealed the day he was to stand on his own two feet. *£20.00 rent, 19th January 1978.*

'How long is he going to be?' Natty finished organising the table for his farewell gathering, wearing her best dark corduroys and a pretty pink blouse with long collars and large cuffs. She had made sure to spend as long as possible on her hair.

Glenn and Ruth had also come over to say goodbye. They had argued in the kitchen since they had arrived: who was doing what chore and how many times Ruth had forgotten to bring her washing down. They all waited together for his arrival.

Glenn was interrupted in her dispute with her sister.

'Oh, Billy Bear, how did you manage to get hold of that?' Glenn rushed forward in a panic, watching George run into the kitchen holding her mother's china doll by its delicate arm. The doll swung back and forth.

'Sorry, Dad!' Glenn looked guiltily at her father.

Her father placed the warm plate of sausage rolls on the side. 'Glenn, that's fine. It's a shame for it to be hidden away; it's too nice for it not to be played with.' He appeared strong; underneath his exterior he felt his stomach churn with nerves and fear, praying the last piece of Eve wouldn't be ruined. Gazing at his wedding ring, he clenched his hand tight.

'Dad, I will cover these.' Natty pulled out a roll of foil and wrapped it over the plate. Her thoughts went back swiftly to the time she had walked into their mother's home; her first diary, a gift from her mother, had been wrapped in the shiny aluminium sheet, and she had witnessed her mother's rare pretty smile.

'Dad, he'll have the eyes out and hair knotted in no time at all.' Glenn giggled nervously. 'Give Mummy the doll, Billy Bear.'

George gripped the doll hard.

'Billy Bear, give it to me!' Glenn's voice was stern as she started losing patience with him, knowing her family were staring at her lack of authority over her small son.

'Will you get off the Billy Bear stuff?' Ruth snapped at her sister, rolling her eyes.

George held on to the doll as if his life depended on it.

'George! Lucas is home.' Glenn wanted to scream at him.

George finally dropped the doll, the face cracking onto the kitchen tiles.

Glenn scrunched her face, fearful of picking it up just in case its perfect features had smashed.

Her father bent down and took it from the floor. Wiping its face and rubbing his hands over the black ringlets, touching the shiny rose-coloured cheek, the sharp edges of the cracked porcelain on the tips of his shaking fingers. His shocked body began to rattle as though his organs were dancing inside, his heart thumping with intensity as if its desire was to push its way out of his chest. He stood frightened as there was no way his denial for his Eve could ever stay hidden, the fractured figure finally making him accept his Eve, his beauty and love was damaged and truly broken inside her unique perfection. Breathing in steadily he placed the

353

unrecognisable doll into the cupboard, unable to reveal her imperfections to their daughters. Closing the cupboard door, he watched the doll going into the darkness, the shadow drowning its face, his head throbbing with acceptance and truth. He prayed Lucas would find the image and fix her with his gentleness and wonder. Help her as he had them.

'Hello, little fellow, what a lovely surprise. I can feel the warmth from you already taking the chill from me. Sounds like we have a full house. It makes me happy for you all to be here.' Lucas leant over and picked George up, kissing him firmly on his soft pink cheek. The house was extremely warm; the heating must have been on full.

'Hello, everyone. I've paid my first rent, all ready to go.' He kept his voice light, not allowing them to see what he was really feeling about the move deep down.

'Well done, Lucas,' they all said in unison.

'I so love his scarf,' Ruth said as she went to boil the kettle.

'You're not nicking it,' Natty snarled at her.

'Keep your frizzy wig on, Natty, it's only a scarf.'

To Natty it wasn't; it was something she knew Lucas would always wear. And, more importantly, it was a gift from her. She watched him as he spoke to her father and Glenn; he was so handsome, and belonged with them all.

'Look, Lucas, we have made you some lovely sandwiches; Ruth even made you a cake. She hasn't done that for a long time.' Natty gazed at Ruth, knowing how much she had loved to bake when she was small.

Natty saw Lucas taking off his coat and dashed forward to help him. Standing in the doorway of the kitchen, seeing them all together from afar and feeling as though her tears were going to burst from her heart, she squeezed his coat and scarf in her arms. He was leaving; she knew she'd be heartbroken the minute he laid his key to their home on the table. And no writing in her diary would bring him back.

'Hold on, Ruth, I have a little thing for you.' Lucas made his way past Natty and smiled as he did so.

As he went inside his bedroom he saw his suitcase still unzipped, filled with all the new belongings he had been gifted with. Rubbing his hands over the soft brown leather, he felt lucky. He had come

354

with a box with a few dirty newspapers and some blankets. He now owned far more than he ever could have imagined, his head held high, and the stylish case and clothes to match.

Taking the small photo from the front of the case, he gazed at himself standing with his parents. Closing his eyes, he thought about his dancing; he was sure he wasn't doing the wrong thing.

Pushing the creased photo back again, Lucas realised the blue plastic bag was still in the pocket of his coat. Feeling as though he wanted to scream through the fear she may have found it, he hastily made his way back down the stairs. His coat still hung on the coat hook, blending in with the others. Before making his way back into the kitchen he pressed his coat secretly, hearing the crumpling of the plastic. It was safe; he could tell her when he was ready. Feeling as though his heart was throbbing in his head, he prayed with all his might she'd understand. He'd kept this secret for so long. He could cry later alone; he had his new door key in his pocket.

'Ruth!' Lucas remembered as soon as he saw her again and made his way back up the stairs as quickly as he could. Feeling out of breath, he reached the kitchen once more.

'Here you are, Ruth; I hope you keep it safe this time.' Lucas breathed hard.

'Lucas, you fixed it.' Ruth looked at the paper flower she had ripped, the Sellotape around the edges carefully placed. She was going to treasure it forever.

'It was a pleasure, Ruth. You see, everything that has been broken can be mended.' Lucas began to get his breath back as he glanced at Natty.

Ruth pushed her lips onto Lucas's hot cheek. 'Going to miss you, man who came into our home. You know, Lucas, I'd always feel so stressed and angry and in some crazy way it's like magic dust is sprinkled over me when you're around.' Ruth felt as though she wanted to cry. A sudden surge of affection overwhelmed her as she slung her arms around him, giving him the tightest cuddle ever.

Lucas was overtaken with flattery, standing holding his cheek at Ruth's affection.

'The sun will always shine on you, dear Ruth, taking the shadows from your heart. You will do just fine. All your beauty wrapped up into your youth and inquisitiveness: it will be the making of you.

Please don't allow the sadness from the times gone to set you on a path you truly aren't meant to follow. I am going to miss you too, very much.' Lucas smiled, his eyes sparkling.

Natty's feelings were confirmed at that moment as she overheard his gentle voice. She was completely in love with him. And he was now going. He wasn't going to be sleeping in Glenn's old bedroom, taking ages in the bubbles in the shower and draining all her shampoo. Searching for her locket for her was the kindest thing for him to do.

Natty began to feel uncertain as to why Ruth was taking all of his attention. She'd been living with Glenn, so she had already left him. *Trust her,* she thought.

Ruth fixated on George. She'd be keeping her mended flower away from him; he'd eat it if he was given the chance.

Staying with Glenn was not as fulfilling as Ruth would have liked. If she wasn't taking care of George then Glenn would hand her a pile of ironing each Sunday. And each time Stanley and Glenn went to bed, the thought rushed through Ruth of what they might be doing now they were married.

Matthew, Natty and Glenn looked at each other in amazement at Ruth's honesty with Lucas.

'All these things look amazing. Are they for me? It feels like my birthday.' Lucas clapped his hands together as he gazed at the table. He leant over and touched each item carefully, absorbing the beauty of each and every one. His hands went across a few tins of beans, and four bottles of apple shampoo. Popping the lid from one plastic green bottle, Lucas inhaled the fragrance into his nostrils. 'Apples. It's undeniably fascinating. Do you think they can put oranges and strawberries into a bottle too?'

They all laughed as they moved forward to him, they wrapped their arms around him, they all huddled together in the centre of the kitchen. He had been the best friend in the world to all of them, the man who came into their lives hidden behind tramps' clothing. Their days had been turned around. He had brought them together as a family once more; he was the piece that had been missing since the day their mother and wife took her life. He had repaired part of their broken hearts.

Pulling away from each other, they all dried their eyes.

'Right, let's get this party started.' Matthew wiped his eyes on a tea towel, handing Lucas an envelope. 'Lucas, you go and get yourself something nice, things which you deserve.' Nodding his head, Matthew walked away a little as his tears began to fall.

Lucas looked into the envelope; there must have been at least £100 inside.

'Oh dear, Matthew, I cannot accept such a gift from you; it's far too much. Everything you have done for me. How can I ever repay you?' Lucas knew he wasn't *bad*, the word his parents had pushed through his veins. He was amongst his family who cleansed him with kindness and love.

Matthew moved forward and pressed Lucas's hand, hoping he'd take it with grace. 'You have done more for us than you know, Lucas. We shall be eternally grateful to you. What's in there can never touch on all you have done.' He smiled with sincerity.

'Right, I have a gift for you.' Natty passed Lucas a box wrapped in brown paper. 'Keep the bow, won't you?'

'Yes, Miss Natty, I am certain to keep it all. Always.' The pangs in his stomach were beginning to hurt; how was he to hold such feelings in? Studying the parcel, he glanced at her, wishing he could simply take her face in his hands, pull her soft lips to his. He breathed in hard, aware she didn't want him in such a way. Placing the bow in his cream trouser pocket, he carefully removed the brown paper.

'Wow, new shoes. Very shiny new shoes.' Suddenly frightened with his gift, he prayed the day wouldn't come when he'd have to make new steps. He was leaving; did this mean he was never going to see her again? He prayed he'd never have to open the box again.

Natty's thoughts went back to their ordeal in the shoe shop. 'You may never wear them.'

'Thank you, Miss Natty. Maybe they can stay in the box, hidden within the tissue, until the time is right.'

'Let's eat.' Matthew could sense the emotions stirring between them.

'God, I need a fag!' Ruth said aloud.

They all glared at her.

'Oops!' Ruth pulled the foil from the plate and pushed a sausage roll into her mouth. She'd attempt to buy ten cigarettes later.

'Would you like me to open my beans?'

'No, Lucas!' They all spoke in unison, laughing together.

357

# 63

'Honestly, Harry, you haven't got to walk me to work.' Suzy moved her handbag further onto her shoulder, wrapping her jean jacket around her as she folded her arms. Proceeding to walk ahead of her irritating boyfriend.

'No, I'm not having it any other way.' Harry stepped beside her. He knew she wanted him really; she always played so hard to get. To a degree he found it an extremely attractive trait.

'Of course you wouldn't, would you?' Suzy spoke quietly through gritted teeth.

'Didn't hear you!' Harry placed his arm around her shoulders.

Suzy pushed her arms more firmly into her chest in a silent dispute.

'Thanks for the takeout last night, Harry. Really nice. I'm here now.' Looking up at the vast glass window outside the bookshop, Suzy smiled reluctantly at him. Leaning over to kiss him, she made her way inside with sheer relief.

She didn't manage to close the door before he pushed on it with his hand.

'See you, Suzy. May pop in later, bring you a cheese roll and that.'

'Oh, cheese, yeah, OK.' Suzy wanted to scream at him; didn't he know by now her favourite filling was ham?

Breathing out hard, Suzy stood inside the bookshop having finally managed to make her escape. Her hands behind her back, she leant on the door, looking around the musty shop. She hadn't been able to get herself together properly since the last time she had seen Matthew. He must have moved town; it'd been months. Things must have changed in his life. Pushing herself from the door and sighing, she knew things hadn't in hers. The same walk, talk and sex each and every day. The only thing that changed was the day of the week.

'Men!' Suzy threw her bag on the counter, speaking harshly.

'Oh, yes, completely dreamy.' Wilfred scampered up to her and tapped her nose with his finger, giggling.

'Oh, my, there's no point talking to you; if they walk, you'll grab them.'

'No, peachy, I have standards. These fine young gentlemen need a wallet to match.' Wilfred rubbed his hands over the pink frills on the front of his shirt.

'Fat wallet to match their fat heads.' Suzy scraped her hair back, taking a bobble from her wrist and tying it up high into a neat ponytail.

'Did you want a nice strong tea, sweetie pie? Still hanging on to the man, eh?'

'Yeah, don't know what's wrong with me.' Her voice was full of desperation.

'Love at first sight, I call it. Need to let your boyfriend know, though.' Wilfred laughed as he went to make a cup of tea.

'Oh, ha, very funny.' Suzy grabbed a paperclip, aiming it at the back of his head as he poured the hot water into the mugs.

The letterbox clanged. Sighing, Matthew went to grab the morning newspaper, yanking the rolled-up printed sheets from the letterbox. He was fed up with being reminded as he stood alone in the hall in his dressing gown, his anxious unsettled breathing almost echoing around him. March 1978: three years and three months since his perfect Eve went away forever. The constant torment consumed him, being unable to simply hold her hand or stroke her face. A reality he knew it was pointless trying to understand, the reality of his broken beauty. He'd placed the doll back onto his bed; before he left his bedroom each morning he'd attempt to pull the soft shiny ringlets across the small features, hiding the cracks he'd always pretended were not there.

Since Lucas had left, the house had been extra quiet. Natty spent most of her time dithering around the phone in the hall, waiting for his call.

Throwing the paper on the stairs, Matthew went to make some

tea. Placing two cups onto the clean side and, of course, tipping extra milk into one.

Sluggishly making his way back to the living room, he placed both cups onto the small table next to his typewriter. He leant back on the sofa, looking at the plain piece of paper, already waiting for his mind to free his thoughts into words. The book had got hold of him just as his Eve had all those years ago. Tapping his fingers up and down on his legs, suddenly aware he'd buried himself in his own space, he felt almost afraid to say hello at the bookshop; he knew he'd left it too long.


'God, what a long day.' Suzy doodled on the side of a small pad as she leant on one of her elbows, her hand on her chin.

'No, peachy darling, it's a normal day with the same twenty-four hours in; it's what you do with it that counts. Long, short, whatever you want to call it, it's the same day.'

'Tell me about it. I wish something exciting would happen.'

The door to the shop was pushed open.

'Hello, gorgeous; got your lunch,' Harry said happily.

'Oh, hi, Harry.' Suzy thought this was as exciting as it was ever going to get, feeling more downhearted than ever. 'Really kind, thanks.'

'Not busy in here today, is it?' Harry glanced around the dim shop.

'No, boring as hell.' Suzy smirked.

'Well, not that it's great on a busy day either, I can imagine.' Harry laughed.

'Actually it's good fun, not that you'd know.' The frustration built further inside her tea-filled belly.

'There's a new movie on at the pictures, meant to be pretty good. Be good to go and see it.'

'Yeah, sounds like an idea. Tell me what it's like.' Suzy found herself chuckling.

'You nearly got me there.' Harry pretended to find her comment funny; he'd bothered to bring her lunch and she was being rude for no reason at all. They'd had a lovely evening together; he was sure he had pleased her. He'd gone down on her for longer than normal. Any other woman would be thankful.

Seeing him looking glum, she felt she had to swiftly make amends. 'I will think about it. I was joking, by the way.' Taking the paper bag containing her hard-crust roll, she pushed her finger into the top, aware all the flaky crust would still be in the bottom of the bag when she ate it. 'Thanks, then, Harry.'

'I was going to stay with you for a bit; not busy today at the garage either.'

'No, I'm OK, got some stock taking to do.' Suzy forced a smile.

'OK, then. If you fancy I will walk you home later.'

'Yes, Harry, fine, just not now, OK?'

'OK, if you insist.' Harry felt rejected.

'See you.'

Suzy felt grateful he'd left, sighing with relief once more at being released from his persistence. She smashed the cheese roll with the palm of her hand, her unwanted flattened lunch now inedible.

'Now, that's not nice.'

'Oh my God, Matthew.' Her mood changed instantly. She stood upright and pushed her shoulders back, ecstatic to be in front of him.

'Is that my head? I'm really sorry I haven't been in.' Matthew stood calm and relaxed to be in her company again. He had missed the bookshop and the young lady who had become very drunk in his presence. It made him smile as he thought of how he had carried her from the car to her front door.

'No, it's my crap cheese roll.' Suzy's voice was gentle, her stomach going nineteen to the dozen with nerves entwined with excitement.

'Lucky me, then.' Matthew giggled nervously.

The door to the shop opened.

'I forgot to give you your chocolate.'

Matthew saw a small chocolate bar placed gently on the counter.

Instantly Matthew's body became immobilised; he dared not take a look. It couldn't be, not in a million years.

Suzy closed her eyes for a second, praying Harry never sensed her feelings for the other man in the shop. 'Thank you, Harry.'

Matthew's temperature began to rise, his visible shaking overwhelming him. She was his and he was hers.

'No way.' Harry moved around the front of Matthew a little further.

'Matt. It's me.' Harry became exhilarated with seeing him. For a moment he forgot what he'd done so long ago which had hurt his brother so much.

Matthew looked to the floor, praying he'd walk away, as a surge of anger rushed through him. Clenching his fist, he could feel the sweat building up underneath his chequered shirt, his skin becoming prickly as his goose pimples were almost burning.

'Matt, it's me, Harry.' Harry raised his voice a little. He'd be all right with him after all this time, surely, he thought.

'You two know each other?' Suzy placed her hand over her mouth, overcome with shock.

'Yes, Suzy, this is my brother, my brother Matt.' Harry spoke as though his introduction would be welcomed by them.

His mouth becoming dry as his throat became thick, Matthew took all the strength he had in his numb body to speak. 'Please don't call me that,' he said with a hostile tone, still staring at the floor.

'Harry, this is *your* brother?' Suzy squinted her eyes with tightened lips, realising what the relationship between them meant for her and Harry.

Wilfred came out of the stockroom whistling. Witnessing the intense situation, he promptly dashed back in, speaking under his breath. 'See, men and women cause all sorts of complications; why don't they simply stick to the same sex?'

'I don't understand how you two can be brothers.' Suzy pushed the cheese roll further into the bag with her fingers, squeezing at the roll until it squelched almost through the paper.

'Matthew, please, it's been so many years.' Harry wanted to shake him, wake him up to see finally he was still his brother after everything. His hands became clammy as he wiped them down the sides of his grease-stained overalls.

'Bye, Suzy. So sorry you had to see this.' Matthew's throat was burning. He could feel the sick building inside him, his mouth suddenly beginning to water.

'Suzy? Oh, on first-name terms, are we?' Instantly Harry went on the defence; he didn't like it very much that his long-lost brother knew his girlfriend's name.

Matthew stared at Harry's face and shook his head, disgusted by his childishness. He made his way out of the shop, his legs like lead, his head throbbing with the adrenaline pumping through him.

'Are you sure it's your brother, Harry?' Suzy was in disbelief at what she was seeing, hearing and of course feeling in the bottom of her stomach. She prayed he wasn't.

'Yes, not that he's ever going to give me a chance to be his.' Harry made his way after him.

'I don't blame him, Harry, do you?'

'Suze, I will catch up with you later!' Harry dashed after his brother, dismissing her comment.

'I can't believe that fucking happened.' Her hands on her forehead, she made her way to the stockroom. She was going to scream at Wilfred, letting him know as all became clear; the whole fucking picture of the dark-haired fucking beauty made sense finally. She hoped Wilfred was man enough to take it.

'Matt, Matthew, please let me talk to you.' Harry's actions mirrored the ones he had made earlier with Suzy, rushing by Matthew's side to keep up with him, wishing he'd stop and turn around and wait for him.

'Matthew, I sent a letter to Ruth.' Harry knew if he mentioned Ruth it'd certainly make him listen.

Matthew stopped in his tracks, his breathing out of rhythm with the thumping in his chest.

'Ruth, I sent her a letter. Did she get it, Matthew? Please tell me.' Harry gritted his teeth, longing for his brother to talk to him, respond to him in some way. He'd been invisible to him for far too long.

Matthew didn't look around, and began walking ahead again with his hands in his cream jacket. Everything around him seemed a blur.

Harry still rushed behind him. 'Matthew, I know you hate me, but please can I see her? She's eighteen now.'

Matthew found the strength to stop once more.

Sighing in relief, Harry stepped forward, seeing Matthew face him.

363

Swallowing hard, Matthew took his time to speak, his tears sitting at the back of his throat, making his voice croaky.

'Whoever you choose to call yourself, I am completely aware Ruth is eighteen. I've been her father for that time and shall remain that way for the rest of her life. I don't know what this is about. You're dead to me, so I take it I'm standing on this busy street speaking to a ghost.' The tears of despair glistened in the corners of his eyes.

Harry held his hands together as though he was about to pray. 'Matthew, my dear brother Matthew. Please, not having you and my daughter in my life is killing me.'

Matthew broke down in tears. The sobs from his stomach felt as though they were bruising his ribs.

'Matt, it's OK.' Harry felt it was time he comforted his brother, moving forward a little more.

Matthew pulled his arm up, swinging it back, punching Harry in the face as hard as he could. The blood from his brother's nose spattered his knuckles and his jacket, his body swaying and shaking with adrenaline.

'Fuck, fuck!' Harry pressed his hands onto his face. 'I think you've busted my nose.'

'Yeah? I think you busted my fucking life.' Matthew breathed in the deepest breath possible, trying to calm down the intense beating of his heart. Without any thought he promptly passed his bloody brother a tissue from his inside jacket pocket. 'Just hold your goddamn head back.' Allowing himself to give the smallest degree of compassion, Matthew shook his head at the fuss his brother was making over a small bleed.

'I didn't, Matt, it was already busted.' Speaking through the tissue, Harry's voice was muffled.

Matthew went to swing another punch; a voice in him told him to stop. He hastily retreated.

He was right; his shitty brother was right.

'Actually, I think you're going to need to sit down; you're bleeding everywhere.' Matthew held his brother's arm and guided him to the bench as Harry was unable to see, looking into the sky.

'You punched me!' Harry's voice sounded squeaky from pinching his nose.

'Yeah, I know. Felt good.'

'Thanks.'

They both sat on the end of the bench, Harry still holding his nose and Matthew looking at the stains his brother had now left on his favourite attire, like the stains on his life.

Tearing off a small clean piece of his brother's tissue, Matthew wiped his eyes.

'See, still sharing.' Harry glanced at him, his face sore, his head feeling as though it was going to crack.

'Do you want another one, Harry? Don't like your innuendo.' Matthew leant forward, his legs parted, his arms on his thighs, staring at the pavement, unable to make eye contact with him.

'No, mate. I didn't think you had it in you. You've got a swing on you.'

'Harry, why are you here?' Matthew's voice was calm, his insides trembling like his hands, rubbing the knuckles of his left hand. 'Why have you appeared in my life again? Why now?'

'You're in mine. That's my girlfriend, you know.' Harry began to dab his nose with the remains of the ripped tissue.

'Suzy? What was it you said about sharing?' The awful thought of such words coming from his own mouth made him feel ashamed.

'Yes. She's too good for me.' Harry giggled nervously.

'You're going to have to make sure you look after her.' Still Matthew made no eye contact.

'She's a great ...' Harry halted in his sentence; his nose was beginning to dry and he certainly didn't fancy ever receiving a punch like that again.

'What made you send my daughter a letter?' Matthew asked, his emotions out of control as he sensed a burning sensation taking over his body.

'Matthew, I know it seems a bit random after so many years. We aren't getting any younger. I wanted to make up for things, finally belong to something solid in my life.' Harry's thoughts went to Suzy.

'You've finally found a conscience over the years, Harry. Oh, my, how commendable of you. I didn't know you sent her anything.' His thoughts went onto Natty. 'I have a funny feeling I know where it is.' There was no way Harry's grovelling was ever going to make up for what he had done. Ruth had to spend her whole life being different from her sisters.

'Matt, I made the shittiest mistake; well, apart from Ruth. What are you doing on this side of town, anyway?' Harry frowned.

Matthew gazed at him for a moment. 'Not sure if you can call anything to do with my wife shitty.' He began to bite his bottom lip, uncertain if he should even be sitting with his brother. 'I don't know what brought me here, Harry; something inside told me to come. I wanted to see the old coffee shop, I suppose. You know, where I met my Eve.' He inhaled a deep breath.

'I remember, you were like a kid with a new toy.' Harry paused and continued trying to explain. 'You know what I mean, Matt? Ruth wasn't a mistake. It wasn't meant how it sounded.'

'Yes, like you said, it was busted. You always broke my toys when we were small; do you remember that too?'

'I didn't really think about what I was doing, Matt.' Harry sighed.

'Everything about it was busted, broken, whatever you want to call it. She was so terribly ill. And when I met her, I was so wrapped in how much I loved her and wanted to give her the best, I never allowed her to just be. To be the Eve she yearned to be. I didn't hear her. I never saw or heard anything I didn't want to. And that's busted. I pushed her too hard. Expected too much. I think I made her finally give in.' Matthew put his hands on his face and cried.

'Matthew, you didn't. She was ill; you did all you could.' Harry rubbed Matthew's back, as the skin on his face began to feel tight from the aftermath of the punch and the dried blood.

'Do you love her, Harry? Did you fall for my wife?' Matthew gulped.

Harry thought before he answered. 'It just happened.'

'Harry. Please tell me you did, please tell me she meant something to you; it kind of gives meaning to it. Eve's too special to be one of your one-night conquests.' The burning sensation overtaking his body became more intense.

'I did love her, Matthew, and in some crazy way I still do.' Harry moved over slightly.

Matthew finally made eye contact.

366

'Me too, Harry. I do with every single pulse in my body.' Matthew wiped his tears on his stained jacket sleeve. The anger and overwhelming realness to love sealed him. Eve's presence and beauty would capture the entire world. It was hard not to love and desire such a person so. 'I've been lucky, Harry; she even wanted to love me for as long as life gave her breath. She was going to spend the rest of her life with me.'

'I know, Matt. I really hope you can forgive me.' Harry began to feel the tears welling up in his eyes.

'Not sure if I can forgive you, Harry. I don't feel I have room in my heart yet. I've held on to torment and pain for so long.'

'Matthew, you're speaking to me; it's a start. And you've only made my nose bleed once since we were eighteen.' Harry chuckled, hoping to prevent Matthew from seeing his obvious sadness.

'That wasn't my fault.' Matthew managed a smile.

'You pushed me off the wall.'

They both sniggered nervously.

'Don't know how you're going to fix it with Suzy. I hope you can. Funny, isn't it? What goes around comes around.' Matthew zipped up the front of his jacket; with all the adrenaline that had pumped through him, he felt chilly.

'What do you mean?'

'Nothing, Harry. You'll get it soon.'

'Eve loved you, Matthew, more than anything in the world.'

'Think her heart was with you.' Matthew huffed and began staring at the pavement again, concentrating on the small weeds growing from the edges of each concrete slab.

'No, her heart was with y—'

'Oh, my goodness, she can't even rest in peace and you're both fighting over her. The poor woman. You are both being completely selfish; stop thinking of yourselves.' The old lady who had sat at the other end of the bench picked up her umbrella and slowly walked away.

# 64

As he opened his black duffel bag, the soft sound of the zip felt as though it was vibrating through him. He smiled softly; he had always loved the way she pulled the covers over so neatly. She'd puff both their pillows up, leaning them on the headboard. Picking up the empty bag he wiped down the covers, making them neat, guilty for ruining her hard work. She always worked so hard attempting to keep it the only way she knew. He wished he'd helped her more.

Gazing around their bedroom as he stood next to the bed, he knew everything in his life had changed for the better. A woman's touch was all he'd ever needed in his heart and home. As she told him each morning when she brought him up a cup of tea in bed, a mother and wife is someone who wakes up the home. She'd kiss him on his lips and take their son from his bed. He was going to miss hearing them both laugh as they went down the stairs together.

Shaking his head in disbelief, he grabbed a few ironed shirts from the wardrobe, pushing them into the bag still on the hangers. He was sure it was the right thing to do; deep down he was sure she'd be grateful one day.

How her beautiful face had shone as she brought out their son's second birthday cake only a couple of months ago. She had sparkled with pride and happiness. He'd never forget how she looked at him; she was going to spend each and every day with him. He felt it.

Taking some socks from the drawer, he pushed them inside the bag. The shirt she liked was now creasing under the weight of his hands as he needed to get as much in as possible.

Staring at her dressing table covered in perfumes and powders, he chose to stop his feelings. He'd never finish what he planned if he thought any more. He couldn't allow his mind to make his decision for him. He had to do what was right. He'd come back one day and explain to them both. He hoped they'd understand.

He was certain each mile further away from them both would only confirm to him how much he truly loved and adored them. He missed them already. His fortunate heart had the chance to finally embrace such a gift. All he had ever wanted was everything he was running away from? She had sacrificed so much for him. It was now his turn to do the same. He would desperately push the love he felt deep inside his ageing body, for her to be the woman she was meant to be.

Standing at the bedroom door, gripping his heavy bag, he glanced once more at her side of the bed.

# 65

He could see the newspaper on the small bristly rug below the door. He wasn't going to pick it up, to let his eyes scour the date. He knew it was July and it would be Eve's birthday soon. He wasn't going to look at it in print. Not today.

Pulling his coat from the coat hook, Matthew was extremely aware he wasn't going to be welcome at the bookshop. The deep reality consumed him, as the young lady who he had become comfortably fond of was part of his family in some strange way. He wondered with a little compassion how Harry had handled it after they'd all been introduced. Knowing Harry, he had probably taken her to bed.

Matthew felt convinced he had done the right thing, gently asking Natty to hand the letter over. She'd denied having it at first and then reluctantly pulled it from under her mattress; she'd wanted to teach Ruth a lesson, how it felt to have something important taken away. She asked him how he knew. He replied that if Ruth had read the letter she'd have told him. He was sure in his heart. She'd have asked to meet Harry before now. Two wrongs didn't make a right, as his own father had once told him, and he now told Natty.

Ruth had only been gone an hour. The thought of allowing her to enter unknown territory without him by her side was hard for him to bear; a heaviness burdened his heart. He'd left her vulnerable in the school, alone and scared, as he had left her with her mother, his Eve. He had believed she was safe, only for it to end in tragedy. He prayed as he looked at the clock in the dining room that she was being protected.

Reluctantly Matthew threw his coat onto Eve's chair before he realised his actions; he promptly removed it. Slumping down hard on the sofa, his body surrendered to all the emotions so very trapped inside. They didn't want to leave him; they were going to be part of him forever.

Watching the small hand on the clock ticking, he waited for her return. The house was so quiet; all the noise and commotion which had surrounded him for so long had simply dispersed, little by little, as the seconds in front of him. He wasn't going to begin the last few chapters of his book. He was determined to be waiting for her when she came in. Ruth had promised she'd see him first. She wouldn't go straight to Glenn's.

A familiar pain rushed through him as he recognised Glenn's despair. Her nights would be long from now on, her days a mass of confusion and emotions. She'd have to push herself from her bed each day, to face the pain she'd never be able to hide from. If only he could take it away for her. It was an impossible feat to even contemplate.

The hands on the large clock above the fireplace seemed to move slower than ever. He remembered watching his Eve cleaning it with a soft cloth, her slim legs showing as she stood on a chair. She was a statue of perfection as she stretched her body across the clock's face. To stop the tears from falling he slowly closed his eyes to remember, wanting to recapture her smile again and again.


'Dad, Dad, I'm back.' Ruth moved his shoulders gently back and forth.

Rubbing his eyes as he woke, he could see she had been crying. He felt comfort seeing her back with him, back where she belonged.

'Can I ask, Ruth?' His voice sounded croaky from his disturbed sleep.

'Yes, Dad, you can.' Ruth felt the warmth of the house and her father all at the same time; it was something she hadn't felt for years. She knew she was safe finally.

'Well?' Not wanting to pressure her he spoke with a gentle tone, almost whispering.

'Well, he cuddled me, Dad.' Ruth felt her emotions stirring. She had never let Harry see her cry. She had only been with him for five minutes. To her it felt like betrayal for everything her life stood for and everything they had all gone through together. As Harry went to get a fizzy drink from the shop, she had to go, walk away and not turn around, as he had chosen not to all those years ago as she had gazed out of her bedroom window.

'And?' He waited in anticipation, praying he hadn't lost her to him, as he had his Eve.

'It was too late; he cuddled me too late.' Ruth pushed herself next to him, ruffling the cushions under her, snuggling her body close to his. He wrapped his arms firmly around her. As they cuddled each other hard, she began to sob into his chest and he kissed her on her head. His breathing became settled as he gazed at the clock and smiled.

# 66

'Let Mummy take her teabag out.' Glenn pushed the water from the bag with a spoon at the side of the cup as George hung on to her legs, pulling and demanding that she give him even more of her time and energy. All she wanted was a strong cup of tea, with plenty of sugar. It seemed too much to ask. Holding the drained squashed bag on her spoon, Glenn placed it into the bin.

'Mummy, Mummy!' George screamed for it.

'George, it's a teabag, God damn it.' Glenn began to feel impatient, huffing as she pushed down hard on the bin, preventing her insistent son from opening it.

'Mummy!' George screamed at the top of his voice and began stamping his feet.

'Oh my God, what's the matter with you, child?' Glenn asked impatiently, feeling her unwanted emotions building; she had been strong for nearly an hour that day.

'Mummy, I want it.' The stamping of his feet became fierce, his screams almost piercing through her already fragile limbs.

'Look, keep the stupid thing.' Glenn grabbed at the dirty rubbish, picking out the teabag and quickly rinsing it under the cold tap. Squeezing it between her fingers, she gave it to him. He had defeated his mother and he smiled, rushing to the back door.

'Mummy, it's raining.' His voice was full of wonder.

'I know, darling; it's raining in my heart too.' Glenn leant over the bin, holding each edge, and cried, praying Stanley would come home and simply put the kettle on. She swallowed hard, attempting to push the pain back into her stomach, her tears being her only form of nourishment. The pains of hunger and uncertainty ate away her insides with relish. Her small son had witnessed her crying so

373

many tears already. Blowing out a huge breath and taking a damp tea towel, she wiped her eyes, forcing a smile as George gazed innocently into them.

'Oh, for goodness' sake, Glenn, stop being so dramatic. Get a grip.' Ruth walked into the kitchen twiddling the gold charm bracelet she had been gifted with on her eighteenth birthday. She knew she was done for; she'd have to stay with her sister now. She was desperate to go home and not be woken by a child each morning. Not have to play peek-a-boo until her voice crackled. There was no way she could say to Glenn what she was really feeling, not while she made such a fuss over everything. She'd simply have to sit it out with her sister.

Ruth gazed at Glenn and huffed. She wanted to comfort her, deep down; she just wasn't sure if she'd say the right thing or help her at all.

Glenn remained leaning over the bin, trying to bring her breathing to a steady pace. She felt her sister's arm around her shoulders and though it was a kind thing for her to do; she only wished she'd get the fuck off her and leave her alone to smash the kitchen to pieces.

'I put his clothes in here.' Glenn touched the bin lid.

Ruth frowned. 'You what?'

'Doesn't matter.'

Ruth knew how much her sister loved Stanley, how much she missed him. It was unfair on her not to know where he was; she had to know he was safe. Ruth wanted to know where he was more than anything, so she could tell Glenn to give her some peace, but more importantly go around and punch him in his grey head.

'I love him so much, Ruth.' Her voice was full of despair, her face tingled, her stomach ached; she felt at that very moment she didn't want to live for another second.

'I know you do, Glenn. At least you can pass wind in bed now, eh?'

They both giggled together as Glenn leant over the bin and Ruth's arm stretched around her shoulders.

Their moment of laughter was disturbed by hearing George crying. Glenn promptly rushed to his aid, pushing her body into auto-pilot yet again; she didn't have time for her own grief.

'Hey, little one, come here. Oh, look at you.' Glenn picked him up, seeing his face covered in tea leaves and the sucked bag sticking to his fingers. Sitting him on the work surface, she wiped his face and his tongue with the dish cloth. 'Hey, blow the hurt into Mummy's hand and we'll throw it away into the sky.' Glenn spoke with a mother's tenderness.

Ruth shook her head, watching her sister.

Hearing the front door, Ruth went to open it, thinking quickly of how much weight Glenn had lost in the last five months. It was a day to remember when she had heard Glenn's screams from the bedroom. The memory had flashed through her of when their father had echoed the same release from his soul, the minute he had discovered their mother's still and breathless body. It was the day they had all taken on their parents' broken hearts and minds. Mirrored fears had surfaced for her as she made her way up Glenn's stairs in uncertainty to see her. Glenn was standing next to the wardrobe. Ruth could see in her eyes a sadness she had seen only once before, at their mother's funeral.

'Hello, Natty.' Ruth was happy she had support.

'How is she?' Natty made her way in.

'Well, apart from being a complete dramatic emotional wreck then, yeah, I'd say she's doing pretty well.'

'Not good, then?'

'No.'

'Hi, Glenn, you look like crap.' Natty kissed her on the cheek. 'Hello, George, you've been sad too?' She placed the full carrier bags on the side, trying to keep her voice uplifted for Glenn's sake.

'Hi, Natty. Did you want tea?'

'Absolutely not; I've brought wine.' Natty took a bottle of white wine from the stripy plastic bag with pride.

'That's unpleasant.' Glenn frowned.

'And beer and lemonade.' Natty raised her eyebrows, feeling cocky in the nicest possible way.

'Actually, now you've gone to the trouble, I think I might have a go at the old squashed-grape stuff.' Glenn smiled reluctantly; she didn't want to upset Natty by refusing her kind gesture.

Natty happily took three long-stemmed glasses from the kitchen cupboard and blew the dust from inside them. Pulling the cork from the bottle with a corkscrew, she filled the three glasses to the brim. She knew Glenn was only trying to keep her happy.

'We are going to be drunk.' Ruth gulped a mouthful and sighed in relief.

'So are not; how is one glass meant to get you drunk? That's why I brought two bottles.'

'Don't know; I don't think I've ever been.' Glenn sipped the wine, screwing up her face at the sharp taste burning the back of her throat.

Natty smiled at Glenn. 'Do you know, if we get Ruth drunk maybe she can give us all the details of going to see him?'

'Who?' Ruth looked confused.

'Your dad.' Natty rolled her eyes.

'Oh, for goodness' sake, need you like a hole in the head. I did see Dad only yesterday, so do you want to get off that with me? Honestly, you never change, do you?' Ruth felt a little upset at the dividing comment from her elder sister.

They all leant on the kitchen sides as they chatted.

'So, Miss Natty, dear Miss Natty, like fluffy clouds and the dewdrops from the rain, have you seen Lucas?' Ruth roared with laughter, followed by Natty; Glenn slowly sipped her wine with difficulty.

'Oh, we had the best time. We went to the pictures. Film was amazing; honestly, you have to go and see it. Such a sad one.' Natty spoke through her giggles.

'Yes, you are, aren't you?' Ruth tipped a little more wine into her glass.

'No, seriously, it was. And when I came out I asked Lucas if he liked it. It was the funniest thing. You couldn't write it. He said he only watches the extras.' Looking confused, Natty held one hand up in the air.

'Extras? I don't understand.' Ruth finished her glass.

Natty giggled. 'You know, the people behind the actual main actor, the people who sit and say "rhubarb" in the background all the time.'

Glenn and Ruth burst into laughter.

'I kept thinking he wanted to tell me something,' Natty said.

'Maybe you should have let him sit behind you and say

"rhubarb".' Ruth grinned and reached for the corkscrew to open the other bottle of wine.

Glenn held her hand over her glass as Ruth went to refill it. Glenn's belly was full of pain desperate to show itself.

Natty looked at Glenn, seeing how weak she was becoming, and placed her glass down.

'Well, I suggest, young Glenn, you get the little man to bed and we can get cosy on the sofa.' Natty turned the radio on low in the kitchen.

A song came on they recognised. 'Oh my God, do you remember this one?' Ruth began to move slowly around the kitchen, holding a glass of wine.

Natty echoed her movements. 'Yes, Ruth; I'm older than you, remember? What number was it in the charts?'

'I've got no idea.' Glenn shook her head gently. 'Not too loud, you two. Say night, George?'

Ruth and Natty pushed their lips hard onto their little nephew's cheek.

As Glenn walked up the stairs she began to cry. She had no care for rhubarb or who was number four in the charts. Once they left she'd release her pain alone in bed, her heart ripping, holding on as tightly as she could to his stripy pyjamas.

# 67

'Did you want another scoop?' Suzy smiled, holding the plastic tub in front of him. Watching him plunge in for another heap of gooey ice cream, she knew she had made him suffer for long enough.

It had been nearly eight months since she had taken his calls. Each night as she lay on her sofa the phone would ring nonstop. It had brought her almost to breaking point; she had thrown her slipper at the noisy interruption finally in a plea for the chimes to stop demanding her. As the receiver had fallen onto her carpet she had heard his muffled voice calling her name. Pushing her cat from her lap, she had finally made the decision to sit on the floor and listen to the bullshit she assumed would come out of his mouth.

She was proved wrong. He spoke to her with delicacy and concern for their relationship. She informed him they'd never had such a thing over and over. He was insistent he'd got it wrong. Sharing all of his feelings with her for the very first time, promising her he'd rip up the photo of his brother's wife which he kept so very safe. He wanted her to help him understand why his daughter walked away that day. As he spoke she felt as though she could have reached into her receiver to kiss him, hold him tight and let him know she understood. He asked her if they could both begin something special, hopefully different from anything else he'd ever been part of: a place to be loved and safe, to take whatever came, good and bad, and still manage to laugh over a beer at the end of the day together. It was too endearing for her to resist. She agreed.

She hit the back of his hand with her spoon as he scooped into the tub deep, taking more strawberry than vanilla; the chocolate section had almost gone, so Harry knew not to touch the pink stuff. There had to be boundaries, after all. Suzy was full of contentment and warmth as she sat with him on her sofa, her legs over his lap.

From the rescue of her favourite ice cream her thoughts went to Matthew briefly. She hadn't seen Matthew for the whole of the eight months either, and it caused a pang to appear in her ice-cream-full belly.

The realisation came to her as she watched the bare-chested man licking the spoon of vanilla ice cream that all along she had only really wanted Harry. She felt happy with the Chinese and nights in together. When she looked at it, it had always really been them. He didn't want to share her with the world, taking her to fancy restaurants and working desperately to make her happy; he was simply being Harry. She chuckled silently to herself as she had believed Harry wouldn't make the cut in keeping her content. She had put Matthew in his place, an image of someone she believed could, only to realise she'd never be so relaxed in his company, unless she was completely intoxicated of course.

Suzy began to laugh out loud.

'What's so funny?' Harry rubbed her legs with his hand as he gave her a gentle smile, the button to his jeans undone, as normal perfectly charming.

'Nothing.' Suzy raised her eyebrows slowly, licking her spoon as she could see him watching her with pleasure.

'Tell me or else.' Harry raised his eyebrows in return, gently moving his hand nearer to the edge of her brown skirt.

'How funny was it when you came back into the shop that day and Wilfred shouted at you?' Suzy lifted her leg a little with an excited laugh.

'Oh, yeah? Can't say I remember.' Harry pushed the cold spoon under her skirt gently.

'Yes, you can.' Suzy's body jerked quickly as the cold sent a tingling sensation through her. 'He said, "You call yourself a man?" She giggled as the spoon touched the top of her legs, finding it hard to speak through her mirth and arousal. 'He said, "Call yourself a man? If you were the last penis on earth I'd close my eyes and sleep with a woman." Suzy held her stomach through her laughter. She knew she'd never forget the look on Harry's face when her camp colleague gave him what-for.

Harry grinned, raising his eyebrows, moving the spoon up and down her soft slim legs. 'So what would *you* do if I was the last penis on earth?' He stared at her alluringly; he felt aroused seeing her so relaxed, her legs slightly apart, letting him see a little of the inside of her legs.

Suzy gazed at him as the throbbing between her legs became more intense. Placing the ice-cream tub onto the carpet she lay back a little. Opening her legs, she pushed her hand slowly and seductively into her peach lace knickers. Knowing he was watching and wanting her, wanting to taste her as he did the ice cream, she waited for him to lick her like she had the spoon. As she closed her eyes he pushed her legs apart a little more, pulling her knickers to the side only enough to taste her warmth. She groaned with pleasure as she became lost within their world.

Her cat hovered around the ice-cream tub, unaware he could help himself to the pink icy gloop.

'Finally. Natty, please tell me you actually feel at home in here.' Matthew leant up against the bedroom doorframe, his arms folded, feeling the warmth from his black cardigan.

'I know; how long have I waited to get in here?' Natty touched the new bedding with her hands. 'Kind of feels different now it's just us, though, Dad.' She sat bouncing slightly on the wonderfully made bed, which had once belonged to Glenn.

'It's taken you long enough to move your stuff over.' Her father gazed at her old bedroom. The rooms in their large family home were lifeless, almost. He felt an eerie sensation overwhelm him suddenly.

'Funny to think Lucas danced in here.' Natty gazed around the tidy room, smiling softly.

'Sorry, Natty, didn't catch that.' Her father gave her his full attention again.

'He danced, Dad. Didn't you hear the banging each and every night?' Natty shook her head, grinning. Whenever she spoke or thought about Lucas she'd always smile.

'I didn't, with my typewriter going.' Her father walked slowly into the bedroom. Pulling out the dressing-table chair, he sat on the soft red velvet cushion.

'How are you getting on, Dad?' Natty opened the drawer next to her bed as she spoke. A few items of perfume and makeup were yet to be put away.

'A month or so to go.' Her father sighed, looking up to the ceiling and then back at her. 'You know, Natty, writing saved my mind, heart and soul. There is something extremely surreal about seeing your mind become real, and knowing it will always be kept. Thoughts pass in and out of us all day long. Some of them can save our lives and some of them can destroy it.' He coughed a little to clear his throat. 'It's all made up, Natty; thoughts are words simply strung together to make some kind of meaning. So we can understand what's actually happening. We don't have to understand reality, Natty; you see, that's where we all get confused. I made some terrible choices; I only wish they were also fiction.' He spoke softly as he could see Natty was listening to every word he said. He was also very aware his writing wasn't real; every letter he typed was simply fantasy. He sat in the precise moment of his own reality, his large home quiet with only one daughter to talk to, his bed empty each night with only his warmth, his heart full of love and protection for them all.

'Dad.' Natty could see he was lost in thought.

'Sorry, Natty. I must say one thing to you: if it wasn't for you then I'd never have written in the first place, never would have contemplated such a thing.' Her father got up from the soft chair, feeling she'd rather be left alone.

Natty chuckled, thinking her father was starting to sound a little like Lucas. 'I think I have to thank you too; if it wasn't for you then I wouldn't have met Lucas. And I do get what you're saying about your writing. Lucas did the same thing to me the minute he walked through the door.'

Her father thought for a moment. Turning to her, he spoke with pride. 'Dear Natty, I believe it's your mother you need to thank. She united us all, remember.'

'Oh, yeah, so she did.' Natty nodded her head in agreement, chuckling to herself as she began placing her belongings in the drawer. Her father had finally made his way back to his saviour.

'What's this?' Natty frowned as she opened an A4 piece of paper which had been neatly folded and placed in the back of the drawer. With eagerness she read.

'Um ... I wonder.' Natty jumped back onto her bed. Taking a pen from the side, she leant on her leg and began to fill in the missing lines, hoping she had a spare stamp.

# 68

1979

'And we end up in your chilly flat under these really itchy covers.' She pulled the musky blanket and her coat over her a little more, the cold beginning to pierce her body. 'Lucas, I think I need another cuppa.' Natty began to laugh. She was really getting cold and the pins and needles in her feet confirmed it to her. She was staying for the day and that was that, even if her small tits dropped off in the cold.

'Miss Natty, I can imagine we missed so much. We could have spent so many more times together.' Lucas clenched his hands as he went to place the kettle on the stove; he could feel goose pimples all over his naked skin. Glancing out of the corner of his eye he swallowed hard, the nerves beating through him; he had to give it to her finally. Another night in the cold sitting with the bag within his hands was too much to bear.

Moving forward to the edge of the bed, he wrapped a blanket which had fallen to the floor around him. Kneeling down he reached underneath the bed, the dread filling him. This was it; there was no turning back now. His hands were clammy on the grungy blue plastic.

He admired her sitting in his bed, barely seeing her face as the covers and her coat were wrapped up around her neck.

'Miss Natty, this is for you.' His voice was shaky. Leaning on his scruffy bed, Lucas took her hand from under the covers. There was no way he'd look into her brown eyes as she placed her hand inside the bag. He didn't want to see her cry, not like he had before. 'No, Miss Natty, please don't look, just let me speak first, eh?'

Lucas sat on the edge of the bed, his frightened body wrapped in the musky wool. Swallowing a couple of times with nerves as the words he was trying to find didn't want to be found. If he started explaining then there would be no going back. He remained silent in thought. He'd never have a chance of sharing life with her, being part of her confusion and her wonder. He desperately hoped one day they could be floating around in the same waters of life together. Entwining their sadness and happiness, the undercurrent of all of the sea blending all the things they both loved and didn't understand within its thrashing waves.

Natty was confused as the bag was handed to her. Her thoughts went back to the feeling of plastic in his pocket as she stood holding tightly on to his coat at the kitchen door in the home he had once shared. Pushing her hand out, she desperately hoped to move it back under the covers.

'What is it?' Natty asked inquisitively, squinting into the bag.

Closing his eyes and biting down hard on his lip, Lucas knew at any second all was going to be revealed. A sensation of sickness sat in his belly.

'I don't believe it! What the hell?' Natty stared at him at the bottom of the bed; she was flooded with disbelief and excitement.

'Miss Natty, I know you must be shocked. I hope you can enjoy such wonder again, certainly as immaculate and beautiful as you.' Lucas began praying it'd be all right. He wanted another chance to share his bed with her, to share every blink and gust of wind swirling around them.

'Lucas, you are naughty.' Her thoughts quickly went back to feeling his body upon her. 'I told you not to buy it. I'm glad you did, though.' Natty chuckled, feeling a sense of warmth rush though her, holding on to the wonderfully crafted butterfly trinket box. Touching the delicate stones and handcrafted purple wings with her fingers, she thought it was an adorable thing for him to do for her.

'You're not upset, Miss Natty, at my actions?' Lucas felt confused and exhilarated in the same moment.

'Why on earth would I be upset? I think you deserve a kiss. Come here.' Natty prompted him over with the movement of her hands, wishing he'd simply get back into bed. Forget the tea and touch her once again. A sense of completeness surrounded her, a comfort and love she had never imagined possible. She couldn't wait to tell her diary.

Looking up at the damp-stained ceiling, Lucas let go of the heaviness he had carried for so long. He recalled her telling him she'd be cross if he purchased it. All the pain and fear had been for nothing; all she wanted was a kiss. A euphoria engulfed his body, as he knew he'd be touching her and holding her close for the rest of the day.

'I know I said I'd be cross. I kind of hoped you'd get it.' She winked at him after her lips touched his, then kissed the butterfly; she was going to treasure it forever. Watching him struggle to make tea as the blanket flapped around his arms, she was also very certain she'd treasure him. He was the only gift she longed to open each and every morning. She waited in anticipation for him to get back into bed so they'd be able to wrap themselves around each other; she was never going to let him go.

Natty saw how hairy his legs were and began to chuckle to herself. She had never noticed it before. When she saw him walking in and out of Glenn's bedroom with a towel around his waist, she'd always make sure her door was open a little, just enough to see.

'Miss Natty, it's very hot; be careful. Please do not move even an inch.'

They both began to laugh as Lucas's attempt to get into the bed without spilling the tea was unsuccessful. Natty was holding up the covers.

'Ouch!' Lucas yelped as the hot beverage stung his legs.

'I'm surprised you felt it, being like a grizzly bear and all.'

They continued laughing together. Lucas leant over the side of the bed, placing the cups on the floor, his hands catching the impact of the draught from under the door and floorboards.

'Lucas, why didn't you do that before you got back into bed?' Natty rolled her eyes in jest.

'Aren't you going to open it, Miss Natty?' Lucas snuggled back next to her, happily waiting for her to look inside. For her face to shine like the glow of the sun. He was unaware of how it was done, but nonetheless he was going to ask her to be his wife.

'You haven't, have you?' It all seemed too good to be true; making love to him and becoming Mrs Dunstable would be ludicrously brilliant. Natty chanted *Mrs Dunstable* over and over in her mind as she pushed open the small gold clasp with her red-painted fingernail.

'I'm too scared to look.' Natty pushed the unopened box back into her chest as the excitement became too much.

'Open it, open it.' Lucas was almost kneeling as he couldn't bear the anticipation, desperate for her to do as he asked. He longed to see her smile, for her to wrap her arms around him in delight. An overwhelming love for her consumed his body, the same way it had the minute he had seen her as he walked into the Hopkins home.

'Lucas!' Speaking with solemnity and vulnerability, Natty placed her fingers into the blue velvet-lined box, carefully taking her heart locket from it, placing it upon her hand.

Lucas happily observed her staring in wonder at her found necklace in her chocolate-stained hand. He felt the chain glistened like her eyes.

'Isn't it fabulous?' Lucas was full of vibrancy and enthusiasm.

'Um ... Lucas, I'm not quite sure. You found it. I am happy, of course; I didn't think you had it.' Natty's eyes began to well with tears, her body numb with shock. 'We've been looking for it for so long.' She moved the chain around her hand, looking at each link in sheer disbelief; the small heart locket and chain meant more to her than anything in the world. A mixture of happiness and betrayal ate away at her like the cold in the room; adrenaline pumped inside her. She was realising that her life had had meaning for only a few moments, and she would have said yes to him.

'Let me help you put it on, Miss Natty.' Lucas moved nearer to her.

Opening her locket, Natty hadn't heard what he said.

'My parents aren't here, Lucas; they are gone.' Natty stared at him, biting the inside of her mouth.

'Oh, Miss Natty, you seem sad. We can surely find you another picture. They are in your heart, Miss Natty.' Lucas began to sense there was something wrong.

Natty scratched her neck as she began to feel irritated with him. Breathing out hard, she pushed herself from the bed and began to dress, stepping into her uniform and sliding her locket into a small side pocket.

Moving along to the edge of the bed on his knees, Lucas wondered what was actually happening, sensing she had thought about the trinket box and his fear was going to be confirmed.

'My parents, Lucas, they're gone.' Tears began to fall from her eyes as she paused for a moment, breathing hard. 'They are gone, Lucas, as are you.' She wanted to erupt as the pain introduced itself to her once more. The pain she had felt the day she knew she'd no longer smell her mother's perfume. 'You knew how much it meant to me, Lucas. And you hid it from me. How could you do such a thing?' It was all a complete nightmare. She wasn't awake; she had fallen asleep with him in the night and she hadn't yet woken. Natty wanted to scream at him, scream for him taking himself away from her and for life taking her mother.

'Miss Natty, please, I don't understand.' Lucas shook his head, everything around him a blur.

'I think my father was right, Lucas. There isn't anything to understand. This is my reality, right here and now in your cold, damp, mouldy-windowed flat, with no lights and dirty bedding, with a stupid butterfly box and my locket. Yes, Lucas, my locket.' Natty began to sob, her feelings hurt beyond repair. 'Please, Lucas, do not stop me from leaving; if I stay I shall shout at you.'

'Miss Natty, I thought you'd be happy, pleased with having it back,' Lucas said in despair, his heart breaking like the floorboards around the bed. 'I wanted to ask you something, Miss Natty; please allow me to.'

'Lucas, please do not say any more.' Her anger began to build, her sadness being bullied into leaving her by the sudden urge to scream and smash anything she could.

'Miss Natty.' Lucas leant back onto his bottom from the kneeling position he had taken up only a few moments ago.

'*Lucas!* You hid it; you pretended to look for it with me, and you had it all along.' Natty wiped her eyes with her arm. 'I don't know what to do or say, Lucas. Please do not bring me any more cake.' Why had she bothered? She had thought he loved her. It had all been a lie; all of it, even the Swiss roll. Her heart felt as though it was going to dissolve in the tears on her cheeks.

*

386

Natty stood outside the door with her coat over her arms, feeling as though she was going to collapse. The tears finally erupting fully from her body, she turned slowly and pressed her hand firmly onto his door, only wishing she had the courage to knock and lie with him once again.

Lucas sat dumbfounded on his empty bed, his body immobilised with disbelief. He didn't understand where she'd gone or why she had become such a portrait of sadness, however hard he tried to work out the reason. He closed his eyes; his tears sat almost on the tips of his long eyelashes, tipping over and flowing softly down his cheeks. Feeling the warmth from them, he knew it'd be his only warmth for a long time to come.

Pushing his hand over his face, longing to push the tears away, he caught a glimpse of the gift she had bought him only a few months ago. Sniffing from his emotions, Lucas slowly moved off the bed and began to dress. Picking up the box she had given him, he leant against the table leg, sitting on the cold floor. He saw a halfpenny piece from the change he had dropped; it seemed stranded in some way. It had no meaning sitting alone next to the green rug.

Staring at the door, he knew he'd have gone after her if his parents hadn't been right; he was possessed by the devil. He had made her cry; he had given her sadness and hurt which would now rest within her for a very long time. He prayed she could hold him, even if it was for the last time.

As he sat lost and frightened, the feeling of isolation he'd subjected himself to in the secure hospital resurfaced; his own solitude flashed through him. He only wanted someone to smile at him, even if they were only pretending to notice him sitting alone in his chair.

Holding his arm up high, he felt for his unopened post on the table. Swallowing his tears down with his legs arched, he began to open it. Tears fell from him again as the fear and trepidation stung his heart.

Putting the half-opened letter on his lap, he flipped open the lid of the rectangular box, quickly looking at the door again as the thought of taking his gift out seemed unbearable. Sniffing and swallowing hard, his tears abandoning his eyes, Lucas took one of the shoes from the box. The shiny shoes with new black laces were another thing he didn't understand. They needn't be in his hands. He only had to keep his other ones; there was still leather on them. The soles were very thin, but they made him feel alive. His old shoes had brought luck and happiness to him; he'd met wonderful people and found the most amazing job and flat. He had to leave them now, place them in the corner of the room for the dust to settle on.

The letter fell from his lap as he leant forward to push the new shoe onto his bare foot. He wiggled his foot and sighed while reaching for the other. Looking at his new shiny shoes, he knew he was now going to have to make new steps; another chapter of his life had been travelled through, and he was more than certain in the belief each one helped to make him the man he was going to be. Only wanting to stay in his old ones forever, he knew it was impossible; shoes needed to be mended like hearts and minds.

Leaning back on the table leg and picking up his letter, his body hurt with anguish. His heart felt as though it had stopped beating as he read the words. Pushing the letter to his face, he wept for the chance to dance, for finally being accepted at the dance school of his dreams. His tears fell and his sobs became stronger as he gazed at his shoes. She had done this for him; he'd have to dance without her now. One day, he prayed, she'd come to see him perform. To stand at the side of the stage as he did and be unquestionably mesmerised by his elegance.

Natty leant on the steering wheel of her car, crying. She knew she had to drive away.

Turning the key in her ignition, Natty frowned as she saw an old lady walking slowly past her car as though making her way into 45 Parkside. The old lady smiled at her smugly as she made her way through the entrance of the not-very-favourable flats.

Natty felt all creepy and unsettled at being looked at in such a way.

The old lady walked slowly, pulling herself up by the creaky bannisters. Her wrinkled hands were almost transparent, the veins beneath the skin a faint blue. Standing outside the door, she banged firmly on it with her umbrella. The stale flakes of paint fell onto the wooden floorboards. She hit the bottom of the door again, this time with more urgency.

Lucas wiped his eyes with his hand and leapt from the cold floor, his shoelaces undone, holding on to the acceptance letter. He knew it was her; she finally had understood him like no one else had before. He looked at the bed, smiling gently, his sadness almost disappearing from his exhausted body.

Inhaling a deep breath, Lucas opened the door. Instantly he became immobilised with fear, feeling as if his heart was slowing down with his mind, screwing up his acceptance letter with the force of the gripping of his fist, his knuckles almost white. The old lady stared at him sternly.

'Mum!'

Natty's tears fell like a stream down her face. She blared her favourite tape in the car stereo as loud as she could, her foot firm on the accelerator, hoping the noise would drown out her own sorrow.

Pushing her finger hard on the eject button, Natty finally arrived home. Getting out of her car, her ribs and stomach ached as though she still had her seatbelt tight around her slim abdomen.

She found it hard to breathe as she hung her coat on the full hook. She missed it in some way, the hassle and company they'd always give her. Smelling Ruth's coat and then Glenn's, she felt the urge to cry again for the intensity of love rushing through her.

'Hi, everyone.' Natty looked straight at her father, who had been in his dressing gown for nearly twenty-four hours; he looked untidy and unshaven, his hair matted at the back as he pushed the cloth over the kitchen work surface. 'Hi, Glenn. What are you doing here so early?' She thought Glenn looked well, a little plumper in her face.

'Hi, Nat. Dad called wanting to tell us all something. God, Nat, you're either burning the candle at both ends or so need to change your job; you look awful.'

'Thanks for that, Glenn; morning to you too.' Natty wanted to tell them they were not going to see Lucas again. As she gazed at them, the words wouldn't leave her mouth.

'You never know, may have my old room back too.' Glenn giggled, pushing a piece of cake into her mouth.

Shaking her head, Natty knew it didn't matter; no one ever took anything from her as she never had anything in the first place. Her thoughts went to Lucas.

Ruth picked up the last remnants of cake and licked her finger, hoping Glenn meant what she said. She was determined to get back to the family home soon; her nephew was doing her head in.

'Yes, Glenn, why not? Of course you can have your room. Brings back bad memories for me anyway.' Natty picked up George, kissing his cheek.

'How is Lucas?' her father asked softly, gazing at her in concern. There was a silent communication between them. They didn't have to speak; they knew they were both in pain. He walked over to Natty and rubbed her arm gently; he wouldn't ask again until she was ready.

Feeling her tears again, her throat hurting through her efforts to keep them back, Natty strolled over to the kitchen window.

'Can you believe it? There it is.' Natty held in her hand her small drawer handle. She had been wondering where it had gone for ages.

She gazed into the morning sky, the clouds resembling small hills in their own land. Briefly closing her eyes, she could almost hear Lucas saying the same thing. Gripping the handle in her hand, she giggled a little at his love for life and every detail around him.

'What's so funny?' Ruth tapped her hands on the table.

'Oh, nothing, Ruth. Things are right in front of your face sometimes.' Natty gave the handle to George, letting him run off and play.

'Well, you can't do shit about shit you can't do shit about.' Ruth folded her arms.

They all stared at her.

'Ruth,' her father said sternly.

'OK, sorry, it was only I heard it once; it made me laugh.' Ruth became lost in her thoughts, wondering where her friend was resting in the January chill.

'Ruth, who do you know who speaks like that?' Glenn went to the cupboard to get some more cake.

Raising her eyebrows Ruth looked in jest at Glenn, who had taught her a few new words since she had moved in with her. Sighing, Ruth began to share her thoughts with them.

'Oh, only a man I met; he's homeless, you see. He became my best friend, he always made me appreciate having my warm bed at night, and, well, anyway, I'd go and see him and take him a few nibbles now and then.' Watching Glenn place another cake on the table, Ruth took the biggest piece before her sister.

'Oh, that's where all the biscuits went.'

They all began to laugh at Natty's comment.

'You should have brought him home,' Glenn said with her mouth full, smiling at Natty and winking.

'By the way, Ruth, you didn't happen to give him your mother's gloves, did you?' Their father's voice was full of humour.

'Oh no, sorry about that.' Ruth scrunched up her face as she had been found out; she had left them on the top of her wardrobe to dry and had completely forgotten about them.

'Please put them back.' Whispering softly and kindly into her ear, their father kissed her on the top of her head.

'Anyway, Dad, what's all this about? You're looking a bit smug.' Natty could see organised paper in the corner and no sign of his typewriter. 'You haven't?' Natty's voice was full of pride and excitement.

'Is that what we got called over for?' Ruth pulled George onto her lap, moving her legs side to side, making him chuckle.

'Well, have you?' Glenn asked in eagerness.

'I, my dear girls, have successfully and painfully finished.' Their father's smile went right across his face. He felt proud of an achievement he had never thought possible. Seeing his three daughters and grandson with him again, all in the same room and all with a knowledge of one another's deepest loves and fears, he had achieved much more. His girls still held such strength and love after everything they had been subjected to. He knew at that very second there was nothing which could ever take them away from each other. Hearing George chuckle, he was sure the little smiling boy could be taught to overcome such obstacles his life might put upon him; Glenn would teach him well. Ruth would finally become part of something she'd always searched for, part of herself; she'd stop looking one day. Natty, he could feel the pain she had inside her as she stood with clasped hands next to him. And the man and woman who were missing from the celebrations were linked in

391

some way, bringing them a learning and belief in themselves that they could overcome it all.

Wiping Natty's tear away with his thumb gently, her father gave her a reassuring smile.

'The title, Dad, we've got to know.' Ruth raised her voice excitedly. She was gagging for a cigarette, wishing he'd hurry.

'You are going to tell us?' Glenn moved her wedding ring around her finger, sighing and wondering why. George pulled on her trouser leg, wanting her attention.

'OK, girls, you've finally beaten me.' Moving over to his neatly piled paper, their father took the first page from the top.

They all rushed to the kitchen table. Natty gripped her necklace in her hand, the sensation of the chain within her fingers.

Their father held the white sheet next to them. As they passed it around, absorbing the words, each one touched the spacious sheet with the tips of her fingers, the precious letters revealing a sense of loss, for them to understand their reality once again.

Natty's hands shook as she touched the paper to her chin, closing her eyes, the title mixed with her already breaking heart.

'*For Eve*,' she read aloud. 'Dad, it's beautiful.' She spoke softly, gazing at him, knowing he'd never let their mother go, she'd run though him always, but sensing with his words he'd made peace somehow. She recognised the torment he'd carried for the very first time. Wrapping her arms around him, her locket clasped tightly in her hand, she was going to cry again as she felt the softness and warmth of his dressing gown on her still-chilly body. The words which fled through her mind caused her distress. How was she going to stop them? How was she going to make them go away? If only she could write *The End* like her father had.